BROKEN PRINCESS

THE BIANCHI CHRONICLES
BOOK ONE

LAURA BENNETT

Edited by: Samantha Swart

Alpha Readers: Sally Brierley, Sarah Baker, Daisy Jane

Cover: Vicki Nicolson Branding

Cover Images: © Shutterstock

Paperback ISBN: 978-1-7384916-0-5

Hardback ISBN: 978-1-7384916-1-2

BLURB

A MAFIA PRINCESS

Sacrificed to maintain the fragile peace between her family and his, only Aurora Bianchi can sate Max De Luca's desires and keep his darkest depravities under control. But now his father wants complete control of The Syndicate... and she's an obstacle to their plans. A pawn her husband is forced to sacrifice.

THE BIANCHI BASTARDS

Enzo and his crew are brought in to dispose of the casualties of war, brutally slaughtered and left for dead. However, the bodies aren't nameless thugs—they're Syndicate royalty... and they're not all dead. He and his crew find themselves drawn into a mafia coup, and there's only one side they would ever consider taking.

Enzo, Sinclair, Nico, and Benedict will raze The Syndicate to the ground to avenge Aurora, but first they must save her.

AURORA DE LUCA IS DEAD...RORY BIANCHI WILL RISE

BEFORE YOU BEGIN...

No book is ever worth more than your peace of mind and wellbeing. I have detailed the potential trigger warnings below and encourage you to read them but leave it to your discretion. You know yourself better than anyone. I have done my best to avoid spoilers.

This is a dark romance at heart. The villains are irredeemable and the good guys, while cut from a similar and equally violent cloth, adhere to a strong moral code. Triggers include torture, physical and psychological abuse, miscarriage as a result of domestic violence, rape, sexual assault, kidnapping, murder, violence, and untreated psychopathy.

In addition, this is an adult romance with elements of BDSM and kink exploration. With these elements, consent, safety and communication are paramount. Content includes MM/MF/MMF, D/s relationships, power exchange, sadism, masochism, impact play, knife play, cum play, orgasm denial, pleasure domming, praise, degradation, aftercare, and sub-drop.

I have done my best to represent all themes responsibly and welcome any feedback if you find anything that I may have missed.

Lastly this book is written in British English so remember we like *s* over *z*, *-our* over *-or* and we put two *ls* in words like levelling. However, if you find an error or issue and want to let me know, visit <u>www.laurabennettauthor.com/books</u> and click on *Report Error*.

DON

MATEO
BIANCHI

UNDERBOSS
MANNY
FERELLA

STEFANO
TIERO

CONSIGLIERE

CAPOS

MARCO
ROMANO

CARLO
BARONE

ANTONIO
ROSSI

DANTE
MANCINI

BEFORE YOU BEGIN...

THE DE LUCA FAMILY

SALVATORE DE LUCA —*married*— EVANGELINE DE LUCA
DE LUCA DON / DECEASED

MASSIMO 'MAX' DE LUCA ·········*married*·········
DE LUCA UNDERBOSS

THE BIANCHI FAMILY

MATEO BIANCHI —*married*— FRANCESCA BIANCHI
BIANCHI DON / DECEASED

ISABELLA BIANCHI / AURORA BIANCHI ·········
'ISA' / 'RORY'

THE ROMANO FAMILY

MARCO ROMANO —*married*— TERESA ROMANO
BIANCHI CAPO / 'TESS'

BENEDICT ROMANO / LORETTA ROMANO —*twins*— LUCA ROMANO
'BENNY' / 'ETTA' / 'LUC'

THE BASTARDS

ARIANNA VERARDI / KATE SINCLAIR

NICOLO VERARDI / CARLA MORETTI / BRUNO SINCLAIR
'NICO' / 'SIN'

GIOVANNI MORETTI / ENZO MORETTI
'GIANNI' / 'ZO'

For the readers who love broken boys,
morally grey cinnamon rolls,
chaotic springer spaniels
& rage bunnies... I got you.

PART ONE

"I do not think that all who choose wrong roads perish;
but their rescue consists in being put back on the right
road."

C. S. Lewis

PROLOGUE

AURORA

It hurts—everything hurts. My right eye is swollen shut, and I can barely crack open the other. I wish I couldn't. The scene I'm met with is the stuff of nightmares. My cunt of a husband stands in the middle of the warehouse. He's positioned behind a body, suspended by the wrists from a meat hook attached to a long, thick metal chain. The chain sways, the weight of the body like a pendulum, making my head swim as I struggle to focus with my good eye.

Max's hands are stained red, his victim's shirtless torso mottled with welts and deep, jagged slashes. Blood drips down to the floor as the near lifeless victim huffs ragged breaths, his head lolling forward—obscuring his face. A small crimson stream has formed beneath him and trickles towards the drain at my feet.

My arms and legs are tightly bound to a chair using zip-ties, my body facing them, forcing me to witness what's unfolding. I must have passed out again, as it had been just the two of us up until now. The addition of this *guest* is unsettling, and a feeling of dread swells within me.

For four years, I've been married to the monster that is Max De Luca. I know exactly what he's capable of, though I've never had to witness the devastation he can wreak on a body as a spectator. When I'm the focus of his depravity, I drift far away, somewhere he can't affect me. Unfortunately, the first time he pushed me to a state of catatonia, it unleashed a beast I'm glad I was never present enough to fully comprehend. When I zone out, I become his ultimate victim. A doll on which he can practise and perfect his methods.

I pity the man before me. He won't last much longer. I don't know when I lost consciousness—or how long I was out this time—but this man has not lasted well against Max's onslaught. He's fading fast and my husband is rapidly losing interest in his toy.

Oh joy, me next.

"Welcome back, *principessa*," he croons. "I knew you wouldn't be out for long. Your resilience never ceases to impress me." His saccharine tone caresses me like a poisonous tendril reaching around my throat, making me want to choke and gag.

I try to respond, but my throat is dry, letting the barest croak escape. "Fuck you, Max."

"Now, now, wife. Is that any way to treat your husband? Especially when I went out of my way to bring you such a *special* gift," he sneers, waving a hand theatrically toward his current victim.

"Half-dead henchman? *Ooh*, just what I've always wanted. How did you know?" I retort, my voice like gravel. We start our familiar dance; one to which we intimately know the footwork. If I crumble or show any kind of weakness, he will tire of me, too. The only reason I have survived this long is by taking everything he has to throw at me. By never letting him see that he's broken me. I am a husk, but I will not give him the satisfaction of seeing how much of me he has destroyed.

At the sound of my voice, the man stirs. My left eye starts to focus, and I realise why my husband has a maniacal grin on his face. I scream with fear, with anger, with desperation. A dread I've never experienced before, settles in my chest and weighs heavy on my heart, paralysing me with terror.

"Say goodbye to daddy, princess." His face lights up with glee, basking in my realisation. He steps behind my father, grabbing his hair to wrench his head up, exposing his throat. My father's eyes meet mine, giving me the slightest squint, and I nod back. There's nothing I can do to help him, and we both know it. This is all we can do. Never has such a slight gesture meant so much to me. His eyes soften and I feel how much he loves me as a lone tear falls down his cheek. *I love you, Dad.*

Max brings his knife to my father's throat, and with one clean sweep of his blade—ends him.

As my father's blood cascades to the floor, I watch the light die in his eyes and drop my gaze to my knees. Tears flood my vision, and my shoulders slump in defeat. I want to wail and scream and break into a thousand tiny pieces. This pain cuts so deeply I can feel it in my soul. He destroyed the most honourable man I have ever known.

Max tilts his head to the side and surveys me. "Have I finally broken you, my little toy?"

I consider his words, trying to wrangle my emotions as my mind wanders. Our marriage was arranged to strengthen the fragile alliance brokered between the Bianchis and the De Lucas. Resistance and infighting had been threatening to destroy the fledgling treaty since its inception. Only through our union could the alliance my father brokered be guaranteed.

My father hated doing it, but being Mateo Bianchi's daughter, I did what everyone expected of me as his last remaining heir—I did my duty and ended the bloodshed. I married Massimo—Salvatore De Luca's only son.

Only then did I learn the truth. I hadn't been married off to a prince. I'd been sacrificed to a monster. A beast I could never escape—an animal I couldn't put down. Being his wife was a necessity, so I did what I had to. I endured. For my family, for The Syndicate.

But Max has just murdered Mateo Bianchi—the head of the Bianchi family. *My father.* Fuck The Syndicate. Fuck the De Lucas. And most of all, fuck my cunt of a husband.

"You're going to have to kill me, Max," I spit out with a venomous hatred, "because if you don't, I will burn the whole fucking world down to make you pay."

"Oh, *principessa*," he purrs, stalking toward me, cutting a track through the river of my father's blood. He leaves a sickening trail of footprints that draws my eyes back to my father's lifeless corpse. Max crouches, then strokes his hand down my cheek. "How I'd love to see you try. You've always been my favourite plaything, but alas, our time together is at an end." His hushed tone is almost mournful. "I wish I was allowed to keep you."

My brow lifts as his words register. His eyes hold mine in a penetrating gaze and they show hunger, obsession, anger. But this time there's more. More than his thirst to inflict maximum pain. I can see it clear as day. There's some part of him that doesn't want to kill me.

As this thought drifts to the front of my mind, a searing pain slices through me and I look down, surprised to see his knife lodged in my chest.

"Farewell, *principessa*," he whispers softly against my ear.

With a strangled breath I hiss, *"Fuck you, Max."*

CHAPTER ONE

ENZO

Hanging up the phone, I walk through to the kitchen. We're waiting for a call and the team needs to be ready to go at any time. Perched on a stool at the kitchen island, Sinclair is engrossed in his laptop while Benedict rummages through the fridge in search of snacks. Sinclair is my resident tech specialist and oldest friend. Surveillance and tracking are his forte, though he's also known for his ability to liberate funds from our targets' offshore accounts. Being self-funded comes in handy for anything not explicitly sanctioned by The Syndicate. Intellectually, he's the biggest geek you'll meet, but physically, he's built like the rest of us. He's just as likely to be found throwing down in a fight as Benedict.

Benny is our demolitions expert. Imagine the excitement of an eager puppy chasing a tennis ball, and that's Benny with a detonator in his hand. The joy he gets from blowing shit up is *immense*. Sinclair is dark; charcoal black hair, Mediterranean complexion, and amber eyes. Conversely, Benny is essentially a vampire. Auburn hair, striking green eyes and skin so pale he would likely burst into flames if he went outside at midday. He's like a taller red-haired version of Spike from *Buffy the Vampire Slayer*, if Spike lived at the gym.

My phone vibrates and I pull it out of my pocket, finding our instructions from Max have come through. "Clean up on Aisle Five," I say, repeating the green light they've given me for tonight's mission.

I have no fucking clue what's going on. Max has been visiting his father Salvatore more and more frequently this last month, so I know the De Lucas are up to something. No one seems to be privy to all the details outside of those two. We've been on standby for a clean-up for the last week. Max has blocked any other requests for our services while we waited for his call.

"Do we have any idea what this is about yet?" Sinclair says with a sigh, not taking his eyes off the screen. His rigid posture is my only indication that he's less than happy with our being at Max's beck and call.

"Yeah, what gives? I'm bored out of my mind," says Benny. He pops his head around the refrigerator door like a meerkat leaving its burrow, his arms overflowing with various foods—none of which look like they'd go well together.

"No, but we'll know within the hour," I respond, "and put that all back. We've got to leave now. I'm gonna get Nico, I'll meet you in the car."

Nico is the last of our team and specialises in inquisition. At six-four he's our resident giant, benching more than me these days and scary as all hell. He's a blond demon and he can get anyone to break. Frankly, I no longer ask the details of how he gets people to talk. So long as they do.

He's also Benny's boyfriend. I'd send Benny to get him, but last time they got... *distracted*, and I had to break them up. Not sure I need to see that again anytime soon. I'm not a prude, but I could have gone my whole life not knowing Nico has a six-rung Jacob's ladder or seeing Benny's cum face after being impaled by it.

Benny mutters and shoves everything back in the fridge as Sin flips his laptop closed, retreating to his room. I can tell from the glower on his face he's not enthused. It's taken years to solidify a peace between Mateo and Salvatore. Whatever the De Lucas are up to, something tells me it's about to cause trouble. Trouble me and my team want *no* part of.

Knocking on Nico's door, I shout out giving him five minutes to get his ass in gear. I grab my go-bag from the hallway on my way to the garage to confirm we equipped our van with anything we might need for tonight's job. Climbing into the front passenger seat, I wait impatiently for my team. Sinclair is first and slides open the side panel of the van, hopping into the back. Nico and Benny appear next. Benny jumps in carrying a fucking meatball sub. Of course, we get a call to go, and he stops to make a sandwich. Why wouldn't he? *Dick.* If we're late, Max will lose his fucking mind.

We take twenty minutes to get to the warehouse, code named *Aisle Five*. It's crude, but it's concise. Having driven the van into the warehouse loading bay, I jump out and yank down the metal rolling shutters.

We walk through to the main warehouse, passing a bank of monitors featuring the external camera feeds. Only a few of the overhead lights are on. Enough to allow the shadows to bleed onto the warehouse floor and make the chains hang from various points throughout the main warehouse gleam. Ceiling, walls, floors. We never know how many guests we might need to accommodate and it's better to be prepared. It's kept mostly empty. As a rule, we always bring what we need with us, so nothing incriminating remains between visits.

That's also why there's a ground level sprinkler system and a large central drain for easy clean-up. Imagine clearing the dip at the end of *Who Framed Roger Rabbit*.

Me and my guys exist to solve problems. We're known as *The Bastards*. Formerly *The Bianchi Bastards*—pre-Syndicate. We're on the bottom rung on the Cosa Nostra ladder. The unclaimed progeny of Made Men. And if we're sent for you, we're the *last* people you see.

But it seems Max started—and finished—without us. In front of us are two bodies in what I can only describe as absolute carnage. *What the fuck happened here?*

Max is crouched down on his haunches, transfixed by the battered body tied to a chair in front of him. He stands abruptly as we approach and greets us with a slight dip of his chin. A mask of indifference falls across his features. Whatever emotion he was just experiencing, slips away and he buries it deep—far away from our scrutiny.

"I want these bodies gone within the next six hours. Do whatever you have to and don't just bury them. They need to *disappear*," he commands, straightening his spine and stretching to his full height like he's assuming a role—playing a part.

As we assess the scope of this job, Max crosses the warehouse floor to the side and drags out an empty oil drum, pops the lid, and strips. Unphased by his audience, he throws in his blood-soaked clothes before walking over to a faucet on the side wall which has a hose attached, rinsing off the remaining viscera and stalks back to the bay of monitors to retrieve a bag. Riffling through it he pulls out a towel followed by a small, neatly folded stack of clothes.

He came well prepared.

I peer up at the man strung up from the hook. Whoever he was, Max doesn't want us to know, since he appears to have skinned him. His face, at least. I know Max is a violent fucker—he likes to get his hands dirty in the more brutal aspects of The Syndicate's business— but I've never seen him go this far.

Nico lays out the woman on the floor, having cut the zip ties at her ankles and wrists. Her face is unrecognisable, battered black and blue, one eye swollen shut and features distended in a grotesque caricature.

"Untie the bodies, strip them, add their clothes to the first barrel, and grab me two more barrels. We'll transport them off site for disposal in the drums," I instruct the team, then I turn to Max. "You don't normally... handle things personally. What don't I know?"

"You know everything you need to. Make them disappear. Call me when it's done," he barks.

"Who are they?" I push, wondering who could warrant the personal attention of the De Luca underboss.

"I thought I was clear. Who they were is none of anyone's concern," he growls, squaring off against me. At six-three, I have at least an inch on him, more now since he's standing barefoot, but I know better than to fuck with him while he wears this glassy expression. It's like he's not there. Detached from reality.

"Whatever you say, sir. I'll call you when it's done." My words are respectful, but my tone screams, *fuck you*.

"Make sure you do," Max shouts as he storms off to the loading bay. It's tough to look threatening whilst barefoot and wearing sweats, but if anyone pulls it off, it's Max De Luca. There's something about him that's always set him apart from other Made Men. All that I find in his eyes is darkness and ruin. I've never trusted him, and I detest having to do jobs for him. But we're not exclusive to the Bianchis anymore.

The Syndicate was born out of a metric shit-ton of bloodshed and a realisation that working together suited the interests of the competing crime families better than constantly interfering with each other's business. When the families merged, I can't say I was happy. The De Lucas controlled their crews with fear. The Bianchis managed theirs with respect. But largely, the transition was smooth, and the organisations merged resources successfully. There's a balance, it's fragile, but it's there. Mateo Bianchi tempers Salvatore De Luca's volatility and in return, Salvatore inspires more ambition in Mateo. We all benefit from the alliance.

The last piece of the puzzle was Aurora. Isa's little sister was the pawn sacrificed to maintain a continued peace. For four years, I've watched as she shrank away from everything and everyone. For fuck's sake, she used to run her own fucking crew and now she's this cunt's arm candy. Trotted out for special occasions like christenings, weddings, and funerals. It's fucking criminal. Her team was one of the best.

They were largely focused on liberating funds and reacquiring *misplaced* items. She had some of the best thieves and hackers working for her—excluding Sinclair, that is. She tried to poach him, but that was never going to happen. He's mine, and I told her as much. I think that's the last time I spoke to the now Mrs. De Luca. Wife of Salvatore's little psycho.

I hear the metal gears of the garage door churn, wheels tear through gravel, and I know... he's gone. "Benny, go close the shutters after him and we'll get to work here."

"He's a fucking maniac," Nico growls. He may be the most violent member of our team, but he has limits; lines even he won't cross. "Whoever these people were, was this level of overkill necessary? It's fucking psychotic and you know it, Enzo."

"I'm not disagreeing, Nico. Sin, take fingerprints and blood samples before you seal them up. I want you to find out exactly what Max is involving us in and whether we need to cover our asses."

We've been keeping tabs on the heir apparent for years. From time to time, we've been called upon to monitor or vet certain *family* members. We know he has extra-curricular activities outside the organisation, but we've never had enough to track what he's up to. All we know is daddy dearest is aware and doesn't seem to care.

"Yes, boss." Sinclair gets to work letting the faceless corpse down from the meat hook. The guy took a beating. Looks to be about mid-fifties from the greying hair and physique, but that's all I can glean. He's shirtless and wearing dark slacks—he could literally be anyone. When Sinclair is done, he drags a barrel over and with Nico, heaves the body in feet first. With some repositioning, the lid goes on and they drag over the next one for the woman. Best I can tell, she's in her twenties, maybe thirties, with long raven-black hair. She's in jeans and a shredded, slouchy, long-sleeved hoodie. She doesn't fit this picture.

There's no reason for a woman to be at this scene. Certainly not one who looks like they were snatched off a sofa mid sitcom binge. She's even wearing fluffy house socks. Sin kneels to get her prints, and as he lifts her hand, the body jerks. With a loud rattle, she tries to breathe, desperately gulping as her battered lungs fight her.

"Shit, Enzo. This one's not dead!" Sinclair grunts, as he falls back, trying to avoid the arc of blood she's showering him with.

She stills, her breathing is so slight her chest barely

rises. I kneel at her side and one eye opens wide and immediately I know. It may be ringed with red, but I'd know that colour anywhere. The same verdant green as Isabella. Deep emerald with flecks of gold arranged in a halo.

"Aurora," I breathe. Sin's head snaps up and his eyes widen in horror.

"No fucking way, Enzo. He wouldn't," Nico snarls. Sin remains quiet.

Benny runs back to stand beside us. "You've got to be fucking shitting me?" he roars.

"There's no fucking way! The De Lucas wouldn't possibly be this stupid? It would mean *war*," Nico adds.

As I stare down, cataloguing the extent of her injuries, I'm horrified. She's barely recognisable. "It would only start a war if anyone knew about it, and if her body could be identified. Hence, this guy's missing a face, and she's been beaten to a pulp. Without a body— she's missing. Without a body, Max has a reason to go after any organisation in the city in search of her."

"What the fuck do we do?" asks Nico.

"We go to Mateo. This can't stand, Enzo," Benny growls out, his jaw clenched and his chest heaving, obviously seething with anger. "This isn't right. Mateo needs to know. The De Lucas can't get away with this."

He may be one of us now—part of a crew of bastards either by birth or circumstance—but he was once part of the Bianchi *family*. Son of a Made Man working under Mateo. That is until Benny fell in love, came out to his father and was unceremoniously disowned. His father may have cast him out, but Mateo felt differently. He took Benny aside and told him he valued loyalty above all else and that it was none of his business who he fucked as long as Benny didn't fuck him over. While he couldn't force Benny's father to accept him, he could find a place for him within his organisation. With us.

Mateo approached me with an offer to expand my crew, and thus *The Bianchi Bastards* found their fourth.

I take a deep breath and survey the scene. "Right. Nico, Benny, you're staying here. You'll burn the clothes and then activate the hydrants and clean-up the floor. Standard sweep and spray like usual. Sin, we need to call in medical, someone we can trust. We can't turn up at Mateo's with her dead."

Sin takes a moment to think and then adds. "Can't have anyone come here, boss. Max has access to the external camera feeds. Equally, we can't be seen to be leaving mid-job. I could loop the feeds, but it's a risk if he's paying attention to them."

"Do it, Sin," I order. "Benny, monitor her pulse and breathing. I need to find something to help us move her. Whatever you do, don't remove that knife and if it starts bleeding, apply pressure."

"She's unconscious, boss, and her pulse is slow, but it's steady." Benny's breath hitches. "How the fuck could he do this to his wife? To Aurora-*fucking*-Bianchi?"

I dash to the door at the back of the warehouse. It's a storeroom and I'm hoping to find something we can carry her out on. The best I can come up with is an old shipping pallet, but it's narrow enough to fit in the truck, so it'll have to do. I drag it out to find Benny stroking her hair back from her face, shaking his head, whispering something in her ear. I can't make out what, but I can see how affected he is from the pained look on his face.

We're in so much fucking trouble. Whatever we do from here on out, we're fucked. We will betray one family no matter what we do. But it's really no choice for us. We started Bianchi, we'll end Bianchi. We'll do whatever it takes to save Aurora.

And I'm not telling Mateo his daughter is dead. Once was enough.

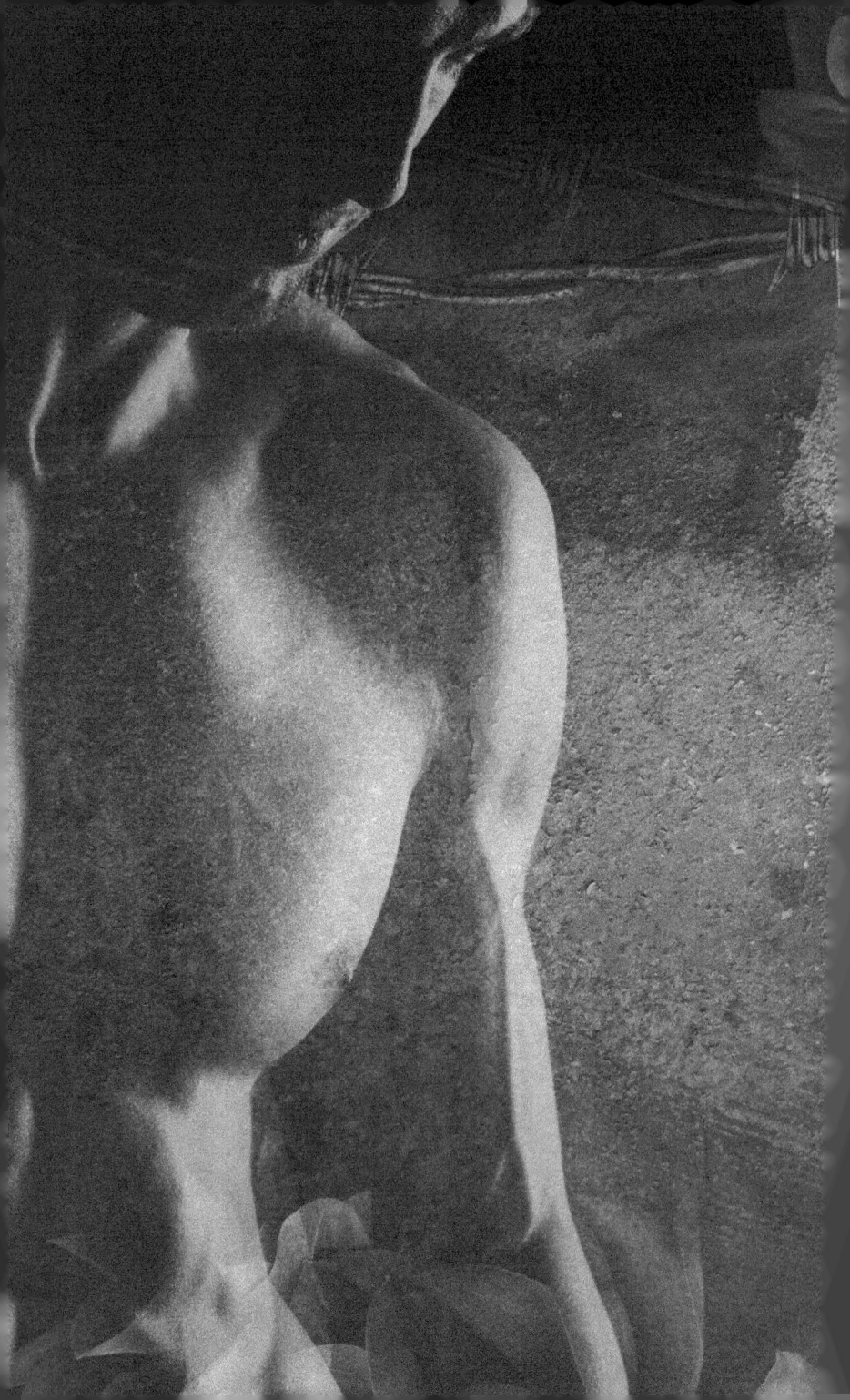

CHAPTER TWO

SINCLAIR

Aurora Bianchi. That sadistic fuck tried to kill *Aurora Bianchi.*

We transferred her to the pallet and got her into the van as quickly as we could while Enzo called the doctor. He's driving us to our safe house while I stare at the near corpse-like form of the most broken woman I've ever seen.

Sometimes I hate what we do. Well, the clean-up element, at least. We're who you call when things have gone so far south you've found yourself somewhere close to Antarctica. Our key skills lie in research, investigation, interrogation, and covert operations. We're also the best at burying the bodies, and un-fucking the most fucked-up situations.

Yes, we kill people, and yes, we—as Nico puts it—*interrogate people vigorously.* But we don't accept jobs that target women and children, or jobs that require collateral damage of innocent parties. We sure as shit don't inflict pain for the sake of it... Well, most of us don't. Nico can get carried away, but not like this.

Leaning over, I listen for her breath. I press my fingers to her pulse, which is slow but determined, but her breathing is so faint it's hard to fathom how she's still alive. I'm no expert, but that doesn't seem like a normal response to the beating she's taken. The longer I stare, the more injuries appear—bruises on bruises, burns, slashes, and cuts. And that's just the exposed skin. I see crimson pools forming under the hoodie. I want to check, but with the knife, any movement is a risk.

This isn't like the beating the man took. This is hours, if not days, of torture. I swallow audibly at the realisation, choking back bile and unexpected emotion.

We need to get her to Doc Em now, but we're still thirty minutes out from the safe house. Nearly all the equipment we need is there, and it's our most concealed and defensible option. We can't risk taking her back to ours. If Max finds out she's still alive, and that we're helping her—we're all dead. I trust Doc Em to protect Aurora. She's paid extremely well for her discretion but also because she's a Bianchi to the core, daughter of a capo, and that makes her our best option right now.

As I pull away to sit back against the side of the van, I see Aurora's breathing grow laboured. Her lips are moving, but words fail her. She's trying to speak, but I wouldn't hear her over the engine even if she found the words.

"Enzo, stop," I shout, lifting my head to return his gaze in the rearview mirror. "Turn off the engine, now." I turn back to Aurora. "What is it? What do you need to say?"

Again, her lips move, but she's too quiet. It hurts to see her like this. My chest aches and I reach to stroke her hair but realise there's no where I can touch her that won't cause her pain.

"You're not in good enough shape for us to be stopping like this. We need to get you to a doctor, Aurora. Last chance before we get moving. What do you need to say?"

I see her take what must be the most agonising breath in history. The knife rises and she winces, and with great effort she forces out, "Dad..." before losing consciousness.

"What did she say?" demands Enzo. "Tell me now, Sin."

Enzo's hands are gripping the wheel so hard I can hear the leather creaking in protest. He's staring out the windscreen like he's slipped into a trance, his implacable glare boring into the void.

"Nothing useful. We don't have time for this right now. We have to get her to Doc Em. I shouldn't have asked you to stop. Start the car, and just get us to the safe house." I say as forcefully as I can. It's not often that I challenge Enzo's authority or order him around, but he's so close to breaking point right now, I know he needs someone to snap him out of it.

I've known Enzo for close to two decades. I've been on one crew or another with him since I was eighteen. He's my oldest and closest friend, and because of that, I know that seeing another Bianchi daughter die will destroy him. When Aurora's sister Isabella went missing, they brought in everyone working for Bianchi to search for her. When we failed and found her body, it destroyed Mateo. It affected us all deeply.

But there's no denying it hit Enzo hardest since he was the one to tell Mateo. His brother couldn't face it, so as he always does, Enzo stepped up and delivered the devastating news for him.

The police investigation had been a joke. Given who her family was they didn't dedicate enough resources to it and when they ran out of leads it became a cold-case. The evidence didn't suggest it was mob related, but they didn't care. She was just another whore found dead in an alleyway behind a dumpster. Mateo has had various crews—including us—investigating it ever since.

Enzo's eyes flick from the road to mine in the rearview and he nods, snapping himself out of it, starting the engine and pulling away carefully. Aurora is still out cold, and I hope to God that's not a bad sign. She's not showing any outward signs of further deterioration, but that means nothing. I'm not a fucking doctor and she looks half dead to me. It's eerie, almost unnatural. I've never seen anyone with injuries this severe maintain a consistent pulse. It's slow, but it's there.

TWENTY-FIVE MINUTES LATER, we're pulling off the deserted road down a driveway with an entrance barely visible from the road. If you didn't know it was there, it wouldn't exist. Doc Em's car is already here, but she's left the garage doors clear for us. Enzo flips the visor and grabs the remote, opening it up for us to pull in. We stop a moment later, and Doc Em pulls open the back doors of the van. She takes one look at Aurora and her eyes go wide.

"What the fuck is this? We should be in hospital, Sinclair. She needs more than sutures and tape. She needs a CT," she shouts, waving her arms like a coach berating his players from the sidelines.

"Can't. Too dangerous. If anyone finds out she's *not* dead, we're *all* dead."

"She's nearly dead already, you prick. Well, fuck you very much, Sin. What in the name of hell have you got me involved with?"

Enzo appears, closing the garage door and returning to help us lift out the pallet. There's no way to get it into the house, so we're going to have to lift her ourselves.

When we bend to pick her up, Doc Em raises her voice with a sharp tone, stopping us in our tracks. "Stop! Are you guys out of your mind? Go into the house now and find something we can use to transfer her. Narrow enough to fit through doors and sturdy enough to hold her flat." She stands, pointing at the door, giving us our orders. As we turn to leave, she calls after us. "Is there an ironing board in the house?"

Running into the house, I crash through the utility room door, grabbing the ironing board and wrestling it out to the garage. Doc Em rolls Aurora on her side as carefully as possible and we slide the ironing board into place, then roll her gently on her back. Together we lift, carrying her through the house and down into the basement med-room. Located next to Nico's soundproofed interrogation room—*for convenience.*

Doc Em takes over the room, directing us to ease her down on the exam table before removing the board. She heads to the back wall and begins pulling out equipment and drugs from our stocks. Passing the fluids, she pushes the crash cart back to the bed, finding everything she needs. We keep this room well stocked, but in all honesty, I think we've only used it for stitching ourselves back up. And Nico sometimes borrows the defibrillator when someone he's interrogating tries to 'check out' early.

Enzo's phone goes off and he steps out of the room to answer it. Doc Em is placing electrodes, hooking up the wires to the monitor she's retrieved, taking Aurora's vitals when Enzo calls me out of the room.

"I've got to get back to the warehouse. Benny, Nico and our mystery guest are ready for pickup. We need to be clear of the site ASAP to avoid rousing Max's suspicion. Find out from Doc Em if there's anything else she needs and keep me posted on her condition." He pauses and drops his eyes before returning my gaze again. "How the fuck is she still alive, Sin?"

"I don't know, but we have to be prepared, Enzo. I'll let you know as soon as Doc Em has anything."

"What did she say in the van?"

"She said 'dad' then passed out." I take a deep breath and add. "You need to tell Mateo, boss."

"I know," he says, leaning into me and letting out a shaky breath. He pats me on the back, turns and leaves. Surveying my clothes, I realise Aurora's blood has satu-

BROKEN PRINCESS

rated my shirt and pants. Dashing upstairs to my room, I strip down and take the quickest shower known to man before redressing in sweats and a tee. Returning downstairs, I knock before I step back inside, unwilling to wait.

"Fuck's sake, Sinclair, did you hear me say 'come in'," Doc Em shouts before getting lost in thought, staring down at her patient, brows drawn in a pained expression. She looks haunted but shakes her head, like she's trying to snap herself out of her sorrow, she moves on and leans in closer to inspect the swollen eye. As I approach, she turns and asks, "Who is this, Sin?"

With a soft sigh, I reply, "Aurora Bianchi."

"Holy fuck," she gasps, "do you know who did this to her?"

"Yes, but it's best if you don't."

"That's such bullshit, Sin. I'm not some delicate fucking flower that needs protecting."

I consider her words, and what she's risking helping us before answering, "It was Massimo De Luca."

Her face crumples in shock, looking crushed by the revelation.

"You'd better make the fucker pay," she declares, refusing to meet my eye as she fiddles with the electrode placements. "Grab the scissors from the crash cart. I need this hoodie off to assess the injuries and figure out where the fuck to start with this knife. I'm promoting you from *Enzo's Bitch* to mine."

I smile at her coarseness; it's one of my favourite things about her. Emergency or not, she's always got the warmth of an ice cube. It's familiar and reassuring, espe-

cially in a crisis. I need that right now. My control is
hanging by a thread.

She snatches the scissors, cutting away the hoodie
carefully, exposing the knife wound. My breath catches
at the marred terrain across her collarbones and arms.

Dozens of tiny angry slashes obscure her skin. But
that's only the beginning. Doc Em cuts away her tank
and I'm shocked by the extent of the bruising. Angry dark
red and purple contusions cast dark shadows over fading
blue-green bruises. From out of her upper abdomen, the
knife handle stands proud. It's lower than I'd thought.

"I wish we could x-ray this," Doc Em mumbles to
herself. Turning to me, she adds, "It's low enough that it
looks like it missed the heart and lungs, and the angle
looks like we may have got lucky; it doesn't appear to
have nicked anything vital. Have you got any O-neg on
hand?"

I nod, heading to the refrigerator at the back of the
room and return with what she needs. She puts in
multiple lines, hooking up the blood first, then fluids,
and injects what I assume are antibiotics and painkillers.
Palpating the area around the knife with great care, she
takes a deep breath, collecting herself before removing it
swiftly with the precision of a surgeon. There's bleeding,
but it looks minimal.

"That was an enormous risk," I bite out through
gritted teeth.

"Oh, exactly when did you attend med school? I
know what I'm doing, Sin. Wind your neck in, right
now."

Seizing instruments from the top of the crash cart,

Doc Em studies the wound, grabbing a suture needle and thread and throwing in stitches where needed. It looks like Aurora was lucky, but then I shake my head in disgust. There's nothing about her condition that could be called lucky. It's a fucking tragedy.

"How are her vitals? Are they normal? Her pulse has been consistent since the warehouse, but honest to God, I can't figure out how. Look at the state of her."

"Her pulse is good, but her oxygen is low, and her respiration is poor. I was concerned she had a collapsed lung, but from what I can see and hear, the knife hasn't penetrated the lungs. She has multiple broken ribs, though. I'll know more when I can get x-rays. How did you find her?"

"She was unconscious, tied to a chair. She regained consciousness once in the van but then passed straight out."

"You're right that she's not exhibiting typical symptoms of shock," she says in a hushed tone and a sorrowful look on her face. "What she endured, Sin. This wasn't just a beating. Half these injuries appear to have occurred over days, if not weeks. And the scars... I can't even begin to guess what's been done to her. This is more than shock, Sin. I think she's in a dissociative state. She's completely shut down."

I gaze down at Aurora as she lies motionless, the reassuring beep of the monitor the only clue that she's still with us. "What can I do?"

Doc Em takes another deep breath and starts cutting away Aurora's jeans, exposing more bruises, lacerations and scars. "We clean and treat every wound. You use butterfly strips for the small ones and leave the stitches to me. We get her as comfortable as possible and then I need a portable x-ray and an ultrasound machine. I don't care how—you guys can steal them for all I care, but I need to know what's going on internally. She's not stable enough to move, but you need to understand this is a patch job. She'll need extensive treatment over the coming weeks, preferably in a hospital."

"Understood."

It takes hours to tend to Aurora's injuries. With every cut I clean, and butterfly-strip I apply, my rage grows. A molten fury I don't think I've ever experienced before. Because next to every fresh cut is an existing scar. Cuts. Some deep, some shallow. Burns, some cigarette sized, others wide and gnarled like from a cigar. They run the entire length of her body, back and front, from her ankles to her wrists to her collarbone. The only places unscarred from injuries are places not easily concealed under clothes.

I look up at Doc Em—the most stoic person I know—and notice the tears trailing down her cheeks. Her shoulders betray her as a hitch runs through them, chasing the soft sob that escapes her. Being witness to what Aurora has endured is heart-rending.

"I'll be back as often as I can without raising suspicion, but I need you to change the dressings on the deeper wounds daily, keep them clean and dry. You need to keep a close eye on her. Call me if anything changes. But I'm hopeful she'll recover well." She's heading towards the door and turns back to look at me, adding quietly, "Sin... when she wakes up, I've got no idea what state she'll be in... mentally. She's going to need help. More help than I think you and your brothers can give her. What she's been through..."

"I know. I understand what you're saying," I whisper.

She closes the door, her retreat marked by the soft footfalls up the stairs. Shuffling, exhausted, shell-shocked by what she's seen. I call Enzo, putting him on speaker as I clean up the discarded packaging. We used nearly our whole stock of bandages and sutures. He picks up on the second ring.

"Boss, Doc Em's got a shopping list for you, and we need to restock our supplies. I'll text you the details, but we need it before she comes back. She said she didn't care who you had to steal from—just get it."

"I'll get it done," he replies solemnly. "What's the update?"

"Shit, boss, it's bad. What he did to her... it's not like the other guy we found. It must have taken days." I pause because I don't know if I should say the rest. "That's not all we found, Zo. He's been doing this, judging by the scars, for years." I'm met with a stony silence. "Are you guys done?" I prompt, attempting to divert his focus to something else.

"Just finished the BBQ, we'll grab the supplies she needs and any additional stuff we need to stay at the safe house, and then we'll be with you. What tech do you need from home to investigate this clusterfuck?"

"I have a lot here, but I'll text you what I'm missing." I take a moment and then add. "Grab as many pairs of sweats and T-shirts as you can from the house. She'll need clothes she can wear over her bandages."

"I'll sort it, Sin," he says before ending the call.

I grab the stool and pull it across the floor on its wheels. Taking up sentry at her shoulder, waiting for so many things. For Enzo to return, for her to wake up, and for my heart to stop pounding so loudly in my ears. My adrenaline is wearing off and an exhausted crash is inevitable.

I stare down, hypnotised by the rhythm of her shallow breaths. I hum to distract myself, which turns into a low tenor as I sink into a trance, zoning out as I sing the words my mother sang to me as a boy. In the background, the steady beep of the monitors reassures me she's okay, and the longer I sing, the more pronounced the rise and fall of her breathing becomes.

As the song ends, I hear her sigh. One of her eyelids flutters open and she seizes my gaze.

"Thank you," she murmurs. And drifts back into a sea of unconsciousness.

CHAPTER THREE

AURORA

This doesn't feel the same as the other times I've drifted away. Normally I feel cold, and alone, and lost—right now I feel warm, and safe, and protected. It's different, and in my experience, different is never good. You can't trust different.

I can hear music. It's soothing, but it moves, floating away only to return moments later. I wish it would stay. The low rumbling tones feel like they're swaddling me. Protecting me from what always comes.

When I wake up, he's always there, leering down at me. Marvelling at the tapestry of destruction he's woven on me. Something was different this time, though. I know this time I'm not supposed to wake up. So why am I still here, trapped in my personal purgatory, tortured by my own thoughts?

I felt the knife go in. The searing agony wasn't

different from any other he's inflicted, but the look in his eyes was like a goodbye.

One that pained him.

You could spend an eternity trying to figure out what goes on inside Max's head and you'd still be no closer to understanding him. He's a straight up psychopath. Or maybe I mean sociopath, because he can mask himself so well only I know the true depth of his depravity.

That's why I retreat here. A place in my mind that protects me while he ravages my body.

When I dissociate, I'm numb except for occasional flashes—barrages of forced awareness. Memories that surface no matter how much I will them to the darkest recesses of my mind. When I'm here, I'm forced to face my fears and contemplate my cowardice. But it's better than whatever reality Max is usually presenting me with.

I open the front door and step inside, finding him waiting for me in the entryway. With just one glance at his vacant eyes, I know what's coming. He pounces, grabbing my hair and wrenching me inside while kicking the front door closed behind me. I'm hurled down on our unforgiving tile floor, and for a moment, I'm stunned, completely overwhelmed by the pain throbbing in my temple. He lurches forward and grabs my right ankle, dragging me towards the basement door.

Behind the basement door is where Max unleashes his beast. Something he hides from the rest of the world. The persona he presents is that of a ruthless Cosa Nostra prince. Maybe some would be afraid of that, but I grew up around plenty of monsters. When you think about it, I am my very own monster. I grew up tough. My father made sure I was strong enough to handle a life like this. Strong enough to run my own crew. And after my sister died, he was determined I would be indestructible.

I am a force to be reckoned with, in my own right—trained in multiple martial arts to varying degrees. There are very few people I can't fend off and many I can leave in a ruined heap on the floor.

I used to fight. I used to kick and scream and bite. Hurting him—while satisfying my need for retribution—never stopped him. Screaming didn't work, as no one ever heard me. And my cries only fuelled him. Strengthened him.

But the type of monster Max turned out to be, that's an extraordinary beast. Despite my talents, every ounce of strength I have—I need it just to survive him.

I learned quickly that if I wanted to survive Max, I'd have to fight differently; protect myself. So, I hid in plain sight—floating away where he couldn't reach me. The problem was, he discovered he enjoyed that more. Pushing me to a point of catatonia left him with a truly blank canvas. One he could play with for hours. Something on which he could hone his skills, improve his techniques. It was his ultimate pleasure and greatest reward.

Another memory forces its way to the front of my subconscious.

I'm strapped to the table, staring up at the bright surgeon's light he had installed. From here I can see hundreds of tiny reflections of me, rivulets of crimson trailing down the sides of my body where the barbed wire has cut into my thighs and torso. He whispers in my ear how much he enjoys using me as his canvas, how he found the perfect doll, and how he's never letting me go.

I can feel his icy fingers stroke a featherlight touch around my ankle, caressing the cuts. He brings them to his mouth and slides them past his lips. Groaning in satisfaction as he savours my blood, his dick straining at his fly as he does.

I was eighteen years old when I was told I was to marry Max. The prince and the princess, *what a fairytale.* My youthful naïveté had me thinking I was the luckiest woman on earth. This sophisticated older man, gorgeous by anyone's standards, was going to be mine. I'd had a schoolgirl crush on him for years. Yes, he was once the enemy, but who wouldn't find the forbidden enticing? Impossibly tall, with sun-kissed skin, dark blond hair topped with piercing blue eyes. Although you rarely saw both his eyes since his impeccably styled hair was long on top and fell forward across his face. I thought it made him look mysterious.

Things that seemed so attractive before, now remind me of every sinister aspect of him. His voice, which I once thought was commanding, now sounds like a venomous sneer. Just the rasp of it makes me shrink away with dread. I used to gaze into his eyes, finding depths of the Mediterranean Sea, but all I see now are the faded hues of icy barren glaciers. The curtain of hair that swept across his face, once so alluring and mysterious, now looks like a mask he hides his monster behind.

Max De Luca has been controlling my life for so long that this haven within me is the only place I have any agency over... *anything.*

I'm chained to the wall by the heavy iron collar, eyes

covered with a blindfold. I can hear him pacing at the back of the room. There's the occasional hitch in his step. Like he's jumping. Like a prize fighter pumping himself up before a bout. There's a quick shuffle before his icy claw is wrenching me down to the floor. His knee pins my chest to the ground while he unlocks the collar and releases me. I try to take my first full breath in hours, but it's stolen from me as he grasps me by the neck and drags me across to his workbench, throwing me down. The edge of the table cutting into my hip.

I'm bent over, my hands pulled forwards and strapped to the table with thick, rough leather cuffs. Ripping the blindfold from my face, he grabs my chin, wrenching my head back so I'm forced to meet his eyes.

"You never cease to impress me, wife. No one has ever withstood me. You truly are the best gift I've ever received."

He releases my chin, and my eyes take in the view of his neatly hung tools on the back wall. I hear the clink as he undoes his belt. That's one of my cues to leave, to slip away. But before I've fully checked out, I hear...

"Not only are you the perfect toy, but you are also such a dutiful wife. You will be the most spectacular mother. Breeding you, principessa, is my fucking pleasure..."

I feel the first ruthless thrust and then I withdraw to my haven.

Once introduced, our parents afforded us a long engagement—for an arranged marriage. Partially because I lost my mind at the suggestion of giving up my newly formed crew, but mostly because agreeing the terms of a merger this size takes a long damn time. Merging the two largest Cosa Nostra families on the East Coast was an involved process. Trying to agree the terms of truces, carve out territories for different business interests and solidifying hierarchies for our crews was an arduous task and stressed the already tenuous partnership.

If they'd invited just one woman to mediate the negotiations, they'd have resolved it in half the time. But I wasn't about to point that out. I needed the extra time. Leading a crew had been my dream for years.

They let me live my dream until the day I got married.

We were engaged for three years, and we dated. Hell, I even believed I was in love. The only problem is, I fell in love with an illusion. And by the time I knew who I was married to, it was too late.

"Did you think you could keep this from me, principessa?"

He throws the pregnancy test across the room. I hear it ricochet off the wall then skitter across the floor. I stay silent. Any answer will be the wrong answer. He walks around the chair I'm bound to, pacing back and forth.

"You know, my father has insisted for so many years that your only worth is as a vessel to further our lineage. He promised that the moment this happened it would fill me with a pride beyond anything I could imagine; bringing another De Luca into the world." He pauses, like he's thinking about this. He tracks a hand down my neck, through the valley between my breasts, and stops at my navel, stroking it thoughtfully.

"I did so enjoy breeding you, princess." His eyes flick to mine. "But my father overestimated my attachment to the De

Luca name. He was wrong. Nothing compares to the pleasure you give me... and I will not share you. Not with anyone."

Without warning, he strikes my stomach hard. Balling his fists, he lands blow after blow as I drift further and further away.

I've been married for four years. That's forty-eight months he's owned me. Two hundred and eight weeks he's experimented on his favourite toy. For one thousand four hundred and fifty-eight days, I've wondered what will trigger the beast today. And every minute of every day I've fought with every fibre of my being to make sure I can do enough to make sure I always wake when he's finished with me.

I've asked myself a million different times in an infinite number of ways. Why do you stay?

The answer is simply—for the greater good. My abominable marriage is the keystone of an unstable bridge between two warring territories. Without it, everything crumbles. If I left, Massimo De Luca would burn down the world. Not out of an all-consuming love for me, but driven by a burning hellfire of pure evil.

One day I'll figure out what I need to destroy him, not simply survive him.

For now, the soft, deep melody has returned, and it pushes my consciousness out of my safe space.

I try to resist.

I need to stay here where I can protect myself, but it's no use. I'm forced out of my head and lulled into a deep and restful sleep.

CHAPTER FOUR

ENZO

I open the med-room door and find Sinclair slumped over the bed, snoring. Head lying on the bed at Aurora's side with one arm outstretched, holding her hand. I wheel in the equipment Doc Em requested and leave Sin as he is. Standing on the other side of the bed, I study Aurora.

They've cleaned and treated her wounds. I don't know what I expected, but it wasn't this. With the blood wiped away, the full extent of the injuries is startling. There's not a square inch of skin unmarred. I've seen a lot of injuries, a lot of dead bodies, but rarely have I witnessed torture like this. Not even Nico inflicts this on his victims. It's hard to look at, and that this is Aurora is even more jarring. She's fucking *royalty*.

How did we not know about this? Her body is a tapestry of scars upon scars upon scars. This is years of abuse. Some marks are an angry red—newly healed and raised—but others are older. Glistening with a faded silver, almost like ghostly projections of everything she's experienced.

I've been trying to get hold of Mateo, but he's not answering. It's common for someone in his position to be unavailable from time to time. But I've been calling his priority line for hours with no response. Several of his capos have proven just as elusive. My stomach lurches, but I don't want to pay attention to this creeping dread settling in my gut. As incomprehensible as Max trying to kill his wife is, there's no way he'd go after Mateo... would he?

With her eyes fluttering, she rolls her head towards Sin, as if she can sense a calming presence nearby. Her lids cease their movement, and her state seems to calm, leading me to believe he must actually soothe her somehow. Stepping back as quietly as I can, I leave for the corridor, and take the stairs.

Nico and Benny sit at the kitchen island, staring blankly at beers they've yet to open. They look shell-shocked. They're significantly younger than Sin and me. Benny grew up with Aurora. He blows out a ragged breath. He folds his arms around himself and appears to shrink back a little, as if the weight of the evening is finally hitting him. Nico crosses to him around the counter and pulls him into his arms, running his hand down Benedict's back.

Benedict has always been the only person to calm Nico's soul, but when Benny's hurting, Nico is his rock.

"I can't believe he did that to her..." he whispers, hiding his eyes on Nico's shoulder.

I cough to announce my presence, causing Nico's eyes to lift to mine. "How is she?"

"Doc Em called from the car. Aurora's stable, but she'll be back in a few hours with more medication plus any supplies she can grab from the hospital. The knife appears to have missed everything vital, which is a fucking miracle, but she needs to monitor for any complications that might arise from the stab wound."

Nico nods and continues, "How do we play this, Zo? We need to check in with Max, and soon." His hands absently stroke Benny's lower back, still holding him.

I huff out a breath and run my hands over my face. It's been a long fucking night. "He can't know she's still alive and he sure as fuck can't know that we have her. By saving her, we've defied a direct order, and if De Luca finds out, we're as good as dead," I say, thinking out loud. "We need to get hold of her father. Fuck, we need to identify whoever we just incinerated and figure out what the fuck is going on. We all know there's no way Mateo approved a hit on his daughter. Which means Max may make a move against The Syndicate, or the De Lucas are staging a coup and somehow, we've ended up in the middle of a clusterfuck of epic proportions."

Benny blows out a breath as he considers the implications. "Holy shit, this is big." Then he turns to me and says, "My money is on a coup. But why, in the name of fuck, would he choose us to get rid of her body? He knows our history with the Bianchis."

"That's what I was wondering. But if she hadn't opened her eyes, I wouldn't have known it was her. He did everything he could to make her unrecognisable," I respond.

"And we are the best. He needed us to make this go away," Nico chimes in.

"Maybe," I muse, volleying my head from side to side as I consider Nico's words. "As far as we're supposed to know, this was a typical clean-up."

"Us holding up in a safe house isn't typical," Nico retorts.

"Well, we have no fucking choice if we're going to keep Aurora safe," I snap.

"Easy, boss. What I meant was we have to cover our asses. Someone is going to notice our absence. Assuming we're not already under surveillance," Nico explains.

"Shit, you're right." He takes a moment to think before continuing. "I need to get Sin to rustle us up some cover jobs. In the meantime, one of you needs to pick up Doc Em. Make sure she's not being watched and get her here *without* leading anyone to us."

"I'll go," Nico says. "Text her now. Let her know I'll be picking her up in three hours." He turns and heads back to his room, reaching out and grabbing Benny by the hand, he pulls him with him. "We need a shower," is all he says, and they're gone.

I lean over the counter and grab one of the abandoned beers. Using the side of the counter to pop the top, I bring it to my lips and take a long, thirst-quenching gulp. Fuck, I needed that. Well, I'd rather have a whiskey, but I can't right now.

I take out my phone, text Doc Em, and then place the

call I've been avoiding. In a terse tone, he answers, "Is it done?"

"Yes, Mr. De Luca," I confirm and then wait to see how he's going to play this. The silence stretches out until it reaches a painfully awkward level.

"You're not on-call anymore. I won't be needing you for anything else," he says and ends the call in a clipped tone.

If we're lucky, or as good as we think we are, he believes we have disposed of both bodies. But I need to wake Sin up. If we're going to cover our asses, he needs to identify the male body. But I also need him to hack Max's communication systems, track down Mateo, and start doing what he does oh so well, gathering any intel we can exploit. There's a fucking shitstorm coming, and we need to be prepared.

I down the last dregs of beer and head back to the garage to grab the rest of the gear I brought back with me. Clothes for, well, everyone. We have tactical gear here and enough casual gear for brief stays, but we'll be here for the foreseeable future. Lugging the various gym bags I packed, I leave them in the hall. I grab the bag of stuff for Aurora and head back downstairs.

This time, as I approach the door, I hear singing. Low soulful notes that I know can only be Sin. He doesn't sing often, and only when he thinks no one is listening. I creep back to the base of the staircase and stomp loudly enough to announce my presence. The melody stops, and I enter the room. Sin is already leaning back and stretching out his shoulders as I enter. He looks exhausted, his face drawn and eyes bloodshot.

"I got everything you asked for," I start as I drop the bag on the floor at the foot of the bed. "Talk to me, Sin. What don't I know?"

He's looking down at her hand. Sin isn't a talker, but his silence is disconcerting. I wait patiently as he finds his words.

"I helped Doc Em, when she was... patching her up." He takes a steadying breath before he continues. "I've never seen anything like it, Zo." He can't look at me. "This wasn't attempted murder. It was torture. Doc Em says it's like she's in a self-induced coma. She's catatonic or some shit."

"You need a break, Sin."

"Why do I get a break? She didn't get a break for however long it took him to do *this* to her," he lashes out, waving his arms frantically before letting them fall to his sides in defeat.

I surge forward, grabbing his neck with one hand and yanking him towards me, pressing his forehead to mine. "Open your eyes and look at me right fucking now, Sin," I hiss, emotion clogging my throat. "We need you to work your magic. Find out what the fuck is going on. Mateo and his most trusted capos are MIA. I have a faceless dead guy I need you to identify, and I need you to hack anyone you can on the De Luca side to find out why their number two just *murdered* Aurora-fucking-Bianchi. Got it?"

He takes a shaky breath, clenching and unclenching his fists as if trying to regain control of himself. "Y-yes, boss."

"Grab a quick shower, get your head on straight, and

get started. You're the only one who can dig up the information we need. In the meantime, I'll stay with her." My tone may make it sound like a request but it's an order, and Sin knows it.

He shuffles out but looks back when he reaches the door. "If she wakes, call me. I need to hear her voice to know she's okay." I nod and he leaves.

Taking Sin's place on the stool, I sigh and whisper to myself, "She's nowhere fucking close to okay."

Sitting in silence for I don't know how long, my mind races like a torrent of water through river rapids. I'm lost. I'm so fucking lost. When there are things to be done and tasks to complete, I'm fine. But sitting here, staring at evidence of my failure... It's too much. This is the second Bianchi sister I've failed. I wasn't on the crew that was protecting Isabella when she went missing—but my brother was.

Gianni ran her protection detail, and when someone took her, it devastated him. My crew was the first to join the search and we didn't stop until we found her. We searched for three days straight, convinced we would find her alive, but we were wrong. According to the autopsy, we were only a few hours too late.

After that, Mateo had multiple protection details on Aurora twenty-four-seven, and when she got married, the De Lucas took over. Fat lot of fucking good that did her. Turns out Aurora didn't need protection from some unknown attacker. She needed protection from her scum-sucking husband.

I won't let the Bianchis down again—let Aurora down again—I fucking can't.

As I keep my gaze cast down, my hand reaches for the long strands of ebony silk fanned out on the pillow. I pull them back and lean in, resting my lips by her ear.

"You're safe here, *guerrierotta*. Rest as long as you need to. We'll protect you."

Her eyes remain closed, but her breathing becomes more restful, like she's heard me and finds some comfort in my words.

CHAPTER FIVE

NICO

The scalding water courses down my back as I lay my cheek against the cold tile. The contrast in temperature is invigorating. It's helping me both stave off my exhaustion and temper my rage.

I'm a monster. I know I'm a monster, but there's a limit. There are lines even I don't cross. I can extract information with a blade carefully placed on a nerve cluster, a good old-fashioned beating, or resorting to removing an appendage or two. Three at a push. Because of that, I know the beating Aurora took served no other purpose than to gratify Max. He got off on it. He enjoyed every moment. I thump the wall with the side of my fist, my breathing laboured as I try to rein myself back in.

This is hitting Benedict hard. He's as exhausted as I am, and passed out the minute I made him lie down on our bed.

Growing up, he was the closest to Aurora of all of us.

He's... different. Zo, Sin, and I are all bastards. And I mean that literally. We are a highly respected crew and sought after for our various skills, but we're at the bottom of the food chain. The unclaimed progeny of Made Men who knocked-up their mistresses. We're family. But we're also *not* family.

Benny, however, is different.

He's Cosa Nostra, born and raised. The youngest son of one of Mateo's most ruthless capos—Marco Romano. When Benny came out, he was disowned. I didn't want him to tell his father—I knew what the reaction would be and I'm not worth the consequences he's faced because of it. What he did to my Benny was abhorrent, but when he eventually told me the vitriol Marco spewed at him, it made me want to hunt him down, cut his tongue out, and feed it to him.

Benny vetoed the suggestion. *Spoil sport.*

Even now I want to kill Marco for the pain he's caused my Benny, but it would cause him more suffering if I went after his father. There's nothing I wouldn't do for that man. Even though I don't understand the grace and forgiveness he offers others, I would never jeopardise what we have.

He's the best thing to happen to me. I don't deserve him, I never have.

When we met, I was in the midst of a self-destructive spiral that, had it continued, would have ended with Zo *retiring* me—permanently. I was stuck in a cycle of self-loathing and hating the world. Neither the crew nor the Bianchi capos could control me. More often than not, my targets died long before I could get anything out of them.

What's worse is I didn't care. I was new to Zo's crew. I didn't understand why anyone gave a shit about what I did or what happened to me. One day, a mark got the drop on me and left me for dead. Zo and Sin saved me. They didn't have to. My death would have solved a lot of their problems. And no one would have tossed roses onto my casket; no one would have missed me. Looking back, my stomach turns thinking about how I treated the people I now consider my family.

But they saved me, and I'm grateful. They saw something in me I didn't, and I finally found a place I didn't hate. That's when I found Benny.

We've been together for four years now. In fact, we met at Aurora's wedding. What he saw in me, I will never understand. But he walked up to me—in no way intimidated by my default fuck-around-and-find out glare—and asked me out, broad smile on his face, infectious joy radiating from him.

I thought he was an infuriating ray of fucking sunshine, determined to annoy the fuck out of me. I also thought he was gorgeous with an ass I wanted to ride hard and a cocky little mouth I wanted to silence with my dick.

My complete opposite. He is day to my night, light to my dark, and obedient to my commands.

Just imagining his hands on my thighs makes me hard. I run a hand down my torso, feathering my fingers along the ridges of my abdomen, down to my rapidly hardening length, gripping tight as I imagine my Benny on his knees, eager to suck my cock. I imagine how he runs his tongue along the base of my shaft, teases every rung of my ladder, and takes me all the way to the back of his throat. He has a way of sealing his eager lips around my crown with a sinful technique that coaxes a near constant stream of pre-cum from me. Just as the beginning of an orgasm tingles at the base of my spine, I hear the shower door being wrenched open with a loud rattle. I'm spun around, slammed back against the cold tile, and I'm unable to prevent the strangled grunt that's forced from my lungs.

Benny stands before me, a mix of anger and desire burning in his gaze, so worked up he's practically bouncing on the balls of his feet. "How *fucking dare you* deny me what's mine."

He's sexy as fuck right now, the frenzy of emotion in his eyes hitting me full in the chest. Benny looks desperate and cock-hungry; it enflames me. But as his Dom, there's no fucking way I'll let this behaviour stand. He's *mine* to command, not the other way around.

I reach out slowly, running my hand up his neck and in a quick jerk I grab his hair, pull his head back ruthlessly and force him to his knees. His chest heaves, and his eyes shine with lust. His tongue traces his lower lip before he bites it. Benny is waiting for me to make my next move—like a good fucking boy.

"Fucking brat. Who do you think are? My orgasms are mine to do with as I please. If you want my cum, then you can beg for it. Beg for my dick like the dirty little whore you are." I run my other hand along his upper lip as my cock twitches eagerly in front of his mouth. "Tell me what I want to hear."

"Let me suck your dick, Nico. I want to taste you on

my tongue and drink you down." He's panting, squirming, and desperate. Fuck, I love this gorgeous little brat. I'm going to spank his ass so hard later for daring to control my pleasure. There's a lot I'll do for Benedict, but taking direction when it comes to sex is not one of them. He is mine to own, and it's his pleasure to obey my every demand, to satisfy my every desire.

"I'm not sure you deserve it. Why should I reward such bratty behaviour?"

"Please," he begs and licks his lips, the pink tip of his eager tongue peeking out as he pants. "Nico, *please.*"

I thrust forward, forcing his mouth wide, his tongue sliding under my dick, while I bottom out in his throat. He's wet and warm and feels like fucking heaven. He swallows, eyes watering as I gaze down at my man gagging on my cock. "Fuck yes, Bambi, you'll take what I give you and beg me for more."

I piston savagely, chasing my orgasm as he moans. I can feel it through my cock, little vibrations that spur on my release. He's careful to avoid catching the barbells with his teeth while also caressing them with his tongue. He's so fucking good with his mouth, but I don't want to come down his throat. "That's all you fucking get, you ungrateful brat. Stand up," I grunt, dragging him up and spinning him round. I grab his arms and place them against the wall. "Don't move, and *maybe* I'll let you come."

He whimpers in protest, but his body obeys.

I step out of the shower to retrieve what I need and when I return, I run my hand down his spine to cup his ass. Leaning forward, I nibble and kiss the side of his neck. He shudders and nearly drops his arms but stops himself. "Good boy," I whisper.

I squeeze the lube onto my fingers and massage his tight little hole. With my other hand, I reach around and stroke his cock. At his entrance I press forward to the knuckle with one finger in shallow thrusts, timing them to match the pace I'm setting on his cock. "Does my filthy little fucktoy enjoy his master's gifts?"

"Fuck yes, sir. More, please give me more," he says, whining pitifully.

He takes my finger all the way to the last knuckle, and I ease out to drive the next finger in and give my eager little slut what he wants. I surge forward with both fingers—filling him, fucking him—then curl to tease his prostate, causing him to let out a strangled moan of pleasure. I lean into his body so he can feel my length against his ass. While I scissor my fingers to stretch his eager little hole for me, I run a thumb over the tip of his crown, coaxing out fat beads of pre-cum.

"Is this all for me, Bambi?" I say, bringing my thumb to my lips to taste him. Teasing a cry of both frustration and near-feral lust. I grab his hair, pulling his head back to my shoulder, forcing him to arch his back and his ass to jut out. Removing my fingers, I notch my cock at his entrance. Thrusting forward, I let out a choked moan as his tight ass welcomes me. I release my grip on his hair to grasp the front of his throat, letting the weight of my palm rest there without squeezing—just the way he likes it. "So fucking perfect wearing my hand like a collar."

He trembles as I yield my hold on his throat to grab the base of his cock, applying enough pressure to deny his release. "Did I say you could come?" With my free arm, I grip him across his torso, taking as much of his weight as I can as I'm pounding into him, mercilessly.

"Please, sir, please let me come." He tries to buck his hips, desperate for release, but my grip prevents it. "Please, please, *please*," he begs, almost delirious with need.

"Good boys do as they're told and get what they're given. You will take every fucking inch I give you and will thank me for it, *Benedict*."

With those words, I fuck him deep. He bites his lip, stifling his mewls as the metal ridges of my piercings rumble against his rim. "Don't you fucking dare come without permission."

"Please, Daddy. Please."

His tight ass grips me like a vice as I growl out, "Come for me." He detonates, coming in thick ropes that follow the cascading water down the tiles. I join him, coming in hot pulses, filling his ass, throbbing as he milks every drop from me. Leaning forward I kiss the side of his cheek and whisper, "Stay still, Bambi. I got you."

Pulling out, I turn him to allow the jets of water to rinse him off while I drop to my knees and lather a cloth to clean him with reverent care. Rising to stand, I turn him round and take him in my arms. "You were supposed to sleep. Come with me."

I walk him out of the shower stall, wrap him in the nearest towel, and dry him off. Once I've dried myself off too, I lead him back to bed and lie down, pulling him with me. He burrows into my neck, and I pull the covers over us both. "Sleep, Bambi."

"I love you, Nico," he says sleepily, drifting off with a satisfied sigh.

The rage I was feeling has subsided thanks to this beautiful man. I'll slip out once he's asleep, but right now I just need to hold him. I want to make him feel better in any way I can.

"*Ti amo*, Bambi," I murmur into his just-been-fucked unruly, auburn tendrils. They tickle my nose and it's a feeling I adore. It's peaceful, like home. Something that is characteristically Benny. My sunshine guy, with the chaotic energy of a springer spaniel and a heart so full of love, it awes me. He is my opposite, but he soothes me like no one can. Calms my demons.

I MAY HAVE POWER NAPPED, but I tore myself out of the comfort of Benny's arms—eventually. Right now, I'm driving Doc Em back to the safe house. I wouldn't say I like her—I don't like many people. I respect her, though I'm not sure what her deal is. She's someone that gives off a perpetual vibe of *touch me and no one will ever find the body*.

She doesn't talk much, and she's not interested in what other people have to say. I find it refreshing—she's a kindred spirit.

We drive in comfortable silence while I run a non-standard route to make sure we're not being followed. She blows out the occasional huff of frustration as she glares down at her phone.

"Everything alright?" I ask, regretting my decision

immediately. I don't chat. The residual calm from my time with Benny appears to have weakened my ordinarily stony façade.

"Someone at work who won't take 'fuck off' for an answer."

I glance over at her, anger emanating from my eyes at the idea that someone is crossing a line with her.

"Down boy, I can handle it," she laughs out. "I forget there are men out there who respect the word *no* sometimes. Calm down and get back in your box."

"I meant no disrespect. I'm sure you've got it handled." I tip my chin, impressed by her moxie.

"I'm sorry, Nico," she says quietly after a few minutes. "A nurse at the hospital seems to have developed a fascination with me. He made it extremely difficult to borrow what I needed for Mrs. De L—" she stumbles on her words, pulling a face as they appear to sour in her mouth, as if choking her, "Miss Bianchi, I mean."

"Do we need to worry about him?"

"Danny is harmless. A complete narcissist with delusions of grandeur, but otherwise harmless."

"Last name?" I push.

She hesitates, considering the implications of giving his details to a man of my... talents. She shrugs before giving in. "Costello, his name is Daniel Costello." She takes a breath and then adds, "Don't kill him, Nico. The guy's a prick, but not a threat."

"Understood." I nod, accepting that I'm not supposed to kill him. Doesn't mean I won't, but I will pass his details on to Sin to have him checked out.

Ten minutes later, we're pulling into the garage. She heads down with what she can carry, and I transfer the rest down to Sick Bay. It's what I call it, or at least it is since Benny forced me to watch what must be every fucking episode of *Star Trek* ever made. It's fortunate the man sucks cock like a vacuum cleaner, because if I never have to watch another episode, it will be too fucking soon. Unless it's *Voyager*—Seven of Nine is hot. She could join us any fucking time.

While I'm bisexual, Benny hasn't quite figured out where he lands yet. He's only really dated me. I've tried to encourage him to explore how he feels, but he thinks it's a betrayal of what we have. He'll figure it out when he's ready. I couldn't give a shit what our labels are. I'm secure in our relationship.

That man is it for me. Now I've found him, I'm not letting him go. And I'll keep telling him until it sinks in.

I'm on my third and final trip down to the basement. I knock on the door this time and pop my head in, letting her know everything she requested is here. As I look over the scene, I'm taken aback. Doc Em raises her finger to her lips, so we don't disturb them.

Strewn on either side of the hospital bed are Zo and Sin. Hunched over, Zo perches on a stool, resting his head on one arm by her side while the other is reaching forward, holding her hand at her waist. Sinclair's fallen asleep in the armchair on the other side with one hand on his laptop keyboard and the other on her pillow, stroking her hair.

Fucking pussies. I take out my phone and grab a photo

to wind them up with later and Doc Em giggles at me. She approaches, then shakes them awake.

"Out of my way, boys. I need to take her x-rays. In the nicest possible way, all of you fuck right off," she asserts.

Enzo rises, tilting his head to chivvy Sin along. We all head out of the room as Enzo calls back, "I'll be back in fifteen."

We enter the kitchen and stop to circle the island. Enzo looks about as well rested as usual, which means he looks like a zombie. Sin doesn't look much better.

"I'll grab a shower and head back down. You two need to sleep. Nico, tell Benny to take over from me when he's ready. We'll take shifts. Someone should be with her always." Enzo commands, shifting easily into boss-mode.

"What about now?" I ask.

Enzo drops his eyes and brings them back up, debating what he wants to say. We've worked together for years, we read each other like a book. "Doc Em needs the room for x-rays—"

"Cut the bullshit, boss. What gives?" I ask.

His eyes flick between us, not nervously, but considering his options. Taking a breath, he concedes. "She needs to examine Aurora. Without us present. Stuff that's not our business, alright?"

"Shit. Understood," I reply, "but are we sure we can trust Doc Em, given the circumstances? We don't know for sure who we can trust, do we?"

With that, Sin punches me in the shoulder. "Shut the fuck up, you prick. Doc Em is solid."

I raise a questioning eyebrow and Enzo growls out,

"She was one of Isabella Bianchi's closest friends. She's known Aurora since she was born. There's no one I would trust more with Aurora's care."

I nod and hold my hand up in apology. "Wasn't questioning your authority, boss. I didn't know. Before my time, you've got a decade on me."

Running his hand down the back of his neck, he volleys his head, conceding my point.

I turn to Sinclair. "I need you to add a name to your list of people whose asses you need to crawl up. Danny Costello. Nurse at the hospital giving Doc Em trouble. Persistent fucker that seems to have a problem with the word *no* and was butting his nose into her business while she was grabbing the stuff we needed." He takes out his phone and makes a note.

"I'll do it first thing." With that, he nods at Zo and heads to his room.

I face Enzo and see his brows drawn in... confusion, anger, sadness? "I meant nothing by it, Enzo."

He shakes his head as if trying to shake off whatever was haunting him. "I know, Nico, I know. We're good."

"Talk, boss."

He cants his head, considering his words before he says, "Everything is about to change. No one knows it yet, but Max just declared war on the Bianchis. We've picked our side and now it's our job to protect her," he rolls his shoulders as if trying to manage the weight of those words, "But it's *my* job to protect all of us."

Well, shit, when you put it like that, I don't envy him right now. But I do trust him.

I'd trust Enzo with my life.

CHAPTER SIX

AURORA

Why is it so fucking loud? It's never this loud in the *after*. After the beating, after the cutting, after the torture. He leaves, and it's peaceful. So, what the fuck is all the clattering and beeping and why, even with my eyes closed, is it so fucking bright? He always keeps the basement dark.

"Turn it off..." I groan out. But my voice breaks, growing raspy, and the noise that escapes sounds more like air escaping from a punctured tyre.

"Please, make it stop. Turn it off," I try again, but my words still sound distorted.

The beeping is getting faster, and it's disorienting. I hear footsteps all around me and hands trying to touch me, making me jump and flinch. I'm not restrained, not tied down like usual. When I startle, I lose my balance and begin to tumble off something, making me cry out in panic.

There's a sharp pain in my arm, and then something breaks my fall. It's warm, but solid. It's unfamiliar.

That's when my voice kicks into gear and once I start screaming, I can't stop.

This isn't right. Nothing is the same. Everything feels different, and every sense I have is telling me not to open my eyes. What if he's still there, and it's not over yet? What if he's not there, and this is something else? Something new. What if Dad's body is still hanging in front of my face?

No. I don't like it. Make it stop, make it stop, make it stop!

There's another stinging pain in my arm, and then the beeping subsides. The shuffling noises quieten. The light fades.

This is better. Everything is numb.

CHAPTER SEVEN

ENZO

"*M*ake it stop, make it stop, make it stop!*"

Aurora's screams are relentless. I got to her just in time, as she was sliding to the floor from the gurney. She's ripped out her IV, leaving a fresh wound and a trail of blood streaking down her arm. I don't want to hurt her by holding too tight, but I don't want her to hurt herself either.

"Hold her steady," Doc Em commands. She seizes a syringe and gives Aurora something to calm her down. It works fast. Her body relaxes, shoulders dropping and the mask of pain slipping away. Aurora passes out again, sinking back and allowing me to release her on to the bed and take a step back.

"What the fuck was that?" I demand.

"Her coma was self-induced. When she came round, she was confused and disoriented. I didn't want to give her anything other than pain meds until we had more information on her injuries. Hand me that bag on the chair. I need to give her something else before she wakes up again."

Judging by her agitated huffs, Aurora's condition is hitting Doc Em hard, but she's holding it together. She's doing a better job of that than me.

I toss her the bag, trying to take a deep breath to calm myself down. The door swings open with a sharp bang and Sinclair crashes through, shouting at the top of his lungs, "What the fuck is going on?"

I barrel into him and push him back against the wall. With all the restraint I can muster, I grind out, "Take a breath and reign yourself in. She came round and was confused. Doc Em gave her something and now we're going to carry on treating her. Do you think charging in like a bull would have helped the situation? What the fuck are you doing? I expect this shit from Nico and Benny, but you? Walk it off and don't come back until you can control yourself, Sin." He nods, but to be sure, I grab him by the collar and hoist him out into the corridor, shutting the door in his face.

For fuck's sake. Sin is supposed to be the stable one. I straighten my henley and return to the gurney.

"You drama queens about done?" Doc Em smirks. "Take this and clean the wound while I get a new IV in," she says, handing me antiseptic, gauze, and med tape. I get to work. It's hard to focus. Every time my eyes wander across her skin, I find a new bruise, a different scar. There's an ache in my chest that grows with every mark I find. *Pull it together.*

"Cut us some slack, Katerina—"

"Cut *me* some fucking slack, Enzo," she snaps, her voice thin but her hands steady as she focuses on the new IV site. Her professionalism wins out until she secures the cannula and then I watch as she releases a shaky breath before rubbing her temples in slow, small circles.

"Of course," I concede, realising that Doctor Katerina Mancini is finding this more than a little difficult. She wasn't just close with Isabella, Aurora was like her little sister, forever tagging along after them. Given her connection to the Bianchis, she's called in frequently for *family emergencies*. Mostly, it's bullet wounds and patch up jobs far beneath the talents of a surgeon of her calibre. From the pained look on her face, it doesn't look like it's easy working on those you know and love.

After administering various meds, she retreats to study the x-rays and images from the ultrasound. I busy myself tidying up and return to my sentry post on the stool by Aurora's bed soothed by the steady, even beeps of the monitor and the rise and fall of her breathing. It settles me.

Doc Em looks up at me and asks, "Are you going to assign a specific member of your team to care for her, or will you divide it into shifts?"

"Ideally, I'll split it across the team. Why? What's the issue?" I ask. From her pensive expression, I see she's worried about something.

"I'm debating how much you need to know to care for her when I can't be here, or I'm in surgery and can't reply. There are things you have no right to know, but may *need* to know," she says, then worries her lip. It's not like a mob doctor is normally concerned with patient confidentiality, but usually she's not considering the long-term care of mafia royalty.

"Until we can get hold of Mateo, treat me as her next of kin. I will take responsibility for her medical care. Her fucking husband did this to her and believes her to be dead. As far as I'm concerned, Aurora De Luca is dead." I look down at her and a thundering cloud of possessiveness sweeps over me, urging me to say, "This is Aurora Bianchi, and she's our responsibility... until we can locate her father."

Unease practically radiates off her as she fiddles with the pages of the makeshift chart she's put together.

"This is bad, Zo," she says candidly as she shows me her notes, "For right now, she's stable. We were lucky with the stab wound; it just missed the spleen. However, she has extensive bruising across her abdomen, and there was minor bleeding from blunt force trauma to her liver. From the ultrasound and observations, it appears to be resolving itself and shouldn't require surgery. She will need extensive bed rest, painkillers, and antibiotics. I'll leave you a detailed schedule for meds."

"Okay, sounds pretty straightforward. What's got you nervous?" I ask.

"The biggest problem is her mental state. We can't have her freaking out like that again. Now that we know she can wake up, we're going to need to medicate her. The abdomen is the most pressing concern, but she also has dozens of bruises, stitches, and a few serious fractures—some I'll need to splint. When I say bed rest, she needs to be immobile and calm. I need to keep a handle on her blood pressure."

"What about her other injuries?"

"Fractures to the right eye socket, left wrist, right ankle, and her collarbone. She's got two broken ribs, and a dislocated knee-cap. They'll heal, but Enzo," she takes a steadying breath and looks down at her notes, "from what I saw on the x-rays. This is nothing compared to the historic injuries. There wasn't a bone I scanned that didn't show remodelling."

"Fuck, I'm going to kill him," I grind out, balling my fists finding it hard to temper my reactions. Doc Em doesn't react, but from the way she's fiddling with her sleeve and avoiding my eyes, I know there's more. "What are you not telling me?"

She blanches before dropping her shoulders in resignation and says, "Whoever did this... raped her."

My eyes slam closed as my anger bubbles over. I need to scream and rage and hurt something... but not here. Not in front of Katerina. Turning and stomping out of the room, I throw the door wide and storm into Nico's chamber next door. Slamming the door behind me, I bellow in frustration, up-ending the nearest bench. I send Nico's favourite weapon display flying and lose track of what I'm holding. I don't know what I'm doing, but it involves throwing a lot of things.

From the doorway, I hear Sin barking at me, but his words don't register. Everything is hazy. My heartbeat pounds in my ears as I try and fail to regulate my temper.

"Turn around. Look at me right now, Zo."

I turn and meet his eyes, realising I'm panting like a

feral beast. Shoulders rising and falling in exaggerated movements, I feel like my anger is running rampant like a wildfire through my body. I clench my fists as I attempt to get myself back under control.

Sin's presence affects me like it always does. He dowses the flames, cooling my temper and comforting me in a way I can't explain but will never question. I focus on my breathing, slowing it down and using his unwavering gaze to centre myself.

"Thank you. Stay out here, give me five minutes," I say. "No arguments, Sin."

I return to Doc Em, unfurling my fists as I assume the mask of a man in control. I rub my face and shake off my outburst. "Sorry," I say, ashamed of my behaviour. "Is she going to be okay?"

"I treated the abrasions from the—" she swallows, her throat bobbing harshly as she tries to get the words out, "rape. So physically, yes, she will be alright. But mentally?" she adds, "Enzo, you and your guys, you're not trained for this. I don't know what her mental state will be. I need you to promise me you'll look after her. That you'll get her help if she needs it. If you can't give me your word, I will take her and have her admitted now."

"You know that can't happen. The minute you admit her, she's traceable. Even if we used a fake name, it's too big a risk. She has to stay here," I declare, and Doc Em's brows furrow with worry. "But if we need to, we'll bring help to her. Hell, I'll kidnap a shrink if I have to," I joke, trying to reassure her with a smile.

Her frown doesn't shift. "You may have to, Enzo."

She distracts me by taking me through the meds in minute detail. As she finishes, there's a soft knock on the door before Sinclair appears. While he seems to have dealt with his earlier outburst and is back to his usual calm and considered self, I still feel overwhelmed. I'll have to ask him how he does that, because the rage I feel every time I look at Aurora's injuries is all-consuming. I'm so wound up, I can hear my pulse racing, pounding my ear drums.

Sin has a knack for reading people and knowing what they need. I can see all the cogs in his head turning as he senses the tension radiating out of Doc Em, whereas my skill has always been in making the hard choices and following them through.

I'm not an inflexible guy. In any situation, I'll listen to the available information and assess the issue at hand. I'll listen to my crew and consider their suggestions. But the burden of responsibility is mine. They place their lives in my hands, and it's my job to take that trust seriously. Right now, Aurora is in our care, and that makes her my responsibility.

I'll do whatever it takes to keep her safe, but we can't move her.

"Walk me through the plan," he says, steering Doc Em to the back counter as she repeats the instructions and the medication timings.

I'm drawn back to Aurora. My shoulders drop and I let out a breath and relax back into my perch on the stool again. After a few minutes, Sin is up to speed and Doc Em shows us how to administer the meds into her IV. We've botched it before when one of us has needed patching up, but I'd rather know how to do it right. The last thing I want is to do anything that causes Aurora more pain. Doc Em grabs some things from a hefty-looking bag she brought with her. She's careful as she puts Aurora's wrist into a reinforced splint and secures the Velcro strap. "Be sure this isn't too tight," she instructs Sin, and moves on to the plastic boot for her ankle. "This one needs to be loose enough to allow for circulation, but tight enough that it's stable when she starts walking on it. Give it a week before she removes it at night."

Doc Em packs up her things and checks the makeshift patient chart before crossing the room back to me.

"You should be good to go. Call me when she wakes up and text me if there are any changes. I'm on shift for the next four days, but if it's an emergency, you call me. You have enough meds until then." She packs her medical bag. "Who's taking me home, Enzo?"

I'm not paying attention as I stare down at Aurora. Sin takes this as his cue to volunteer. "I'll take you." They retreat from the room and we're alone.

I stare down at her for I don't know how long. I furrow my brow at her hair. Fanned out on the bed, it's stained crimson. Her dark tendrils streaked with blood. It angers me that she still bears the evidence of Max's depravity. I can't move her, but there's got to be a way I can wash her hair.

I take out my phone and send a text to Benny. He should be up by now. Nico needs to sleep, and I need an extra set of hands.

I whisper in her ear, "Sleep, Aurora. I promise we'll keep you safe until you're ready to wake up."

CHAPTER EIGHT

BENEDICT

What the fuck does Zo need all this for? I dig out the last of the items on his shopping list and balance it all as best I can, heading down to the med-room.

I've been up for about an hour, but I didn't want to get out of bed when I woke and found my limbs wrapped up in a tangle of Nico.

When you see us separately, nothing about us is believable as a couple. But when we're together, particularly alone, he is as undeniably mine as I am his. Every hard edge he has softens for me and only me. And there's no demand he could make of me I wouldn't gladly obey.

But when he sleeps, I get glimpses of a side of him even he's not aware of. I'll never tell him—it's my guilty pleasure and I enjoy it too much. At night, I bask in this secret Nico. The one who seeks my warmth, holding me tight like he'll never let me go. The Nico that burrows into me and whose shallow breaths tickle my neck, sending satisfying vibrations down to my core and straight to my dick.

Nico has never thought to ask why he wakes up so often to my mouth wrapped around his cock. But that's why. Because that's the only time I'm in control. When he seeks comfort from me.

I wouldn't want to trade or change our dynamic. I bend to his command, willingly and eagerly. But every now and then there's a part of me that longs for control. Though I know he'd never allow it.

I knock quietly and hear Zo tell me to come in.

With a level of coordination I didn't think I had, I wrestle open the door and manage to not drop the towel, bowls, and jug he requested. "Where'd you want all this, boss?"

"Go grab that trolley and set everything out. I'll be right back... keep an eye on her, Benny."

He rushes off and I wonder if he's hurrying because he doesn't want to leave her side, or perhaps he doesn't trust me to keep her safe. Don't get me wrong—Enzo trusts me. But this need to protect Aurora borders on obsessive. Looking at him now, I barely fucking recognise him. His brow is etched with worry, body tense, like a coiled spring. He's shutting down, locking us out.

I don't think he'll ever forgive himself if anything happens to Aurora. *Shit*. If anything *more* happens to her. Fuck, how did we let this happen to her?

He's wrong. She is *our* responsibility.

I glance down at her and I'm momentarily transfixed. It's overwhelming taking in the brutality she's withstood, but even now there's something about her presence that mesmerises me. Her whole life, I've witnessed the effect she has on people. Aurora has always had a presence that captivates everyone around her. Like a star with her own gravitational field, she pulls everyone into her orbit. The only person to ever dim her light was Max. Like a black hole, he tried to consume her and crush everything about her.

A loud thud of the door announces Enzo's return, and I do a double take as he produces bottles of shampoo, conditioner, and multiple brushes.

He must see my face of confusion as he explains, "I don't want her to wake up again still covered in blood. She woke up earlier and freaked the fuck out. This is one thing we can do to help," he practically growls.

His words only highlight her trauma and leave me nauseous.

"You going to help, or just stand there all day? I don't have time to hold your hand through this, Benny."

I instantly flare my nostrils at his tone, and I find myself toe to toe with him, grinding my teeth. "Fuck all the way off, Enzo. I'm allowed to be affected by this. It's not easy seeing her this... broken."

He's holding up his hands, realising his mistake. "I'm sorry, Benedict. I wasn't thinking."

"No. You fucking weren't," I mutter. "You've had your head up your ass since we found her. You've been behaving like you're the only one who's feeling this, you dick. Like you're solely responsible for her or some shit. We're all taking this hard; I grew up with her, for fuck's sake. We *all* have a duty to her. Cut it out and stop being a prick."

He nods and then smiles. "Fair." His shoulders drop, and the tension he was carrying seems to drop away like a weight has been lifted. "Calling me a prick might be a step too far though, Benny."

"Prick," I say, returning his smile.

He heads to the sink to start filling the bowls with warm water. After some deliberation, we figure out how to gently manoeuvre her up the gurney until the majority of her hair hangs over the top. With me stabilising her head and neck, Enzo rinses out the seemingly endless lengths of dark hair. They coil in the bowl, staining the water red. Her onyx tresses had hidden the extent of the blood. We repeat this again and again until the water runs clear.

This is the most random thing I think I've ever done. It's unexpectedly intimate, but I'm not uncomfortable. I take the time to search her face, observing every microscopic movement, making sure we aren't causing her pain or discomfort. The flutter of her lashes, the occasional purse of her lips.

"What's Doc Em got her on? Like, this isn't hurting her, right?" I check.

"No. We had to give her something after she woke up earlier. She'll be out for a while."

"You going to fill me in, then?"

As he continues tending to her hair, he keeps his eyes down but talks. "She's got a ton of injuries, Benny. In addition to him torturing her for days," he coughs awkwardly, "it looks like he's been hurting her for years."

My eyes flick up to the ceiling and I bite down on my cheek until I taste the tang of copper. *"Motherfucker."*

"We have another problem. I can't get hold of Mateo."

My eyes dart down to his. "That's not good, Zo. Even if he's out of contact, Manny or Stefano should be answering for him."

"Well, Mateo isn't picking up and I don't know whether I should be going to his second *or* his consigliere with this. Firstly, the fewer people know, the better we can protect her, and secondly, how the fuck do we know we can trust them? You know them better than any of us. Would you trust them, Benny?"

I stop for a moment and think. "Fuck, boss. I don't know. If they can't be trusted, then contacting them with any of this is the quickest way to get her and us killed. Even asking after Mateo will rouse their suspicions."

"That's my thinking." He stops rinsing, replenishes the bowl again with warm water from the corner sink, and reaches for the shampoo. He goes quiet, seemingly getting lost in thought as he lathers and rinses, but he takes care to avoid any injuries. His movements are trance-like as he repeats the process again. I take the opportunity while his focus is on her to analyse him in more detail. His care and reverence for the task takes me aback. I've never seen him like this.

It's both unfamiliar and peaceful. The way he gently combs through the conditioner, strokes it down the lengths with a feather-light touch. It's an act of care I would never have expected from our closed-off and emotionally barren leader.

The silence stretches out as we both consider our situation. Working on together, we carefully move her back down the gurney and I take the bowls and jug to the sink while Enzo resumes his perch at her side and towels off her wet hair.

Enzo starts rambling, working through his theories. "What if there's a rat in the Bianchi family? Did Max do this alone, or was he under orders? Is Salvatore involved? What if the De Lucas have Mateo? What if Mateo is a target? What if Mateo is already dead?"

My head snaps up again, and the ball drops, realising what he's spoon feeding me. "You don't think...? The other body?"

He looks me dead in the eye and speaks solemnly, "I really fucking hope not. Right now, our biggest problem is a Syndicate underboss who's attempted to kill a don's daughter. If he's killed Mateo..." he shakes his head and scrapes a hand over his scruff, "it's definitely a coup. And we're fucked six ways from Sunday."

I'm shocked. We can't be *that* fucked... can we? I mean, there's fucked, and then there's *fucked*.

I wander out and head back up to my room to search for the only thing that will soothe me. Opening the door, I find him. Still a mess of limbs and dead to the world. I crawl into bed and encourage a sleeping Nico to entangle me.

An unsettling sense of dread settles in the centre of my chest and I can feel it spread throughout my bones.

We. Are. Fucked.

CHAPTER NINE

AURORA

I'm drifting again. But this time, there are no memories clawing at me. No thoughts wandering through my consciousness. No sense of inevitability that more pain is coming.

There's... nothing.

And it's glorious.

I stand corrected—there *was* nothing. The annoying beeping is back, and it's still brighter than the sun behind my eyelids. I try to crack open my eyes and this time I'm not feeling scared. My vision is blurring and only one eye opened, but it's staring straight up at two blurry pools of midnight blue—dark and hypnotic. They momentarily distract me from the brightness, but I shut my eyelid quickly to stop the harsh light bombarding my senses.

"Enzo." I breathe out his name like it's a prayer. Zo can't be here. I've lost my mind. Max finally broke me.

"I'm here, *guerrierotta*."

I feel like I'm losing it. There's no reality in this life or the next where Enzo Moretti is here, let alone calling me *little warrior*.

I try to sit up and am met with more loud beeping, an alarm of some sort, and pain... *everywhere*. "Holy shit, that hurts," I cry out. "Got me good this time, you fucker," I mutter under my breath.

"I need you to listen to me, Aurora. The last time you woke up, you ripped out your IV. I need you to stay still while you're coming round. You're safe, he's not here."

"Well, now I know I must be dreaming, Imaginary Enzo. Next, you're going to tell me you can make the alarm fuck off and stop the lights from burning out my retinas," I reply, tone dry and dripping with sarcasm.

There's some shuffling and the alarms stop, the beeps fade away to a tolerable volume, and the light dims enough for me to open my eyes again. Well, eye. My left eye opens, but the right is being decidedly disobedient. I lift my hand to reach for it, but firm yet gentle fingers stop me.

"Your right eye is swollen shut, Aurora. Doc Em says it will hurt like hell for a while, but there's no permanent damage." His tone is a familiar rumble, the timbre reassuring me as it always has. It chases away any of the usual fear that normally accompanies waking from whatever torment Max has subjected me to.

The obedient eyelid may have opened, but focussing is beyond difficult and is making my head swim. Given how I'm feeling, it's probably for the best. Not sure I'm ready to see what I look like—see what state he's left me in this time. I can't figure out if it's good or bad that Enzo is here. On the one hand, I've been taken to a doctor, but on the other, no one ever sees me *after*. I always wake up alone, where no one can witness my shame.

"Keep your eyes closed if it's too much," I hear Enzo whisper. "Aurora... we didn't know it was you when he brought us to the warehouse. Please believe me. If I'd known you were in any danger, we would have—"

"Done nothing, Enzo." I cut him off abruptly. "People have been doing nothing for four years."

My words choke me, stealing my breath.

"We had no idea, Aurora," he says, voice heavy with regret. There's pain and sorrow in his tone and I'm sorry, but no. I will not sit here and listen to self-deprecating platitudes.

"Cut it out right now, Zo. I don't have the strength to survive another round with that psychopath *and* hold your hand as well." It's a battle to force out the words, but I have to protect what little dignity I can muster. I need him to shut this shit down, right now. I have a way of dealing with this and it does not involve being plied with unwanted pity.

I can feel his unwavering stare. Hear the gentle pant of his breath as he collects himself. Finally, in a more detached and considered tone, he speaks. "Max called us to the warehouse for a cleanup. He asked to dispose of some bodies and as we were moving you, you woke up."

"Wait a minute, after you saw it was me you were going to carry on? You were just like, 'Cool, let me just get rid of your wife's body?' What the fuck, Zo?"

"We still didn't know it was you," he says, his

pleading tone returning, like he's begging for me to hear him out. "Your face is—well, it's so swollen—we couldn't tell it was you."

"Go on," is all I can bite out in response to that. I can't bring myself to assess my injuries in full, so I'll have to take his word for it. I can lose my shit over it later.

"When you tried to open your eyes, we realised who you were, got you away from the warehouse and to a doctor. Given the situation, we called in Doc Em."

Shit, how many more people know what he's done to me? Fuck's sake. "Makes sense," I deadpan. "So, am I dying?"

"Aurora, it's not a joke."

"Oh, if anyone is aware of the seriousness of the situation, I think it's me, you sanctimonious prick." My blood is boiling. I'm guessing my blood pressure is through the roof because an aggressive beeping has begun behind me.

Excuse me for having an inappropriate trauma response.

"It's never a joke. It's not funny when he beats me. It doesn't make me giggle when he locks me up or ties me down. Not so much as a smirk when he cuts me, sure as shit not filled with glee when he burns me, and I wasn't fucking laughing when he stabbed me!"

I'm struggling to catch my breath, heaving like I've just run a marathon, like my heart is about to beat out of my chest. Everything is just too much. I close my eyes tightly, wishing the ball of emotion growing in my chest would just go away.

I can't breathe. I can't breathe. I can't fucking breathe.

With that thought on repeat in my head, I burst into floods of tears. Full on, hysterical tears.

What fresh hell is this?

I feel hands pulling me up and a warm, solid body slides behind me. I sink back into his chest and cry until I can't cry anymore, and my wails die down to whimpers. My incoherent ramblings are reduced to one sentence that I can't help but let escape.

"I want my dad."

"I know *guerrierotta*, I know," he whispers into my ear as he holds me close and strokes my hair. "We're working on it."

I still in his arms. He doesn't know... I don't think I can do this. If I say it out loud, it's real. It happened. Turning my head, I crack my eye open and force myself to hold his gaze. Taking in his features, I can see that he knows what I'm going to say.

"I hoped it wasn't true. When I realised it was you... I prayed that it wasn't him," he forces out, hanging his head in defeat.

"You don't have to say it." He pulls me back to nestle into his torso. "I won't make you say it."

His hand returns to stroking my hair and there, cradled in the safety of his arms, I fall asleep. But this time isn't like all those others. I'm not drifting away to hide from a monster. I'm falling asleep under the protection of someone I know won't hurt me. I don't know how I know, but I feel it.

Enzo is here. Enzo will protect me. Enzo will keep the monsters at bay.

I DON'T KNOW how long I slept for, but this time when I wake up, the monitors are muted, the lights are low, and I hear gentle snores emanating from a sleeping giant trying to take over my pillow. There's a part of me that wants to evict the intruder, but there's also a bit of me that wants to crawl back into his arms and hide there. Perhaps forever.

Enzo Moretti—a man I've wanted to climb like a tree since I was seventeen years old—is who shows up to dispose of my body. The universe has a twisted sense of humour. Of course, the guy I've dubbed Henry Cavill's more attractive Italian brother finds and rescues me at my lowest. Now he's aware of how weak I am... What a coward I've been.

Fucking typical.

He stirs, and the movement brings my focus back, snapping me out of my bout of self-loathing. It's easier to focus now.

"How long was I out?"

"We found you Friday night. It's Sunday morning now. Although I'd argue it's still yesterday. Four AM is not a reasonable time to be waking up, woman," he gruffs out as he rubs his far-too-enticing stubble with his palms.

Snap out of it, Rory. Now is not the fucking time.

"I've been asleep for a day and a half. I'll wake up when I damn well please."

He's more awake now and considers my words before finally nodding in agreement.

I take a deep breath to snap myself out of whatever mood this is when I catch an unfamiliar scent. "Why do I smell of coconut, Enzo? It's freaking me out."

I hear a nervous cough before he clears his throat and says, "We cleaned all your wounds with the doctor, but... but your hair was covered in blood, so Benny and I washed it." For some reason he's awkwardly frozen, looking guilt-ridden.

I blink at him in astonishment. I have a vague recollection of feeling cared for, of someone singing, someone talking to me, someone stroking my hair. In all honesty, I had assumed it was a new enhanced feature of my favourite coping mechanism—a lucid dream or, I don't know, some kind of hallucination. Makes more sense than someone coming to my rescue and looking after me.

Caring whether I lived or died.

That's technically not true. Max cared a lot about whether I died. He just wanted to know how far he could push me without killing me. He screwed that one up a time or two. Admittedly, my memory is hazy, but in the early days there were instances when he "misjudged" as he put it. My most hated way of being resuscitated is good old-fashioned CPR. Hurts your ribs like a bitch. Adrenaline and defibrillators aren't fun either. Hmmm, stab me in the chest or electrocute me... *tough choice.*

I'm really not normal anymore, am I? No one else considers their favoured way to be saved. I don't think I've been normal for a long time.

"Thank you, Enzo," I say with as much feeling as I can convey. "So, first things first, coffee, then we should talk... about everything."

I'M DANGEROUSLY close to feeling numb again. I've been sitting, staring at Enzo for thirty minutes, willing myself to speak. Every time I think I'm getting up the nerve, I bottle it and take another sip from my mug. Doing anything with my mouth other than talking him through what happened.

I *really* don't want to do this. It's bad enough having it in my head; I don't want it in someone else's too. He already looks at me like I'm broken. Damaged somehow. I don't want him to know *how* damaged.

He leans forward and inspects my mug. "You need a refill. I'll be right back."

It feels like he's gone a while. He reappears with what appears to be a coffee, covered in whipped cream and chocolate sprinkles. I can't stop the tiny smile the gesture entices from me.

I take a deep breath, gearing myself up when he cuts me off. "Aurora, I think we should start with timelines. Sinclair and I need to start putting one together so we can track Max's movements over the last week. To help us trace him when he was away from you—when he was making the arrangements for whatever they're up to. It will help narrow down who's helping him." He pauses, reaching out featherlight fingers that brush the back of my hand enough to feel supported yet not pressured. "We can start with that. You don't have to tell me anything else."

I feel like a caged animal who's been freed from a

trap, freed from the dread that's been clawing at me. He just needs dates and times, no details.

"Well then, we're going to have to start with what day it is?"

"Like I said, Sunday."

"Yeah, no, I got that. What's the date?"

He swears under his breath and balls his hands up into fists. I don't catch everything, but the gist was something to the effect of *gonna kill that motherfucker when I get my hands on him.* I appreciate the sentiment but not if I get there first.

Giving me today's date, he grinds it out with such force I swear I can hear his teeth creaking under the strain.

"Huh, short stint this time," I muse. "He locked me up last Thursday, so eight days in all."

Focussing on the logistics is sort of liberating. I can be useful, without having to relive it. I'm guessing that the future therapy I'm going to need in abundance will find this approach entirely unhelpful. But you know, needs must and all. While I'm safe for now, if that psychopath finds out I'm alive, he will come after me with everything he has. He decides whether I live or die, and my living when he decided it was my time to die, is going to leave him unhinged.

Shit, I went off track and now I've got feelings creeping into my consciousness. *Rein it in, Rory.*

"Where were you before he took you?"

"Took me?" I'm confused for a minute. "You're not understanding, Enzo. I wasn't in the warehouse for eight days; he locked me up in our basement eight days ago. I guess it's essentially a torture chamber. Don't know how else to describe it. I imagine it's a lot like the room you have set up for Nico, if I had to guess."

His forearm strains and I hear a small grunt moments before the mug shatters and coffee cascades over him. Enzo runs to the sink to deal with the scalds. It shouldn't be funny. Here's me revealing details that are obviously upsetting him and yet, it's hilarious watching him try to appear manly while also hopping up and down, fanning his crotch. *You've got to laugh or you'll cry, right?*

"Ow, ow, ow," he cries out before rushing to undo his belt and shove his jeans down. I'm met with a vision of one gorgeously tight ass. *Note to self: Zo goes commando.* I strain my neck, trying to get a better view and get busted eyeing him up as he looks back over his shoulder. He gives me a disapproving eyebrow lift. A man's chastising eyebrow should not be that enticing.

Yummy.

Shaking my head, I look at anything and everything else I can as he says, "I'll be right back."

As the minutes stretch out, I reach out to pull the cart thingy over. There's a pen and some paper on a clipboard. My medical chart, it would appear. I flip through the pages and my breath becomes shaky as I read. I don't feel any worse than any other time I've made it through. But that doesn't reassure me like it usually does as I read the near endless list of injuries. Several catch my eye. Broken ribs, a few fractures, and then I stop at the stark words written in typical doctor's scrawl. Barely legible, but I know what it says.

I propel the chart across the room, wanting it as far away from me as possible. It flies toward the door and ricochets back into the wall, deflected by Enzo's return. He's found a pair of sweats that look far too good on him, and don't stop me remembering his trunk like thighs beneath the soft drape of the fabric.

He grabs the clipboard and glances down at the doctor's notes and asks, "Did you read this?" He goes to say something else and stops himself.

"Spit it out and stop pussy footing around me," I bark. Exhaling half in confusion, half frustration. I study him, and say, "Sorry, I know I'm all over the place but... but this is a lot, alright?"

His expression darkens, and I feel like an asshole. I'm doubling down on saying all the wrong shit right now.

"Don't fucking apologise," he grinds out, and then softens his tone. "I mean, I could do without you laughing your ass off at my expense, but don't apologise to me for anything. You understand?"

Relief floods me, and I relax again. "Got it." I hate the thought of disappointing him. He's done nothing but help me. Enzo shouldn't have to be here, babysitting a broken freak.

"But you don't get it, do you?" he says, continuing his study of me. "Whatever you need, it's yours. However you act, it's fine. You've been through seven levels of hell and you're able to smile, for fuck's sake. You're doing pretty good if you ask me. But if you're not... that's okay too. You wanna scream? Scream. You want to talk? Great. You wanna hit something? I'll bring Nico down here. Crazy fucker would probably enjoy it."

I chuckle, "We're good for now, but thanks, Enzo." I hesitate and cast my eyes down before continuing. "I read Doc Em's notes. I've not seen everything written out like that before... catalogued. You've read it." It's not a question. I can see he has by the look in his eyes.

I can see him considering his words with care. "Everything written in your notes I have discussed with Doc Em."

"Fuck," I choke out as breathing becomes more and more difficult. He approaches me with caution, like you would a wild animal.

"None of the team knows the *full* details of what's written there. Sin knows some things because he cleaned and dressed your wounds. But Nico and Benny weren't here. They only know as much as they observed when we found you."

That helps. My heart slowly calms and the pounding returns to a dull thud.

"So, only you know..."

"Yes."

"Oh," is all I can say. I can't bring myself to look at him. This man, my rescuer, my protector, my saviour, knows everything.

"Aurora, I know this is difficult. But I need to know about *before* the warehouse. Anything you can tell us about when he was with you, when he went away, and how long he was gone for?"

The change of subject is a relief for me, and I wonder if that's the point before I take a steadying breath and walk him through it.

"It started on a Thursday night. He came home late,

took me downstairs and left when he got tired. Friday, he let me be until the evening and then it was the weekend, so he was there all day, and I didn't hear him leave the house. After that he would fit me in around Syndicate business. He'd leave around eight thirty in the morning, return for an hour or so at lunch, and then be back after dinner. It was Wednesday, I think—I passed out after eating the lunch he brought me and woke up in the warehouse."

I can hear Zo muttering under his breath and when I look up at him, he apologises and instead starts grinding his teeth. I'm transfixed by the muscle in his jaw that's straining to contain his emotions. He types out everything on his phone as I speak. "I'm sending a summary to Sin," he explains. I nod and continue.

"When I came round, it was dark. I don't know what time it was. I fell asleep again as the sun was rising, but I don't think it was for that long—Max woke me up shouting at someone on the phone. The sun was high, so I guess that was Thursday lunchtime, maybe?"

"What was he shouting about?" Zo asks.

"It was muffled because he was in his car in the loading bay, on speaker phone. I couldn't make out what he was saying, but it was loud. And when he got out of the car, he slammed the door and shouted about 'incompetent fucking Bianchis'." More nodding and typing from Zo.

"Then what?"

I hesitate, thinking about that day in the warehouse. I'm sick to my stomach remembering the weight of the chains. The sting of the knives. How I prayed to a god I've never believed in to simply let me die. Enzo's silhouette approaches me and snaps me out of that memory. "He left at sunset and returned the next morning with my... dad. He was with us all day."

"Thank you, Aurora," he says as he tries to school his expression. But he's too slow. I see the pity and I can't bear it.

"I'm tired," I say meekly, and roll over as best I can, turning away from him. Pulling the covers up, I hide in a cocoon of blankets and wish the world would swallow me whole. I don't like this after. An after where someone else knows how far I've fallen, how broken I've become, how filthy I am.

"Sleep, *guerrierotta*," he quietly responds and assumes his sentry position on his stool.

"I'm no warrior," I reply in the barest of whispers. I feel like a failure. Like someone who has had everything taken from them.

My pulse quickens as I feel his breath on my ear as he utters, "Aurora Bianchi, you have been and will always be the most courageous woman I know. Never doubt my words. You may not feel like it right now, but you are a warrior. *Una regina soprattutto.*"

CHAPTER TEN

SINCLAIR

Enzo texts me to let me know Aurora is awake, and more worryingly, that Mateo is dead. While it was way too quick for my contact to get results on the DNA I'd given them, the longer Mateo was unreachable, the more likely it was that the other body was his.

I don't really know how to process that. You know when something so big happens, your brain simply can't comprehend the enormity of it? That's this. Max, an underboss, killed a rival don. His fucking father-in-law. I've never heard of something like this happening in any family, certainly not in recent history.

But so many things don't make sense. What's their plan? Pin Aurora and Mateo's death on a rival gang, and everyone falls into line? Then why get rid of the bodies? Don't they need them for proof of death? That's what makes no sense to me... how are they going to assume control of the Bianchi forces without that?

My head hurts.

I'm supposed to be the strategist in our group. A role that's driven by educated deductions based on solid information. Only I can't get any fucking information. My existing taps and traces have produced nothing. Unless you count Salvatore having a new mistress as useful information. Quite frankly, I don't need to imagine that decrepit fossil screwing anyone, thanks. The fact she's a Bianchi capo's wife, though—that might come in handy.

I've tried hacking various capos and their minions in the De Luca family, but whatever Salvatore and Max are up to, they're not sharing or they've covered their asses well. I have links into the Syndicate servers, but anything that would be useful to us is buried behind a firewall that's currently kicking my ass.

My next route is hacking Bianchi sources. We can't talk to any of the remaining Bianchi leadership in case we tip off the De Lucas, who are undoubtedly watching them.

Did I mention my head hurts?

─※──※──※──※──※─

HEADING DOWN to the kitchen for lunch, I find Benny with his head buried in the fridge. *Shocker.* He pops his head up and I bust him with half a sandwich hanging out of his mouth while he's rummaging for his next snack.

"I'm not gonna lie, man. Sometimes you disgust me," I say as I grimace at him.

Benny shrugs, unable to respond for fear of losing his sandwich. I love the guy, but it would be great if just once when I opened the fridge, half-eaten food and milk that I know he's drunk straight from the carton didn't greet me. It's like living with a stray dog.

I grab the left-over pizza, whack on the oven, and chuck it in to reheat. I head upstairs for a shower, and by the time I'm back, it's ready. It's the best you can expect from safe house food, to be honest.

Heading downstairs, I'm greeted with an appreciative smile by Enzo when he sees the food I'm bringing him, but he quickly brings his finger to his lips. "She's sleeping."

"How was she when she came round this time?" I ask.

"Better. She's talked some, gave me shit like the Aurora of old. Got a bit overwhelmed when she went over the timeline. Have you taken a look at it yet?"

"Yeah, it's helped me focus some of my searches."

I take his shoulder and pull him towards the door and essentially shove the pizza slice into his hand. "Eat, shower, and sleep. Everything I'm running will take time to compile. Come back in a few hours. I've got her until then."

He goes to object, and I arch a brow at him. "Even if you don't sleep, you need to go and deal with Tweedle-Dum and Tweedle-Dee. Nico's getting restless and Benny will eat us out of house and home if he's not given something to do soon." I point at the door. "Take your pizza and go."

He grabs a couple more slices and leaves.

I take the pizza with me across to a small couch we brought down earlier. It was meant to be for Enzo but apparently, he wouldn't leave her bedside. That man may be a goddamn saint, but he's also a martyr sometimes. I scarf down the pizza and pull out my e-reader. I could read *History of Programming Languages,* or I could read *Tales from the Slaughtered Lamb*. I'll be staring at code for hours later, so a book where a group of misfits fight the neighbourhood monster infestation and plan their attack at the local pub, wins. *Beer and monsters always win.*

I don't know how long I'm reading for, but I put my e-reader down when I hear her stirring.

"Enjoy your nap?"

She shakes her head but smiles before she nervously looks around. "Erm, I need help." Oof, that looked like it hurt to ask.

"Whatever you need," I reply, crossing to the bed and taking her elbow as she starts to shuffle gingerly to the end of the bed. The occasional wince appears as she moves.

She's blushing hard, mortified about something and then it clicks. "I'll carry you to the bathroom and wait *outside.*"

Her relief is palpable as she meekly says, "Thanks, Sin." She won't make eye contact as I disconnect her IV bag and try to lift her bridal style, but she yelps and her eyes dart to mine. "Fuck, that hurts."

I stop dead and wait for her to catch her breath before trying again. This time she straightens her spine and pushes her shoulders back to avoid compressing her ribs and stitches, her head resting as far back on my shoulder as she can while still being supported. She smiles weakly and says, "I'm good. Go slow."

Slowly and with the utmost care, I take her out of the med-room, down the hall to the bathroom. When I go to put her down, I don't know where to put her. I'm looking around as I ask, "Can you stand?"

She smiles and then laughs. "I have no clue. We should probably have figured that out first."

I lower her legs, and she winces as my arms tug at the cuts and scrapes on her legs and torso as she cautiously puts weight on her booted foot. But when I let her go, she doesn't topple over, so that's a win. She clutches the sink for balance and meets my gaze in the mirror. "We're good, Sin. Can you grab me a coffee and give me five?" But as she drops her eyes, she stops and sees herself for the first time and gasps.

"Shit, I'm so sorry, Aurora. I should have thought, covered up the mirror until you were ready. Idiot," I chastise myself.

But she's not listening to me, she's enthralled. Like she's Medusa, trapped by her own gaze. I can see her eyes wander as she moves the hospital gown further up her arms. Assessing the damage and reviewing each injury and then moving on. If I'm being entirely honest, it's slightly disturbing. Her vacant stare is unnerving. Her head tilts and pitches as she carries on, considering herself from different angles. She's completely detached.

She brings her hands up to the ties of the hospital gown and then realises I'm still here.

"Make it ten, Sin." When I make no move to leave, she reiterates more firmly. "Give me ten minutes. Bring me coffee. Get out."

I turn for the door and head down the corridor, up the stairs and make a move towards the coffee pot, quite bemused. I don't think I've ever met anyone quite like Aurora Bianchi. She's a badass by every definition. I am amazed she's not in pieces, given the state we found her in and what she's endured. I do, however, expect her to break down at some point. Spectacularly so.

She puts on a brave face, but she doesn't have to. Maybe given time she'll realise no one here thinks any less of her. She doesn't have to protect herself from us.

After grabbing some sweats and a t-shirt for her, I make myself useful tidying the kitchen until it's time to get her back in bed. Leaving the clothes in the med-room, I go to open the bathroom and find it locked. Knocking gently doesn't work, so I slide down the door and rest my head back against it, resting my elbows on my knees.

"We've got all the time in the world, Aurora, but you should probably note that your coffee is going cold."

I can hear shuffling and sniffling and rustling. She sounds like a burrowing animal until it's followed by what could easily be mistaken for a foghorn but is actually her blowing her nose. It makes me chuckle. I could never accuse Aurora of being... typical.

The lock clicks and a hand appears, making a sort of 'gimme' gesture.

"Oh no, little one, back to bed and I'll help you get changed."

"Any excuse to see me naked, right? Creepy much?" she says, trying to break the tension, but the smile doesn't reach her eyes.

I turn and reach out, gently pulling her chin up. "Let me make one thing perfectly clear. Nothing, and I mean nothing, will happen to you without your consent. I just meant that if you're going to try to hold your balance and get changed, I'd rather someone was there to help. Fuck, you could blindfold me for all I care."

"It's weird having you guys be so attentive. It's much easier when you're cold, ruthless bastards."

"We're all still cold ruthless bastards, Aurora. Just not when it comes to family."

"Fair," she says, volleying her head in agreement.

After returning her back to her room, I lower and leave her perched on the edge of the bed.

"You dressed all my wounds, right?" she says, and as soon as I nod, she undoes the tie at the neck of the hospital gown, it falls, pooling in her lap. "So, there's really no reason to ask you to turn around then. You've seen everything anyway. Hand me the tee," she demands.

I'm dumbstruck and for a minute I don't know where to look. I'm definitely not studying her injuries. I try hard not to gape, but I'm hypnotised by the curve of her luscious tits. I definitely didn't clock those before. *Stop looking, you perv.* I force my eyes up to hers and the cheeky little minx is laughing at me.

"It's very boring down here, Sin. Can't blame a girl for making her own entertainment now, can you?"

I frown and jokingly growl at her in response. She holds up her hands in apology but as she tries to lift them to put on the shirt, she cries out. I step forward, taking the t-shirt out of her hands so I can pull it over her head. It's completely oversized on her so it's easy enough for me to stretch it and allow her to put her arms through the sleeves without lifting them too high. The actions elicit a few winces and sharp inhales, though, and it doesn't sit right with me that in helping her, I'm also hurting her. The shirt is almost as long as the hospital gown. I think it's Zo's, so it's no wonder.

"I can't face trying to wrestle on sweats, but under-wear would be fantastic, Sin."

"I'll see what I can do. Anything else you can think of?"

"I'm guessing this is my room for the foreseeable?" I nod. "In that case, the coffee machine lives here now. And I need something for streaming and... a book."

"On it," I say and turn to get started on her list of very reasonable demands. As I pass the couch, I pick up my e-reader and take it to her. "Don't fill it up with girly shit."

"Don't tempt me," she smirks. As she skims through my library, she raises an eyebrow in judgement. "What is all this closed-door bullshit?" She starts tapping away at the screen. "Time to completely fuck up your recommen-dations algorithm."

I roll my eyes and leave her to it, heading upstairs to forage for her supplies. I make a pit stop in my room for a tablet and make sure my streaming accounts are logged in. After which I swing by Nico and Benny's room. Technically, Benny has his own room but he's always in Nico's. It's more theirs than his. I knock and wait until I hear Nico shout for me to come in.

"Is one of you free to take some stuff to Aurora and keep her company?"

Nico stirs from his slouched position by the headboard. "I am. Enzo has some jobs for Benny, so I'm this afternoon's babysitter."

"Don't let her hear you say that," I snap. "She does not need to think we begrudge her anything, you got it?" I shout a little more aggressively than is necessary. I know him well enough to know he meant nothing by it, but Aurora isn't an imposition, and I won't have him implying she is.

"Sorry," he grunts, sounding pissed-off but his expression is sheepish.

I shake my head and glare, but ultimately it fades away as I hand him the tablet. "She wants to watch something so, I don't know, take some snacks and hang out."

"I swear if I get stuck watching *The Notebook* or some shit, you'll pay for this, Sin," he half jokes.

"Like you didn't love watching it," Benny pipes up, walking in from the bathroom, towel slung low round his hips.

"Watch yourself, Bambi," Nico says, glaring hard as Benny curls himself around him. "Quit dripping all over me, you dick." Nico squirms out of Benny's hold.

There's a bit of me that smiles internally at watching these two bicker like teenagers. Nico can be one of the meanest, most lethal bastards I know, and Benny's fascination with blowing stuff up borders on compulsive. How they behave may appear immature on the surface, but they have a deep respect for each other. They truly care and it's... I don't know... reassuring, comforting, refreshing... It's *something*. I like that they're a part of our family.

That's what this is—a family. A collection of the discarded and unclaimed. No one wanted us, and somehow we found each other—and more importantly —we kept each other.

"Anyway, go watch some trash and bring her snacks. Oh, and her med schedule is on the chart down there. In a few hours, she'll need more painkillers and antibiotics." I turn to Benny. "You got a full schedule, or can I add something to your list of errands?"

"Whatcha' need, Sin?"

"Underwear for her," I cough out. "But you can't be seen buying women's underwear."

"Judgemental fucker."

"I don't mean like that, you twat. You can't be seen buying provisions for a woman right now."

"Oh, yeah, well... that makes sense. I'm on it." He nods and turns to grab his gear—dark pants, black tee.

"What are you up to tonight?" I probe.

"Recon. Locating and observing some of the capos to help us figure out their current loyalty. Seems a bit pointless in my opinion. I don't think we should trust anyone. But information is power, I guess."

"Be careful, you're beginning to sound like Zo. And

here I thought you'd hang on to your Peter Pan complex like a security blanket forever," I mock.

"Fuck all the way off, Sinclair."

"I'm out of here. Copy me in on any info you think could help my surveillances."

"Already got that order from Zo," he confirms.

As I leave the room, I can hear the unmistakable sound of someone shoving their tongue down someone's throat and I shake my head with an amused grin on my face. *Ah, young love.*

Time to get to work. We need information. We need leverage. We need to know what the fuck we're up against.

No matter what it takes, Max will pay for this. I'm going to make damn sure of it.

CHAPTER ELEVEN

NICO

Benny's off, doing his best spy impression. I told him to channel his inner Ethan Hunt, but apparently suggesting *Mission Impossible* over *Bond* was the wrong thing to say. Neither character or actor is ideal, but I'm still traumatised by the Bond film where he walks out of the ocean in blue hot pants. Just no... no.

If she's gonna be stuck down there for a while, bringing her a tablet is bullshit. This is exactly why women say the bar is so low for men. The least we can do is move the TV for her. Now, I will not sacrifice the living room TV, that's crazy talk... So currently, I'm stealing Benny's. He's never in his room anyway, though I'm sure he'll whine like a motherfucker about this. He'll brat, I'll punish him, but either way he'll end up sucking my dick... It's a win-win, really.

I lug it all downstairs and as I'm trying to hoist it all

through the door—I kick it open with more force than I intended. The door slams back against the wall and a startled scream hits me like a punch to the gut. The guilt I feel is unexpected and unwelcome.

"Shit. Sorry. I couldn't balance the TV," I grunt out, trying to peer over the TV covering my face. I can't tell if she's okay or not. "Hang on, let me put this down."

When my hands are free, I hold them up in apology but I can see that she's giggling. I quirk a brow, baffled and intrigued by her reaction.

"Don't apologise. It was an accident. You guys are sweet, and I do really appreciate the kid-glove approach, but I don't know... Could one of you treat me like I'm not about to shatter into a million pieces?"

"Got it, give you shit like I always have." Catching myself smiling at her, I shake my head, trying to snap myself out of the spell she's cast on me. The curve of her smile, the tone of her snark, and the delicate huffs of her breath have me biting the inside of my cheek. She's intriguing and enticing—just like Benny.

I haul the TV around only to realise... "This won't work. I need to do some rearranging. Hold tight." Unlocking the wheels on her hospital bed, I spin it round to face the countertop at the back of the room as she squeals in surprise, gripping the sides of the bed firmly. Hauling the TV and its stand up onto the worktop, I hook up cables, switch it on and start setting up the Wi-Fi.

"Is it like, a male default for guys to make setting up electronics look ten times harder than it actually is?"

"Less sass, you, or I'll put the parental age restrictions on all the streaming services."

"You wound me, Nico. That's just cold."

Once it's all set up and the home screen has loaded, I produce the remote from my back pocket, presenting it to her with a gruff nod.

"Thank you, Sir Nico. My gallant hero," she mocks, and I huff a grunt, tamping down the desire to join in with her banter. I'm not naturally a playful person but I find myself having to stop the smile that's threatening to creep across my face. It's almost unnerving how at ease I feel with her.

"I'm off to retrieve supplies. You start the eternal search for something to watch," I complain.

"Any hard nos?"

"Nah, you get twenty-four hours of your choices, no judgement, no complaints. Then it's my choice and your terrible taste is fair game for me to ridicule. Now, what's your snack preference?"

"Chips and dip."

"I make no promises, but I'll see what we have."

—※—※—※—※—※—

I'VE ALWAYS ADMIRED AURORA. Anyone who can run a successful crew deserves respect. But more than that, despite her position, the fact she wanted to run a crew at all was badass. Like so many other Cosa Nostra daughters I know, she could have just ridden on her father's coattails and spent her days doing nothing except spending other people's money.

Mafia wives and daughters' lives are usually dictated by either their father or their husband. But Aurora pushed to be a part of the family business. She was determined she was going to not only work but earn her crew.

And she did. With her father's blessing she learned the business and to no one's surprise, excelled. She showed a natural talent for thievery, which served her well once she commanded her own crew.

She's an impressive woman.

Back with the snacks, I settle into my spot on the couch, having rearranged the rest of the furniture in Sick Bay. The couch, the table, her bed—again. I'm tempted to throw this shitty couch away. It's like sitting on bricks. I could bring down the living room sofa, but I think Zo would have a fit.

I'm pleasantly surprised by her choice. I came back down to find that she'd queued up *Shaun of the Dead*. I must admit, my already good opinion of her is now bordering on excellent. Few people outside Zo's crew ever tip the needle on the meter this high. It's equal parts refreshing and unsettling.

In the glow of the television screen, her jet-black hair absorbs the light, making it appear almost ethereal. The way the light flickers from the screen, dancing along her tresses is distracting—and beautiful. It's a rarity that I find women attractive, but it's not unheard of. For me it's not about the anatomy, it's about the personality. I may be a callous bastard with questionable morals, but I'm a sucker for someone loyal and honest, highly skilled, and who can spar with me in every sense of the word. Besides that, I'm a lot to take. Most women can't handle my... tastes.

I demand a lot. But I also give a lot. When I fall, I fall hard, and I will never give up on someone I have dedicated myself to. Benny is a testament to that. He also makes me a better person, not that I'll admit it to him.

When I say better person, it's not like I'm quitting my day job any time soon. I'm fucking good at it. Spectacular even if I say so myself. But before Benny, while I was part of this crew—I respected them—they weren't part of me.

Since finding Benny, having Zo and Sin accept him into the crew—us giving him a home when his own family rejected him—that changed my perspective on a lot of things. Made me see Enzo and Sinclair for what they were.

My family.

And it looks like we've just found our latest stray, and she has phenomenal taste in movies. So that's a win right there.

"You know," she says, not taking her eyes off of the screen, "your vacant stare is getting creepy, Nico. Do I have something on my face?"

"Sorry, I was just thinking about Benny."

"You were staring at me and thinking about someone else. Gee—way to make a girl feel special there."

"I was thinking about how he's no longer the baby of the crew. You're one of us now."

"First, I'm two years older than him—baby, my ass. And second, if you lick me to stake your claim, I will dick-kick you so hard."

"I'm not a child. That's not the way a grown-ass man stakes his claim. But I make no promises that I'll never lick you." *Wait what?* Tell me I did not just flirt with her? What the hell is wrong with me?

An alarm goes off on the monitor, and her eyes dart to the readouts. "This fucking thing is really beginning to piss me off now," she says, wincing at the noise.

"It's just the timer for your painkillers. Pause the film a minute." I get up, reset the alarm and head over to the variety of drugs I need to sift through. After finding what I need, I head back to her and hand her the pills and a glass of water. Then, returning with a fresh fluids bag, I hook that up too and inject the antibiotics.

"How is it you all seem to know what you're doing with all this?" she asks with a hint of meekness that doesn't feel right coming from her.

"Doc Em showed Zo, and he spent a ridiculous amount of time explaining everything. Multiple times. Although, you understand that we have this room for a reason. We know how to use it. The guys get injured and with what I do for the crew, sometimes we actually need it."

"Of course, I get that. I'm not stupid." Rolling her eyes at my faux condescension. "I understand the need for medical supplies and the knowledge of first aid. I just meant that you guys make pretty decent nurses. I didn't expect it. You're looking after me when I expected to be down here on my own."

"We may be murderous cunts, but we're not assholes, Aurora. We look after our own."

She considers my words. "It's been a long time since anyone has taken the time or cared enough to help me, Nico. It's a little overwhelming," she whispers, lowering her eyes. The swelling on the right side of her face is going down, allowing me to see the glistening at the corners of both her eyes.

I lift her chin and hold her gaze. "Listen here. Helping you is not a chore, it's a privilege." I pause, not sure how to express myself. "We are so sorry we let this happen to you. There is no excuse." I can't maintain eye contact as I drop my chin to my chest and start fiddling with the rings on my fingers, straightening them one by one.

"You talk like you have an obligation to me. You don't." Then, lowering her voice further adds, "I had the obligation to marry him—to stay with him." My head whips back up, my eyes meeting hers with a renewed intensity.

I growl and raise my voice. "Bullshit. I've seen the scars. Nothing is worth that sacrifice. Nothing." Seething, my breathing becomes more harsh. "We will kill him. No one does this to Aurora Bianchi and gets away with it."

Her eyes go wide as the force of my words wash over her.

"Also, don't expect me to maintain this angelic behaviour forever. Always remember, I'm the psychotic murderer of the group. I can only rein myself in for so long."

She looks at me with confusion in her eyes and in a voice so muted I can barely hear, she says, "I know a monster when I see one. You are not one."

Stooping down, I bring my lips to her ear and my hand to her throat, gripping with the barest pressure. "Let me make myself perfectly clear, Aurora. I'm despicable, depraved, demanding and debauched. I'm ruthless, merciless, and remorseless. I am truly a monster. But now... I'm *your* monster."

I have no idea where those words came from—but I feel them to my core. A deep sense of possessiveness overtakes me, and I flex my fingers. Aurora lets a small gasp betray her and I catch the subtle flare of her pupils dilating. It tells me how much that thought pleases her. She bites her lip, a look of awe on her face as she appears to reflect on my words. After a long pause she says, "Understood, Nico."

I uncoil my grasp, leaving me free to pick up the remote. I press play and we return to Simon Pegg battering a zombie to the tune of *Don't Stop Me Now* by Queen. "We're watching the next one after this, right?"

Any tension present a moment ago evaporates into the ether. She flicks her gaze away from me and gets consumed by the screen.

"Of course, we are. Don't ask stupid questions."

—※——※——※——※——※—

WE'RE HALF-WAY through *Hot Fuzz* and I notice Aurora drifting into a fitful sleep. I get up to check on her and as I approach the bed, I see her brows draw and her lips are moving. She's saying something, but I can't make it out.

From behind me I hear a cough and Sin says, "If you sing to her, she settles down."

"Erm, that is definitely not happening, old man."

He shrugs and eyes up the changes I've made to the

room. "Good thinking, although whose TV did you steal?"

"Benny's," I say with a smirk, and he chuckles too.

"He's going to give you hell for that."

"It'll be worth it. I like it when he's feisty."

"I'd say too much information, but the walls aren't that thick here or at home. I already know exactly what you guys like."

I saunter up to him, taking advantage of the two inches I have on him, looking down and teasing, "Oh, you do, do you? You may think you understand our dynamic, but you most definitely do not. Maybe we'll show you sometime." For a moment, I think my words are enough to embarrass him until he straightens up, and it's like his presence has grown. He steps into my space and slowly walks me back to the wall. *Interesting.* I let him simply to see how this plays out.

"Ah, Nico. I understand your dynamic perfectly well. Sometimes I think we're alike in so many ways, but so different in others. I'm glad you found your perfect bratty little switch." He backs off and thoughtfully adds with a wink, "Maybe one day I'll find mine." He turns, heads to the couch and flops down.

Well fuck me, our mild-mannered super geek is a closet Dom.

There's a rustling of sheets followed by, "When you two are quite done having a mother's meeting about your kinks, any chance of a coffee?" Aurora asks, her words laced with sleepiness as she stretches and rubs her eyes.

Sinclair nods. "I'm amazed he didn't bring the coffee machine down here as well."

"Was going to, but I got distracted by her excellent taste in films," I say as Sin glances at the screen, and I can tell he's confused. "Please tell me you know what this is?"

Sinclair shrugs and before I can launch into a lecture of epic proportions, Aurora chimes in. "Sin, I judge you. You've forever damaged my opinion of you, I don't think I'll ever be able to look at you the same again. For shame, Sinclair," Aurora says, her tone thick with sarcasm.

"She's not wrong, old man."

"Fuck you both. I came down to ask you if you guys wanted anything from the shop."

Both Aurora and I say in unison, "Cornetto." We lock eyes and then burst into fits of hysterical laughter. He's a heathen if he doesn't get the reference, they're called *The Cornetto Trilogy* for a reason.

"What are you on about? What's so funny? Stop laughing at me. Gah, I'm surrounded by children!" With that, he storms out the door and we hear his boots stomping up the stairs.

"Should we explain it to him?" she giggles.

"Nah, fuck him. He'll get over it." I smirk and wrestle my laughter under control. "Are we carrying on?"

"Yeah, but coffee first."

CHAPTER TWELVE

AURORA

M y head is a chaotic and confusing place to be right now. It feels like it's engulfed by a fog. One that is suppressing my ability to feel anything. As ever, my handy defence mechanism has hidden the bulk of Max's abuse from my consciousness, but the fog is stopping me from feeling anything else. I lost my dad, yet I feel absolutely nothing right now. That's not right. That's not how a daughter should feel.

But I know the minute it hits me; it will annihilate me. I'm definitely not ready for that level of emotional damage right now. I can barely handle the physical pain as it is. The aching in my ribs ebbs and flows. Sometimes it's overwhelming and the painkillers barely touch the sides of it. I've got to admit, the laughing didn't help. Fuck, that hurt.

Nico brought the coffee machine down with him this time so he may be my new favourite nurse. Nurse Nico. I keep stealing glances at him while I'm drawn in and out of the film.

Of all of Zo's team, he's the biggest mystery to me. I've known the members of this crew most of my life and before I got married, it was only Zo, Sin, and Nico. They were an elite team, but they weren't close. Yes, Zo and Sin were like brothers—they came through the ranks together—but Nico, he was younger and not tight with them. I want to know what's happened between then and now that has turned that trio of teammates into a family of four.

I've been absent for four years, trapped in a prison of my own making. I wonder what else I missed?

It's like I don't know them anymore. We weren't close friends before, but we've run in the same circles our entire lives. Even did a few jobs together before I got married. I guess I know Enzo best, but mostly through his older brother. Gianni was on my sister's protection detail for years. He was like family. He was devastated by my sister's death.

What I remember most is how loyal they were. Bianchi through and through, and my father recognised and rewarded their dedication to him. I also know back then he protected them from many attempts by the capos to relegate them to less high-profile work. Made Men are all about tradition and hierarchy. For them, having a well-positioned team of unclaimed mafia bastards—men who remind them of the indiscretions they'd rather keep hidden—is unnerving. It upsets the delicate balance.

Personally, I never understood why skilled men are

overlooked because of the origin of their birth. Why should children be punished for the sins of their fathers? It's idiotic. Don't get me started on how the *family* treats women. Chauvinist pricks.

"What has you so distracted? You have one of the best action sequences playing out and you're not even looking at the screen," Nico pipes up.

"I was thinking about how much has changed in the last four years."

"Like what?"

"I don't know... you guys, The Syndicate, and me. Only it feels like you guys changed for the better, the families for the worse, if recent events are anything to go by, and me? Well, that's just a clusterfuck of epic proportions," I say, accidentally snorting out a laugh at my expense.

"You get that I'm not the touchy feely one in the group, right?" he says, looking awkward as fuck.

"No shit."

"When you're healed, if you want to punch something, I'm your sparring partner. If you want me to hunt someone down to avenge you, that's me. But the talking? That's not me, Aurora."

"I'm not looking for a heart-to-heart, you idiot. You asked me what I was thinking, and I told you," I huff out. "I'm not a complicated woman, Nico. I get cut and I bleed. I fall down and I get back up. My psychopathic husband kills my father, and you know what? I might need a minute to process that. Excuse me for being honest."

"You make a good point," he says, nodding and holding his hands up in defeat.

"Are you telling me you don't talk with Benedict?"

A warm smile creeps over his face at the mention of Benedict. "That's different. Of course, I talk things through with Benedict. He's mine."

It makes me smile that a man as intimidating as Nico is unravelled at the mention of someone he loves. His permanent scowl has evaporated, and his facial expression softening makes his tattoos and various facial piercings less intimidating.

I rub my temples as the low thrum that has been torturing me all day threatens to turn into a full-blown headache. I've been skimping on the drugs because they were making everything hazy, but I'm tired and I hurt and I'm still a little grouchy.

"Can you grab me some painkillers?"

He's up in a flash and brings them straight to me. I smile as I take in Nurse Nico, fastest med slinger in the West. I thank him but don't make eye contact.

"Hey," he says, bringing his hand to my jaw. Gripping it firmly, but with care, making me look at him. My breath catches. The last time someone grabbed me like this, I was stabbed. I should be having some type of trauma response, freaking out in some way. So why am I squeezing my thighs together and wondering what it would feel like to have Nico's firm hands holding me in far more intimate places?

What the fuck is wrong with me?

My eyes widen, and instantly Nico drops his hand

BROKEN PRINCESS

with a look of horror on his face. "Fuck, Aurora, I'm so sorry. That will never happen again."

"Nico—"

"If I hurt you, I promise I didn't mean t—"

"Nico—"

"That's just how I get Benny to get out of his head when he's withdrawn. It was an automatic response."

He finally stops rambling long enough for me to get a word in. "Are you done?"

"Yes," comes a soft, very un-Nico-like reply. His brow is furrowed, and his jaw clenched tight shut as he tries to rein his emotions back in. Looks like he's losing that battle, though.

I take him in, watching as he lowers his head and swallows hard. He looks genuinely disappointed in himself for crossing some arbitrary line he'd drawn. For touching me. This is a version of Nico I don't know. I feel terrible that I've caused him this anguish. The last thing he needs is an emotionally damaged crazy person confessing their sexual fantasies to them. Besides, he and Benny are together.

Gah, I'm a twat. These men are helping me and here I am with all my screws loose, wanting to climb them all like a tree. *All?* Nico. Just Nico.

"You did nothing wrong, Nico. You didn't upset me. You didn't hurt me."

"I shouldn't have touched you." He tries to get up, and I've had enough.

"For the love of God, Nico, sit down and cut it out." His eyebrows shoot up at my outburst, but he takes a breath and stills.

"Yes, Ma'am," he says and a strange raucous laugh bursts free from him, expelling any tension he was clinging to. "Never tell Benedict I let you get away with telling me what to do. That little brat won't let me live it down."

I laugh, loving that he's devoted to Benny. They make a good couple. They don't need my crazy ass interfering with their relationship.

"Press play, and let's watch the *Sanford Neighbourhood Watch* get their comeuppance."

NICO FELL asleep before the end. He's lying in what looks like the most uncomfortable position known to man. Half on the couch with his long legs slung over the low table. He's the largest of them, and by rights he should scare the shit out of me. But there isn't a single one of Enzo's crew that I fear.

I've been sitting with only the residual glow of the TV screen illuminating the room, thinking about my current situation.

I'm safe. For the first time in so long, *I'm safe*. I don't know how to feel about that. I'm used to a life of isolation. The more time I spent on my own, the easier it became to prepare myself for what Max threw at me. I built up walls. I like my walls, but it's hard to keep them up when you're being bombarded with care and attention.

It's getting harder and harder to breathe, and no matter how hard I try to retreat into myself, I can't.

What's the point of developing an unhealthy coping mechanism if it abandons you when you fucking need it?

Images of Max invade my thoughts, taking over and reminding me that as long as he draws breath, I'll never be free of him. I'm still his wife, and if he finds out I'm alive, if he discovers that Enzo is hiding me from him, we're all dead.

The room is spinning. That can't be good. *Fuck, I need to get out of here.*

I mute the snitch that is the monitor and start picking off the wires I'm hooked up to. Nico freed me from the IV bags earlier, so I only have the boot slowing me down. Inching my legs over the side of my bed and using my good foot to take my weight, I start hopping over to the door. Only my hops become more like a limp shuffle as the movements jostle my other injuries, forcing me to suppress a whimper.

Nico may be a fantastic nurse, but he's a terrible guard dog. It's pretty difficult for a patient with all the grace of a drunk elephant to be silent, but I make it to the door without waking him up. I open it and continue my shuffle-hop down the hall to the bathroom. I just need to be on my own. Somewhere entirely less people-y.

Is this what a panic attack feels like? My chest feels tight, and the corridor appears blurry. I think I'm going to throw up. From behind me, strong hands wrap around my upper arms and squeeze softly, turning me with the utmost care. "Where are we going, Aurora?"

Calm washes over me and I can finally take a breath. "I need to be somewhere smaller, darker. I need everything to be a little less... everything."

"I got you," Sin whispers, sweeping me up into his arms as gently as he can. After learning my lesson earlier, I quickly brace my back to keep my ribs as open as possible while he carries me. Thankfully, the drugs I took earlier are kicking in, so that helps. He walks us in the opposite direction; up the stairs. Taking in the ground floor, I notice it's entirely too bright, so I burrow my face into his shoulder and close my eyes.

He nudges a door open with his hip and delicately sets me on a chair. We're in a small dark windowless room full of computers emitting varying frequencies of whirring noises as the hard-drives process whatever Sin is currently working on. He leans over, switching off all the monitors to eliminate the light.

"You have twenty minutes," he says, then leaves.

I whisper a thank you as he shuts the door and darkness envelops me. It's soothing and reminds me of my safe space. The computers are both loud and quiet. Enough noise to drown out everything that's swirling around my head, but quiet enough that I'm not overwhelmed. The hum from the machines vibrates around me, calming me to my core. No wonder Sin likes it in here.

I close my eyes. I sit. I breathe. *It's bliss.*

By the time Sin returns, everything feels better. I'm not entirely sure what that was. It's been years since my personal limbo has failed me. And if I'm being honest, I don't understand what freaked me out.

"Don't overthink it. Time to sleep," is all he says, and it soothes me. A part of me yearns for more of Sin's attentiveness. I feel protected—almost nurtured. He took charge of me when I couldn't, but at no point did I feel like I had no control. This is a surprising and disconcerting feeling.

And Nico... we had fun today. He made me feel normal for the first time in years. But it was a lot for me. I haven't spent so much time with anyone other than Max for what feels like an eternity.

Sin carefully picks me up again, returning me to my room, and I see that Nico has gone. I feel like some kind of precious cargo. I'm tucked back up into my bed and unfortunately, reattached to the monitor, but Sin mutes it. He grabs the stool and pushes it out the door and turns. "I'll be right outside, Aurora."

Dimming the lights first, he then closes the door, and it's perfect. I can sleep.

And I do.

CHAPTER THIRTEEN

ENZO

I jostle Sin's shoulder to rouse him. "How come you're out here?"

"She needed to be alone. She had a panic attack. I calmed her down, but she just needed some space. I've been checking in on her every hour, though, Zo."

His words ease my concern. I know if anyone can help her, it's Sin. He has a knack with people. I feel bad, but one of his most vital roles in my team is anticipating the needs of everyone. The turnaround we saw in Nico was predominantly down to him. Without Sin's endless patience, I think minor quarrels would end up in fist fights far more often than they do.

In my defence, that one time I punched a member of my team, I was justified. Benny took my last beer from the fridge.

"Go check where we are on the searches you have running. We need a meeting to review what you've got."

"Give me two hours. I still have a *tap and trace* that's causing me issues."

I nod and dismiss him as I push the door open. Aurora is awake and staring at her hands, picking her nails, looking like she's lost in deep thought.

"Ah, this is where my coffee machine has run off to?" I accuse with a broad grin on my face. She snaps out of her trance and an odd feeling settles in my gut as she returns my smile. I have always respected Aurora but I don't think I've ever taken the time to appreciate her as a person.

She has always been the mafia princess, the crew leader, or Mrs. De Luca. Right now, she looks like a goddess. One I have failed and need to prove myself to. Every part of me is screaming out that she is precious and needs me, needs us, to stand by her, to have her back. I feel an overpowering need to protect her. To be there for her, in whatever way she needs.

"Well, there have to be some perks to being bedridden."

"Fair," I chuckle. "Want one?"

"Always."

I bring her over a coffee, and she snatches it from me like some sort of feral animal. The bruises on her face are still as angry, but the swelling is going down some. "How are you feeling?"

She stares into her mug, refusing to meet my eyes. She sighs and with a small voice I don't recognise she says, "Alright. My ribs hurt like a son of a bitch, the painkillers make me loopy, and I flipped out for no reason."

Hooking a finger under her chin and forcing her to look at me, I say, "You have every fucking right to freak out. You can justifiably freak out every hour, on the hour, and you'll hear no judgement from any of us." I lean down closer, so we're nose to nose and lower my tone. "I don't know how you survived—all I know is there isn't a person alive with the strength you have shown. You are astounding."

Her eyes glisten, and her lips part at my words.

"It will take time, *guerrierotta*. But I know that once you're recovered—once you're ready—you will burn his world to the ground, and we will be right there to help you."

My heart rate picks up and I can feel my neck flush as it chases the surge of emotion to the blush on my cheeks. *Where the fuck did that come from?* It's like I'm drawn into her orbit. I feel the urge to get down on my knees and pledge myself to her.

Staring into her jewel-like eyes, I am mesmerised. I can see every emotion she's experiencing play out in her gaze, and it's doing nothing to quell these feelings that have come out of nowhere to consume me. I need to step back now. This is wrong. She's in no condition to be dealing with my bullshit right now.

Who do I think I am? I have no right to be confusing things like this.

I close my eyes attempting to pull myself out of this trance but just as I start to lean back, her delicate lips press against mine and, in that instant, I'm lost.

I am hers.

Every inch of my body, every thought in my head screams at me to surrender myself to her. To protect her against any enemy, to submit to her, body and soul. I have never felt more like myself, and it throws my entire world out of kilter.

As quickly as I felt them, her lips are gone, and I open my eyes to find that her guard is back up. She schools her features, trying to hide her thoughts. But her eyes betray her. It doesn't matter that with one tiny action she has felled me—she's not ready to confront whatever just happened between us.

With a reassuring smile I say, "Like I said, little warrior, you astound me." Before she can respond, I raise a finger to her lips to stop her. "Now is not the time, Aurora. And you don't need to say a thing."

She releases a breath and I see her worry dissipate. My gut tightens as a feeling of pride at soothing her in any way swells within me. Hers. *I'm hers.*

"We have a couple of hours to kill until Sin can update us. What are we watching?"

A small and impish smile appears before she picks up the remote and says, "*Bridgerton* today, I think."

Fuck... who gave her the remote?

THREE EPISODES LATER, and I'm royally pissed off with Daphne's brother for trying to marry her off to that pompous twat. I feel like I've entered a parallel universe because after forty years on the planet, I might have just realised I enjoy period dramas. *What fresh hell is this?*

"Don't pretend you're not enjoying this," I hear her tease as the credits roll.

"You tell a single member of the team, and I will—"

"You'll do nothing, Zo. I own you now."

Holy shit, why did those words just feel like a shot of adrenaline coursing through my veins? I can feel the weight of them settling into my bones. My throat is so dry it makes me wince, and any response I have dies on my lips. The idea of her owning me makes my pulse race and cock twitch with excitement. I don't know if she senses how her words have impacted me, but I need to pull myself together—fast.

Mustering all the flippancy I can, I finally respond, "Technically, you own all of us, princess."

The instant the words leave my mouth, her countenance shifts. Her face drops. A mask of emotionlessness replaces the humour from moments ago. It's like she's not here anymore.

Fuck, this isn't good. I broke her.

I text Sin, and he appears at the door almost instantly, Benny and Nico peer in behind him. He takes one look at her and curses.

"I don't know what happened. One minute she was mocking me and the next she just zoned out."

Sinclair stares at the monitor and flicks his glance between it and her. "We should call Doc Em." His shoulders slump and I see the worry etched across his face.

Sinking onto the couch, I enjoy it a moment before leaning forward, resting my elbows on my knees, and hang my head in my hands. This feeling is alien to me, feeling like I'm not in control of the situation. Not only that, but I roil at causing whatever *this* is. I'm the leader. I'm supposed to protect the people I'm responsible for, not harm them. In my periphery, I hear Sinclair on the phone, see Nico hovering by the counter, and Benedict sitting by her side, holding her hand. But I'm frozen.

Sin crosses to me and leans down, close enough so that only I can hear him. "Doc Em says she can't get here, but that her vitals are fine and to call her if anything changes. We'll watch her. Go upstairs, shower, and be back here in twenty." His words are deferential, yet I'm under no illusion that they are anything other than an order.

While his influence in this situation seems to help me, it's also unsettling. I'm the boss, so why am I doing nothing?

I nod and retreat out of the room before casting a quick glance back at Aurora. *What the fuck did I do?*

WHEN I RETURN, I've wrestled my unease back to a manageable level and to my surprise Aurora is sitting, reclined in the hospital bed talking in hushed tones with Benny, who's perched on the edge of her bed. I freeze in the doorway, stunned. Aurora's presence is like an aura that surrounds us all, both a distraction and a driving force at the same time. She makes my heart race yet takes my breath away.

"I-I... You're awake?" I stammer.

She looks at me and blushes, "Yeah, about that. I probably should have given you a heads up." She smiles meekly, her body language sheepish and demure—I don't like it. "I—uh, have a habit of phasing out when something triggers me."

I don't know what to say. I'm reeling at the thought that I did something that scared her that much. "What did I—"

"It wasn't you," she quickly interrupts. "Honestly, Enzo. You didn't know. I still can't believe you saying it triggered me at all." She takes several deep breaths and refuses to look any of us in the eye. In the smallest voice I've ever heard her use, she says, "Please, don't call me princess."

Shit. Okay, so yeah, I couldn't have known she'd react to that, but equally I'm filling with rage. My mind running wild, torturing me with images of all the things he might or might not have done to her, calling her princess as he hurt her. I'm grinding my teeth, but I don't realise I'm growling until Nico comes over and nudges me with his shoulder.

"Sorry," I mutter, unable to find more words than that.

"You couldn't have known, Enzo," she reassures me, finally glancing up to meet my eyes and giving me a wan smile.

Finally snapping out of it, I walk over and lean in to say, "Like I said, it will take time, *guerrierotta*." My tone is faint enough that only she hears my words.

She doesn't have to explain any further. We can all determine why she hates the moniker. Every cell in my body yearns to wring the life out of Max De Luca for everything he has done to her—for all the ways he's tried to break her. I would never rob her of the satisfaction, though. Vengeance is hers to seek. But I will make damn sure that I do anything in my power to make sure that we exact her retribution.

If she wanted his head on a platter, it would be my pleasure to serve it to her. Admittedly, I'd probably get Nico to plate it up. He'd enjoy that. I hear a cough behind me, and I turn to see Sin is raising an eyebrow at me, a not-so-subtle reminder to get me to focus and get on with it.

"So, we should get started then..." I look around at my men as they give me their undivided attention. "We've been playing catch up from the minute Max brought us in and made us a part of whatever the fuck is going on. It's time to figure out how fucked we are and what we are going to do next. First up, Sin. What do we know?"

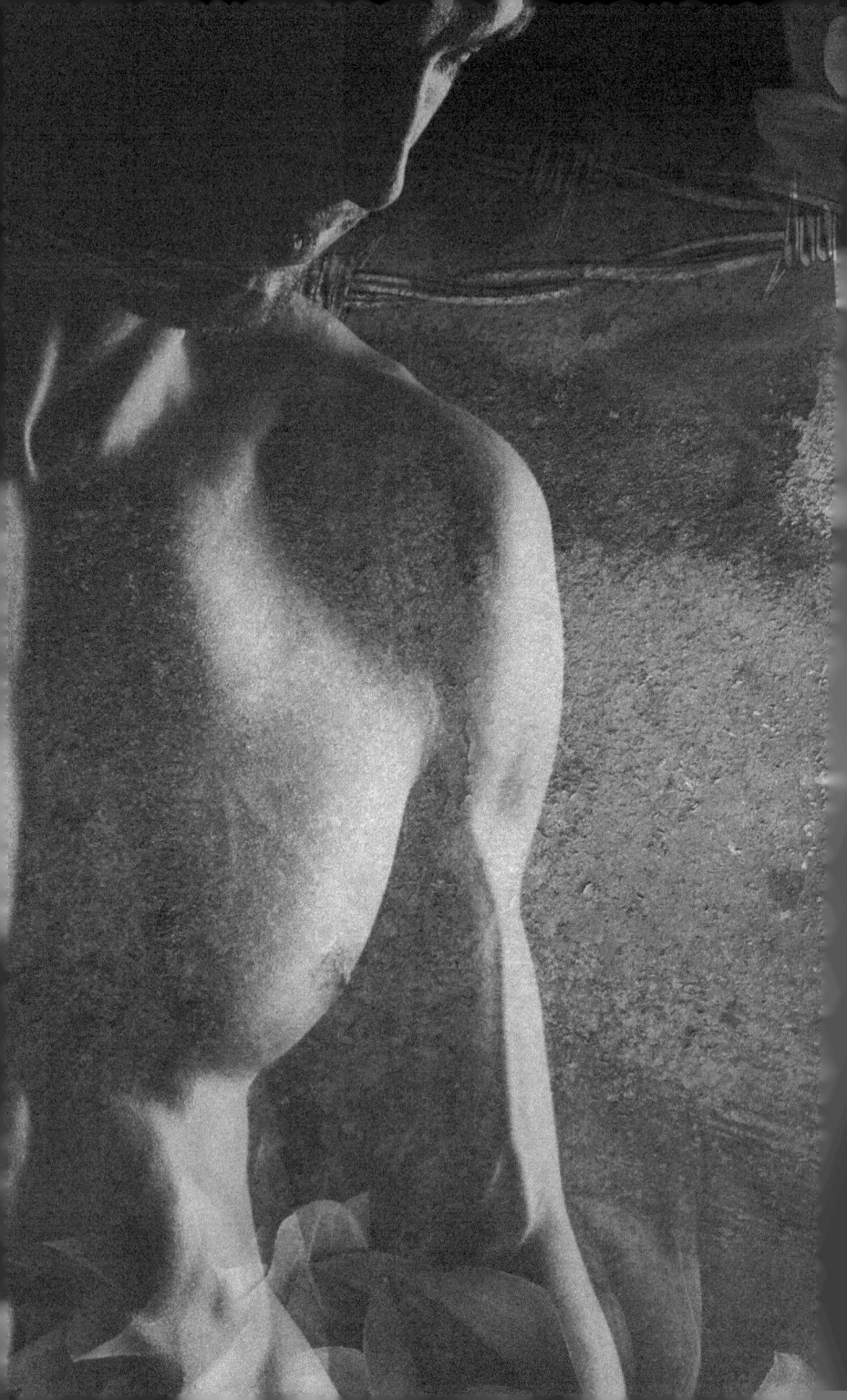

CHAPTER FOURTEEN

SINCLAIR

Earlier, I walked them through everything I had. There's been no unusual chatter in the regular channels. My snitches had nothing for me, but the wiretaps—that's where shit got *real* interesting.

About a month ago, communications on the De Luca side started being encrypted between a select few of the De Luca capos, Salvatore, and Max. Once I identified the days where they were talking on encrypted channels or sending encrypted data, I took a look at the Bianchi side of The Syndicate. What I found was enough to make me want to channel my inner Nico and go on a murderous rampage.

Out of eight Bianchi capos, three of them are communicating with the De Lucas outside of standard channels. That's three rats that betrayed Mateo. Three dogs I'm going to take enormous pleasure in putting down.

While I was running everyone through my intel, I monitored Aurora. When I began, her expression had been that of embarrassment at her reaction to Enzo. All parted lips and pink tinged cheeks. But the more information I revealed, the straighter she sat, a veneer of brazen fury falling over her features. Like witnessing the inception of a super villain—you could see her thirst for vengeance awaken, and it was simply breathtaking. Any hint of weakness receded as she absorbed the names of the men who had betrayed her father. Had betrayed her. She didn't let this information destroy her. She took it into her soul and let it fuel her.

Conversely, when I revealed the names, one person in the room crumbled. I had checked and double checked, but no matter how many times I went through the call logs, one name always floated to the top. Marco fucking Romano—Benny's father. When I said his name out loud, it detonated like a bomb, decimating Benny to the core. Nico took him out of the room, shell-shocked and silent.

Now I'm sitting on the couch, looking into the murderous gazes of Enzo and Aurora. I realise I need to let them process what I've said, regardless of how much I wish it weren't true.

"So, you're telling me, three people who've watched me grow up—who I've trusted with my life—plotted with the De Lucas to not only kill me but also my father?" she spits, her tone laced with incredulity.

"I'm telling you, they're communicating with Max and Salvatore, yes."

Aurora's scowl deepens and her eyes darken until

they look almost as black as her pupils. Her head turns to Zo. So slowly, it looks almost otherworldly, like her head works independently from her body. He's staring at me with so much intensity he doesn't hear what she's saying.

"Enzo," she shouts, forcing his attention to her. With a tone void of all humanity, she repeats, "I don't care what we have to do to make it happen, but I want them dead."

She stops, pursing her lips as she thinks, considering her words carefully. "What the fuck am I saying? I want them brought here. You're fully equipped. Nico filled me in on the room you built for him. I want them interrogated for whatever information they have, and then I want them slaughtered. Hell, I'll do it myself."

"The lady has a decent plan there, Zo."

She continues, "I know Max and Salvatore need to be dealt with, but we have to clean house first. We can't source any additional resources, or trust anyone else to help us until we bring them in and nail down exactly how fucked we are."

Zo is nodding his head before his mouth catches up with him, "Agreed."

A rough cough at the door alerts us to Nico's presence. "There's no fucking way you're all in here deciding on the fate of Benny's father without him."

"Careful, Nico," Zo warns.

Aurora's furrowed eyebrows and tight grimace betray how conflicted she is. She looks pained. She casts a steady gaze around the room, taking each one of us in before landing on Enzo. "We go after him last. We use whatever we can get from the first two as leverage against him." Turning and levelling her eyes on Nico, she adds firmly, "Benedict gets the final decision on Marco's fate."

Nico tips his chin in agreement. I can tell he's thrown by Aurora, giving the orders. While it feels peculiar, it doesn't feel wrong. We all sense it.

I don't really know how to react. There's been a shift that my mind can't fully process. Zo is our leader. He is who we follow—who commands us. But Aurora is who we're protecting—who we'll lay our lives down for and she is calling the shots today. Besides, she outranks us.

Zo moves to stand at her side like a centurion, back straight, head held high and arms rigid at his side, nodding his agreement. That's when he takes back control and enacts the details of Aurora's plan. "Sin, we need to know our first two targets' whereabouts and upcoming movements. Any locations we can exploit so we can pick them up cleanly. Ideally, we need to find somewhere both Tony and Carlo are going to be and grab them together. Otherwise, we're going to have to grab them simultaneously, which is a tactical nightmare without a larger team. Sin, any way you can engineer a plausible reason to get them together?"

"I'll work on it. What's my deadline?"

"Picked up within two weeks; we'll all need time to prepare. And we also want every scrap of dirt we can dig up on them. Nico, I know your methods are effective, but nothing scares men like these more than secrets they want to keep buried."

Nico considers Enzo's words and nods his agreement, then retreats back out the door. "I need to check on Benny," he says as he turns toward his interrogation room instead of up the stairs. As he opens the door, I hear Benny screaming out a tirade of endless rage. I assume it's directed at his father and as Nico slams the door, I'm thankful. Thankful that someone is there for Benny, but also for the soundproofing. Fuck, Benny is loud.

Turning and heading back up to my cave, I call out, "I'm on it, boss," and leave Aurora and Enzo to figure out whatever is going on with them.

CHAPTER FIFTEEN

BENEDICT

Ripped in two. Torn apart, decimated, betrayed. I'm a raging storm of anger and despair. *How could he?*

The man cast me out like trash under the banner of *honouring the family*. A family he has betrayed in the most unconscionable of ways.

What starts as a mumbled rant ends in a rage filled outburst. "Unprincipled, dishonourable, corrupt, amoral, fucking *cunt*." My throat burns as I vent my ire like an erupting volcano of profanity.

I'm pacing the interrogation room like a captive tiger. Itching to pounce, dying to attack something. Nico grabs the back of my neck, forcing my forehead to his and forces my eyes to his. "Breathe, Bambi."

I surge forward to kiss him, and he swerves my advances, pushing me away. The rejection stings and I struggle to suppress the tears that threaten to well in my eyes.

"Uh-uh. Not a chance, Benedict. That is most definitely not going to help you feel better, and I refuse to be a rage fuck. It's more insulting than a pity fuck, and twice as quick."

I open my mouth to argue with him and stop myself as I realise, he's fucking right. Of course, he is. That's one of the most infuriating and contradictory things about Nicolo Fiero, despite how unreasonable he can be in nearly all things—when it comes to me—he's usually right. *Dick.* I flex my neck, easing the tension as I roll my shoulders. "Alright then, smartass. What do I need right now?"

A knowing smirk rolls over his features and he replies, "You, my tantrum throwing little brat," he leans in and kisses the pulse point at the side of my neck, weakening my knees and distracting me, "need to beat the ever-loving-shit out of something. Let's go hunting."

I DO LOVE A HUNT. Nico has various side hustles, my favourite of which is making problems disappear for businesses protected by The Syndicate. He got me up to speed on his current mark on the drive over. It seems there's a group of local college guys who've become tired of having to put in the effort to meet a woman. Our clubs have footage of them spiking drinks before 'helping' their dates home.

Syndicate businesses aren't exactly keen to call the

cops and let them trawl over their CCTV footage, so shit like this we handle in-house. Drug dealers, traffickers, and general scum encroaching on our territory need a swift reckoning. Otherwise, who the fuck will respect us if we can't keep our own shit in order? There would be challenges to our authority left and right.

Nico does jobs like these to channel his less socially acceptable predilections into something more constructive. I'd love to say that the club in question has engaged him because they care about their female clientele, but the bottom line is, they're a business. Hot women bring in more customers, and if word gets out our clubs aren't safe for women, it hurts the bottom line. Callous but true.

Nico opens his door, stepping out into the dimly lit parking lot. He's seen something I haven't. Understandable, given how distracted I am. I'm not the look-out tonight. I'm the attack dog he's going to set on our quarry.

Like lightning, Nico darts across the lot and lays in wait amongst the shadows for our target. I follow, blanketed by his massive frame. There's a loud bang as a door crashes open against the brickwork. A girl stumbles out from the club's back entrance, swiftly followed by a smarmy looking twat who's eyeing her like she's some wounded animal he's going to pick off and devour. I'm right behind Nico as he steps out from behind the corner and takes the woman by the elbow and says, "Taxi's this way, sweetheart." Before turning to me and winking with a smile, "He's all yours, Bambi. Go nuts."

This is going to be fun.

"What the fuck are you guys doi—" I silence him with a cross to his jaw, throwing my full weight behind it. That's enough out of him. I feel the give in his jawbone as the force dislocates it, effectively silencing him.

"I wouldn't try to speak if I were you. You'll only piss me off." His eyes go wide with terror as he realises how absolutely fucked he is. He turns to run, but he's a fool for thinking he can outrun me. He makes it maybe three strides before I have him by the hair, wrenching his head so his neck strains backwards at an unnatural angle.

"I hear you and your friends have been up to no good, Jack." His eyes, now wide as saucers, as I reveal the extent of my knowledge about him. "Oh, not only do I know all about your little ring of rapists, but I know where you live. I know where your family lives, your friends too, Jackie-boy. How do you think your mother would react if I sent her the footage we have of you drugging your dates?"

My prey tries to respond and yelps in agony as his sagging jaw protests at the movement. "I said don't talk. You just don't listen." I spin him round and back him up to the wall, body checking him before taking half a step back and throwing a punishing jab to his abdomen, targeting his liver. My plan is to fuck him up, *just enough*.

"I detest sleazy womanising scumbags like you. Is it that you lack the personality and intelligence to get a woman to connect with you, or are you just plain lazy?" I grunt as my fist finds his left kidney. "I'm going to guess you and your sorry collection of assholes hit the trifecta. Dull, stupid, and bone idle."

This goes on for a while. I talk, Jack cries, I punch,

Jack pisses himself, I kick, Jack passes out. Oops... I went a bit too far. I look up and notice Nico shaking his head at me, but he's also smirking.

"My Bambi and his impulse control issues," he says with a chuckle, clearly enjoying watching me toy with Jack. Relishing me unleashing my monster. I can see from the outline of his hardening cock that my display has turned him on. "Are you done?"

"The shit-head passed out on me, Nico. Help me get him in the car, since he's not conscious enough to take the message back himself," I turn and spit on him, "like I said, just plain fucking lazy. I have an idea."

"Why do all your bright ideas end with me having to get my car detailed, Benny? I'm fed up with explaining this shit to the guys that clean it."

"You only ever complain like this when it's blood, you know. You never seem to object to having my cum all over your back seat," I say, a shameless smile on my face now. This brief excursion seems to have done the trick. Nico was right. I feel a shit-ton better—like I've exorcised some demons.

Nico huffs out a grunt, which I'm going to assume is agreement. He can't deny it. Nico loves to take me on road trips, only they're nearly always kinky. He'll take me somewhere he can chase me or park his car somewhere public and edge the fuck out of me until I can't take anymore. We didn't realise cum stains some leathers. Now we do. Nico was pissed when we ruined his last car's interior. We scotch-guarded this one, but it never holds up against blood.

"Where are we taking this cunt, then?" Nico asks.

"Home, of course, but we need to stop at the store first."

—※——※——※——※——※——※—

I'm ADDING the finishing touches to my special delivery. I picked up some chunky red ribbons and a *get well soon* card at the store. We've positioned him naked on an Adirondack chair in the backyard of his frat house. Tied in a pretty bow that's woven through the slats around his torso and legs, making sure he's not going anywhere until his pathetic disciples rescue him. Hopefully not until morning. While we didn't technically sign the card, Nico and I are certain that they'll all get the message.

> *Dear Date-raping Cunts,*
> *We catch one of you again and we will deliver all of you to the police exactly like this... gift wrapped and with the footage we have.*
> *Watching you always.*

"Are you about done? I know you're having fun, Benny, but we can't stay here all night." His tone is weary as he runs his hands through his hair.

I concede defeat and follow him back to our car. Sliding into the front passenger seat, I sit back and take a breath. But now I'm done with my little distraction, I'm faced with the cold, hard reality again.

My father betrayed the Bianchis. To be connected in any way to Mateo's death—to what Max did to Aurora?

It makes me sick to my stomach. It's been a long time since I had any respect for him, but this is a level of shame I find hard to bear.

"I see all your cogs turning, Bambi. Stop it. We're not responsible for the sins of our fathers. I may not know much, but I know that." His words are comforting and warm me from the inside out.

He doesn't make eye contact as he starts the car, but he rests his hand on the top of my thigh after he pulls out of the alleyway behind the frat house. He soothes me, stroking his thumb back and forth as a sign of reassurance. He's a hard bastard, but when I need him, even if I'm not aware I do, he becomes my rock.

"I know you're right, but to think that I'm in any way involved in this, even by association, is repulsive," I say, trying hard not to be overwhelmed by the shame that creeps its way through me, making my skin crawl.

"I know you were fond of Mateo, especially after he backed you joining our crew. But there's more to this, isn't there?" Nico asks, his tone probing but not accusatory.

"You can read me too well, Nico," I say, a lump forming in my throat, voice thick with emotion. "Sometimes I wish you couldn't."

"Benedict, there's nothing you could say to me that would make me think any less of you."

I take a deep breath and consider how to phrase what I'm about to say. How the love of my life will take it. Steeling myself, I open my mouth and let the words fall out as they will.

"Before you, I was confused, Nico. And while I know

exactly how I feel about you," I turn to him and watch him as I say, "you know I love you." He smiles. It's a devilish smile reserved only for me. "But I'm still quite confused about what I felt... *before you.*"

He nods. A simple acknowledgment with no reaction, and it bolsters me with enough courage to say the next bit.

"I was in love with Aurora for years. At least, I thought I was. I pined after her. When she got married, and I met you, I figured my feelings weren't real. They were exaggerations I'd imagined based on our friendship. A sort of delusion I'd leaned into to avoid accepting myself and embracing that I was gay."

Nico continues for me—because of course he does. How does he figure out what's in my head before me? Every. Damn. Time. "And now you're realising that you always had feelings for her, and you still do." It's not a question.

I swallow audibly and in a meek voice that I don't recognise, reply, "Yes."

It feels so dishonourable to say that to my partner. Someone I love with everything I have. But I continue, "When I realised it was her on that warehouse floor, it all came flooding back, and I don't know what to do with it all." Unable to look at Nico, I avert my gaze to the landscape passing us by.

Nico pulls the car over, switches the engine off and turns to face me. "You love me."

Panicking, I snap my eyes to his, my voice almost shrill as I say, "Of course, I do. How can you say that to me?"

"Calm down, you twat. It wasn't a question. I love you, Bambi, but sometimes you can be so dense. I know you're not only attracted to men. I've been waiting for you to figure it out for years. I have no issue with whatever you're feeling for Aurora. You need to figure it out and how that affects you. Are you planning on leaving me?" he asks and gives me a rare, sweet smile. He'll deny it later, of course.

His loving look brings me back down, calming my fraying nerves. "Of course not. You're perfect for me. Who else would gift me a rapist to beat the shit out of when I'm having a bad day? Best present ever, by the way." I lean over and grab the back of his neck and kiss him savagely. Claiming his lips and showing him just how much he means to me. Our breaths mingle and I feel the familiar warmth in my chest. One that feels like home.

I break our kiss and hold his gaze. "I love you, Nico. It's just I think a part of me has always loved her, too. And I don't know what to do with that."

"Do you need to do anything with that?" he asks, with no hint of anything other than support and honesty.

"I guess not," I reply, unsure of myself. "Doesn't it worry you I'm so confused?"

"Bambi, you're confused, but not about me or us."

His understanding and endless support doesn't shock me like it used to. This man is amazing. It annoys the fuck out of me that most people don't see it.

"You continually blow me away, Nico." I lean in to steal another kiss, more gently this time, and his eyebrows raise in surprise at my tenderness. "I wish you'd let other people see this side of you."

"I reserve this for you," he growls, taking control back and placing his hand around my throat, squeezing just enough to allow me to feel my pulse throbbing under his thumb. "You're mine." Then he tilts his head and pauses before leaning closer. So close, I feel his breath dance along my jaw and across my earlobe. "There's a part of you that will only ever belong to me. That glorious submissive part—that's mine."

I nod, dropping my head back, elongating my neck for him. Enjoying the weight of his palm at my throat, the rasp of his tone, the dark possessiveness that bleeds out of his every pore.

"But there's a part of you that may also be hers. One that wants to protect her the way I protect you, Bambi. The way I look after you... in *all* ways."

I'm so confused, "And you're okay with that? Are you saying what I think you're saying? You'd share me?"

I've entered a parallel universe, where up is down, left is right and someone who doms the ever-loving fuck out of me and is the most possessive man I know just suggested he'd let me fuck someone else.

"Yes." His expression shifts to something foreign. He's unsure, and for just a moment, his fuck-around-and-find-out demeanour slips. He looks vulnerable as he says, "I need to talk to you about something."

I feel my eyes flare as panic seizes a tight grip on me. Those words sound so ominous. My posture shifts and I become rigid, waiting for my fight or flight instinct to figure out which way it's leaning.

"Easy now, Bambi. It's nothing bad."

"Promise?" I slump in relief while my tone softens, sounding more like a prayer.

He captures my gaze and refuses to release it. "I promise," he says with a dominating tone that embodies the ownership and power he has over me. Releasing the breath I've been holding hostage, I relax back into the passenger seat.

"It's not that I'm saying I'd share you. I'm saying I think I would share you with *her*." He pauses and heaves down a breath of his own to help him force out what he doesn't look ready to say. But whatever it is, I will understand. "There's something about her. She doesn't just call to you. That woman brings out something in me I've only ever felt for you. It's confusing, and unwelcome, and infuriating. It pisses me the fuck off, but it's there."

I'm staring at him, trying to figure out how to respond to this. The silence grows and becomes more and more awkward. When it becomes close to unbearable, he rambles just to fill the gaping maw that is this silence.

"I'm not saying I'm in love with her, just that we had a moment, and I overstepped and tried to dom her, a reflex and it was unexpected, and I thought I'd hurt her and it was a clusterf—"

This is not like him. Nico does not discuss feelings. I lean across and cut him off with a hungry and adoring kiss that stuns him into silence. *That's better.*

"Shut up, you twat," I mumble against his lips, failing to suppress a smirk. From the way his brow is furrowed I'd say he's more than a little confused. He's emitting a low growl, disappointed in himself for letting his armour slip.

"You're attracted to her, too. How about we just leave it at that for now? I love you; you love me. Nothing affects that. You reassured me. Now it's my turn, Nico. Whatever you feel for her now or in the future, I know you're mine and I'm yours. Right?"

"Right," he says, breathing out a sigh of relief. He turns over the ignition and pulls away. One hand on the wheel, the other curling round my thigh. He strokes up and down the seam of my jeans, and while it soothes me, I can tell from the way his shoulders drop and the contented little moan he releases that it comforts him too. "Let's go home."

CHAPTER SIXTEEN

AURORA

Benny and Nico have been gone for hours, and Sinclair has yet to emerge from his tech-cave. Which has left Enzo and me alone. We've been sitting in a comfortable yet strange silence while I torture him with more episodes of period dramas. He's had the same odd expression on his face for the last two episodes, and if I didn't know better, I'd almost say he was enjoying this.

Every muscle in my body is protesting at the ordered bed rest they're insisting I adhere to. Yes, nearly everything hurts, but the bits that weren't injured are now aching and making every joint seize. As the credits roll on the latest episode, I try to massage out the knots in my shoulder, forgetting about my fractured collarbone for a moment. I squeal in shock as pain lances through me.

Enzo is quick to jump up from the couch and appear

at my side with his trademark look of concern. I appreciate it, but it was my own stupid fault. Guess I have no patience with being a patient. I'm healing at a snail's pace, and though I can feel a tiny improvement since yesterday, the painkillers I'm not rejecting aren't touching the pain.

"Why won't you take any of the stronger painkillers, Aurora?" Enzo asks, with deference in his tone.

Balls, I don't want to have this conversation. Keeping my eyes focussed on my hands in my lap, worrying my fingers together, I reply in a small voice, "They make me loopy—I can't think clearly when I'm on them and I don't know where I am. Right now, the only thing keeping me remotely sane is knowing that I'm safe here. If I take them, I won't know that for sure... and it's been a long time since I've felt anywhere close to safe."

Zo takes a moment to study me and absorb my words. "I can understand that. What can I do to help?"

This version of him feels like an entirely new person to me. Every time our eyes meet, I feel seen. Understood. Supported. He understands my boundaries but knows when to push them to give him what he needs to control the situation. I trust him, and because of that I feel compelled to share more with him than I think I have with anyone other than my sister. The sensation is foreign, but not unwelcome.

"Nothing, to be honest. Aside from my obvious injuries, everything just aches. I'm stuck on bed-rest and my muscles are protesting. *A lot.*"

He pauses, considering something, but releases a

sigh and looks like he lost a battle within himself. "Shit, barring the heavy-duty meds, there's nothing Doc Em will let us do. Until your stitches dissolve, I don't think we can even put you in a bath."

"Don't be ridiculous, Zo. I'm just feeling sorry for myself. It's not like I haven't done this a hundred times before. Just got to suck it up," I say with a bravado I'm not sure I feel inside.

"Don't do that," he whispers, leaning in and brushing an errant strand of my hair behind my ear. "Don't belittle your pain."

Well shit. What kind of wizardry is this? How does this man disarm every defence mechanism I have? I hold his stare, trying desperately to tamp down this unwelcome bubble of emotion that refuses to be suppressed. A garbled cry escapes from my throat and before I know it, I'm crying.

What the actual fuck?

Enzo says nothing but leans in, lifts me from the bed as gently as he can, and carries me to the couch. With the utmost care, he settles in the centre, cradling me in his lap and positions me so my head rests on his shoulder and allows me to nuzzle into his neck and breathe him in. His rich, oaky scent overwhelms my senses and the strength that he exudes envelops me. The warmth of his body encourages me to nestle into the soft fibres of his henley.

"Let it out, *guerrierotta*,"

And I do. I cry until I drift off to sleep, sniffling into his shirt.

—※──※──※──※──※──※—

I WAKE up in his arms. It feels exquisite—better than I have any right to feel. He's still asleep, his head is tipped up leaning against the back of the couch. His unruly dark hair sweeping off his forehead gives me a chance to study the planes of his face. If you were to sculpt the definition of *masculine* out of marble, it would be this man.

As I continue to study him, I trace the lines etched in his face. Even when sleeping, he looks like he's concerned. Taking responsibility for something and never letting the mantle of leader slip. I reach out without realising it and run my hand up the back of his neck and thread my fingers into his hair. Scraping my nails through the soft hair at the base of his scalp absent-mindedly. It's just long enough to rake my fingers through without getting them tangled.

Who looks after you, I wonder?

"No one, Aurora."

"Fuck, that was out loud, wasn't it?"

When he lifts his head to nod, I realise I'm still fondling his hair, so I pull my hand away, mortified to be caught manhandling him. This blush broadcasting my embarrassment seems to burn a path across every square inch of my skin.

An unexpected twinge of pain surprises me and I grimace as it ebbs and flows through me, making me realise it's about time for my painkillers. I wriggle on his lap trying to get comfortable, however I stop abruptly when my movement alerts me to Zo's rather impressive hard-on announcing itself beneath me and I'm left dumbfounded. *Sweet Jesus*, that can't be an accurate impression of what he's packing?

He falters for a moment as he clocks my reaction and looks equally embarrassed. Lifting me swiftly but carefully, he returns me to my bed. Coughing awkwardly and turning away from me to face the counter, he adjusts himself as discreetly as possible. Which is not at all. If I were a better woman, I would look away.

I am not a better woman.

He glances over his shoulder, and I try to hide my smile but I'm not quick enough and again he throws out one of those, *ohmygod*, eye rolls of mortification.

I giggle—I can't help it. I always find it amusing how some of the most masculine men I've ever known get spooked when it comes to natural bodily functions. "Grab a shower, Zo, and take care of that. Send down this morning's nurse-come-babysitter."

He huffs and grunts, refusing to meet my eyes, and shuffles towards the door, attempting to *hide his shame*. Which turns my giggle into a guffaw.

I hear a muffled, "for fuck's sake," and try to suppress the full-blown laugh that threatens to decimate my broken ribs.

"Happens to everyone, you big priss," I call after him and give in to the pain that assaults my ribs as I laugh with abandon at the six-foot-three-inch Adonis storming off with a very large and very loaded weapon. The full-belly laugh surprises me, making me feel lighter than I have in years.

A few minutes later, Nico wanders in and makes a

beeline for the coffee machine. I'm stretched back, nursing the ache in my ribs from my giggle fit.

I'm surrounded by people that make me happy, that care for me. While this thought is alien to me, it's not unwelcome and I can't hide the smile that blossoms on my face.

"You're going to have to tell me what you did to break Enzo."

"And give away my secrets? Never. I will learn everyone's weakness and use it for evil... well, not evil, but definitely for shits and giggles."

"Brat," he accuses.

"Of course. What's your point?"

My retort causes him to do a double take, but he shakes it off and returns to playing with the coffee machine. Thank fuck it's one of those pod-style ones. Mamma needs her lattes, and it would creep me out to see any milk being stored in the med-room fridge next to the frankly sinister-looking pouches of blood that stare back at me through the glass door.

It's fucking distracting having blood bags on display below the TV.

While I'm lost in thought, wondering how many of those bags were pumped into me by Doc Em, a heavenly waft of java snaps me out of my thoughts. Nico hands me my mug and returns to the machine. He has lined up a little procession of cups.

"Are you the designated barista today?"

"I just got here first. Sin called a meeting and every now and again, I'm not a complete and total prick. Besides, you put Zo in a foul mood, and I'll resort to bribery by coffee to make sure I'm not on the receiving end of his wrath."

I roll my eyes. "You're all a bunch of drama queens," I say in a light tone.

"And you woke up sassy and itching to start a fight, apparently." He approaches me with the swagger of a wild animal stalking its prey and drops his voice to a raspy growl. "There are many people in this house that would gladly take a brat in hand, Aurora." He has a sinful smirk on his lips, but something causes it to drop, and he looks back at me sternly. "Enzo is not one of them—be careful you don't push him too far."

Well, that's cryptic as fuck and in no way informative. What does that mean? Before I have time to dwell on it, I hear feet pounding down the stairs and the loud voices of Benny and Sinclair. They're joking about something, but I can't make out what until they come through the door with wide grins on their faces.

"Okay, you little hellion, what did you do to wedge a stick up Enzo's ass already this morning?" Benny asks with a chuckle. "Sin and I can't figure it out. Spill, Aurora."

"Me?" I say as innocently as I can muster. "Absolutely nothing, my dear Benedict." I smirk at him and for the first time since I arrived here, I feel like the old Aurora, when we were kids together and I was Rory and he was Benny. Like I'm not a stranger to someone I used to know so well. Taken out of the banter for a moment, my face must drop because Benny's face looks worried now. I tip my head, encouraging him to come closer, and when he's close enough that only he can hear me, I say, "I've missed you, Benny. Please forgive me for disappearing on you. And what's with calling me *Aurora*?"

He shakes his head and leans into me, hugging me as much as he can without causing me any pain, and whispers, "Shut up, Rory. I missed you too, but I had my own shit to work through. And we're both here now. We can talk another time. Just hug me and let's get started on our plan."

I squeeze him back as much as my injuries allow and pull away to take in this much calmer Benny than yesterday. "I take it Nico's distraction helped?"

"If you mean I'm no longer experiencing violent bouts of rage, then yes... I'm angry still, but I have it under control." He pauses and shame washes over his face. "I'm sorry, Rory. What my father has done to y—"

I place my index finger over his lips and glare at him. "You are not your father. You are not responsible for his actions any more than I am responsible for Max's." I give him a broad smile I hope is reassuring, and he nods, retreating to the couch and sitting next to Nico, who winds his arm along the back of the cushion behind him so he can stroke his arm. A part of me envies their connection and how obviously and effortlessly they comfort each other. I don't know what Nico did to pull Benny out of his funk, but whatever he did, it's impressive.

I catch Sin watching me, but he doesn't look away.

Sin watches everyone, and he uses any information he gleans to diffuse tensions within the group. That man is the glue that holds them together. Just like he knew what to do when he found me freaking out, I've seen him—when he thinks no one is watching—act in similar ways with the others. His greatest talent is making sure the team has Enzo's back. I know Enzo sees everything he does, but right now I wonder if Nico and Benny understand the pivotal role he plays, or do they just see him as the grumpy geek he pretends to be? They have to know, right?

Enzo returns, breezing into the room with his shields back up. Nothing about his countenance reveals how he dealt with his *little* problem. He appears strong and rigid, and in no way relaxed. But that's what he always looks like when he's getting down to business.

Everyone has a coffee mug and is assuming either a perch on the counter or the couch as he calls this meeting to order.

"Sin has found something that will work, but it's risky. If we get caught, we'll be enemy number one to all Syndicate members. I can't stress enough how much I need you all to follow the fucking plan." He levels his gaze on each of them and then stops on me.

"You will not be involved in any part of the pickup." There's a pregnant pause, as if he's expecting me to disagree with him.

"Zo, I may be ready to tear their throats out through their assholes, but I'm not fucking stupid." He smirks at my colourful imagery. I pause and lift my chin, ready to stand on the hill I will die on. "But I will be involved with the interrogation."

Zo considers my words and glances at Nico, who's not known for sharing his targets or working well with others. However, he surprises me with a nod of acceptance.

"Nico, you'll spend whatever time you need explaining your plans for our guests and making sure that Aurora's presence won't derail the process."

"Jesus, Zo, I know how to question a rat," I growl, venting my frustration at his complete lack of confidence in me.

"Fucking hell," he mutters and steps in to lean down close to my ear. With complete authority yet utmost respect, he admonishes me. "I need to know you can take being witness to what Nico is going to do to make them talk. Bearing in mind what you've been through, I need to know first and *fucking* foremost that anything you witness will *not* harm you any further. I need to fucking *know* that you can hold it together and be a show of force alongside us so you can help us place the fear of God into them. I don't doubt that you can question a rat. But I'm not stupid enough to place a member of my team in a position they're not *fucking* prepared for. *Got it?"*

His outburst has stolen my breath, but I shake off. "Yes, Enzo," I say with conviction.

Fuck. Me. That's a lot to unpack. I squeeze my thighs together at the show of strength *and* support. He's a formidable leader. I can see the genuine concern he has for me—for all of his team. But I can also see the toll it takes on him.

Right now, it's time to go over the plan. I sit still as a statue yet alert, observing and absorbing the details. Everything they need to source, where they need to be and when, and what I need to prepare for.

In two weeks, we'll strike. We'll take the first step in going after my father's killer. We have questions we need answered before we make my darling husband pay for what he's done. There's a larger play happening here by the De Lucas, and we need to know more before we can unravel whatever plan they've activated.

END OF PART ONE

There's a sinister feeling crawling beneath the surface of my skin. It feels like something is trying to break out, ready to rip me apart and claim its first full breath in years. This dark demon, sated for so long, is furious—it's ravenous and desperate.

I scrape my nails down my neck and pull at my collar. I feel like it's choking me from the inside out. My lungs burn and a fiery heat thrums through my veins, making my skin itch. It needs to be set free. Free to chase, free to capture, and free to play.

It's been so long, but nothing else will keep this monster at bay. Its favourite toy is gone, and while we can never replace it, someone must sate this hunger.

Something intriguing has just caught my attention. A meek little lamb has wandered away from its herd. Tripping and stumbling away from the crowd towards a dark alleyway leading away from the club.

Perfect...

Foolish little lamb, I think to myself as I reign in the chaos within me and focus on my prey. The beast smiles, happy with its new focus. Following behind, my footsteps are delicate, and I remember the joy of the hunt. I stalk him, waiting for my perfect moment to strike.

This one is nothing like my last, but it's not about how they look. It's about how their fear tastes. How they quiver and tremble as I toy with them. It's about how long they can last.

I doubt this one will last long. I'd be surprised if he makes it until the alcohol wears off. The idiot doesn't even flinch as my foot nudges a rock, announcing my presence. This is going to be too easy, and part of me is disappointed. This won't be satisfying, but I need this. Just a little something to take the edge off.

I wonder what his screams will sound like? Will he cry? Will he beg?

A cruel smile snakes across my face as I cast off the internal shackles that have restricted me for so long. I reach out and coil an arm under his arm and around his torso, reaching up to muffle his startled holler. He's so focused on the hand silencing him, he doesn't notice the hypodermic syringe in my other hand until it's embedded in the side of his neck.

Night-night, little lamb... time for your slaughter.

PART TWO

"It isn't what we say or think that defines us,
but what we do."

Sense and Sensibility, 1811
Jane Austen

CHAPTER SEVENTEEN

AURORA

TWO WEEKS LATER...

I have at least an hour to kill until they'll be back with our targets, so I'm taking advantage of the opportunity to have a shower without one of my guard dogs standing sentry. In their defence, they have been perfect gentlemen and always keep their backs to the shower stall, but it's nice to be alone and be able to savour the hot water pelting my back and easing my aching muscles. It soothes my soul.

Doc Em lifted my bed-rest restrictions a few days ago. She seems pretty happy with my progress. Most of my injuries are healing okay save for my ankle. While I'm allowed to move about more, I've been told to use a crutch. Hence the guys not allowing me out of their sight when I need to stand for any length of time.

When I've exhausted the hot water supply, I shut it off and step out, balancing on one leg while I reach for the towel. Last thing I need is to slip in the shower—Zo would bench me in a heartbeat. Once I'm wrapped up, I manoeuvre across the bathroom to perch on the closed toilet seat. Towelling off, I then start the ordeal of trying to get dressed. I live in Benny's sweats these days as they're easy to get on and they have drawstrings to keep them up. But lifting on t-shirts is still more of a struggle than I'd like.

While they're healing, my ribs and collarbone complain at the imposition of lifting my arms above my head. They also make it impossible for me to wear a bra. I will never admit this to another woman, but *fuck*, I miss wearing a bra. There's no way in hell I can right now until my collarbone is more fully healed. For years I've savoured the feeling of removing a bra after a long day. Now, all I want to do is get them strapped down and under control.

Our *guests* should be here soon. I need to get a move on. I abandon the protective boot and swap it out for a compression bandage. It'll have to do. There's no way I can show weakness in front of the capos. I'll lose the room before I've even started. I grab my crutches and start my ungainly lollop back to the med-room.

I love that I'm more mobile now, but I can't hide how much it takes out of me. I constantly feel like I'm wading through treacle. Everything requires more of an effort than you expect it to. At least I'm looking more like myself. The swelling on my face has gone down and all my superficial stitches have dissolved. The stab wound is still tender as fuck and my skin looks like a rainbow of mottled hues; angry reds and purples are morphing into camo greens and yellows.

I try to avoid looking at myself in the mirror. Not because I'm ashamed, but because the Aurora I see in the mirror isn't an accurate reflection of the way I feel inside. The Aurora in the mirror looks broken—a shadow of her former self.

I lean the crutches against my bed and gingerly place all my weight down on my ankle—it's not unbearable. I've maxed out my pain meds for this and I've been practising without the boot for the last few days. Doc Em's going to kick my ass if I fuck this ankle up further. *But that's future Rory's problem*, I think as I wrangle on a pair of sneakers the guys picked up for me and make my way to the interrogation room to prepare.

Nico had me set up everything I wanted to use tonight on a table of my own, next to his. I hand-picked everything, although in all honesty, I'm not sure if I will use them all. Every item on this table is something I have an intimate knowledge of. I know how each object can be used to our advantage. A couple of my choices confused Nico, but he'll find out soon enough how I plan to use them.

I trail my fingertips over each tool and my mind drifts. This room, while it serves a similar purpose to Max's basement, is very different in its appearance. It's bright and clean and almost clinical. It helps me compartmentalise what I'm about to do. How far I'll go to get the answers I need. The men coming here tonight betrayed everything they stood for, betrayed me, betrayed my father. For what? To hoard scraps of power?

They're traitors. Whatever happens tonight, they had it coming.

-×--×--×--×--×--×-

I DON'T KNOW how long I've been sitting staring at the empty interrogation chairs, but I snap out of my trance when I hear the dull thuds of heavy boots coming down the stairs and approaching the door. They're back. The unease I didn't realise was weighing so heavily on me lifts at the thought of them returning to me. This is the first time I've been alone in the house since I arrived, and I hadn't realised how much it would affect me.

They've all sacrificed more than I had a right to expect to save my life. And besides that, they seem to have pledged themselves to helping me avenge my father's death. They have an immense amount of loyalty to my father's name and legacy, but sometimes... it feels like there's more to it.

Since I've been here, their care, their reverence, has awakened parts of me I thought were long dead. For years, the only way I survived was to shut down parts of myself. The more walls I erected, the more protected I was. To know that there's anyone, let alone four people who will stand by me—will help me—it's quite frankly staggering. I've been alone for so long.

While they've been gone, I've felt exposed and raw, like every barrier I had built before is vulnerable. When they're here, I feel safe and protected. Without them, I feel... lost.

Sin opens the door and holds his index finger to his lips, reminding me not to say a word. Behind him, Zo and Nico carry a blindfolded Antonio Rossi. He sounds groggy and twitches as he fights against their hold.

"Where the fuck am I? What's going on?" Tony slurs his words, getting more and more agitated. I can almost smell the fear rolling off him as he's forced into the nearest chair, his arms and legs strapped down. He struggles, but it's pointless. Zo has all his weight behind the bear-hold he's got on dear old Tony. Nico nods a hello at me and crosses the room, standing beside his table as Sin and Zo retreat from the room.

It doesn't take long before I hear everyone returning with Carlo Barone. He's unconscious and decidedly heavier than Tony, so it takes Benny, Sin and Zo to carry him comfortably. The stale smell of sweat emanates from his every pore, and I can't help but sneer as his stench hits me. Carlo is every inch the archetypal corpulent Mafioso, a grotesque caricature that makes me ashamed of my heritage. He represents everything that's wrong with the traditions and the institution.

He's tied into the second chair with speed and efficiency, and they leave Nico and me to it.

Nico and I have planned this as much as we can. We can't predict exactly how this will go or how long it will take to break them. But break them, we will. Phase one of the plan is easy though. We're going to do nothing. Just sit here and wait. See how much they'll talk when they think they're alone in here.

Tony is fidgety. He's twitching his head around in all directions like he's surveying his surroundings despite being blindfolded, trying to figure out where he is and why his captors have left. He looks like a disgruntled pigeon on crack.

Tony jumps as Carlo stirs, groaning and pulling against his bonds. "What the fuck is this?" he moans like a mean drunk waking, only to be greeted by their familiar hangover.

I steal myself, tamping down my rage and forcing the vengeful thoughts deep down. I have to maintain control, no matter how much every part of me is screaming to make these fuckers pay. I may have to be rational right now, but there's no part of me that will ever understand how these men—men I considered family—betrayed me so heinously.

I sacrificed everything for their precious organisation, and it meant nothing to them. It takes everything in me not to unleash the fury that's scorching my soul just being in the same room as them.

I glance across at Nico and can tell from the devilish glint in his eyes that he's holding himself back as well. He tips his head towards me, his near maniacal grin turning to something warmer. Something I know means *we got this.*

It's time, boys... show us just how stupid you are, you traitorous cunts.

"Carlo, is that you?" Tony says in a shriek that matches his manic energy. He's going to be too easy to break. "What the fuck is happening?"

"Tony, shut the fuck up, you imbecile."

"Don't you fucking talk to me like that. We're alone. The fuckers that took us left."

I take my time assessing the differences between our two rats. I can almost see the threads I'll pull to unravel Tony, but Carlo surprises me. Despite my distaste for him, I can tell there's more to him. He's stoic in response to the unexpected. Since he came round, he's already started erecting what he thinks will be an impenetrable wall against whatever is to come. He will be harder to crack, but there's no way he'll withstand us both. But it also tells me that while we'll get *something* from Tony, my diabolical husband is an intelligent man and won't have trusted him with anything vital.

Carlo remains silent while Tony continues to run his mouth. "One minute, I was in the john and the next thing I know, I'm waking up in the back of a van. Who do these cunts think they are?"

If I was a betting woman, I'd put money on Carlo rolling his eyes under his blindfold at Tony's histrionics. And I'm already wondering how this idiot was ever promoted to capo under my father. My best guess is that he knew where too many bodies were buried to deny him advancement. I'm trying to remember a single job Tony's crew has been involved with that was vitally important to our operations in recent history and I'm drawing a blank. He deals with enforcement for the protection racket we run in the neighbourhood.

We look after the businesses that turn a blind eye to our more audacious criminal practices. They don't pay us —much to the De Lucas chagrin. They keep their mouths shut and facilitate our alibis when necessary. Perhaps even provide the odd safe-house on occasion, and in return we have their backs in whatever capacity that might be. Anything from chasing off the upstart gangs or thugs trying to strong-arm them, to discouraging developers from edging them out of the old neighbourhood.

Sometimes it's just that we like them. My dad's favourite bakery has been under our protection for three decades because it's the place that made my mother's favourite cannoli.

"You think Manny and Stefano are on to us? This has got to be them, right? No way this is Marco. We did everything he told us to." My ears pick up at the mention of Benny's dad, Marco Romano. I hope Benny's okay. I know the rest of the guys are watching this on Sin's monitors, and he's still reeling from finding out his father is involved in this.

"Keep your fucking mouth *shut*," Carlo growls. Under his breath, he almost comically adds, "How I ever let myself get involved in anything that required your participation I'll never understand."

Interesting. What does Tony bring to the table?

"Fuck you, without me you'd never have got access to the—"

He's a total fucking idiot. I'm thinking I won't need any of the tools I prepared at all at this rate.

"Shut the fuck up!" Carlo roars, and that's our cue. Show time. I nod at Nico and take the lead.

"Oh, I wouldn't listen to Carlo here," I pipe up finally. Stalking towards Carlo, I yank off his blindfold and I see the flare of recognition before he schools his features and shuts down his facial expressions.

Of course, he knows who I am, and he's clever enough to know he's fucked, no matter what. We're not getting anything out of him anytime soon. And that's fine with me. I run my fingertips along his shoulder and then walk them up his neck before grabbing his jaw and jerking his head back. Digging my nails into his jowls hard enough to leave angry crescent-shaped divots behind. "You can just watch for now. Gag him, Nico. He doesn't speak until I say so."

I slap Carlo clear across the face and hold his hostile gaze as it returns to me.

This is going to be fun...

CHAPTER EIGHTEEN

NICO

This should not be turning me on. The moment she stood up and approached Carlo, her shift in demeanour was remarkable, like a phoenix rising from the ashes. A mythic and wondrous creature evolving before my eyes. She's running on adrenaline, burning with anger and giving no fucks that I was supposed to take the lead. However, her timing and flair for the dramatic is impeccably executed. There's no good cop, bad cop here. There's vengeance and wrath. And she may well be both.

I'll take on whatever role she needs. For now, she's in control.

I reach back to my table of toys before hopping off and approaching Carlo with a spring in my step and a smirk on my face. I'm swinging a rather-large ball gag at my hip by the strap, but he doesn't baulk and holds his mouth firmly closed in defiance. "You either open wide and take it like a good boy, or I use those pliers over there to extract every single one of your teeth, shove this in, and watch as you choke on your own blood."

Carlo doesn't flinch. However, my words are not intended for Carlo. They're meant for Tony. My phoenix has removed his blindfold, and my performance is having the desired effect. Tony's crumbling before our eyes—he's pissed himself. Such a pathetic weasel.

Grabbing Carlo's hair, I rip his head back, forcing him to open his mouth. I ram the ball gag in and start buckling the leather straps before he can spit it out. Holding eye contact the entire time—my favourite maniacal grin plastered across my face like a twisted masquerade mask —it has the desired effect because, for a moment, Carlo falters. I can see it in his eyes that a sliver of fear has embedded itself under his skin.

His bravado comes crashing back, and I'm sure he thinks he's saying actual words but while he fights against the gag, all we're hearing is unintelligible gibberish. That's fine. He can waste his energy while I grab the hose from the industrial sink in the corner.

Is this sink big enough to carve up a body in? Why yes— yes, it is. I'm lazy by nature and detest having to take bodies out whole. It's far easier breaking them up into more manageable pieces. When we kitted this place out, I requested an industrial garbage disposal, but Zo said that was a step too far. He's probably right.

I turn on the hose and spray down Tony's trousers and chair, and use the flow of water to encourage everything towards the central drain. We'll be here a while, and I don't need the stench of piss assaulting my nostrils for hours.

Aurora has returned to her table and picked up a large, serrated hunting knife. She's using it to pick out the dirt from under her nails and then admire her talons. She flicks those long lashes up and smiles at me. That grin does something to me. Lights me up from the inside out. Her eyes are bright, but there's a darkness in them that calls to me, like I see a reflection of myself mirrored back at me.

"Mind if I go first?"

Shaking her head, she proffers her hand in Tony's direction. "Be my guest, Nico."

Tony's snivelling is now a low-grade incoherent babble. Maybe Sin will make some sense of it when he reviews the video feed footage later, but it's useless to me right now. I slap Tony around with little conviction. Knowing me, I'd knock him clean out if I put my full weight behind it. He's stunned into silence, and I watch him as his eyes dart between Rory, Carlo, and me.

He's the very definition of a startled deer caught in the headlights, only whatever road he takes to save his skin—he's fucked. We're going to run him the fuck down.

Carlo shakes his head at him in warning and rolls his eyes in disgust as Tony cracks. Well, this is no fucking fun what-so-ever. I didn't even get to use my knife. I sharpened her specially. Aurora laughs as I huff in disgust, folding my arms over my chest and leaning back against my workbench as Tony blurts out everything he knows.

The long and the short of his verbal diarrhoea is that he facilitates locations for Marco, Carlo, and Tony to meet under the radar to discuss unsanctioned jobs. He uses the premises of a select few of the businesses under Syndicate protection after hours. The owners think it's Syndicate business and are none the wiser.

I glance at Carlo, who maintains his silence, refusing to make eye contact with Tony.

"I swear, it was just a few things we ran outside of The Syndicate. A few heists, shipping containers mostly. Nothing big and everything fenced straight away to a black-market buyer. We stored nothing using Syndicate resources."

What the actual fuck is he talking about?

"I know we're not supposed to run unsanctioned jobs, but the money was too good to pass up."

I glance at Aurora. She doesn't look as confused as I am. She slides off her bench and approaches Carlo. Bending forward, she pats his jawline in a patronising little tapping motion before gripping his chin and tipping his head back to force his eyes to hers. "Should I tell our gullible friend here what you actually used him for?"

Carlo glares back at her, spittle escaping the corners of his mouth, his neck straining as his ire rises. But it's obvious from the sheen of sweat that's bursting forth on his brow that he's not as confident as he's trying to appear. He has no fucking clue how to play this situation —how to tackle Aurora. *Oh, this is going to be fun.*

Tony looks more confused than ever and I'm doing my best impression of someone who knows what's going on. I don't have the first damn clue at this point, though I'm intrigued to see it play out.

Aurora pulls her phone out of her back pocket and places a call. "Come and pick up Tony. We're done with him for now." Ending the call, she turns back to Carlo and smiles. "I underestimated you, Carlo. That won't happen again."

"What the fuck is going on? What do you mean, he used me?" When Aurora ignores him, he turns instead to Carlo. "What don't I know? What's she talking about?"

"Who else was at these meetings, Tony?" She arches an eyebrow and looks like a mother scolding a sullen child. "Was it just you three? Or were there other Syndicate members present?" His gaze darts down to the floor and he looks sheepish. "Come on, Tony. Whatever happens, you're fucked six ways from Sunday. Speak."

"Max would sometimes come," he says, now looking as baffled as he is petrified.

"Uh-huh," is all she says as Sin and Benny appear at the door. They enter with speed and precision, gagging and blindfolding Tony, who struggles and whines behind his restraints. They untie and manhandle him out the door. Presumably, they'll knock him out again and keep him stored in the back of the van.

I'm a little thrown that Aurora has dismissed Tony and gone off script. She must have a valid reason, but we had two toys to play with and now there's only one. *Not. The Fucking. Plan.*

I take a few deep breaths and turn to face my work bench. It glistens and gleams, almost overflowing with sharp blades and serrated edges, pliers and bone saws, even my favourite nail gun. There are sewing needles, curved fishhooks, and knuckle dusters. Just a cursory glance over my tools and I'm centred again.

Aurora walks to the side of the room, retrieving another chair, since the one Tony vacated is still dripping wet. She drags it right in front of Carlo and settles back, getting comfortable. I can see that she's favouring her ankle, but it's not obvious and she's doing a fucking excellent job of masking any weaknesses.

"He's got no fucking clue what he's involved with, does he? Would make a decent enough patsy though, if shit went sideways," she ponders out loud and then glances back at me. "They used him so they could meet face-to-face without suspicion. Tony's crew was probably running fake heists, stealing empty shipping containers. He would leave with his team to run the job; they would stay and chat at the locations he arranged." She glances at Carlo. "Please, correct me if I'm wrong."

An icy stare is all the reply she's granted. It's obvious he's galled that she's worked out Tony's involvement. I, on the other hand, am fucking impressed she put it together. I mean, I'd have got the same result eventually and would have enjoyed torturing it out of them, but I can't deny that this is a far more efficient use of our time.

"He kept his mouth shut about the meetings because he thought he was running unsanctioned jobs, while also feeling he was being trusted by senior players. I assume they would have offed him and pinned anything they needed to on him if anything went awry."

I watch her closely, fascinated by every movement she makes. You can practically see the cogs turning as she mulls over all the possibilities. I can tell when she considers a scenario she thinks has merit. She volleys her head from side to side as she follows her theory to its conclusion. When she reaches a dead end, her head stills and she casts her eyes up, and they bore into Carlo's in a predatory fashion. His shoulders are still, jaw clenched, and chin jutted out. He's doing his best to maintain his composure—as much as he can with a ball gag in his mouth—but I can see him faltering under her scrutiny. The muscles in his jaw twitch under the strain, and he swallows hard.

Aurora retreats to her workbench and continues to taunt our guest. She fondles and strokes her slender fingers over the tools as she makes her selection. I quirk a brow as she hums a tune. She's a dramatic little minx, I'll give her that. Her penchant for showmanship is intoxicating, and it does nothing to quell my raging hard-on when she emits a little gasp and lights up from within as she makes her selection.

What the fuck is she gonna do with that?

Aurora has picked up what looks like a flogger. *Where the hell did she get that?* I can only assume Sin has sourced it for her because I sure as shit didn't. I catch glimpses of something else embedded within the leather tails as she swishes it out from her hip. Don't ask me how a woman in grey sweats is channelling Catwoman right now, but as she prowls back to Carlo, that's all I can think of.

Focus, you idiot. I chastise myself, shaking my head and returning my focus back to our target. Aurora leans forward and cocks her head. "This simply won't do. I need a blank canvas."

She reaches into her pocket with her other hand and retrieves a switchblade. Flicking it open, she makes a show of rotating the knife to take stock of the blade. With speed and precision, she sweeps the blade across Carlo's button-down a few times and then rips the front apart, exposing his rotund torso to us.

Not drawing it out, she slices the air with the flogger, and I realise from Carlo's pained reaction that she's altered the flogger in some way. *Oh, she impresses me.*

Every time the ends glide across his skin, minor cuts appear, and it doesn't take long for dozens of tiny slices to flood with rivulets of blood and drip down his chest. There's no gushing, he's not in any danger of bleeding out. His torso just cries dozens of copper scented tears.

Whatever is embedded in her toy must be excruciating because Carlo is grunting against the ball gag. Tears slipping from his eyes, splashing on his chest, and cutting streaks through his agony. I can see the strain in his jaw as he bears down on the silicone ball. His face red and engorged.

I need to know more. Crossing to her, I stare down at her weapon and ask, "May I?"

"Be my guest." She smirks as she hands over her vicious little implement, unabashedly proud of her invention.

I inspect it thoroughly and soon realise she's embedded strips of guitar strings between the soft suede strands. "Oh, this is delightful." I can see her studying me as I review her handiwork and I can see a flash of sadness cross her features, drawing her brows together as if haunted by a memory before she masks her expression again.

"It has its uses," she deadpans before turning her attention back to Carlo. "But it's definitely not the main event. Time to warm you up before we can really get going." Holding out her hand, she crooks her fingers at me, demanding it back before she returns to her table, puts the flogger back in its place and retrieves a pair of G-clamps.

Who is this Aurora Bianchi and where the fuck did she come from? She's dark, near demonic in her movements and she's never been more captivating to me. She has yet to ask him a question. He couldn't answer even if he wanted to, but it's not looking likely she'll take the ball gag out anytime soon.

She unwinds the clamps, designed for securing timber, and then places the first one at his knee, ensuring that the metal plates are situated around the knee joint. As she winds the mechanism tight on the first leg, she continues until it can support itself, repeating the process with the second G-clamp, this time on the ankle of the same leg.

She checks the position of both clamps and then, using both hands, winds each one clockwise—setting an agonisingly slow pace. A quarter turn at a time. Carlo pulls against his restraints, and it's followed by loud huffing snorts as he tries to breathe through the pain.

Rory's face remains impassive as she focuses on the handles and watches the movable jaw of the clamp tighten on the joints. She is focussed on the task at hand and is unaffected by Carlo's increased struggling.

The moment she breaks him is spectacular. There's a sickening pop that draws my focus to his knee before he cries out in anguish. But she doesn't stop. She continues to tighten both, and I realise that she's dislocated his knee and is targeting his ankle next. His noises have returned to snorts of discomfort but are soon replaced by loud muffled cries of agony as his ankle emits a loud crunching sound before he passes out.

I stare in wonder at the little villain before me as she unwinds the clamps and returns them to her bench.

"I guess we'll have to wait for him to wake up," she says. Her tone is hollow. She returns to the seat and watches him.

Shit, this isn't good. I've been marvelling at her technique and dropped the ball. I walk around the chair to look at her and it's like she's returned to the trance-like state we found her in. She's here, but she's not *here*. I mean, thank fuck this time she at least appears to be conscious, but it's like I'm looking at a mannequin. She's completely vacant. Void. Empty.

Shit.

CHAPTER NINETEEN

AURORA

When Carlo finally stirs, his head bobs and dips as he battles his consciousness. I can tell the moment he comes to, by the harrowing cry he heaves out. Though, with the ball gag still in, his pitiful wailing has nowhere to escape through.

Tears fill his eyes, causing snot to stream out of his nose. As his nasal passages block, he coughs and splutters violently, transforming him into a fountain of mucus.

Delightful.

It really fucking hurts when someone dislocates a joint with a compression clamp. I should know.

Carlo's cries are growing more urgent. I stalk around the chair and remove the ball gag. "No no no, Carlo. That simply won't do. I can't have you choking on your own tears before Nico gets his turn."

I lift my head and hold Nico's gaze. He's obviously concerned about me, but now is not the time to discuss the state of detachment I find myself in. It's new. Not like the other place I go. I'm here, I'm present, and I'm filled with a rage I've never felt before. The man in front of me is complicit in my father's death and as much as I would like to torture him endlessly, I know that this is Nico's area of expertise.

Nodding slowly, I hand off to Nico and step back, returning to my chair and dragging it back to my workbench so that I can give Nico space to work. My ankle is aching, bombarding me with dull but persistent throbs, reminding me I will feel it worse tomorrow.

It's fascinating to watch Nico. In his arena, he doesn't walk, he prowls. He's a predator circling his prey. Calculating the most efficient way to capture and devour its target. It's clear from Carlo's general demeanour that he believed himself to be at the top of the food chain, however he is not the apex predator in this situation. He's beyond fucked.

"We know it was Marco who was communicating with the De Lucas, not you. How long before you realised you were working for the monkey, not the organ grinder?" Carlo flinches at my words and it tells me a lot. As Nico circles our captive, he swings by his bench and grabs his first weapon of choice.

"How long have you been doing Marco Romano's bidding, Carlo?" Nico asks, stalking towards him, grabbing his chin and forcing it up, demanding all of Carlo's attention. I observe Carlo and see him biting down hard, clenching his teeth together in rage.

"Fuck you, bastard scum," he spits out between pained breaths.

"Well, that's not very nice, is it Carlo?" Nico deadpans and then I catch my first glimpse of the implement he's brandishing. It's a pair of large pliers, the kind used to wrench out nails from timber. Nico levels the tool at Carlo's raw and exposed chest. Lining the open pincer up at his nipple, Carlo's eyes widen in horror as Nico closes the pliers over his nipple and wrenches upwards, tearing it clean off and discarding the lump of tissue with a flick of his wrist. It lands flesh side down with a pathetic sounding slap on the tile.

Huh, that's a new one for me. I'm impressed, and it's fucking effective. Carlo howls in agony but it doesn't afford him any leniency as Nico crosses to his other side and rips off the other nipple, letting it fall to the floor. I cannot suppress my smirk as this one bounces and rolls under Carlo's chair, like the strangest little spinning top.

"How and when were you recruited by Marco?" Nico barks.

Carlo, while in tremendous pain, continues to hold his ground against Nico, and I shake my head at him. His resistance merely makes Nico's eyes come alive; they glisten with glee. His malevolence has a twisted beauty to it, and I watch in awe as he unleashes a beast.

I remain in my chair for the entire performance. Nico breaks his victim down, cell by cell, until he no longer resembles the man they dragged in. He uses a selection of knives to carve intricate patterns into Carlo's skin. It's hypnotic, watching the swish and flick of the knife as drops of blood trickle off the tip in mesmerising arcs.

Nico seems quite lost in the art of his torture as he moves from one method to the next. After the blades, he drags Carlo's chair back to the sink, covers his face with a rag and pulls the overhead faucet down, allowing him to waterboard our rat to his heart's content. Carlo gasps and splutters, unable to catch a half-decent breath between barrages of water.

Nico doesn't ask a single question.

Ripping off his now sodden shirt, Nico hauls Carlo back and carries on, this time choosing the knuckle dusters to tenderise the smirk on Carlo's face. The ripple of his tattooed muscles as he punches and pummels Carlo's torso has me transfixed while the rhythmic dull thuds of fists meeting flesh soothes me. This isn't a reaction I was expecting, but I lean into it. I'm dimly aware that Carlo's howls of pain have died down to exhausted grunts, more like responses to each punch forcing air out of his lungs, than deliberate cries.

I'm equally impressed as I am baffled at Carlo's resilience to this onslaught. I've known this man for years and in that time, nothing about him has impressed me. He may be clever enough to be a capo, but not much else. What's in this for him? Taking out my father wouldn't progress his ranks, at least not by much.

"You're most likely dying today either way, Carlo. The question is—how painful do you want that process to be? Tell us what we want to know, and it will be quicker," I say.

Nico glares at me, and I realise I've overstepped. It's not my turn, and the ire in Nico's pitch-black eyes is palpable. *Note to self: Don't interrupt Nico when he's working.*

My interruption seems to spur him on to a new level of viciousness. Still, he asks no questions, and continues his torture. I watch in fascination as Nico finds and pulls at Carlo's threads, knowing he will unravel. Eventually.

—✳—✳—✳—✳—✳—✳—

IT TAKES LONGER than I would have predicted for Carlo to break, and it wasn't for lack of trying on Nico's part. As destroyed as Carlo is, Nico almost looks as haggard. Nico is breathing like he's run a marathon, and Carlo... Well, he's completely destroyed. He doesn't have the strength left to lift his head to hold my gaze, but when he speaks, I know he's talking to me, not Nico.

"It would never work long term—having two dons in one organisation. When Marco approached me, he told me that some of the family had been talking—that many of them felt The Syndicate would be better off under a single leadership." He tries to rally, but every slight movement elicits a cry of agony. He has my attention but when our eyes meet, they don't show the emotion I expect them to. There's a sorrow there, but I don't believe for one minute it ever outweighed his desire to further his own agenda.

"Being a Bianchi, obviously I assumed the plan was to eliminate the De Lucas. The first few times we met up, it was Marco, Tony, and me. We spoke in generalisations and after a few meetings, Max joined us. I knew then who the target would be, but I was too far in to back out without being killed by Max. If I'd told your father, he would have executed me on principle for my initial betrayal." He drops his head, but as he does, the faintest whisper of a smile flits across his face and I realise with absolute certainty, the sorrow he displayed before was fake. I have to give Carlo credit. He nearly had me for a second.

Sonofabitch.

While he's not looking, I gesture to Nico to back off, and he nods, retreating to the sink at the back of the room. He busies himself by grabbing a cloth to wipe off the viscera coating his chest and arms.

I approach, forcing down the bile that rises in my throat caused by the bold-faced lies spewing from this cunt. I lean forward and lift his chin, softening my eyes in a show of empathy as if to offer him absolution for his sins.

"I'm sorry, Aurora," he says meekly. "I should have warned your father and paid the consequences for betraying the family the minute I was aware of the De Lucas involvement."

I cup his face and stroke my thumb on his temple softly, praying I can muster my resolve to follow this through. "I understand, Carlo."

He tilts his head towards my touch, and the smug bastard doubles down. "Do you, Aurora? I'm *so* sorry, I never meant for this to happen. I should have protected you. I never thought Max would try to kill you, too."

How stupid does this prick think I am?

I can see Nico over Carlo's shoulder, faking retching at the sickly-sweet performance Carlo is putting on. I walk around the chair, patting his shoulder and squeezing in reassurance.

"What can you tell me about how they got access to my father, Carlo? There's no way you should have been able to get him alone for long enough to get him to Max. He was never unguarded."

"That was Marco. He met your father to discuss his son."

"Uh-Uh, Carlo. Try again. My father knew Marco would never go back on his casting out Benedict, and he would still have taken bodyguards to any meeting with Marco." He pauses, realising he's gone a step too far with the web of lies he's trying to weave.

"I can only tell you what I know. I wasn't involved with that side of the plan, but that's what they discussed. The only other person it could have been is Max."

"Here I was thinking you were going to be useful." I lean in close and bring my lips near to his ear. "Someone else is involved here, Carlo. Because neither you nor Marco would have been granted unprotected access to my father, certainly not to discuss a person who was under my father's personal protection. As far as my father was concerned, Marco no longer had any rights to discuss, let alone dictate, anything regarding Benny—"

"It must have been Max then," he insists, dropping the act as his growing unease sneaks out.

"Also, not possible, you fucking traitor," I grind out as my ability to stomach his lies disappears and is replaced with a vengeful growl. "He was with me when my father went missing." I grab a fistful of his lank, greasy hair and yank his head back, forcing him to meet my eyes.

Based on phone records and orders he gave that day, Sin narrowed down the time when my father was taken to the day before the guys found me. A day that Max spent with me. The same one where he took the call that sent him into a blind rage which he took out on me.

"Try again, Carlo," I snarl. His eyes flare as he realises he's talked himself into a lie he can't get out of. Just like that, it's like a switch has flipped—a vicious snake replaces the reverential toad.

"This would never have happened if your father hadn't got us all involved with the De Lucas. The stupid old fool brought it on himself. He brought shame on the family by going in with the De Lucas," turning to sneer at me he adds, "whoring out his daughters," then throwing a look of sheer disgust at Nico, "approving of full-blooded sons sucking the cocks of worthless bastards. Allowing them to flaunt their ungodly sin in front of *the family*. Your father was a disgrace to his own name."

He turns to face forward, but not before spitting in my face. I wipe it off with my sleeve as I drift to a place somewhere so far past rage it makes my skin itch. The feeling is like nothing I've ever experienced, but I feel like I need it. I cling to it, like it's grounding me. Turning towards Nico, it conveys everything I need it to.

Don't. Fucking. Move. He's mine.

Nico obeys, despite the fact I can see him vibrating with pent-up fury. I hate to say it, but I'm playing the *my pain is worse than yours* card. I realise Nico has bones in this fight, but this cunt is complicit in my father's murder, and I will get my answers.

How the older *family* members view queer people is archaic, but I honestly did not know there was this much resistance within the leadership. My father didn't give a shit who people fucked as long as they were loyal, and the blatant hypocrisy of the old boys hating any of Enzo's crew sickens me.

Men like Carlo vilify the progeny while honouring pigs who can't keep their dicks in their wives. It's despicable.

These *bastards* Carlo hates so much have more loyalty, more devotion and more respect to the family than this ignorant cunt can fathom. I round the chair, grab his chin and squeeze until my nails draw blood. "How did you get access to my father?"

"Fuck you, whore," he grinds out before I backhand him. My collarbone screams at the exertion, but it's well worth it.

"You brought this on yourself, Carlo." My breathing is heavy, punching through the air that hangs heavily between us. My eyes are wide as they bore into his. "I won't stop until you answer, and I sure as shit won't let you pussy out and die before I allow it."

Marching to Nico's table, I grab his nail gun first. With no ceremony or preamble, I shoot a nail through each thigh, mostly guessing which area will cause the most pain but is least likely to nick an artery. Carlo squeals like a stuck pig, hurling endless vulgarities and insults my way.

I don't even register the words. I'm too busy selecting

my next toy. *Fuck it, time to channel my inner Harley Quinn.* I snatch up the baseball bat at the back of the workbench and chaotically swing it around. I have to use both hands to get the balance right, but once it feels like a natural extension of my body, I return to Carlo and a feeling of peace descends over me as the first swing connects with his corpulent flesh. First the stomach, then the chest, the collarbones, the *good* leg, and not to forget the bad leg, of course. I cycle through the same areas a few times, all the while singing *Don't Stop Me Now* in my head. By the time I reach the chorus for a second time, I cock the bat out to the side and lean on it like a crutch, making sure I cock my hip out as playfully as possible, looking as unhinged as I feel. My collarbone and torso are howling in protest at this exertion, but I refuse to buckle.

It appears Carlo has finally learned some manners and has stopped spewing his vitriol in my direction. He looks ruined. And I feel glorious.

"I will ask you one last time, Carlo." I punctuate my threat by pulling the bat back up and jabbing him square in the dick. "How did you get access to my father?"

His wheezes offend me and turn my stomach. They're wet, and each hitch in his breath causes a gurgle that expels a mist of blood towards me. Everything about this man disgusts me. He can't even die right. Using the fat end of the bat to maintain a distance from the mess he's creating, I force him to tip his head back and meet my stare. He's done, he's got nothing left.

Using what remains of his dwindling strength, he croaks out, "The graveyard. Your father would visit your sister's grave once a month." A ragged hacking cough interrupts him as the heartbreaking reality barrels through me.

As he mourned his eldest daughter, my father's most trusted men sacrificed him to a psychopath. An unrelenting flurry of emotion assaults me and nothing can quell it. Garden-variety violence will not sate it. All rational thought leaves me, and only vengeance remains.

I remember nothing after picking up the machete.

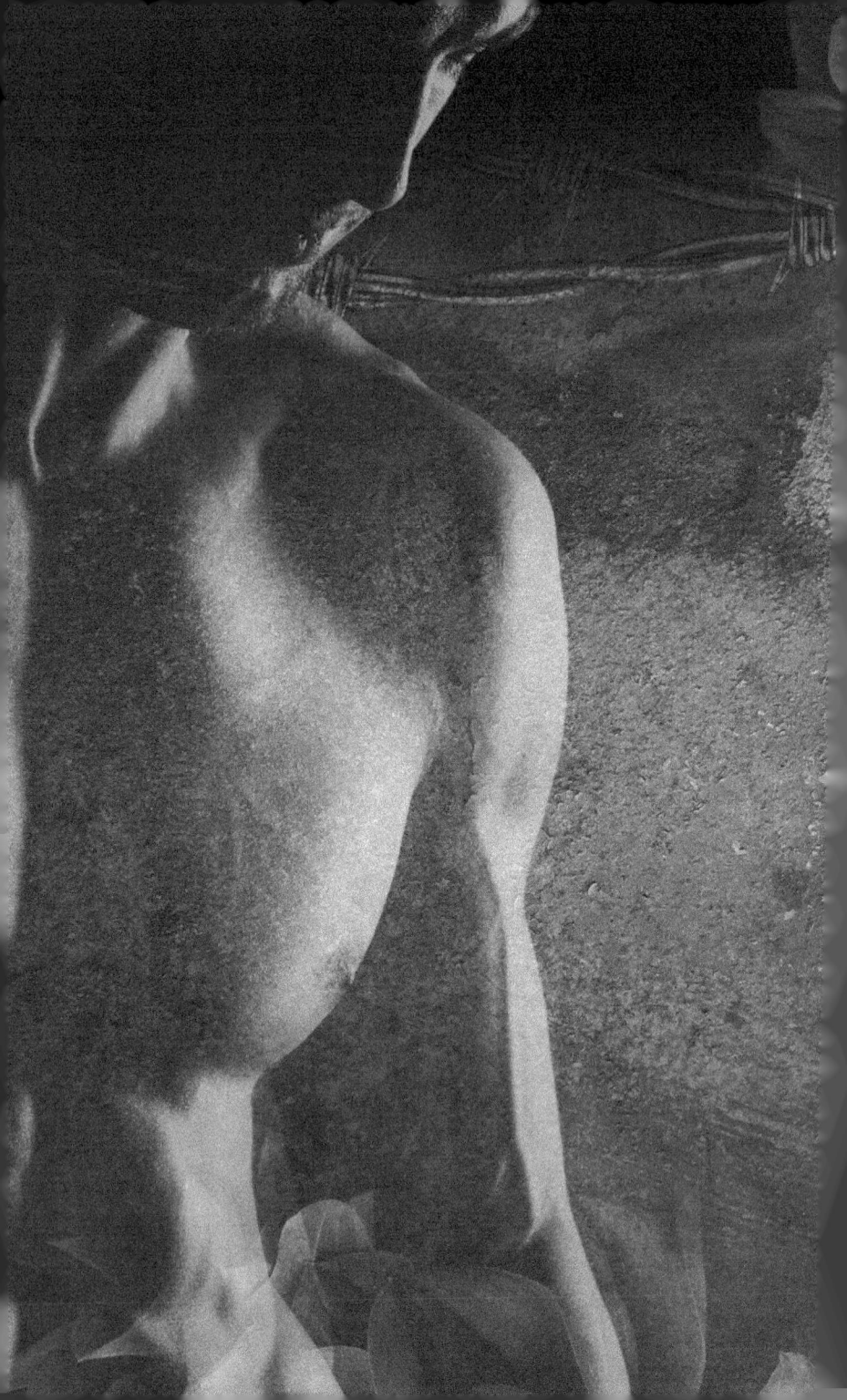

CHAPTER TWENTY

SINCLAIR

As I enter the interrogation room, I am staggered by the carnage that greets me. I mean, it's not like I wasn't watching on the monitors. We all were, but I don't think I've seen anything like it before. Even Nico usually stops before things reach this level of... gore.

Dibs on not cleaning this shit up. Fuck no.

There's not much left of Carlo. She picked up the machete and hacked him to pieces. She even started on the limbs, so he was alive for at least the first onslaught. At some point, she nicked a femoral artery, and he was gone pretty quickly after that, but it didn't stop her. Hacking and slashing with the blade, carving him up in chunks, she took her literal pound of flesh.

Right now, Aurora's sitting back on the chair that faces Carlo's carcass, staring vacantly at the aftermath of her wrath. She's out of breath, swallowing the air in large gulps, grappling against the adrenaline that's thrumming through every inch of her body. Frozen in place, Nico stares at her with awe and wonder.

I don't fucking blame him, though. That was... something. The power she wielded—the raw, unhinged strength. It was spectacular. However, right now she looks like she's on another plane of existence—while still holding a foot-long machete.

I crouch down in front of her, close enough to get in her line of sight, but far enough away that I stand a chance of dodging if she takes a swing at me. "Drop the blade," I whisper.

Her eyes remain glazed over, but my words must register because she drops the machete.

"Come with me, Aurora," I command in an unwavering tone. Holding out my hand, she takes it and I help her stand. Stepping forward, I lean into her personal space and place my forehead against hers. "Let's get you cleaned up." I scoop her into my arms, sweeping her off the floor.

As we're about to pass through the door, she calls back to Nico and I pause, turning her to face him. With a disturbingly monotonous tone and an empty expression, she instructs him, "Make sure you salvage his head and keep it on ice. When the time is right, I will serve it on a fucking platter to Max."

A Machiavellian grin creeps over Nico's face and I know it's euphoria at finding another person with a deviance to match his own. He nods, obviously happy to carry out her command, and I retreat from the room.

Aurora hasn't retreated into herself like before. She's not broken—she's not devastated. She's apoplectic—incandescent with rage. No words can mollify her, but there's something I *can* do.

I can take care of her—for at least the next few hours—I can shoulder the burdens and give her a break from... everything.

As I watched the feed, I was in awe of her. Her cunning, her strength, and her power. She owned that interrogation room, and she brought one of the most powerful capos in the Bianchi family to his knees. And even when she had defeated him, she did not stop. She showed him the mercy he deserved. Absolutely none.

It took my breath away.

Every second I spend with her makes me feel things I haven't allowed myself to in years. Anything I can do to help her, fulfils me. When she lets me support her, I feel... complete.

Bringing her upstairs to my room, I place her on the mattress. We don't speak and she doesn't question me as I head towards the attached bathroom to fill the tub. I make sure it's not scalding before returning to her.

"Stand," I say, and she obeys, staring vacantly behind me like she can't focus on anything directly in front of her with her pupils as wide as saucers. I can barely make out the emerald halo circling them. She hasn't dissociated from reality, but it's like she's in some kind of violence-induced subspace.

Taking her hand, I lead her into the bathroom and

position her in front of the bathtub. Moving to stand at her back, I lean in, basking in the warmth of her before bringing my lips to the shell of her ear. "I'm going to take care of you. If you want me to stop at any point, say red."

As my breath melts over her skin, she releases a soft sigh, and I see her shoulders drop in relief, taking comfort in the realisation that she's not in charge anymore. She leans back against me, and that gesture makes me feel like a king. It's a privilege that she's allowed me to do this for her.

Ever since we found her, each day I've daydreamed about her more and more. She's truly formidable and I can't fathom the depths of hell she's experienced, but I want to know everything about her so I can be everything she needs to help her overcome it.

Bringing my hands to the hem of her hoodie, I lift it off, careful not to catch her hair as I do, but I hear a small gasp as she pulls her arms from the sleeves. I hate that I can't take that pain away.

Hooking each index finger into the waistline of her sweats, I pull them down. Her apex is bared to me, and I'm reminded that she has no underwear here. I crouch behind her on my haunches, removing her sneakers and lift each foot out of the pant legs. Finally, I take care to remove the compression bandage on her right leg. It's swollen and discoloured, angry at her over exertion and having been forced into a shoe all evening.

She stands naked in front of me, and while I'm sure there's not a square inch of her I wouldn't find attractive, that's not what this is about. She needs my care, not my desire.

My eyes wander across her skin, scrutinising the wounds I tended when she arrived. They're healing well, but now that the angry welts are fading, I can appreciate the history of abuse she's suffered. I will never forgive myself for the pain she has endured because of the neglect of every family member who could have intervened. Had we been vigilant, this never would've happened.

Turning off the faucet, I lift her into the water, encouraging her to recline and let the warmth soothe her —body and soul. Kneeling at her side, I pick up the sponge and shower gel.

"Close your eyes, Aurora."

With the utmost care, I buff the lathered sponge across her silken skin. I move her gently, her limbs first, then pull her forward to rinse her back, washing away the burden of tonight's events. Leaning her back down, I sweep across her torso in careful unhurried passes. The movements relaxed, meant only to comfort.

We no longer need words. Her body surrenders to every movement I demand of it. Sitting her up again, I wash and rinse her hair and slather it in conditioner, then leave her to relax and soak in the tub while I retrieve some things I'll need.

I've never indulged this side of me so much before. This urge to tend to her is almost oppressively aggressive as it howls to be let loose. When she first arrived here, these urges were easier to sate because she rested so much. No one noticed how eager I was to watch over her.

Watching her sleep calmed me and making sure she had everything she needed was my purpose, not a chore.

As the most home-based team member, I was around more, while the guys were out keeping up the pretence and running our regular jobs for The Syndicate.

The more time I've spent with Rory, the more consuming the urge to protect her has become. Having to stand back and watch on the monitors as Carlo called her a whore was gut wrenching. But then this little spitfire did what she always does—survive and persevere. She decimated Carlo, expelling every ounce of her strength in the process.

I know that my purpose is to bring her back to life. I can feel it in my core.

Aurora Bianchi deserves to be cherished, not tortured, and I—we—will annihilate anyone who stands against her.

Returning to her, I rinse the conditioner from her hair and then lift her out, bundling her in an oversized towel before taking her through to my room. Setting her down on the end of my bed, I arrange myself behind her so I can towel-dry her tendrils and brush out the ebony strands cascading down to her hips. She can't keep her eyes open as the soft bristles stroke across her scalp. Soft moans fall from her lips as she leans into the movement of the brush strokes.

Standing her up, I encourage her into a pair of my boxer briefs and an oversized hoodie. I'm more careful of her injuries this time and though she winces, she doesn't cry out. An almost primal sense of ownership swells inside me, seeing her in my clothes, and I clench my jaw as I suppress a groan.

Winding my fingers through hers, I pull her back on

the bed, leaning my back against the headboard as the soft pillows envelop us. I encourage her to curl into my side and rest her head against my chest. As her cheek comes to rest, nestled below my thundering heart, I curl an arm around her and stroke her hair.

Tipping her chin up, she opens her eyes again and whispers, "Thank you." Her tone warm and relaxed.

"There's nothing to thank me for."

She frowns and places her delicate hands on either side of my jaw. With a serious look, she says, "I mean it, Sin. I have a lot to thank you for. Not just you, all of you. For the longest time I've been alone, and so very broken. You all saved me." Her thumbs are stroking my stubble as she gets a faraway look in her eyes. "But what I cannot understand is why you keep on saving me."

I growl at the heartbreaking realisation that our failure to protect her has left her doubting her worth. Every fucking Bianchi member, including her father, failed her the minute they married her off to that fucking psychopath.

"I'm not worth it, Sin." Shaking her head, she refuses to look at me and closes her eyes. The powerful creature she's been channelling all night has abandoned her. Right now, she's succumbing to every bit of self-doubt that only years of abuse can breed.

Her words hit me like a punch to the gut. Clutching her around the waist, I roll her underneath me and tower over her. Glowering like a feral beast, I loom over her with hands on either side of her head. "If I ever hear you speak about yourself like that again, I'll have you over my knee, spanking your ass so hard you won't be able to sit for a week. *How fucking dare you, Aurora.*"

I move to straddle her hips and ease my hand around her slender throat, squeezing gently until I feel the rapid thrum of her pulse, like the delicate fluttering of hummingbird wings—rapid and exquisite. She swallows hard and I can feel every movement as she tilts her chin, a defiant glint coming to life in her eyes as she tests the limits of my hold on her. Her pupils are blown wide, and she peeks out her tongue to wet her lips.

"We failed you, *colibrì*. You sacrificed yourself to a monster, and every single one of the Bianchi Family let you. It is us who are not worthy of you." Leaning down with my eyes boring into hers, I add, "You were spectacular tonight."

My guttural tone betrays me, declaring just how much I admire her.

Her eyes flare open wide—filled with shame. "I lost it, Sin. I couldn't even hold it together through one interrogation."

"How can one woman be so fucking dense?" I say with a smile. "You undid Tony in minutes, you got everything we needed from Carlo, and then you obliterated him. It was glorious." Just thinking about the look on her face as she took her vengeance out on Carlo has my dick stirring. It practically stands to attention when I stroke my thumb along her neck and a blush chases its way down her body. Her skin heats in flourishes of goosebumps, trailing behind my fingers. She writhes, her body chasing my touch.

The shame fades and disgust creeps across her features. "But what I did to him—"

"He had it coming, Aurora. He deserved to die," I say with as much reassurance as I can instil in my tone. Then, stifling a chuckle, I add, "But you may owe Nico an apology. You kind of stole his thunder and then left him with the cleanup."

A brief grin appears at the corners of her lips. It satisfies a part of me deep down that I can make her smile. But there's another part stirring that wants more from her. I want to make her laugh. But it doesn't end there. I want to make her moan. I want to watch her shatter for me again, and again, and again.

A low rumble escapes from my throat, and my expression causes a little hitch in her breath. Wetting her lips, she bites down on her plump bottom lip—her eyes veiled, her pupils blown wide. She is stunning, and I'm lost to her. Releasing her throat, I lean down, bringing my lips to the shell of her ear.

"Tell me to stop, Aurora."

She shakes her head. I reposition myself, pressing my thigh between hers, forcing her legs to part. A shiver moves up my spine as she grinds against me, rolling her hips and squeezing her thighs around mine.

"But I don't want you to stop, Sin." Her confession is barely above a whisper and dripping with need.

As soon as the words leave her mouth, I'm done for and I descend on her, stealing a kiss from her eager lips and sealing our fate.

CHAPTER TWENTY-ONE

AURORA

oly Fuck!

H After four years of hell, I feel like I'm in heaven. It's been so long since I was last touched with any tenderness or true passion. I was by no means a virgin when I married Max, but his cruelty has been my whole world for what felt like an eternity. I'd forgotten the bliss of being lost to someone you want with such intensity.

I can feel my pulse thundering and blood rushing through my veins as his lips clash with mine. Our tongues collide and do battle while my hands fly to his shoulders and pull him closer. He tastes like coffee and his scent is fresh and clean, almost citrusy. The combination is intoxicating, and I lean into the sensation of being conquered.

The anticipation is almost too much to bear, and the way Sin's hands have tended and caressed every inch of my body has left me desperate for more of his touch. As he grasped my throat—the most gentle of my four protectors, dominating me with not only his words but his presence—everything in me surrendered.

I can feel the subtle undulations of his lean body along me and his breath as it tangles with mine. I'm gasping for air as he pulls back to trail kisses along my jawline. What started as a dull ache as his masterful hands bathed me is now a persistent and insatiable thrumming. I squeeze my legs around his thigh again, trying to slake this need.

"Uh-uh, *colibrì*. You're no longer in charge tonight."

With a tilt of his pelvis, he teases me with the slightest increase in pressure against my core before retreating, forcing a desperate whimper from my lips. Back to straddling my hips, he's staring down at me, fully aware of the effect he's having on me as a smirk warms his features before he buries his head back into the crook of my neck, running his nose along my collarbone and inhaling me. It shouldn't feel as filthy as it does —like he's about to consume me.

His mouth on my skin feels ravenous, his touch is reverent. It's nothing like Max's lascivious torture. Every feathering of Sin's breath on my skin, erases any memory it holds of past cruelties.

I'm wearing entirely too many clothes right now. I try to move my arms down to the hem of my hoodie, but he bats them away. "What did I say, Aurora?" he asks with a glower.

"Er—"

He tuts at me with mock disapproval and wags a

finger at me. Sin takes my wrists and brings them above my head, holding them tenderly but firmly together with one hand. My injuries not hampering my position, the bath having done me the world of good. My pain is less, and my muscles are relaxed. Returning his attention to my neck, he nips and bites, punctuating each one with his words.

"You..." he bites my earlobe, "are not..." his teeth nip at my throat, "in charge. Any pleasure you experience is mine to give you, not yours to take."

He bites down hard at my pulse point and pulls against my skin, teasing me with his tongue in a way that sends a jolt straight to my clit. It's not enough to leave a mark, but the pressure is delicious. Little pulses of heat radiate up my neck in ripples, making the hairs on the back of my neck tingle. A soft moan escapes my lips, and I can feel his satisfied smile against my skin.

I strain against his hold, wilfully testing his patience. Not because I don't want to submit to him—I do. I adore the way his control is making me feel free for the first time in so very long. However, I'm intrigued to know how far he'll take this role he's assumed. The idea of surrendering to someone I can trust—with not only my body, but my welfare—is seductive. But that doesn't mean I'll make it easy for him.

A hand drifts down my side, a featherlight touch glancing over the swell of my breasts and delving under the hem of the hoodie at my hips. He slides both hands behind me and leans back on his haunches, pulling me up with him. Sin is careful as he relieves me of the hoodie and tosses it aside.

With one hand, he wrenches off his henley.

I wasn't deceived when he pressed against me earlier. His lean physique is a sight to behold. Broad shoulders that taper into a slim waist and a tantalising happy trail that dips below the waistband of his jeans. He has sharp angles that make it look like someone carved his hips from stone. He observes my blatant appraisal and drops his hand to adjust what looks like a rather impressive and very hard cock.

"I don't know what makes me harder, seeing you in our clothes, or seeing you out of them."

I study his eyes as they explore me in return. They are unlike any I've ever seen. Brilliant amber, with metallic flecks that subtly contrast each other to catch the light, burning in varying tones of gold and bronze. They're mesmerising, and when they capture my gaze again, I feel compelled by them. He doesn't need words to control every movement I make. Leaning into me, I recline back on my elbows and watch as he lowers himself to his hands and knees and prowls backwards.

I pant as he steps back off the end of the bed and reaches forward. Avoiding my injured ankle, he hooks his hands under my knees and pulls me to him. His movements are animal-like. They feel predatory, but at no point do I feel like anything other than a willing sacrifice. Pulling the boxer briefs down my legs and falling to his knees, he spreads me wide for him. I feel exposed, but in the best way.

One of the most worthy men I know is on his knees for me and that realisation takes my breath away. Thinking on the possibilities of everything he could do next holds me hostage, and I can't help but whine as I feel his breath inching its way up my thigh. It tickles and teases me, skipping back and forth from my thigh to my hip, inching back down, and then finally, he devours me.

Parting me with the flat of his tongue and drawing it through my slick folds up to my clit where he stops and tongues the sensitive bud before nipping and sucking, varying the sensations so I can't anticipate what's coming next. It's overwhelming and when I hear a growl in his throat and feel the vibrations thrum through my core, I lose myself to the sensations and surrender to the pleasure he gives.

Throwing my head back, I fall against the bed and grasp the sheets tight as his tongue explores me. My orgasm builds, but I'm not giving it to him. He's taking it. I feel his fingers at my entrance, teasing, exploring, and savouring how wet I am for him. First one, then two fingers plunge into me and curl forwards, hitting my g-spot before pulling back. With slow, deliberate thrusts, he tortures me by drawing out my bliss, making sure I come only when he allows it.

I've never been held so close to coming like this. It should be torture, but it's paradise. Right now, there's nothing else in the world, only this. Only him. Only us.

I'm flooded by a cacophony of debauched sounds as Sin continues to tease me. His fingers fuck my pussy in time with the way his clever tongue rolls against my clit. A string of incoherent mewls escapes me, announcing how close I am to the edge.

"I'm not sure I should let you come yet, *colibrì*," he

teases, pulling his mouth away from my greedy pussy and I cry out at the loss of his skillful tongue.

"Sin. Please."

"Be a good girl and beg, Aurora."

Whether it's being called a good girl or the level of desperation I feel, but I'll gladly beg this man if it means I get more of him. "*Please, Sin.* Please let me come."

I stare up at him, desperate for his mouth to finish what it started. His arm is still moving, pumping his thick fingers into me, stretching me perfectly and grazing against my front wall with the perfect pressure. But it's not enough. My hips roll, desperate to chase my release, and he brings a hand to my hip to hold me in place.

He pulls his fingers from my now drenched cunt and immediately replaces them with his mouth, fucking his tongue into me, drinking me down and savouring every drop. "Fuck, you taste good, hummingbird. Like the nectar of the gods."

The mouth on him is fucking filthy, and I love it. Words are eluding me, and I can only focus enough to remember to breathe. With one arm wrapped under my thigh, gripping me tight and pulling my pussy to his lips, the other moves to allow his thumb to massage my clit. I feel my centre clenching every time his tongue breeches my entrance and I shatter.

I feel... everything and I come harder than I ever have. As waves of ecstasy roll over my body, Sin doesn't stop, his tongue is back on my clit and three fingers are filling me gloriously, fucking me hard, demanding I come again.

"Sinclair, please. Please fuck me. I need you inside

me," I plead with him, lifting my arms to bury them in his hair and wrench him from his ministrations. The interruption is both a relief and a loss that makes me cry out as my orgasm fades away.

Climbing up on the bed, he hauls me back to its centre and kneels, tugging at his belt and popping his fly. He shucks down his jeans, pulls them off and throws them to the floor.

"I warned you, Aurora. Repeatedly. You are not in charge here. On your knees and face the headboard. Now."

His words send shivers through me. They promise so much, but there's nothing about them that makes me feel threatened. Quite the opposite. I'm eager to obey him.

"Your only job was to lie back and take everything I chose to give you. You didn't do as you were told, Aurora."

I've lost the ability to form words, struck speechless by his commands, but I nod. Once I'm on my knees, he's next to me arranging the pillows under my chest and abdomen, encouraging me down with a soft stroke along my spine. His makeshift bolster takes my weight, leaving my wrist and collarbone protected. Sinclair growls his approval, and I feel his warm palm brushing across my cheeks.

"You can say red at any time, Aurora."

Whatever happens next, I trust him. He wouldn't do anything to harm me. But before I can prepare myself, a sharp smack lands at the top of my thighs. I hear it before I feel it. I'm startled and then hiss at the sting before rolling my hips as the pain gives way to a warmth that radiates through me and sparks something in my core I've never felt before. He keeps going, maintaining the same force and making sure never to hit the same spot twice.

It feels so good.

I've experienced more pain at the hands of someone I should have been able to trust than I will ever come to terms with, but this is not the same. The sensation is reassuring, restorative. It's like a release I didn't know I needed. I feel Sin's hand connect again, and I cry out, unable to contain myself.

"Fuck, you wear my handprint well. Such a good fucking girl, for me."

He massages each spot he's marked, drawing out an unexpected moan and a rush of emotion. I feel so many things all at once. I'm not happy or sad, but I'm feeling everything. Turning me and pulling me into his arm, he leans back against the headboard, and I straddle him. Rolling my hips, I can feel every inch of him against me.

He caresses my cheek, "You okay there, hummingbird?" Shaking my head at him, I lean down and lay a tender kiss on his lips.

"Not yet, Sinclair, but I will be." Quirking a brow at him, I add. "I need you... all of you."

Cupping my cheek, he checks in with me. "Are you sure? Today has been a lot, Aurora."

"I need this, Sin... please." I feel like I'm taking advantage of him. I've got no idea what any of this means. I just know that every time he touches me, every time he tends to me, I feel safe and free. Like the Aurora I was before I married Max.

He looks deep into my eyes, and I see a flurry of emotions run riot across his face before he nods and leans into a tight embrace, pressing his lips to mine with the utmost care. It's both too much and not enough. He pours all of himself into this kiss.

Fuck. I am not in the right headspace for the emotions he's stirring in me, but that doesn't mean it's not happening. Sinclair quiets all the noise. The urge to retreat into myself is no longer present when he's close. When any of them are, for that matter.

He reaches across to his bedside table and grabs a foil package from the top drawer. I tilt my head, observing him. It feels surreal to watch him open and unfurl the condom. It's been so long since I've even had to consider using protection. I reach forward, taking it from him, and use the opportunity to explore Sinclair.

Pushing him back against the pillows, I nuzzle into his neck, trailing open-mouthed kisses across his chest, savouring the taste of him. Dipping down, I trace my fingertips over his subtle abs until I find myself face to face with what I can only describe as a delicious looking hard-on.

It's not that it's some kind of enormously oversized monster-cock. It's thick, with prominent veins that leave a pattern of ridges that make me shiver, wondering how they'll feel inside me. How his bulbous head will feel as it stretches my pussy and strokes my walls. I've never thought of a cock as beautiful before, but this one is a work of art.

Wrapping one hand around the thick base, I lower my head and flick my tongue across his weeping slit. Taking as much of him as I can, I run the flat of my tongue along the underside, making sure to flick along his frenulum on my upstroke. As I twist my hand in tandem with my mouth's torturous pulls, he throws his head back and cries out.

"*Fuck*, Aurora. What the fuck are you doing to me?"

Lifting off his dick, I stare up at him through my hooded eyelashes. "You're not the only one here with skills, Sin. Now shut the fuck up and let me suck your cock like a good fucking girl."

He rewards my filthy mouth with fat drops of pre-cum beading at his tip. His hand grips my hair forcefully and he pulls me forward, thrusting into my mouth with his needy cock.

"Are you a good girl, Aurora?" he grinds out as I take him as far back as I can. Deep throat has never been a skill I possess, but what I lack in anatomical dexterity, I more than make up for in technique. "Because right now you feel like my eager little whore, desperate for my cum."

His words make me clench my core, which complains at the absence of his dick. Hearing my bereft whine, he pulls me off him and takes charge, moving my hands to roll the condom over his crown and down his shaft. Guiding me, he encourages me to straddle him, and I moan as I feel him glide along my swollen lips, notching him at my entrance. I pause for a moment before sinking down slowly, savouring the feeling of being impaled by him, inch by inch.

It's rapturous, and I can't help myself as I roll my hips to make sure there's no part of me that's left untouched by his length. The motion does something to Sin that ensures words are lost to him. He's nothing but a sweating mass of straining muscles and animalistic groans, and I realise his cock is having the same effect on me. I writhe and grind myself on him until my legs give out on me and his hands fly to my hips to take over.

This orgasm barrels towards me at an astounding rate as he pumps up into me with a new angle that triggers a flood of arousal that takes me by surprise.

"Come for me, Aurora. Let me feel your pretty pink pussy quiver around my cock."

A strangled groan slips from Sin's lips. His jaw is clenched, neck straining and just when I think my pleasure is at it's peak, he starts fucking up into me, punctuating his thrusts with his gloriously filthy mouth. "Make me come, *colibrì*. Take what's yours."

A flurry of euphoria rolls through like an avalanche, and this time I feel a new pressure building. My pussy feels like it's engorged and swollen in a way I haven't experienced before. Sin's pace increases and it triggers a chain reaction. My orgasm tears through me and I feel an unfamiliar gush of wetness spread across my thighs as he swells inside me and cries out his own release. "Fuck yes, such a greedy little pussy."

My cum warms my thighs and I feel a contentment like no other I've experienced. I'm an exhausted, quivering mess. Sin pulls out and deals with the condom, reaching to toss it in the trash, then pulls me into an embrace, cradling my head to his chest.

"You did so good, *colibrì*." His words wash over me, and I feel lighter than I have in years. There's a part of me that almost wants to cry. Not because I'm sad, but because I feel... content in a way I can't begin to explain. I try to speak, but I can't think of what to say. I've never felt so overwhelmed by an orgasm. But it's not only that. It's the connection we have forged here.

It's meaningful. It's real. And as I come to my senses, it scares the hell out of me.

"You don't need to say a word," he breathes out as he nuzzles the top of my head and kisses my temple.

I couldn't if I wanted to.

He rolls us over to place me delicately on my back. Heading to the bathroom, he returns with a washcloth and a towel, cleaning, then patting dry my oversensitive pussy. It's a small gesture that makes me feel more cared for than I ever have been. Like there's nothing he wouldn't do to comfort me. I feel small and nurtured.

"I'm guessing from your reaction, you haven't come like that before?" he asks, lightly stroking my shoulder with his fingers in an intricate pattern. I shake my head, attempting to hide my blush.

Finding my words, I reply. "I've read about it, but I think I'd decided squirting was a myth. But it turns out you are a sexual unicorn, Sinclair," I chuckle. "I was unaware that men like you existed. You should do TED talks."

"There's only one person I plan to educate on the virtues of orgasm play, and that's you," he replies so quickly that from the surprised look on his face, it was an automatic response. He appears worried, concerned he's spooked me. I smile as the calm and ever prepared Sinclair rambles. "I mean—you know—I'm not assuming anything. I know we haven't discussed—"

I bring my hand to his lips to stop him from over-thinking. "I don't know what this is or what it means, Sin. But I know I don't regret a single moment. It feels like you just put me back together again. I feel safe. And the rest? The rest we'll figure out tomorrow."

His shoulders soften and it's like I can feel the brief spell of anxiety seeping out of his every pore. I curl into him, moving my head down to rest in the nook at his shoulder, and his arm envelops me, holding me tight.

"Sleep, Aurora. I've got you," he reassures me as he reaches for the blanket and then bundles us up under it. My eyelids dip, heavy with the weight of exhaustion. This time, as I drift off, it's not into a nightmare. It's not into a world of make believe where I can hide from my monster.

It's a peaceful and contented sleep for the first time in years.

CHAPTER TWENTY-TWO

ENZO

The last thing I needed after helping Nico with clean-up last night was to crawl into bed only to be kept awake by the moans of ecstasy emanating from the next-door bedroom. Having retreated to the med-room, primarily because it's the bed furthest away from Sin's, I thought I'd stand a better chance of getting some sleep. I was mistaken.

I found myself wide awake in Aurora's bed, surrounded by her scent and rock-hard all night. It's now five in the morning and I'm fucking glad she refused to give us back the coffee machine because I feel like I need to hook it up intravenously if I'm going to make it through today. It's not like we have anything that strenuous planned, but I'm finding more and more that the weight of what we're up against is proving to be a lot to carry.

We made progress last night. We know who's pulling who's strings and confirmed how far up it goes. But now we have a dead body to dispose of and a prisoner we've established is about as useful as the male nipple. If he's worthless to Salvatore, he's less than useless to us. The only potential angle we could work is the fact Salvatore is fucking his wife, but that only makes her valuable, not him.

Tony's back in the interrogation room, chained to the wall. After we finished the clean-up, we brought him back into the house. I wanted to sleep, and it's the most secure room we have.

Boy, did Nico complain about it, though. *"My space is not a holding cell. Guests are not welcome for extended stays."* I told him it was this, or he could sit in the van all night and babysit. He caved in... eventually. Benny helped *placate* him.

As I sip my espresso, realising that I'll need another one before I feel human again, I try to focus on the positives. It's looking likely that Mateo's number two and consigliere—Manny Ferella & Stefano Tiero—aren't dirty, so we might bring one or both of them in on this. We've been monitoring them since we found Aurora, trying to figure out why they were keeping Mateo's murder under wraps and covering for their don's absence. Either they're involved or they—like us—are trying to figure out what the fuck is going on within The Syndicate.

What I can't figure out is why the De Lucas aren't outing the information yet and claiming responsibility.

This is a weird-ass coup. It makes no fucking sense and we're missing several pieces of the puzzle. *What else are the De Lucas up to?*

I run my hand over my face, rubbing against the scruff I keep forgetting to trim, attempting to wake myself up enough to figure this crap out.

Fuck, it's too early for this shit.

We're missing so much information, I feel like we are the extras on a movie set who haven't seen the script, yet somehow the director is expecting us to save the fucking day in the third act. And I don't have the first fucking clue where to start.

I GRAB a shower using the basement bathroom since I don't want to wake everyone, but again it turns out to be a mistake since the only toiletries down here are the ones we got for Aurora and now I'm going to smell like her all day. The fragrance is light and floral, but I can't place it. I don't have the first fucking clue what neroli is, but according to the label on the bottle, that's the scent that follows her everywhere and has my dick hard right now.

Fuck's sake.

I find no satisfaction in rubbing one out in a dank shower stall, but since I have to face the guys soon, I'd rather not spend the whole meeting with a hard-on. It's perfunctory and in keeping with the status quo. It's been a long time since I've given much thought to my sexual needs, let alone had any desire to fuck anyone. Until Aurora.

It's not that I can't, it's that I just... I have zero fucking desire to. I'm just... exhausted. My team is the most sought-after crew in The Syndicate, and we have to work twice as hard as anyone else for our position, thanks to our bastard status. Add to that the jobs we ran under the table for Mateo, and there's no fucking time for a sex life. I guess I could have found a willing side-piece or paid someone, but what's the fucking point?

Besides, I don't fucking deserve the respite, given my failings.

My crew has been investigating Isabella Bianchi's death for Mateo for the last fourteen years. When we started, we had tons of leads to follow, but they all went nowhere, and we've found fuck all in the last decade that would help us. It's my greatest failure.

What's worse is Sinclair has turned up a fresh lead for the first time in fuck-knows how long. The police have turned up two unidentified bodies in the last three weeks and one of the autopsy results threw up a red flag on one of the routine searches he runs.

They pulled one victim out of the river, making half the evidence useless. They found the other in a dumpster, protected from the elements. What triggered our interest was the markings that were found on the body. We're working on getting hold of the full autopsy right now, but from the description, they sound similar to the markings found on Isabella's torso.

Dividing my focus right now is the last thing I need, but even with Mateo dead, I won't ever stop searching for Isabella's killer. I feel a familiar ache in the pit of my stomach as I remember how her death destroyed my brother. He never recovered. He lost the love of his life, and when he took his life, I lost *everything*.

If I can't find her killer, I don't deserve happiness.

Stepping out of the shower, I sling a towel around my waist. I left my fresh clothes in the med-room so I head back there, dripping on the floor as I go. I head to the coffee machine first to get that started and then drop my towel. A small gasp behind me has me jerking around, only to be met with a pair of startled green eyes.

"I'm sor—" she starts before covering her eyes and turning on a dime, ready to bolt out of the room. With her limited visibility, she slips on the water trail I've left behind me and goes down hard, crying out in pain.

Running to her side, I bend and pick her up and bring her back to the bed. She pulls down her hands and gasps, immediately covering her eyes again.

"Er... Enzo. You're still naked."

"You saw quite a lot of me the other day, Aurora."

"I did not." She peaks through her fingers and then closes the gap, pretending she didn't peek. "I saw your thighs when you spilled the coffee. I did not see... all of... do you live in the fucking gym?" She's blushing and looks mortified, but she's smiling—and that takes my breath away.

She carries on babbling about not meaning to barge in and apologising for invading my privacy while I extend her arm and check for any fresh injuries. She winces as I turn over her hand. It looks like her wrist took the brunt of it when she fell.

"Can't you be more careful? We only just got you

back into one piece, woman," I chastise with a friendly tone. "Did you injure your ankle again? Why aren't you wearing your boot? Where are your crutches?"

"I'm fine, Zo. I came down to grab another compression bandage. I was fine without the boot last night and I'm taking the painkillers like I'm supposed to. I'm done with the damn crutches." Taking her hand back, she stares back at me and opens her mouth to continue but shakes her head and thinks better of it. She smiles contritely and says, "I'll be more careful."

I reach around her to grab my clothes from the bed, and she leans back as I do. She may avoid my closeness, but I don't miss the subtle dilation of her eyes at my invading her space. She closes her eyes as I get dressed, but the smile remains on her lips, and it's hard not to be warmed by it.

"I'm decent," I call out as I head back to the coffee machine and grab my espresso. "Want one?"

"Please," she replies as she heads to the little dresser we brought down for her. Rummaging through the drawers, she grabs some clothes. "Be right back. Just gotta get changed." Then she pauses at the door, before adding, "Er... Sinclair said he'd be right down for the meeting."

I chuckle a little. She's nervous to admit where she's been all night. I can see her neck and ears colour as she tries to hide her blush from me by turning and walking out the door. Does she think I'll judge her? She's a grown-ass woman and she can do what she wants. I would never judge her for that. Heaven knows she's had far too little autonomy over her own life or her own body for far too long.

But I am jealous. It was difficult hearing her with Sinclair.

There's not a cell in my body that believes I'm worthy of Aurora. But that doesn't mean I don't wish I were.

CHAPTER TWENTY-THREE

BENEDICT

Entering the med-room, my eyes clock each one of the guys and noting Rory isn't here, I can't help but smirk at the state of my friends. They look like they've been up all night—they probably have. Fuck knows why Zo looks like death, but I can only assume he was up all night planning our next steps. I know I kept Nico busy most of the night, and from the noise coming from Sinclair's room, Rory was being *taken care of* extremely well.

I don't begrudge Sinclair his happiness, but it was hard to listen to them together when these feelings I have for her won't subside. It drove me wild and triggered some of the most profound orgasms I've ever experienced.

It unlocked a part of my submissive side that had me whimpering on my knees, begging for Nico's dick like a needy cum-slut. I blush as I remember how I used the soundtrack of Sinclair and Rory fucking to imagine the filthiest of scenarios. Last night, when he finally let me come and took me to bed, I quickly passed out, dreaming of the things I wanted to do with Rory—and Nico.

How he'd sit in his armchair and impale Rory, her back to his chest, grinding on every rung of his ladder. How he'd spread her wide and have me on my knees for both of them. Demand that I tongue her clit, lap at her pussy, tease his balls, and finally lick them both clean, savouring every drop of their cum.

I feel a sense of guilt fantasising about her. How would she feel if she knew the things I imagined? Would she feel violated? Fuck, I hope not.

Sinclair catches me staring at him and glares at me. "You got a problem, man?"

"Sorry, I was miles away," I say, shaking my head to drag me out of my concerns.

Nico brings me a coffee and steers me to the couch. He leans close and whispers to me, "Stop overthinking, Bambi." He captures my jaw and turns my face to his so he can hold my gaze. "Are you okay?"

I cast my eyes down, ashamed. "I feel... lots of things."

"I know." He moves his arm behind me across the back of the couch and gently strokes the back of my head. It instantly soothes me and dampens the thoughts running through my mind like a herd of wild horses.

I don't know what last night means—whether she's with Sinclair now. What I do know is that she's not mine, she's not Nico's, she's not ours, and it feels like she never will be. That causes a dull ache in the centre of my chest that no amount of rationalising seems to quell.

It's ridiculous. The chance of her ever being mine and Nico's to share were non-existent to start with. Now it feels like all hope is lost. She's the only person other than Nico that's made me feel this way, and it's hard to process.

"Have patience, Bambi," he whispers so softly I nearly miss it.

I have no time to dwell on his words as Rory enters the room, looking fresh faced with her slick ebony locks trailing down her back, dripping on the back of an over-sized hoodie. I have no idea whose sweatshirt it is, but it's one of ours. It's really fucking difficult not to fantasise about a woman who walks around in your clothes.

She looks far too refreshed for someone who remorselessly slaughtered a traitor and then spent hours being fucked six ways from Sunday. Nico's a shining example of what she should look like. Haggard and exhausted.

Bless him. I tuckered him out last night. After Rory commandeered his kill, it left me with a wound-up rage bunny in need of release. And I'm precisely the type of brat for that job.

She looks like a weight has been lifted—like she's coming back to life.

She catches me staring and smiles, looking a little sheepish. Deciding to put her at ease, I avoid mentioning Sinclair. "Next time, you're helping with clean-up. When you're choosing weapons, the answer is rarely a machete, Rory. We found pieces of him all over the place."

For a second, I think I've gone too far as her expression falters. Just as I'm about to back pedal, she bursts out laughing.

"There's never *not* a good time to use a machete, Benny. But you're right. Next time I'll clean up after myself." Her smile is magnificent—breathtaking. It does nothing to help me tamp down my feelings for her.

She glances across to Sinclair and sees that he's taken a seat on the armchair. She hesitates, obviously not having a clue where her place is. Enzo steps forward and takes her hand, pulling her up onto the gurney that has served as her bed since her arrival. Since we now hold all our meetings down here, it feels like a throne in its elevated position. Something that uplifts the person we value.

I realise after last night's demonstration, this person we revere may be precious to us, but she is no longer the fragile victim she was when she arrived.

"We need to figure out the next steps," Zo says, calling our focus to him. "We have a body to unload, and a rat problem."

Throwing my hand up, I say, "I'll get rid of the body. I have some charges to test out. It might be fun to put them inside an oil drum with our friend Carlo and see what kind of soup he makes."

"While I appreciate the enthusiasm, Benedict, I need all trace evidence vaporised. I dealt with enough gore last night. I just need it all gone," Zo responds in a weary tone that makes me realise the implications of last night's events. We have serious problems to face.

"Sorry, boss. Of course."

Sinclair adds, "I'll go with you. Got an idea where we can test your charges and dispose of Barone." I tip my chin, encouraging Zo to continue.

"I think our best bet now is bringing Manny and Stefano in on this. They have to be in the same situation as us—trying to figure out what the fuck is going on. We need to know why the fuck they've not told anyone Mateo is missing."

Sinclair interjects, "They're working with half the information we have. What else would you expect them to do? It's not like they trust the De Lucas and announcing it to everyone only creates panic. In Manny's position, I would do the same. Gather information and wait until I know more."

Nico nods along as the grownups talk. This is how our crew works best. Zo and Sinclair hash it out, and then Nico and I act on the plans.

"We need to go to them with Rory and Tony to back up our claim that Salvatore is behind all this," Zo suggests and then lets us consider his words.

"How do we know one or both of them isn't crooked, too?" I ask.

"Carlo gave us what he knew. I have no doubts that Rory and Nico got everything out of him," Sinclair interjects.

"You're assuming it stops at my dad and Carlo was trusted enough to know of every Bianchi traitor involved?"

"I see your point, but it's a risk we have to take. We need help, Benedict. They have resources we need, and we can't take on the De Lucas without support. We'd be dead before we started," Zo posits.

"Are you willing to gamble Rory's life on this?" Nico asks.

A subtle cough has us all snapping our head around to stare at Rory. "If you're quite done deciding for me," she takes a moment to glare at each of us, making sure we each feel a heated flare of embarrassment before continuing, "I think you're right, Enzo. As it stands, we've just kidnapped two capos and killed one of them. If Manny finds out, he'll be forced to order a hit on you. They may continue to keep quiet about my dad, but someone's going to miss Carlo and Tony soon. Without the underboss's support, we'll be defending on two fronts."

Rory runs a hand over her face and huffs out a frustrated sigh. "This is a clusterfuck. What the fuck is Salvatore waiting for? Why initiate a coup and then fail to seize power?"

"I don't fucking know, and that's why we can't do this shit alone. We can protect you here if we hide and do nothing. But if we're going to stop the De Lucas, you need more than us. You need a fucking army at your back."

"You're assuming a lot there, Zo. Dad's loyal soldiers were happy to sacrifice me to a De Luca in the first place. Why the fuck would they be loyal to me now?"

Sinclair stands and crosses the room, stopping directly in front of Rory. Hooking his thumb and forefinger under her chin, he demands her focus. There's something understated but so unbelievably dominant about the move, and it stirs a submissive response in me. *That's new.* I'm looking at Sinclair and suddenly seeing him in a different light. Daddy Sin. Commanding, gentle, and dominant as fuck.

I squirm in my seat next to Nico and he chuckles at me, realising my response.

"It's not fucking funny," I grumble at him under my breath.

His lips are at the shell of my ear and his words dance across it, forcing a shiver down my spine. "Maybe I'll try to channel my inner Sinclair later. Would you like that, Bambi?"

"Shut the fuck up," I push him away and volley my head between Sin and Nico before coming back to his eyes. "But yes."

Nico's sinful smile warms my cheeks, and I return my focus to Aurora.

Sinclair starts in an even tone, "Because a majority of us thought we were agreeing to an alliance—a partnership. We thought you would be protected, not sacrificed. Why did you think that your safety was the price that had to be paid for The Syndicate? Why didn't you ask for help?"

Rory takes a breath, and it makes me nervous. I know I will not like what comes next.

"Sin, you are overestimating the motivations behind our pact with the De Lucas, and you are underestimating the significance of the agreement we made when The Syndicate was forged. We were sending good men to their deaths in a pointless war, arguing over territories, and losing millions diluting revenue streams between the two families. My freedom was the price the Bianchi family had to pay to stop the bloodshed and secure a financially stable future." She lifts her hand to cup his cheek. "My father was aware of the consequences of the sacrifice I made."

"*What the fuck do you mean he was aware?*" Zo roars, charging over and pushing Sinclair out of the way. Enzo's heaving frame blocks Aurora from my view, but I can see that she's cowering at his outburst. I'm up in a flash with Sinclair next to me as we each grab one of Zo's arms and pull him back.

"Calm the fuck down, right now, Zo," Sinclair growls while Zo looks distraught.

"Are you telling me your father knew? Knew what Max was doing to you?"

Rory straightens her back and pushes her shoulders back. "Not in the beginning. But he figured it out. There were too many times I couldn't see him, usually because I'd spent an extended stay in our basement, and I had to heal. He never saw my injuries, but there were weeks, sometimes months at a time, that I couldn't leave the house. I don't think he realised the extent though until..." her breath catches, "the warehouse."

She casts her eyes down to her knees and shoves her hands in the kangaroo pocket on the front of the hoodie. "Besides, there was nothing he could do short of declaring war on the De Lucas. It's not like I could divorce Max. The only way out was death and like fuck was I going to give that cunt the satisfaction."

The stilted cadence of her words makes it obvious

how affected she is. She starts to fiddle with her hands inside her pocket nervously.

Zo takes a deep breath and kneels before her. "I'm sorry, *guerrierotta*."

I don't think I've ever seen him apologise like this. Like he feels it with every fibre of his being. It feels wrong witnessing it.

Rory shakes her head. "You don't need to be sorry, Zo. You just need to realise that while you guys know a lot, there's always more to family business than you are aware of. Whatever we do next, we cannot do it without more information. We need to talk to Manny and Stefano, and you're right—I need to go with you. I can promise you, whatever it is you think we know—we don't know everything."

Zo starts to interject, but she's off the gurney and covers his mouth delicately with two fingers.

"And whoever it is you think we can trust, we can't."

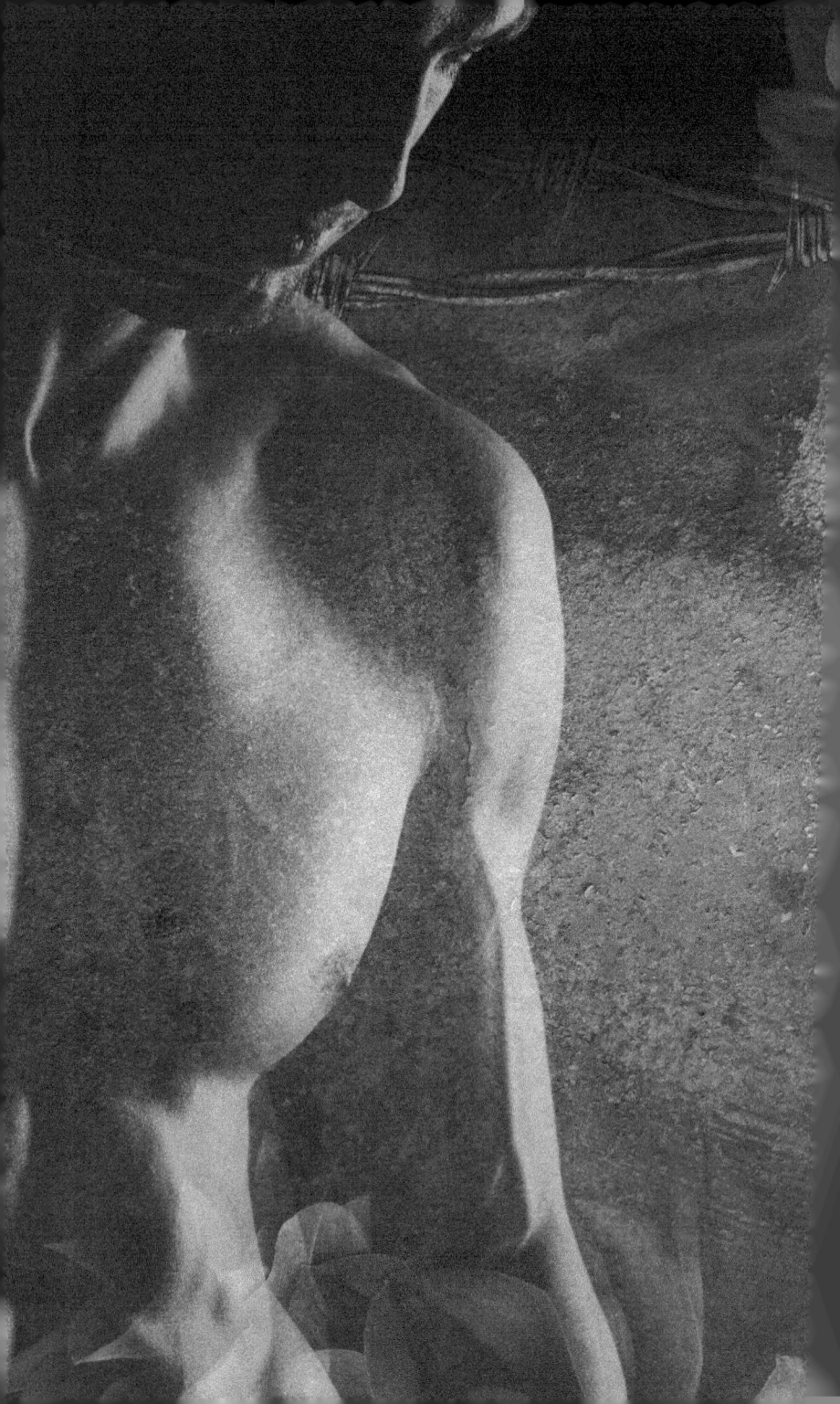

CHAPTER TWENTY-FOUR

SINCLAIR

We've been driving for about thirty minutes, but we're not far out now.

"How'd you find this place?" Benedict probes.

"It's a target for a Syndicate job. I found a job to demo some outbuildings a while back, and I noticed the contract hadn't been picked up by any of the crews yet. The building schematics show they have an incinerator on site. When you mentioned testing your latest designs, it occurred to me this way we could get paid, and you would get to blow shit up while we dispose of our little problem. Win-win." He shrugs.

"Your knack for details worries me sometimes."

I smile and tease him back. "Just be thankful you've never pissed me off, Benny. There are so many ways I could dispose of your body."

He laughs at my harmless threat, and it reminds me

how fond I am of him. I've known him most of his life, although we've only been working together for a few years. He's eleven years my junior, so unlike me and Zo, we didn't get to hoon around together as teenagers. We've had less time to cement a firm friendship, but it's there.

I respect Benedict. He had a rough run of it for a while and it took guts to hold his head high when his father disowned him. Made Men aren't known for their forward thinking and acceptance. Mateo was an exception to the rule, and I'm thankful he encouraged us to bring him into the team. That's why I find it hard to believe that Mateo did nothing to help Aurora.

There's no way the Mateo we all knew would forsake his daughter, no matter what obligations he had to The Syndicate or duty he felt to the family. She was all he had left. It makes no sense.

While I mourn Aurora's loss, I curse that Benny is still being haunted by his sonofabitch father. It guts me that Marco is involved in this. I thought Benedict had caught a break and was free of him.

"You doing okay with all this, Benny?" I try to ask as nonchalantly as possible, very much missing the mark as I watch his posture stiffen. Before I have the chance to prompt him about his father, he punches the steering wheel and I'm hit with an unexpected tirade.

"You'd better do right by her, Sinclair. I don't know what the fuck you think you're playing at, but that woman has been through enough. She's not some nameless fuck. You better look after her or I swear to fucking

Christ, Nico will have to pull me off of your cold dead corpse when I'm done with you."

Where the fuck did that come from?

"You about done?"

Benny looks just as surprised by his outburst as I am.

"I meant, are you okay with the fact we're going to go after your father? But it would seem we have something else we need to discuss." I bristle at this. Like fuck do I wanna sit with a twenty-something and discuss my sex life. I'm too old for this bullshit. However, we are brothers-in-arms, and it would seem I underestimated Benedict's interest in Aurora.

So did he, apparently.

His face is bright red. I'm unsure if it's rage or embarrassment, but either way, it appears to grip him tight and render him speechless. He keeps opening and closing his mouth, like he has lost the thread of his previous rant.

"Okay then." I draw out my words, trying to figure out where I'm going with this. "Look, I don't know what your problem is," he makes a move to interrupt me, but I hold up a hand to stop him in his tracks, "but you have every right to be concerned about her safety. However, it is not your place to question my honour. You know me better than that."

He doesn't speak and I see him nod out of the corner of my eye as I glare at the white lines whizzing past the window as we drive.

"I know I would never intentionally hurt her, but I don't have a clue what she wants from me..." I can't think of what else I can say to convince him of my intentions.

"Are you guys, like, together now?" he asks in a meek voice.

His question takes me aback. It's not because he asked, but rather because I'm unsure how to respond. So, I hedge. "Look, I don't know. It's not like we've had a moment to talk about it. When I woke up this morning, the meeting had already started, everyone was there and then I had to come straight out with you. I don't know what we are, and I'm not being funny, but the person I want to talk to about it first, ain't you."

"Fair," he grunts out after a few moments. "Look, I don't know where that all came from, but... just... look after her."

That's all he says before an uncomfortable silence settles over us. There's only five minutes to our destination, and every one of them is awkward as fuck.

IT DIDN'T TAKE LONG to get the body in the incinerator, and Benedict seems to be catharting the fuck out of his mood by blowing up various small sheds throughout the property. He'll be a while, so I take out my phone and pull up my message thread with Aurora. I slowly scroll back through the messages from the last few days and as I'm reading, my phone buzzes, making me jump while the screen flicks to the new incoming message.

HUMMINGBIRD:

Soooo...

Another one pops up almost immediately.

HUMMINGBIRD:

Last night...

Three dots. No dots. Three dots again.

HUMMINGBIRD:

...please respond and select option

a) was fun

b) was a mistake

or c) never happened

I laugh out loud. Only Aurora could inject so much of her personality into her texts.

But then I realise she's giving me an out, and I hate that. It wasn't a mistake, I don't regret it and I can't wish it never happened. She's worth so much more than that.

a) was fun.

I'm sorry we didn't have time to talk this morning.

HUMMINGBIRD:

No worries, I'm sorry you woke up alone. I needed coffee, and I didn't want to wake you.

You don't need to apologise. I understand how out of hand your caffeine addiction is in the mornings.

Will you be there when we get back?

HUMMINGBIRD:

We're heading out in ten. Talk later?

CHAPTER TWENTY-FOUR

Count on it, hummingbird.

Shit. I was hoping to be back before they head out to see Manny and Stefano. Bodies never burn as quick as you think they will. Guess it's time to track down our resident fire-starter. As I'm setting off across the back of the industrial factory yard towards the perimeter when another alert comes through. Expecting to receive another message from Aurora, I'm surprised to see an alert from the subroutine I have monitoring the local police channels.

MURDERBOT:

ALERT > John Doe

If any murder victim matches Isabella's autopsy results in these categories, I'm notified. Age, sex, location, unusual or ritualistic marks, etcetera. I click to open and see that we have another body with 'unusual markings from an unidentified weapon'. I need to get back to my laptop and see what I can uncover in the Medical Examiners digital files. I need to know what these marks look like.

My criteria are broad, and I've received thousands of these alerts in the years we've been investigating. These leads rarely end up going anywhere, but it's unprecedented to have two bodies with "unusual markings" discovered within days of each other.

As I look up, I see Benny jogging towards me. "We need to head back. There's something I need to work on back at the house. You get the job done?"

He nods. "Yep. Sheds A through D, and F through G,

all demolished. You sure the owners won't mind I've left craters?"

I smile. "I'm sure they will. The job was from their competitor."

I CAN SEE that the other car is gone as we pull into the driveway, and it makes me uneasy. I should be there. I should have Zo's back. We've never faced anything like this, and it leaves an acrid taste in my mouth that burns every time I swallow. With Aurora under our protection, the stakes are impossibly high. If anything were to happen to her because of our negligence—well, it doesn't bear thinking about. We cannot fail her.

I make my way back to my office and start trawling through the information on the latest body. At some point Benedict must have popped in, as there's a hot cup of coffee on my desk now, but I don't recall him being here. I zone out when I'm working. The hum of my machines lulls me into a trance and my focus sharpens.

No matter how much digging I do, what I need is not in the Medical Examiner's files. Either the servers haven't refreshed or they're keeping information back so it can't be leaked. Which would imply they are working under the assumption that this is a serial killer and have classified information behind a firewall I haven't hacked yet. *Fuck.*

It wouldn't be difficult for me to hack. Not much is beyond my skills. It'd just take time and focus I don't have right now. However, it would be faster to see for ourselves. I pick up the cup of coffee and sit back in my chair.

No point going now. We'll have to wait until the night shift. After searching through the personnel records, security in the Medical Examiner's office looks to be minimal overall, but from the looks of the scheduling, it's a skeleton staff at night. That's our best bet.

I head to the kitchen in search of Benedict, but shockingly, I don't find him with his head buried in the fridge. He's not in any of the communal areas either. Heading down to the basement, I find him in the interrogation room. He's set himself up on the corner with Nico's tattoo gun.

"Nico's gonna be pissed when he finds you've been playing with his toys," I say, leaning over to see what he's working on. "And he's going to be even more pissed you didn't ask him to mark you."

"I'm just brightening up the colours. I was getting restless waiting for them."

He's focussed on touching-up the shading here and there on his left forearm. Without looking up, he continues, "Sorry about unloading on you in the car."

"It's okay. You care about her."

His gaze darts up and his eyes betray him. He's nervous, but he honestly doesn't need to be.

"Listen, whatever is going on with Aurora and me? That's between us, but whatever you feel for her—or her and Nico. That's between you guys."

His expression shifts to one of confusion.

"That woman has survived hell. She can have whatever she needs from me, for however long she needs it. Whatever, and *whoever*, she needs—is hers."

Benedict's entire demeanour alters as the weight of my words settles on him. His posture softens and his shoulders drop, like the worry is seeping out of him.

I mean every word. I would do anything for Aurora, and I can see in Benedict's eyes he would, too. He loves her, and even though I don't understand to what extent, I feel no jealousy.

I meant what I said. I don't expect a happily ever after with Aurora. But whatever I can say or do to ensure she gets hers, I will do.

CHAPTER TWENTY-FIVE

AURORA

The buildings flit past the window in a blur. I catch a glimpse of my reflection every time a dark silhouette in the street turns the car window into a mirror. It's not me I see staring back. Well, it is me, but at a glance, in this wig, I look alarmingly like my sister. From the furtive looks Zo is casting at me in the rearview, it's evident my appearance is throwing him off too. He has a haunted expression that sends uneasy chills through my body.

While we were very similar in appearance, as soon as she was old enough, she had dyed her ebony hair red. The only wig Nico could find at short notice was from a nearby sex shop as part of a dominatrix costume—a mid-length auburn wig with rich burgundy lowlights frames my face while allowing me to hide behind a heavy curtain of bangs. I'm impressed with his ingenuity on such short notice.

It's my first time leaving the house in weeks, and I'm more nervous than I thought I would be. I thought I'd feel more comfortable in a disguise, but in the muted light of the tinted glass, the spectre of my sister unsettles me.

Before we left, Sinclair had texted Zo about a potential lead relating to my sister's death. I'd been surprised to learn that my father had people investigating her death still. Despite all these years, he persisted. I lost hope years ago, but that wasn't because I gave up on her, it was because once I married Max, I gave up on everyone.

I didn't have the capacity to hope for anyone other than myself. It was the only way I survived.

That thought makes me feel selfish. My father and these men dedicated themselves to finding Isa's killer, while I was consumed by my own survival.

I'll never forget the day my father told me Isa had been murdered. I was eleven years old when she died and as soon as the words passed my father's lips, my childhood died along with her. My loving, outgoing, gentle sister had her life snuffed out and dumped in a filthy back alley. Tortured and left for dead.

My father only told me she had been murdered, but in the days and weeks that followed, as Mateo Bianchi mobilised an army of his foot soldiers to hunt down the monster that killed her, I overheard plenty.

I hid in the shadows, sneaking about the house to glean any piece of information I could. Thinking back, that was the first time I realised my natural talent for reconnaissance. However, they found nothing and over time, I accepted that we would never discover who took her away from us. I assumed my father had given up, too.

Isa was nine years older than me and after my mother died, she was my entire universe. She became both my sister and my confidant. We shared every secret we had with each other. I glance up at Zo in the rearview mirror and he's looking at the road. We need to talk about my sister's death. I need to know if he's uncovered things I don't know.

If I know things, he doesn't.

"We're here," Nico says, pulling me out of my thoughts. As morbid as they are, it's oddly refreshing to have something to think about other than the monumental clusterfuck we're currently trying to navigate.

We're meeting Manny and Stefano in the basement of a parking garage in the city. Fuck knows if it's a good idea. Whether we meet in a densely populated area, or in the woods, the risks are still monumentally large if I'm seen. If the De Lucas find out I'm alive, they'll murder me and anyone with me.

Zo pulls into a space and turns around in the front seat to take me in. His expression is serious, his tone authoritative yet reassuring. It soothes me. "Stay in the car until one of us comes to get you. I need to check if it's safe first and get a feel for Manny and Stefano before we share what we know. Nico, you run the perimeter and keep your eyes on the car."

I nod and let out a breath. Feeling protected. Every one of Zo's men makes me feel safe, but Enzo... makes me feel protected in a way I cannot explain. His words inspire absolute faith in his intentions and abilities.

He pops the door and heads out, Nico following his lead but taking a different route, scouring the layout and whipping through the parked cars, checking for anything out of place. From behind the darkened glass, I feel like a spectator—a bystander in my own story.

Enzo heads to the back of the lot and approaches a dark town car. The front doors open and two men I've known my entire life get out, cutting Zo off at the hood of the car.

The last time I saw Stefano was at my father's house a few months ago. During one of my rare injury-free spells, I'd visited Dad for dinner and Stefano had been there when I arrived, going over some of the day-to-day issues. You know, thugs encroaching on territory, foot soldiers that needed an attitude adjustment by their capo. I've always had a lot of respect for him. He's even tempered, hyper-rational, and has a naturally empathetic disposition that makes him the perfect consigliere.

Manny has always been a highly-proficient underboss. His ability to wrangle the capos is impressive, and he's always been fair with them. That's probably the greatest compliment I can pay him. Other than that, he's a misogynist pig that spends too much time sticking his dick where it doesn't belong. Every interaction I've ever had with him since I turned sixteen has left a horrible taste in my mouth.

I watch their rigid, inexpressive faces as mouths move, but I can't infer anything from their interaction. I wish I could read lips. A shadow moves in my peripheral vision, and I startle before Nico's frame appears from behind the back of a panel van. A sudden gasp from Stefano and the jerk of Manny's head to glance at the rear window I'm hiding behind, and I know Zo has told them.

Told them that my husband tried to kill me. They walk towards me and Zo nods, giving me the signal.

As they approach, I step out, brazenly projecting a strength I don't feel. Feet planted firmly on the ground, shoulders back and head held high, I greet them with a nod. "Gentlemen, thank you for agreeing to this meeting."

Stefano takes in the fading bruises still very visible on my jaw and the cuts that are obvious, despite healing well. Although I avoid the mirror and I can feel the aches and pains, the guys never look at me the way Stefano is right now. The blatant shock etched into every line on his face takes me aback and reminds me of the reflection I so often forget.

It makes me feel like a victim.

Manny looks me up and down and turns back to Enzo. "I can see why you've been lying low recently, Enzo. I noticed your crew hadn't been taking as many contracts and was getting suspicious. This explains it." Turning his eyes back to me, I bristle at his business-like demeanour. "What happened?"

"I only told him you were here, and that you were attacked," Zo says.

I nod, understanding that the rest is on me to explain. "I need to explain, but I need you not to interrupt me until I'm done. It will be tough to get it all out, but I'll answer your questions afterwards."

CHAPTER TWENTY-FIVE

They both nod and I take a deep breath. *Here goes nothing...*

Starting from the day Max locked me in our basement, I cover everything up to the moment I stepped out of the car. As I talk, I can feel the anger radiating off Stefano while Manny remains cool, calm, and collected. Nodding at every revelation while Stefano either growls or grinds out another, "Motherfucker," in response.

When I tell them about how Max killed my father, that's the only time my breath hitches and they both cry out in shock. Stefano lets out an anguished cry while Manny brings his fist down on the roof of the car next to us with a loud bang. I tell them how he slit my father's throat. How he mutilated his corpse.

What I don't say is how I prayed to a God I no longer believe in that I would slip away as he cut into my father's face. I don't say that no matter how tightly I screwed my eyes shut, I still heard the knife scraping against my father's skull.

Not only will I enjoy watching the light fade in my husband's eyes as I kill him, but I will also take down every corrupt motherfucker that had a hand in helping him.

"If we are going to find out what's coming next, we need support. The Bianchis. Family we can trust." Stefano nods at my words. "We need your support if we're going to go after the men—and I use that term loosely—that betrayed him."

While Stefano is nodding, Manny holds up his hand. "Aurora, the severity of what you've been subjected to is obvious, and I would never doubt your word, especially when it relates to your father, but you've killed the only people who can corroborate that there is a larger conspiracy. If we're going to garner the support of the family—challenge the status quo within The Syndicate —then we need more."

Enzo moves to the trunk of the car and pops it open.

"Tony here, while oblivious to the implications of his involvement, can clue you in to the connection between Marco, Carlo, and Max. Even if he can't validate Carlo's intel, he can act as a witness to the four of them colluding outside of sanctioned Syndicate channels. That still warrants investigating."

Both men peer into the trunk and Stefano produces a gun, while Manny rips off the duct tape as aggressively as he can. Tony squeals until the barrel of the gun is pressed firmly against his temple.

"Speak," Stefano barks, his temper fraying at the edges.

"I didn't know they would go after Mateo! I swear to God I didn't know. I thought we were just running jobs for extra cash. I would never have helped them if I knew they were gonna kill Mateo."

"Holy fuck, you weren't wrong. This one is an idiot. I knew Mateo liked to keep him close so he could better manage him, but I didn't realise it was because he was a fucking liability anywhere else in the organisation. Fuck me," Manny huffs out running a hand over the back of his neck and nodding to Stefano.

Stefano has squeezed off a shot between his eyes before Tony even realises he's been judged and found wanting. The silencer doesn't do a lot, bearing in mind the acoustics of the parking garage and the sharp clang of the trunk closing is just as loud.

"You need more before we can act on this," Stefano chimes in. "Before, we had to keep our mouths shut because we didn't know what had happened to Mateo. It would have caused tensions in The Syndicate. But this? We tell the family this now, it will cause an outright war. We need to know what the fuck the De Lucas end goal is, and we need to know who the fuck we can trust."

"Your only lead outside the De Lucas is Marco. You can go after him with my blessing and any resources I can provide." Manny pauses and leans in to shake hands, but grabs Enzo's forearm, forcing Zo to reciprocate in some sort of secret handshake that denotes a sacred accord. "But if you can't get him to talk or get any tangible proof of this plot you suspect, you're on your own. You don't have long, because we now have two Bianchi capos and a don MIA with no way to explain it. Whatever you do, it has to be done quickly."

"I am at your disposal. Whatever you need, I will make it happen," Stefano says. I'm not sure if he's talking to Enzo or me, or both of us. But his support feels like a facsimile of the way my father used to comfort me. It's not the same and it should make me feel uneasy, but instead I sink into that feeling and let it surround me like a warm blanket.

"Thank you, Stefano," I lean in and hug him. I feel his chin rest on my head as his arm bands around my shoulders, squeezing me slightly too tight as he whispers, "I'm sorry we failed you. You shouldn't have been in his clutches to begin with."

I lean back and hold his gaze. His words were just for me. I know there's more I need to ask him, but with an almost imperceptible squint of his eyes he tells me now is not the time.

Manny steals me from Stefano's warmth, and I'm wrapped in a hug that's about as reassuring as a steel trap. "I'm so sorry for your loss, princess."

Zo hears the word and watches me carefully, expecting me to freak the fuck out. That word only incites a boiling rage that makes me want to grab Manny by the hair and introduce his nose to my kneecap. Plus, I'd probably tear any remaining stitches I have, and I'd rather not deal with a tongue lashing from Doc Em if I can avoid it.

I step back and naturally seek Enzo. He doesn't touch me, he simply stands at my shoulder.

"Thank you. I know you both had great respect for my father. I'm sorry I couldn't stop Max—but I *will* stop him now."

Nodding one last time, Stefano and Manny retreat to their car and Nico appears, pulling Stefano to one side. Nico hands him something, and Stefano nods before turning back to the car to catch up with Manny.

"You're driving," Zo grunts at Nico before opening the rear passenger door and ushering me in, following me into the back seat.

As we head home, I replay our meeting, processing what they said, how they said it. Trying to think of the next step and how we best go after Marco. More information is necessary before accusing the De Lucas of anything.

Outside the new normal of the safe house, everything feels so surreal. In the space of a few weeks, my entire world has shifted on its axis. One that is no longer a living hell, a victim to my tormenter. My world is now centred in a very different reality, protected by men who have pledged to help me avenge my father. I crave their protection and comfort. All I want is to go home to them all, because here in the outside world without them all at my side, I have to be a very different version of myself.

The Aurora Max brutalised was broken. The Aurora that woke up surrounded by Zo and his team, is healing. The Aurora that had to explain how her father was slaughtered? She's not quite ready yet.

It was difficult to say everything without breaking. But it had to be done.

The sooner we return home, the better.

I need... to go home.

CHAPTER TWENTY-SIX

NICO

When Sinclair first mentioned the assignment, it sounded like it would be more fun. Or maybe I just heard the words *morgue* and *break-in* and made a false assumption. In reality, it's cold-as-balls in this freezer, and if I can't find the bodies we're looking for soon, I may end up losing one of them to hypothermia.

Since we returned from the meet, Aurora has been withdrawn. Seeing her retreating into herself, unsettles me so when Zo asked Benny and me to run this assignment for Sin, I asked if I could bring her with us. She seemed reluctant to leave the house, but after the incentive of being able to dust off her lock-picking skills and the promise that she didn't have to wear the wig again, we eventually convinced her to leave Sick Bay.

Aurora headed straight for the file room when we got here. She's trying to see if there's anything in the physical files we didn't get from hacking the digital ones. Fuck knows where Benny is, but I'm guessing he's running a perimeter sweep while I'm stuck staring at corpses. I hear a metallic snick of the door as it opens and the gentle padding of feet that are way too light to be Benny's. I go to duck down behind the gurney but stop as a familiar, soft voice calls out my name.

"You done already?" I ask Aurora as she approaches me, her petite yet sumptuous frame concealed by over-sized clothing. I lent her one of my black hoodies and a baseball cap to keep her at least partially disguised. She looks like she's playing dress-up, the hoodie stopping just shy of her knees, and the sleeves so long the cuffs act like mittens. It has me biting my cheek in frustration, knowing she's wrapped up in my clothes. All I can do right now is try to suppress my cravings for this vicious little thing, but some dark possessive side of me revels in the fact that she chooses to wear my gear more than anyone else's, and it's not like it's because it fits better.

I'm the tallest of the team, and anything of mine practically swallows her whole. Aurora's almost a foot shorter than my six-foot-four frame, yet when I think back to the strength she channelled in the interrogation, there's nothing *small* about her. She projected an air of power so irrepressible she appeared godlike in her command of Carlo and Tony. Not small, or fragile, or weak. Aurora dominated the room.

She's breathtaking, but... *she's not mine.* I need to get out of here. I need to find Benny. *I need what's mine and I need it now.*

"Yeah, the files aren't there, it's annoying as fuck."

"Help me find these two bodies, and then we can get out of here. We only need to see the marks. They probably won't even be a match."

Shaking off my wandering thoughts, I get back to the search. We both have the case numbers memorised, so we keep searching and checking the medical identification bands on the cadaver ankles.

"Got one," she shouts after five minutes. There are a surprising number of John Does backing up the Medical Examiner's freezers right now.

I head over and pull back the sheet fully, wincing at the extent of the injuries. The bloodlessness allows me to take in every jagged edge and deep gouge in the flesh. Whoever this was, died a very violent death. I glance up and see that Aurora is studying the marks they have sent us to photograph. They're strange—uniform and yet not. In places, the criss-crossing striations alter their pattern and become inconsistent. The markings alter depending on the undulation of the victim's flesh. We've all studied the description and photos of Isabella's autopsy. These seem very similar, but I'm no expert. I don't think Sin has shown Aurora her sister's file yet, though, so she has no frame of reference.

Her head pops up, and she directs me. "You take some photos of these. I'll find the other body." She's turned her back to me and started her search before I can object to her commanding me. I *only* tolerate orders from Zo, occasionally Sin, and the authoritative tone she takes with me rankles and festers at the base of my neck and sits uneasily in my chest.

This is not one of the ways I desire Aurora. She is a

strong woman, and I love that. But I want to be a place where she doesn't have to be. I want to be where she feels safe enough to give up all control. To me...

Shit, I need to cut those thoughts out right fucking now. I am not what she needs. *I'm an asshole.*

I take out my cell and start taking pictures of the marks across the body. They wrap around the wrists, the arm and the torso. There's a flow to them in places where they curve around the ribs, but in others they're like staccato notes, jabbing at the flesh and leaving uneven and jagged marks.

The heavy thuds of Benny's boots coming up the corridor have me releasing a calming breath. I'd recognise his gait anywhere. Knowing he's returning to me always fills me with a tranquillity that's hard to explain. Every part of him is mine, and nothing in me ever doubts that. When he's with me, I own every part of him. He is a part of me—part of my soul—and vice versa. Our dynamic is not frivolous, it's meaningful.

How I bring peace to Benny, I long to do for Aurora. I wish I could. He wishes the same.

Fuck, I have to stop dwelling on this.

Benny barges through the door, completely oblivious to Aurora's presence, and proceeds to plant a rough kiss on me, despite his lookout duty. His hands gripping the collar of my jacket tightly. Pulling me into him, his lips slip from mine and he nuzzles across the scruff on my jawline, coming to rest at the shell of my ear.

Before I can alert him we're not alone, he grinds out, "The only thing that I want more than your cock in my mouth right now would be to see your cock in Aurora's mouth while I ate her pussy."

A small cough from behind us alerts Benny to her presence. The mortification that burns a trail across his cheeks would be hilarious if he hadn't made me complicit in his blunder. I don't think Aurora needed to know that she has become a guest star in our sexual fantasies.

Before Benny can apologise, Aurora cuts him off. "Get over here. I found the other body." Benny tries to open his mouth again, but she holds up her hand with a firm, "Ah-ah-ah."

It's hard not to laugh, as he whines when she shuts him down. His darkened green eyes turn to me, wide and disappointed, seeking some kind of reassurance. I take him by the hand and tilt my head, encouraging him to follow me over to the gurney she's been hovering at. I squeeze his hand and intertwine my fingers with his, feeling the tension leave him as his arm relaxes beside mine.

"These marks are the same, can you take shots of these too please, Nico." Her tone is distant and detached. She's so entranced by the kerf marks on the body that I'm wondering if she heard what Benny said at all.

Without touching the skin, her fingers float across the marks, and I watch as she straightens and rolls up the sleeve of my hoodie. She's ignoring us as she holds up her arm and makes the same movement with her fingers. I use my phone to take photos of the second victim, but out of the corner of my eye I watch her.

Something's wrong.

I pass the phone across to Benny and move around to stand beside Aurora. I'm curious to know what has captured her attention—and that's when it dawns on me.

She's not comparing the wounds on the bodies to her recent cuts, she's comparing them to her scars. The faded silver steaks that wind around her forearm and biceps.

I raise my arms and take her by the shoulders, steering her away from the body. She doesn't stop her survey, so I pull her hand towards me and take over the inspection. This pulls her focus to me as she speaks in a monotonous and disconcerting tone.

"There are many things that can mar the skin permanently." She lifts her hand and points at a small burn mark. "Cigarettes," she states. Then her index finger moves to a pink line about two centimetres long and paper thin. "Knives." Her hand dances over her scars as she continues, "Scalpels, scissors, razors..."

She stops and brushes her fingertips along the matching patterns that band her wrist.

"These though," her breathing falters before she steadies it and a disembodied voice that doesn't sound like her explains, "these are barbed wire. These marks happen when you are bound so tightly with it that any movement slices into you. Your only choices are to fight and potentially slice your wrists open, or to remain still."

I draw in a sharp breath as I let the full weight of what she's saying wash over me. Restrained with barbed wire, Aurora had to choose between survival and ending her own life... Repeatedly... For four years.

The rage that fills me is uncontrollable and I can't contain my reaction.

The sound that comes out of my throat causes her to flinch and Benedict rounds the table and stands in front of her. He knows I would never hurt her, but he is also familiar with my temper. "Walk it off now, Nico."

I can see Benny's lips moving, but I can't hear his words. It's like a haze has descended and it's fogging my vision and my hearing. I can't hear the roars that I know are bursting from me, but I can feel them in my chest. The way they burn my trachea and leave an emptiness in the pit of my stomach.

When I get my hands on Max De Luca, I will make him suffer. Every injury he has ever inflicted upon her, I will visit back on him tenfold. I will use the map of her scars as a fucking instruction manual.

When I'm done, I will watch as she snuffs him out of existence. I will not take that joy from her.

I will be Max's judge, and she will be his executioner.

I feel Benedict pushing me towards the door, the gentle squeeze of his hand on my shoulder reassures me even as I'm evicted. I find myself pacing up and down the corridor, trying to will the excess energy out of my system.

There's no denying what I feel for Aurora, and in that realisation is the truth that her pain is my pain. The look in her eyes as she relived what Max did to her cuts me to my core, leaving an ache that buries itself bone deep and threatens to consume me.

I have no idea how long I pace, but eventually my steps slow and I'm leaning back against the wall, sliding down to the floor. Resting my elbows on my knees, I drop my forehead into my hands and take a deep breath.

I take a moment to fall apart—a moment Aurora was never afforded the luxury of—and now I need to pull my shit together.

I hear the door open again, and Benedict drops to his knees in front of me.

"Get up," he demands, and I don't move.

A smile works its way across my face, and I reach out to grab him by the scruff of the neck. "I do not take orders from you, Bambi."

I pull him into me and as the familiar taste of him floods my mouth, I can't help but moan. Pulling back, I add, "But thank you. I needed a moment."

"Anytime… sir."

CHAPTER TWENTY-SEVEN

BENEDICT

Ordering Nico to do anything isn't something he lets me get away with. Unless I'm bratting, and he's waiting for me to test the limits of his patience, poised to punish me. Just thinking about how that man thrashes my ass with a paddle makes my dick wake up.

But I had to remove him from the room when he startled Aurora. I can see how conflicted he is. He's burning with a near uncontrollable need to protect her, avenge her. I feel it too. Only she's not ours to protect.

I've never felt so confused, yet so sure of myself. The dichotomy is difficult to wrap my head around. I love Nico, but how I feel about Aurora is undeniable. I yearn for Nico to overpower me—to surrender to him. But I long for her too. I want to command her body. I want to feel her surrender to me... to us.

Fuck's sake. Now I'm hard.

Nico leans back against the wall and rises to his full height, leaving me staring up at him, kneeling at his feet. He runs his hand from my temple, into my hair and forward, holding his palm at my jaw. He draws my chin up and demands my submission, my affection, my love. And I give it willingly.

Settling back on my heels, I sink into the familiar position. The pose I hold for my master when we're in-scene. I can't adequately describe the feeling of peace I experience at Nico's feet. I lean forward and I nuzzle against his leg, and he strokes through my hair.

"Such a good boy, Bambi." His words steal a moan from my lips and then he pulls me to my feet. That's when we spot we're not alone.

Aurora is staring at us, mouth open, chest rising and falling, and eyes blown wide. Whatever she saw between us, she liked. She liked it a lot. Nico, having centred himself, turns to her and takes her hand.

"I'm sorry, Aurora. I shouldn't have reacted like that."

She swallows and glances at her feet. "Why?"

"What do you mean why, Aurora?"

"Why *did* you react that way?"

I sigh and try to explain. "When you told us how you recognised the marks... the thought of you going through that? It was a lot."

She steps forward, invading his space, "But why, Nico? I'm sure you've seen worse. Hell, you've probably inflicted worse."

"Don't ask that question if you're not prepared to hear the answer, Rory," I warn. I don't think she's ready to hear what Nico and I want to confess to her.

She considers my words for a few minutes and then nods, comprehending enough to know now isn't the time.

Squeezing my hand and then clearing his throat, Nico encourages us along the hallway and says, "Since we got what we came for, we better get out of here."

"HOW LONG HAVE you guys been together?" Aurora's voice asks from the backseat.

I've been watching her in the rearview. She's been flicking her eyes between Nico and me. I can see her brain working—trying to figure us and our relationship out. She thinks she's being subtle, but I see the blushes flushing her cheeks and the way she keeps squeezing her thighs together. When she does, she has the same look on her face from when we spotted her watching us in the hallway.

I could tell from her expression then, and the hungry gaze she's trying to hide now that she saw me on my knees for him.

Fuck, to have her on her knees next to me. Or for us... I smile and bite my lip but nod to Nico, giving him permission to speak for me.

"Well actually, we first met at your wedding," Nico says.

I see her eyes widen. It's like a punch to the gut and makes me wish one of the happiest days of my life wasn't the beginning of a four-year prison sentence for her.

"I saw this sexy asshole at the reception, hiding in the corner like some kind of dark cloud."

"I told you to fuck off three times that night. I still don't understand why you kept asking," he says, his voice gruff but tempered with a wry smile.

"Because you were hot as fuck," I reply and Nico smiles. He's still hot as fuck. Six foot four inches of brooding muscle, with dark, sapphire blue eyes, I could swear were black at times. Throw in the dirty blonde hair and facial scruff that scrapes my jaw when he kisses me and he's a walking wet dream.

"You were fucking hard to say no to."

I can see Rory smiling in the back, and I say, "We should thank you. If it weren't for your wedding and those shots you served at cocktail hour, I'd never have had the guts to ask him out."

Her smile widens. "It's nice that something good came out of my wedding."

"We went out on our first date the following week and we've been together ever since," I say.

"Where did you guys go on your first date?"

Nico takes this one. "Well, he suggested a coffee date... and I laughed in his face. So, we compromised, and I took him to a firing range that had an axe throwing gallery."

"Yeah, I'm not sure it did much to quash my first date nerves when you showed off how lethal you were with an axe."

"Bullshit, it turned you on."

"Of course it turned me on, but it was also my first

date with a guy, so yeah, I was nervous as all hell." I hear a little chuckle from the back seat.

"That's sweet. You bonded over sharp edges."

"Yeah, and I got to see a side of Nico few people have. No one except me and the guys, and now you. Oh, I hear I have you to thank for his sudden interest in bingeing comedy shows. I've been trying to get him to watch *Parks and Recreation* for years."

This easy conversation takes me by surprise and for the rest of the journey we sink into anecdotes about our early days dating. Rory tells him embarrassing stories from when we were kids. It's nice, but it eventually turns when she asks about my brother and sister, Luc and Etta. I answer her questions about them, what they're up to, who they're dating, but then when she talks about my parents, I can't help but go quiet. My mother disowned me the day my father did.

"I'm sorry we have to go after your dad, Benny. We have to do it, but I'm sorry if anything we're about to do ends up hurting you."

The words that come to me flow without a second thought. "Marco Romano will pay for his betrayal. There isn't a cell in my body that will mourn him. He stopped being my father the moment he tried to kill me."

I try not to glance in the rearview, but it's automatic when I hear her shocked gasp.

"What did you say?"

"It always makes me laugh when people say that cunt disowned me."

Nico reaches over and rests his hand on my thigh as if to bolster me as I say the next part.

"What he actually did was shoot me. My sister heard and called Nico, who went all knight in shining armour on me."

"Can you not joke about this?" Nico hates it when I'm flippant about it. He thought I was dead. He walked into my father's house, picked up what he thought was my body, and only realised I was alive when we got outside. Took me to the hospital, called Mateo, and wouldn't leave my side until I was fit to leave. By the time I'd healed, Mateo had agreed with my father that I was no longer a Romano, and just another *Bianchi Bastard.*

As I explain her father's role in my life, Rory nods along.

"Sounds like Dad. He may not have been able to sanction Marco for his actions, but he did what he could to protect you." She catches my gaze in the tiny mirror again. "I've been selfish not acknowledging how much he meant to you all. I'm sorry for your loss, Benny."

Her selflessness floors me. How does someone who's spent years being systematically destroyed have the capacity for this level of understanding? I can't speak, and Nico has my back.

"You don't need to say that, Aurora. But... I'm going to say thank you, anyway. Mateo meant a lot to us." We're left with a lull in the conversation that stretches out until I pull the car into the driveway. It's not awkward, it's just heavy with the weight of the topic. It follows us as we head into the house and go to find Sinclair.

AFTER TRACKING Sinclair down in the gym with Zo, we filled them both in. When Rory explained what she thought the marks were, the tension rolling off Zo was palpable, but he pulled it together as we discussed the meet with Manny.

"When we were leaving, I asked Stefano to take over investigating the nurse that's stalking Doc Em. He's more of a problem than I originally thought. Normally, I'd deal with him myself, but we have too much on our plates right now. I can't guarantee her safety if I can't watch her all the time."

"You think it's that serious, Nico?"

"Yeah, from my surveillance of him, he's definitely a problem. With everything else we've got going on, we need someone else keeping an eye on the situation. Stefano has experience with stalkers and the resources to protect her—he's got it covered."

"Good thinking," Zo says, patting Nico on the shoulder as he heads out of the makeshift gym we've set up at the back of the garage.

I jerk my head towards the door to encourage Nico to follow me out of the room. He looks pained to leave Aurora, but I know that Aurora and Sinclair need to be alone. They haven't seen each other since this morning, and they need to talk.

When we get to the kitchen, I turn around and bring my palm to Nico's chest. "I need—"

"I know what you need, Bambi."

He pushes me back against the counter, fisting my hair and wrenching my head back, exposing my neck to him. I have kept my hair this length since we started dating—just long enough for Nico to grab on to. The perfect length.

He drags his lips from my jawline down my neck and across my pulse point. I let out a whimper when he bites down—the pain shocking me and then morphing into a shiver that trickles down my spine.

"How many times do I have to tell you both? Not in the communal areas. Take it somewhere else," Zo says from behind us, opening the fridge and grabbing the milk.

Oops. Busted.

"Yes, boss," Nico replies and grabs my forearm, dragging me behind him. I assume he's taking me to his room, but as we cross the foyer, we detour down into the basement. I can't suppress my smile when I realise he's taking me to the interrogation room.

We are going to play.

Stalking down the corridor, he throws open the door and pulls me to the centre of the room.

"On your knees and assume the position."

Fuck, I'm already hard.

The room is cool and crisp, but I don't feel its chill as Nico exudes an aura of masculinity that I can feel wrapping itself around me in winding tendrils. It takes all my control to obey and not cross the room to him, into the soothing warmth of his dominance.

I drop to my knees, maintaining eye contact as I tuck my feet underneath me. Placing my hands palm up on my thighs, I break eye contact and drop my chin to my chest, taking a deep breath to centre myself in the scene.

"What's your safe word, Bambi?"

"Midnight, sir."

"And give me your colour."

"Green, sir."

"We're going to play with pain tonight. Get you out of your head."

He stands towering behind me, running his fingers through my unruly hair. I lean into his touch automatically as he radiates a masterful energy that demands my subservience.

"Shirt off, hands and knees."

I try to remove my hoodie and henley without tangling myself up in them, but in my haste my sleeves catch on my wrists, and I'm left shirtless with my arms inadvertently restrained.

"Well, that's just perfect. Change of plan, leave the shirt, get on your knees and elbows. Ass up, Bambi."

I can hear him walk across the room and start pulling open drawers. The metallic snicks of blades being placed on the counter and the whisper of leather straps as he draws them through his fingers make my cock strain behind the zipper of my jeans. They're tight and restrictive, and the slight pinch is as tantalising as it is uncomfortable. If I thought I wouldn't be punished, I'd complain, but tonight there's not a trace of brat in me.

I want to be owned by my man, and I want it to hurt.

I know better than to lift my head up to see what he's doing, but I can hear him. I listen as discarded items of clothing drop to the floor. First his jacket, then his shirt, and then I hear the dull thuds of his boots being kicked off.

When he returns, I can only see his bare feet and the

bottoms of his dark, low-slung jeans. I'm salivating at the image. *Why is barefoot in jeans so fucking hot?* I bite my lip to stifle the moan that wants to erupt from me.

I hear the scraping of a chair across the floor as he places it in front of me. "Elbows on the seat and brace yourself, Bambi."

I do as I'm told.

I say nothing.

I do not have permission to speak.

He moves in a slow circle around me. I can appreciate him now that my head is off the floor. He is a sight to behold. He's monstrous in so many ways. The tallest of us, and the strongest. Every inch of his body exudes power and menace, and the tattoos only add to his intimidating presence.

My favourite of all his ink is the black flames that wrap around his torso and along his shoulder, trailing down his right arm. They wind across his skin like they're alive—like they're licking at his skin and feeding his darkness. Fuck, they're enticing. The tendrils of flame lick at his bicep the way I want to.

I notice that he's tucked the leather straps I heard earlier into one of his back pockets, and several handles poke out of the other, belonging to blades of varying sizes. I know roughly what's coming next, but I never know exactly what to expect.

He comes to a stop behind me, and I try to quiet my breathing. It's loud in my ears and blocks me from being able to hear the brush of his hand against the soft denim of his jeans. It teases me and I can't figure out which pocket he chose first.

However, I don't have to wait long to find out before I feel the leather against my skin, softly dragging over my back. The ends of several wide strands are scraping across my shoulder blade, travelling down my spine in lazy sweeping motions. Repeating the pathway, up and down. This is torture, this endless teasing. He knows what I want. He knows this isn't enough.

With no warning, the soft leather cracks across my skin, burning and making my cock weep. The sting of pain fading almost immediately, transforming into a heat that burns and runs rampant through me, making me want to beg for more. We've played with so many floggers over the years, but my favourite is always these large belts of suede. They leave me streaked with gloriously angry brands, marking me as his and warming me from the outside in.

I stay hunched over the chair, never moving, taking every stroke of pleasure my master will give. That's what he is to me. The master of my pleasure, master of my pain, master of everything. As he continues to streak my skin, I come undone. Near feral noises escape me as I sink into the pain, my words completely incomprehensible as I slip into a state of mind only Nico can put me in.

Subspace is different to everyone and difficult to describe, but as I stare across the room, I focus on the shafts of light streaking down from the recessed bulbs in the ceiling, highlighting the specks of dust that refract the light. Tiny glistening particles dancing in front of me that float away with every breath I exhale. That's how I feel. Like I'm untethered, not bound by the forces of gravity, and moulded by influences outside my control.

Being fully aware of my change in demeanour, Nico checks in with me. "Colour, Bambi."

"Green, sir."

"Can you stand? Or do you need help?"

It's hard to form sentences in this headspace, but if I want to carry on, then I have to rally my senses.

"Help please, sir."

His thick arm reaches around my chest, and he hauls me to my feet. At six-feet I'm not small, but he throws me around like I'm a rag doll—and I love it. He untangles me from my shirt, and I rub my wrists.

"Hands behind your back."

I do as instructed and feel the softness of one of the suede straps being wrapped around my wrists, followed by the tip of a blade being dragged delicately down my spine. I know better than to flinch by now, and I remain impassive as he teases my skin with the scratch of the knife—my cock pulsing, leaking a near constant stream of pre-cum in response to Nico's attention.

As he reaches the waist of my jeans, the blade disappears, and his hand moves to grip my length over the denim. I can't stop the needy words that escape me.

"Please, sir. *Please*."

"Tell me what you want, my needy little slut."

His words only heighten my arousal and inspire my desperate pleas. "I need more. I need to come. I need everything. I want your hand on my dick, your cock in my ass, and your knife at my throat. I want you to savage me. Leave nothing left of me. *Please, sir, fuck me hard and leave me broken.*"

With a beast-like snarl, Nico's response is instant. My

pants are shoved down past my knees, the knife pressed to my throat, as I'm dragged to the nearest counter and bent over it roughly.

"You won't come until I say so." I can feel his hard cock through his jeans, resting in the crack of my ass. It makes me clench, and he steps back while I mewl at the loss of him. He grabs me by my hair and wrenches me back to his chest. "Fucktoys don't get to bounce on my cock until I say they've earned it."

He releases my hair and throws me down across the top of the workbench. I couldn't move if I wanted to. His words have me desperate for everything he's willing to give me. Nico takes my feet out of my jeans and kicks my legs further apart.

I feel the heat radiating off him as he stands behind me, and it's a stark contrast to the lube he drizzles and smooths over my puckered hole. It cascades down over my balls, and I whimper as I hear it drip on the floor.

With his blade at my throat and his fingers breaching my entrance, he continues, "Be careful what you wish for, Bambi."

CHAPTER TWENTY-EIGHT

AURORA

I really shouldn't be watching this.

After talking with Sinclair, I'd come back to my room to get ready for bed. I needed a little time to think about what he'd said. The med-room somehow feels like it's my haven and even though I'm feeling much better, I've been reluctant to take Enzo up on the offer to move me to a bedroom upstairs and out of the basement. I keep saying no because I feel safe down here. It's my sanctuary. It's not just because I don't want to give up the coffee machine, although that's a bonus.

While I was grabbing my next round of painkillers, I bumped into the countertop and the computer Sinclair set up for the interrogation jostled and came to life. What filled the screen has me transfixed. It doesn't help that there's sound too.

Hearing the words coming out of their mouths makes me want to run next door and watch the live show

—join them—but that would be dangerous considering Nico's entirely focussed on finger-fucking Benny at knifepoint.

Now is not the time to distract them.

What the fuck is wrong with me? I've literally just finished talking to Sinclair about seeing where that goes, yet I'm lusting after two of his best friends. Best friends who are in love with each other, *for Christ's sake.*

Am I so fucking starved of attention I'd risk their relationship for my pleasure? I'm a selfish monster.

I set the coffee cup on the counter and fall back on the stool, still not switching off the monitor. They're... *mesmerising.*

I've watched porn before, read about all kinds of kinks, but watching the power dynamic that these two men live, it's eye opening. By rights, the threat of the blade at Benny's neck should scare me, the angry red streaks across his skin should enrage me. But nothing about what they are sharing with each other is sinister. It's nothing like what I have experienced at Max's hand.

What they're doing is enticing. It's sexy. It's so fucking hot.

The way Nico owns Benedict is not threatening. It's loving and nurturing. You can see from the look of ecstasy on Benny's face that Nico is giving him everything that he wants. He's satisfied and safe in the arms of the man he loves.

The idea that pain can bring any kind of pleasure shouldn't be making me feel these things. But I can't look away, and I slip my hands beneath the waistband of my sweats, easing my fingers under the boxer briefs I borrowed. I run my fingers through the evidence of exactly how much I enjoy what they're doing. I'm not just wet, I'm dripping.

As Nico fucks two fingers into Benny's ass on the screen, I slide two of mine through my folds, teasing my entrance before thrusting them into my pussy in time with them. I can't help but cry out at the intrusion. Even though it's my hand, it feels like it's at someone else's command. I match my pumps to Nico's and when he adds a third finger—so do I.

I circle my clit, making sure to catch the sensitive bundle of nerves in just the right way while savouring the burn of my fingers stretching me. It feels like it's too much. I can hear my breath coming in heaving gulps, feel my pulse racing and my blood pumping while my orgasm threatens to erupt. My sounds mix with theirs and as I close my eyes, it's almost like they're here with me.

"You don't have my permission to come. What are the magic words, my pretty little whore?"

My breath stutters, but my hand doesn't stop. I open my eyes to watch as both Benny and I say together, "Please, sir. Please let me come."

Nico smiles as Benny's pleas wash over him and he keens into them like a cat being petted. His sense of satisfaction is tangible in that moment. He speeds up his merciless pounding and I see the slight twist of his wrist that wrings out screams of rapture from Benny. I change rhythm to match and curl my fingers, skimming against my G-spot and I join him, crying out in desperation. Trying so hard not to come.

From somewhere that feels like miles away in my rapturous haze, I hear a voice say, "Come for me."

I shatter. And I don't stop.

Ripples of pleasure oscillate along my spine. My cunt throbs around my fingers, and it feels wanton, and filthy, and euphoric. I'm lost in a trance of post-orgasmic bliss, but I slowly drift back to myself. I start to pull my hand back, tempted to taste myself. Slowly, I draw my hand to my lips when I hear a voice. *"Uh-uh-uh.* That's not your orgasm to savour, phoenix."

I gasp and open my eyes to find Nico in the doorway. His eyes laser focussed on me as he stalks across the room and gently encircles my wrist, cuffing it with his vast grip, and brings my fingers to his lips.

He hesitates and asks, "Yes or no, Aurora?"

I know what he's asking, and right now, in this moment, it's the easiest fucking answer.

"Yes."

He sucks my fingers into his mouth, licking them clean and all I can do is moan out my response as his tongue draws out breathless pleas and desperate whimpers.

"You're ours now," is all he says before he lifts me off the stool and sweeps me into his arms. I can't help but nuzzle into him, and the combined scent of Nico and Benny envelops me. As we get to the hallway, I see Sinclair coming down the stairs and panic. Not thirty-minutes ago we were discussing what happened with us, how we'd take it slow and that there was no pressure and now I'm slung over Nico's shoulder. He must hate me.

I can't bear to make eye contact, so scared of what I'll see in his expression when he meets my eye. These men have pledged to help me. They saved me, and here I am, flitting about from one to the other like a disloyal slut.

His footsteps get closer and Nico stops so he can catch up. He hooks a finger under my chin, kisses me softly, and I'm too stunned to kiss him back.

"That won't do, hummingbird. You can do better than that."

I open my eyes and see his warm smile and it fills every corner of my soul, casting light into the darkest corners where all my fears hide. I kiss him back and revel in the feeling of adoration. Breaking the kiss, my eyes search his golden irises for what this means. Why isn't he stopping us?

"I care about you, *colibrì*. But you should have figured it out by now that we *all* care about you." He smiles, and he only confuses me further. Canting his head, he strokes my cheek. "You have nothing to worry about. I am not threatened by my brother's feelings for you. What I said earlier still stands. I want you. You will set the pace of whatever this is between us, and we'll see where this goes." I'm still baffled by his reaction. That he's not screaming at finding me in Nico's arms.

Nico finally breaks his silence, "You may need to have a similar conversation with all of us, phoenix. All of us want you."

Sinclair chuckles and steals a kiss before I can open my mouth to ask them... I don't know... something. What the fuck is going on? I'm so confused.

"I'll see you in the morning, *colibrì*. Have fun." He's

gone before my brain reboots from the short circuit it seems to be experiencing.

"What just happened?" I ask.

Nico continues on his way and, with his free shoulder, pushes open the interrogation room.

"Well, phoenix, I believe Sinclair gave us his blessing to play together. And considering you just spent the last half hour getting yourself off to a live sex show without our consent, I would say you need to be punished."

I've definitely died and gone to some sort of kink-based hell where the objects of my desire torture me with promises they will never keep.

"You involved yourself in our dynamic without our consent and worse than that, you denied my Bambi his orgasm by interrupting us. What do you have to say for yourself?"

I have no idea what comes over me, but after witnessing the bliss on Benny's face, hearing the stern tone that Nico chastises me with, I fall to my knees, sit back on my haunches, drop my hands to my lap and avert my eyes to the floor.

"I'm sorry."

I hear Benedict gasp, and I feel both of their eyes on me now.

"I'm sorry, sir," he corrects.

Holy fuck, I feel my pussy gush as his words awaken something in me I'm terrified to lean into. "I'm sorry, s—"

"Wait," he interrupts, his expression softening. "Look at me, Aurora. It's not right to demand a title when we have not discussed how we—how this—dynamic works.

Benny, you're going to have to wait a little longer. Come here."

Benny comes to his side, naked and hard. I don't know where to look, so I end up studying my hands. Nico chuckles and unties Benny's arms and sends him to put his jeans back on. This should help, but they're both still shirtless and that's doing nothing to curb the debauched thoughts racing around my head.

I want them both—them all. I want them and Sinclair. *Maybe I am a whore.*

Before I can follow that train of thought any further, I'm being lifted again, cradled to his chest as he sits back in the same chair Benny was flogged over. His corded muscles are covered with a tantalising sheen of sweat that is begging to be licked clean, but I tamp down that urge—for now. He turns me so my back is to his front and his lips dust the shell of my ear.

"Let me explain, phoenix. Bambi, on your knees."

Watching Benny obey Nico is intoxicating. It makes my body come alive and thrum with need. I'm wracked with jealousy as Benny falls to his knees before us.

"Benedict and I explore each other through a power exchange dynamic. He is submissive to me, and I am his dominant." Nico raises a hand and strokes along Benny's jawline, making me bite my cheek. "We've customised our dynamic to suit what we need and based on our hard limits. Everything we explore is with explicit consent. But we've been together for years. I know exactly what Benedict's limits are."

His hand drops to my hip, and his gentle squeeze triggers me to lean back into him.

"We use the traffic light system and I check in throughout a scene. Green for happy to continue, yellow to slow down or when approaching a limit, and red for stop. If I hear red, everything stops immediately. Do you understand?"

I nod my head, but he hooks a crooked finger under my chin and chastises, "Uh-uh-uh, phoenix. You want to play, then we'll play. But I need your words."

I want to reply to him, but he runs his lips down the slope of my neck and words escape me.

Each word out of his mouth is punctuated by a gentle kiss across my collarbone. "Use. Your. Words."

"Ye-Yes, sir."

I can sense his smile from his tone. "Good girl."

His words elicit a response that cascades through my whole body. A shiver of excitement rolls through my body, leaving a trail of goosebumps in its wake and makes me squeeze my thighs together as I feel his cock straining beneath me.

"We need to know if you have any hard limits, Aurora."

His words pull me back to reality and I think about it for a minute. I feel like I should be saying a lot of things in response to this question. I should be asking him not to hurt me. I should be asking him not to degrade me. I should be asking him to treat me with care. But that is not what I want from him—from either of them.

"Don't treat me like I'm fragile." My breathing becomes rapid as I let myself truly open up as I realise what I can't tolerate. "Don't call me, princess. Never restrain me and leave, never use denial of food or water as a punishment, and never..." I collect myself as I say the next part, "never use barbed wire as a restraint."

I can feel Nico's rage at my back, and see the fury in Benny's eyes. They know every hard limit I have is born of Max's abuse, but they remain calm. Benny nods, as Nico responds, "That leaves us with a lot to explore, phoenix. You sure about this?"

"Yes, sir."

"You need to know that this is not a meaningless thing for us, Aurora." I can see when Nico's gaze finds Benny's by the look of pure adoration in his eyes. "Tell her, Bambi."

Benny speaks at his sir's command, "We care for you, and together we want to show you how we want to cherish you."

"Together," is all I can muster, as reality is finally sinking in that these two men want me. They want to share me.

"Together, Rory." With a nod from Nico, releasing him from his submissive pose, he rises off his haunches to level his gaze at me. No longer giving off an air of submission, his voice alters to a more commanding tone. "And you need to know that while I submit to Nico—you, I want to possess, body and soul."

I have no time to process his words before he unleashes himself and steals a kiss from me. Benedict's tongue caresses the seam of my lips, demanding my surrender. Every rational thought in my brain evaporates under the onslaught of Benny's attentions. Nico's hand returns to my hip, stroking tender circles and causing me to grind down on his lap.

Nico runs his fingers back up my spine and his touch evolves from reverent to unforgiving as he fists my hair and pulls back. It's then I realise he has Benny in a similar grip, drawing out the most sinful noises from him.

"There's still the matter of your punishment, Aurora. Watching us without our consent, robbing Benedict of the opportunity to come. That can't go unpunished."

They seem to communicate with each other on a telepathic level because, without words, Benny takes my hand and pulls me off Nico's lap, only to pull me back down again, encouraging me to lie down over his lap. Benny kneels behind me and pulls down my sweats and underwear, leaving me ass up with my pussy on display to both of them.

Instead of feeling the quick sting of a palm across my cheeks, I hear tutting. "What's this, Aurora?" I feel his fingers tracing patterns across my skin.

"It seems someone has already punished you. What did you do to get these?"

A smile warms my face as I remember how Sinclair peppered my ass with handprints last night.

"I didn't do as I was told, sir."

"Well, well, well. Sinclair is a dark horse," Benedict says as I feel his hand join Nico's in its exploration of my prior punishments.

"I didn't realise that he'd left marks."

"Only a few," Nico says. His timbre low—barely audible. "But they're stunning on you."

I should feel self-conscious that Nico is witnessing another man's mark on my flesh, but I'm oddly proud.

For once, the marks I bear are not a shameful representation of my failures. They're an expression of the care someone showed me. And it makes me feel glorious.

Pulling me back to the moment, the full weight of Nico's hand lands on the curve of my ass, forcing a yelp from my lips. As the sting fades and he draws his hand back, I'm startled by a bite at the top of my thigh. Benedict strips off the clothes bunching at my knees and encourages me to spread my legs.

Nico continues his sharp smacks, and my cries of pain morph into moans of pleasure. Nico soothes the sting of his punishments by massaging my ample curves, and it serves as a distraction while Benny lowers himself on his back between my legs and then steals my breath as his tongue finds my clit. He wraps his hands around the top of my thighs, and spreads me wide for Nico, whose palm now lands across my pussy.

The sound that escapes my lips is somewhere between a whimper and a wail. I've never felt anything like it. The pain radiates through my cunt and leaves me throbbing while Benny's tongue relentlessly builds my orgasm.

"Colour, Aurora," whispers Nico, tantalisingly close to my ear.

"Green, sir. Oh, so very green," I ramble, lost in the sensations that are assaulting me.

"I think you're enjoying your punishment far too much. Poor Benedict has had to wait so long to come."

"I'm sorry, sir," I force out and then whine as Benedict's head disappears from between my legs.

"I could come from the taste of her alone." Benedict

CHAPTER TWENTY-EIGHT

walks around Nico and pulls my head up and off his lap. Tugging down his zipper, he pulls out his cock, and I salivate at the prospect of running my tongue along the veins and ridges of his length. "Look how hard you've made me, how my cock weeps at the taste of you."

His pre-cum beading and falling to the floor makes me lick my lips, eager to taste him, but he pulls back. "Ah-ah-ah, temptress. You don't get to play with my dick until sir gives you permission."

"Please, sir."

Nico pulls me up and turns me, sitting me back on his lap facing outwards, legs held wide outside his. It's now that I realise I'm still wearing my shirt and I pull at the neck, feeling wildly overheated. Nico frees me from it, throwing it to the side, and I sink back into his torso, completely content to be at his mercy.

One hand moves to my pussy and the other grabs my hair, but instead of pulling me back into him, Nico pushes me down. Forcing me to fold at my hips, his elbow at my back flattens my spine and his grip elongates my neck, leaving my mouth wide open and waiting for Benny. Presenting my throat to him.

"Don't squander my gift, Bambi. Fuck our filthy little fucktoy's face and paint her with your cum."

His words are so degrading, but they ignite a desire within me that makes me want to be a vessel for their pleasure any way I can. Benny's glistening crown pushes past my lips and slides over my tongue at the same time as two of Nico's thick fingers push past my sopping entrance and impale me.

My incoherent groans vibrate along the steely shaft,

stroking the back of my throat. I swallow and hollow my cheeks, enveloping his crown and holding him tight in my mouth.

"*Holy fuck,* I won't last, *Jesus Christ, Aurora.* Don't stop, *fuck, don't stop,*" Benny snarls, losing all control, pistoning erratically and fucking my throat with abandon. He is at my mercy and the feeling is intoxicating. Every swirl and flick of my tongue over his crown draws out wild and incoherent cries.

"I didn't say you could come yet, Bambi," Nico warns.

"Please, may I come, sir?"

"When she comes, you can come." As the words leave Nico's lips, he stills his hand inside me, and I protest the loss of stimulation with a muffled whine. Benny halts his thrusts, attempting to stave off his orgasm. "Keep his cock warm, Aurora."

Nico releases my hair and strokes gently down my spine and reaches around to toy with my clit, and then pauses. I try my best not to protest, but my mewl betrays my desperation.

"You're both doing so well. Such obedient little cock-whores." I can't figure out which I like more, Nico's praise or degradation. Both settle over me like a blanket and warm me from the inside out.

The minute my body relaxes, Nico restarts his assault on my cunt, fucking the fingers of one hand into me in long languid strokes, while the others tease my clit in little circles that rip my orgasm from me in seconds. Benny reaches with both hands, twining thick tendrils of my hair between his fingers, taking control and fucking my face. He bottoms out in my throat and I swallow around him.

He is undone, and I am destroyed.

Pulling out, he grips his shaft hard to buy himself the second he needs to command me. "*Fucking hell.* Open your mouth and hold out your tongue."

I obey and he runs the head of his cock over my lips before pumping his straining cock and erupting on my tongue. He comes in thick ropes that try to escape from my swollen lips.

"Do not swallow," he commands before falling to his knees before us.

I am lost in a head space I did not know existed, but from somewhere Nico's rough growl and firm grip of my jaw keep me grounded in reality as he demands, "Give me what's mine."

His meaning is lost to me until he turns my face to his, and lips find mine. His tongue teases my mouth open and he takes his prize. Our tongues dance together as he claims Benny's cum, leaving me a boneless mess of limbs held together only by Nico's powerful arms.

He lets me up for air long enough to catch Benny's gaze. "Such a good fucking boy."

He then taps my thigh and Benny shuffles forward, stopping at our feet and laying his head down to rest on my thigh.

"Thank you, sir," I say as an abundance of emotion courses through me, but before I can begin to process it, I am consumed by exhaustion and sleep takes me.

CHAPTER TWENTY-NINE

ENZO

After I left the gym earlier, I had to get out of the house to clear my head. We need a plan. We need to go after Salvatore and Max, but we can't do it yet. If Benny's dad is working with them, then no loyal Bianchi is above suspicion. Fuck, there may not be many loyal Bianchis left if that's the case.

And the last fucking thing I need right now is Isa's murderer resurfacing, but if you consider the details in the autopsy and the markings, it has to be a copycat or the same guy. It's unlikely anyone would copycat a four-teen-year-old cold case, so we need to double our efforts there. Not only to honour Mateo's wishes, but also for Aurora. Fuck... for my brother. *For me.*

Her death destroyed what little family I had. I need to close this chapter of my life. Fourteen years is too fucking long to chase a ghost.

My feet pound the sidewalk as my breath puffs out

thick clouds of mist into the frigid night air. The air tastes fresh, almost crisp, with every ragged heave I make. My headphones blare out a monotonous playlist chosen based on its tempo. I could be listening to K-pop for all I know, as long as it matches my stride and drowns out my thoughts, I couldn't give a fuck.

The thud, thud, thud of my soles sends jolts up my calves, my joints are screaming at me for the punishing pace I'm setting. Running used to calm my thoughts, but nothing works these days. I've run this circuit far more times than I planned and it's getting late—I need to head back to the house.

Slowing my pace, I bounce on my toes before coming to a stop. Reaching down, I stretch out my hamstrings while the sweat I've built up rolls off my forehead onto the asphalt below. I need a shower. Fuck. I need to rest. I can't keep this up. Either I'm awake all day and exercising all night, or I'm feeding my newly gained unhealthy addiction to bingeing tv shows.

I blame Aurora entirely.

I've not slept well for years. My mind is always a buzz with thoughts and what-ifs, trying to anticipate any scenario that may impact me or one of my team.

While she was recovering, I'd been getting some decent sleep, often passing out on the sofa in her room to her latest favourite show. She was feeling better, so she didn't need to be monitored constantly anymore. It would be weird to hang out just to sleep near her.

Aurora doesn't need to deal with some fucked-up old man taking advantage of her and using her as some kind of security blanket or sleep aid.

So, I do anything I can to push myself to the point of exhaustion where sleep finally takes me. All night I run, I hit the weights, or I follow Nico's insane conditioning circuits. If I keep this up, I'm going to start out-lifting him.

The stretch I feel down the back of my legs is painful, but soothing. Standing, I stretch out my shoulders by pulling each arm across my chest, then roll my head from side to side to work out the kinks in my neck.

I take off again, completing the final circuit before heading home.

It's funny, having Aurora with us at the safe house makes it feel more like home than any other place we've ever lived. As much as I dread the hours I will spend awake and alone while they sleep, I'm eager to return.

WHEN I GET BACK, I head downstairs to hit up the coffee machine before everyone turns in. I need to move it back to the kitchen, but the last time I tried, Aurora adamantly refused my request. Her exact words were, "Touch my coffee machine, and I'll cut your balls off." Since then, I've been reluctant to push the point.

It's late, but she's usually still up at this time, so I don't worry about disturbing her. As soon as I step into the med-room, I instantly regret it.

I had assumed the flickering blueish lights sneaking under the med-room door were from the TV. I was wrong. They are, in fact, from the computer monitor and I am greeted with a vision of Aurora bent over Nico's lap

having her luscious ass spanked while Benny eats
her out.

Whattheactualfuck.

Her cries of ecstasy assault me from the monitor
speakers and I stop dead in my tracks. There's nothing I
can see or hear that is not consensual and it's none of my
fucking business. Backing out of the room, I decide
retreating is my best option.

I head up to my room, taking the stairs two at a time.
Once I'm inside, I shut the door and lean my forehead
against the wood. I can feel the rise and fall of my shoulders and the thrum of my pulse everywhere as it slows to
a gentle throb.

I keep myself busy because when I stop, or rather
when I try to stop, there's no peace. There's no respite
from the chaotic muddle of endless possibilities that race
through my head. At least when I was caring for Aurora, I
had something to calm my mind. But now it races, and
now there are fresh worries, more problems we have to
face.

I fear I'm not good enough at my job to protect her.

I push away from the door and force myself to ignore
my doubts. There's no room for any uncertainty right
now. We must find a way to separate Marco from his
men. Tony and Carlo were relatively easy to isolate,
largely because of their hubris. But Benny's dad isn't
stupid, and we have to act fast before he finds out they're
missing.

I throw my phone on my bedside table and strip out
of my running gear, forcing myself to have a shower. Not
because it will help relax me, only because it's necessary.

The pounding of the water against my skin doesn't soothe my aching muscles, and the heat does not help me unwind. When I step out, I wipe the mirror clear of steam and stare at my reflection.

My dark hair falls forward in sodden waves, trickling water down my face and highlighting that it's about time I shaved—the droplets disappearing into the mess of hair that is more beard than scruff now.

Another necessity.

After taming my facial hair, I grab a pair of sweats and sit down on the end of my bed. I'm not entirely sure how long I stay there, held hostage by the never-ending scenarios that run rampant through my mind, but eventually I hear the heavy steps of Nico and Benny traipsing up the stairs.

I cross to the door and crack it open. Benny is in front, and Nico follows with Aurora wrapped around his chest like a koala as he carries her to his room. I step out into the hallway, announcing my presence.

The words leave my mouth before my mind objects. "Do not hurt her." They both nod solemnly, and I turn without waiting for any other response and close my door behind me.

As I crawl under my sheets and roll onto my back to assume the familiar position—staring at my ceiling—I prepare to wait the hours it'll take for exhaustion to win out.

My phone vibrates, and I reach out to the bedside table to check it.

CHAPTER TWENTY-NINE

MANNY:

> I have information your guest needs to
> be aware of.

As I'm reading, another text comes through with a time and an address.

Rubbing my face, I mentally rearrange my team's day —I had already decided who was going where tomorrow, but Manny's a priority.

> See you there.

I throw my phone on its charger and rub my hand over my face again. How the fuck are we supposed to take on Salvatore-fucking-De Luca? We are four men. Four men and a fucking strong woman, but five against the full force of the De Lucas?

It's like I can hear Sin's voice in the back of my head. *One step at a time. First Marco, then we see where we are.*

Channelling Sin helps. He's not just my oldest and closest friend, he's my brother. Fuck, they all are. It's my job to make sure they're safe. Whatever we do, my primary objective is to protect them. It's a responsibility I take very seriously and one I feel for Aurora, too.

I will never forgive myself if anything happens to any of them.

Their safety will always be at my sacrifice.

That's the last thought in my head as I finally surrender to sleep. It's always my final thought, and it always will be.

CHAPTER THIRTY

AURORA

I feel warm, cosy, and content. I refuse to open my eyes on the off chance that what I think happened with Nico and Benedict last night turns out to be a dream. I'm praying that the pressure I feel engulfing me is their hot and hard bodies pressed against me.

"I know you're awake, phoenix," comes the low growl at my back that can only belong to Nico. Cracking open one eye, I find Benny sleeping soundly at my front.

"Good morning, sir," I say as I turn slowly to face the man who owned me in every sense of the word last night.

"Benny sleeps like the dead, especially when he's had his cum sucked out of him by a mouth as wicked as yours."

I can't help but blush at Nico's sinful words and I hide my face in the pillow, embarrassed by how much I enjoyed being degraded between these two men.

"You looked stunning taking his cock. No shame here. You were spectacular." His fingers grip my jaw, turning me to face him. "How do you feel this morning?"

"Good, sir."

"Do you trust me, phoenix?"

I never trusted Max. I knew from the second I laid eyes on him he was beyond any level of danger I had ever experienced. He wasn't a walking red flag—he was the embodiment of evil.

But Nico, staring into his midnight blue eyes, I feel a pull to him like a moth being drawn to a flame. Only I have no fear that Nico will destroy me. He is not some raging fire that will burn me. Trusting him feels natural.

He would never hurt me, not one of Enzo's men would. I feel it with every cell in my body.

"Yes, sir."

"Fuck, I love to hear you call me that." The smile that radiates across his face is a rare treat. For all the hours I have spent with Nico while recovering, I have rarely seen a smile like this given freely to anyone other than Benedict. It ignites a hope within me that I can inspire a fraction of what he feels for Benny, for me.

"Is that smile for me, Aurora?" he asks, running his thumb over my lips and catching on my dimple.

I can't speak. Words evaporate on my tongue before I can force them out.

"I wasn't expecting you, phoenix. You came out of nowhere."

"Why phoenix? Why do you call me that?" I ask.

His expression becomes thoughtful as he replies, "Because the other night, I watched you resurrect yourself before my eyes. When we found you, Max thought he'd destroyed you, but in that room, the way you decimated Carlo... you literally bathed yourself in the blood of your enemy and were reborn out of rage. To witness it was a privilege. You rose out of the ashes of your past life, little phoenix."

His words take my breath away, swiftly followed by his lips. He devours me, like he is trying to absorb the essence of me into his soul. It's all-consuming. In these moments with him, I don't have to worry about anything. Nothing exists outside of us, and I am at peace. It is the most free I have ever felt.

Benny starts to stir at my back and I feel his long, lean finger stroking along the flare of my hip, teasing little moans that are swallowed by Nico. Wrenching himself out of the moment, Nico draws back and rises up to his knees. Catching Benny's eye, he commands, "Sit back against the headboard and spread your legs."

He eagerly obeys as Nico gets off the bed and grabs me by the calves, pulling me down the length of the bed. Once Benny is reclined in a sea of pillows, Nico arranges me on my back, my head nestled between Benny's thighs just below his fierce morning wood and my feet just barely hanging off the end of the bed. When I arch my back and try to look at Benny, all I can see is his hard-on and the hand he is using to stroke himself lazily as he takes in every dip and curve of my body.

At the end of the bed, Nico takes us in. Standing proud, like a feral beast about to devour its prey, he slowly works open each button of his fly. I realise now he kept his jeans on last night. As he shucks them off with his boxer briefs, I am awestruck. As I gasp at the sight before me, Benedict chuckles. "Fucking mouthwatering, isn't it, Aurora?"

"How am I supposed to accommodate that?" I choke out, eyes wide and breath ragged.

"You should try taking it in the ass, sweetheart." I giggle, but it's quickly replaced by a groan as I imagine myself watching Nico fuck Benny. My pussy is practically fluttering with eagerness and Nico's heated gaze as he strokes his monstrously-large cock is doing nothing to quell my need to come.

"You can take it, and one day you'll take us both." He leans over the bed and rests above me, supporting his beastly frame on one arm. He's huge everywhere. I never realised quite how daunting Nico was until now, but faced with the very real possibility of being impaled by him, his broad shoulders, wide chest, and chiselled body seem somehow unreal. Every part of him is solid and hard, and every part of me is screaming to be invaded by him.

His free hand travels from my collarbone, tracing a path between the valley of my breasts, curving in lazy sweeps along my ribs, looping down to my hip before delving into the apex of my thighs.

"You will take us here," he buries two fingers into my aching pussy, "and here."

Now the pad of his thumb moves to tease my tight pucker. "But one day, Aurora," he dips down and steals a kiss that's all clashing tongues, "one day you'll take us both here."

With that, he pulls out the two fingers he has buried

in me and replaces them in successive strokes, first with three and then four. I cry out at the intrusion. The pain of the stretch shocks me at first, only to be replaced with an ache of satisfaction as his relentless thrusts trigger a flood from my cunt that gushes across his palm. The orgasm takes me by surprise as I hear his words of praise envelop me.

"Such a good fucking girl, squirting for us."

When he steps off the bed, I cry out at the loss of his thick fingers. I whimper even more as I realise the reason for his departure. He's rifling through his bedside drawers, and I watch as he makes a move to cover his glorious metallic ridges in a condom.

Catching my pout, he pauses and says, "Does my pretty little cumslut want to ride me bareback?"

I bite down on my lip and nod my head vigorously.

"Use your words."

"Yes please, sir. Fuck me bare." I'm trying to smother the whine in my tone, but my desperation betrays me.

"If you want my dick raw, then we need to have a conversation about safe sex and birth control."

I know he's saying words, but I'm distracted by his hand wrapping around his thick cock and pumping his length, enticing pre-cum to pool in the slit of his crown.

Reaching down, he slaps my inner thigh playfully, but hard enough to sting as he admonishes me. "Focus, Aurora."

I love that Nico's taking responsibility for my safety, as well as Benny and Sinclair's. We should discuss protection. Doc Em did a full panel of tests when she was treating me, so I know I'm clean. It was a relief when she told me because who knows who else my husband was fucking?

While he would always fuck me when he was torturing me, once I was completely broken and left to heal, he would never touch me. In his words, "I'm not fucking a broken cunt." I shiver at the memory and Nico sees the moment my thoughts have drifted somewhere dark.

"Where did you go, phoenix?"

"No where, I'm fine. You're right, we should talk." He squeezes my arm and it reassures me. "Doc Em tested me for nearly everything when she started treating me. I'm clean, and I was on the injection for birth control. I have a month until it needs to be done again."

Nico nods as he strokes across my collarbone and down my arm. "That's not the only thing I meant, phoenix. We need to discuss many things, like how I'd love nothing more than to see mine and Benedict's cum dripping out of your pretty pink pussy, whether you're on birth control or not." He runs his fingers over my scars and reaches the angriest red scar on my abdomen. "But we can't risk the possibility of getting you pregnant while you're still healing."

I hadn't even thought of that. The injuries I sustained were pretty serious and while I do a good job of pretending they're not there, it will take time for my body to fully heal.

"But if you're saying that you are on birth control?"

"Yes, sir."

"And you are clean?"

Another, "Yes, sir."

"And I confirm that both Benny and I are clean?"

"Fuck yes, sir."

Nico drops the condom on the side table and crawls across the bed, stopping above me. "Benny, pin her arms under your legs and make your dick weep for me. You're both mine and it's time I got to play with my fucktoys."

His words short circuit my brain, while Benny restrains me. Nico's lips blaze a trail down my neck to the swell of my tits. His tongue teases my nipple to a hard peak as he palms the other, its weight heavy in his hand as he kneads gently. The sensation sends a pulse to my clit that makes me rock my hips against his weight.

Nico's giant-like stature and ruthless nature has earned him a reputation as a monster, one you would never want to see looming over you. But there's nowhere else I want to be right now. His mammoth frame is heaving against me as his weight holds me down and makes me submit to his will, forcing me to take every quiver of pleasure he bestows. He is merciless. He is a beast.

He is mine.

I writhe as his head disappears between my legs and his tongue gets its first taste of my pussy. I am gone. There are no words, and he is relentless. He draws feral moans from my lips as he sends me soaring towards my orgasm. It builds deep in my core as his inexplicably long tongue fucks into me. His thumb circles my clit and I clench in abstract rhythms, screaming out Nico's name as I fall over the edge.

I'm still coming as he moves swiftly back up the bed and impales me in one long excruciating slow thrust, making sure I feel every rung of his ladder. The cry I release is inhuman. As he bottoms out, he rotates his hips slowly, allowing me time to adjust.

It's like he's waiting for me to come back to earth, but I honestly don't know if I ever will. I'm so overstimulated, my swollen pussy refuses to surrender its grip on his cock or the barbells currently pressed tight against my g-spot. A near constant growl slips from his lips as he tries to hold back.

"On your knees, Bambi. Hands behind your back."

I finally get a view of Benny that's not obscured by his hard-on and I can tell from how eagerly he obeys, he's turned on. Eyes glazed and pupils blown, he can't take his eyes off of where I'm joined with Nico. Every pump of his cock has Benny panting and a glistening bead of pre-cum forming on his crown.

I'm nothing but a string of incoherent mewls as Nico leans forward, taking Benny's cock in his mouth and deep-throating him. The roar that Benny unleashes surprises me almost as much as the curl of Nico's hips that drags the barbells of his piercing along my walls, and I join Benny in his cries of ecstasy.

With one arm on the mattress beside me and the other free to roam, Nico grabs Benny's hip and encourages him to fuck his mouth harder. I see the outline of Benny's dick as it breaches Nico's throat and I'm fascinated. It's hypnotic. Nico times his thrusts with Benny and I feel connected to the both of them in a way that transcends reason.

Time seems meaningless, and I feel displaced in it. Nico's thick cock swells further, increasing the stretch and dragging me into an orgasm that will not be denied. I can't come again. I am exhausted, but my traitorous cunt betrays me when Nico releases his grip on Benny's thigh and reaches to tap on my clit.

I shatter.

My pussy contracts and milks Nico's cock, demanding his cum and coaxing his release from him in hot ropes. The sounds are obscene as he fucks me through my orgasm and buries his cum deep.

Benny surrenders to Nico's skilful mouth and comes with a bellow. Nico's hand steadies his hips, demanding that Benny come on his tongue.

Both Benny and I watch in awe as Nico moves down my body and opens his mouth at the entrance to my pussy.

"What are—"

Before I can finish, Nico spits cum into my dripping cunt and leisurely tongue fucks it into me. Benny collapses beside me, releasing little desperate howls prompting Nico to look up with a smile. Stepping back off the bed, Nico heads for the bathroom and shouts back over his shoulder, "I'll be right back. Make sure you lick her clean while I'm gone."

Holy Fuck.

I'm not sure I will survive these men.

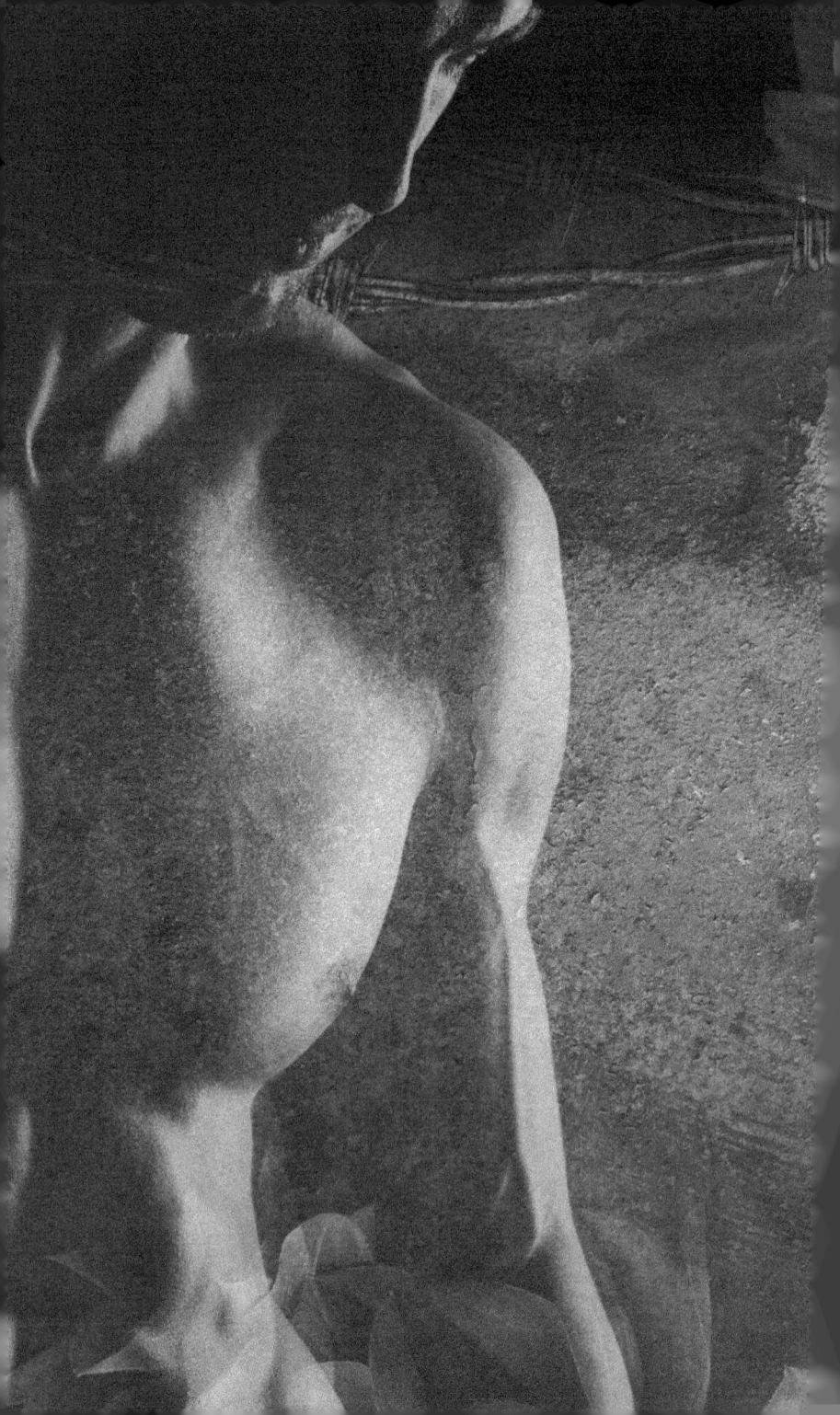

CHAPTER THIRTY-ONE

SINCLAIR

I guess I should be jealous that she spent all night with two other guys, but I'm not. They're not two random guys, they're my brothers. Brothers by choice. And she's not my girlfriend. That title is such an inadequate word.

Aurora feels like a missing piece of me—but not just that—she's like a missing piece of us. I can't fucking explain it. But honestly, do I have to understand it fully? She's here, she's with us, and that feels right. In all ways. I just hope she feels the same way. I took a big risk last night when I walked away and left them together. If it's too much for her, we all stand to lose.

When I woke up this morning, I grabbed a coffee and holed up in my office. I need to check the chatter to see if there's anything we should be worried about. As far as I can tell, the De Lucas are still carrying on business as usual. No one's missing Tony yet—shocker—but it would seem Carlo's absence has been noticed. It's been pretty easy to deal with in the short-term because we kept both their phones.

As far as their crews are concerned, Tony's bedded down for a few days with a new side piece and not to be contacted, and Carlo is dealing with a distribution problem in one of our out-of-town warehouses. I've been replying to his crew's messages this morning, making sure they suspect nothing. This will buy us some time, but not much.

Enzo went out at the crack of dawn to meet with Manny. When he got back, he messaged me a summary of the intel and outlined a schedule for us for the day. As usual, his plan is impeccable, and it means I'm going to have to go and wake up the sleeping beauties. After what I assumed was round two this morning, I haven't heard a peep out of them since.

Pushing my chair away from my desk, I stretch and then head upstairs. I quietly tap on Nico's door and wait. There's no response.

Slowly opening the door, I smile at the pile of limbs that entangle Benny. He's awake and brings his finger to his lips to get me to keep it down and mouths, "Ten minutes," to which I nod, closing the door as quietly as possible.

I can't help but laugh as I head to the basement to make us all some coffee. I would never have pegged Nico as a cuddler. Benny had looked more than content to be trapped under his weight.

I finish making our drinks and head back up to the living room just as Nico, Aurora, and Benny come down the stairs. They each grab a mug and I watch as they try to figure out who's sitting where. I chuckle as Aurora looks around awkwardly, obviously not sure where she should sit. Grabbing her wrist, I pull her down on the sofa next to me, nestling her under my arm. I feel better having her close and she settles into me, tucking her legs to one side and burrowing under my arm.

"Where's Zo?" Nico asks.

"Asleep. I assume he was up half the night as usual and had a meeting with Manny at stupid o'clock this morning, so I'm going to try to let him sleep as long as possible. I'm amazed he actually went to bed when he got in, if I'm honest, so don't fucking disturb him," I say.

"'Kay," is the only response I get. Nico's a monosyllabic prick before he's had caffeine.

"Zo sent through instructions. Benny, I need to know if you can handle what we've got planned for your dad?"

"Depends on what we've got planned, doesn't it?" He keeps his voice even as he sips his drink while Nico strokes his shoulder absentmindedly.

"He has an appointment at his favourite club tonight—"

"By club, I assume you mean *whorehouse*?" Benny snarks out and I catch Nico squeezing his shoulder, giving him a signal to check his temper. I hear Aurora dry heave beside me and arch a brow at her quizzically.

"What? It's bad enough most of the capos can't keep their dicks in their wives, and nearly every one of them has a girlfriend on the side, but some can't even be faithful to their mistresses. They make me sick—bunch of disloyal cunts, the lot of them."

Nico laughs and Benny looks like he's got a sour taste in his mouth.

"Sorry, Benny," she says. "You probably don't want to think about who your dad's fucking, but the old boys are fucking gross, and your father is one of them."

"It's not that. It's more thinking that my mom has been married to him for twenty-five years. I don't know how she stomachs it."

Aurora's bravado fades fast as she mumbles, "She may not have had much of a choice, Benny." His gaze snaps to hers and he nods in understanding.

"So, what's the plan?" he tosses my way.

"We're planting a girl for him. His regular girl is calling in sick tonight."

"Shit, Sinclair. How much information do you have on the capos?" Aurora asks, expression confused.

"Enough, nowhere near everything. Stefano and Manny helped me fill in some blanks. I'm limited only by my time and resources. But what we do find out, Enzo is exceptionally skilled at exploiting when we need to."

"Good to know."

"Anyway, someone else will be waiting for him in his usual room and we should have about an hour before anyone becomes suspicious."

"Who's going in?" Nico probes.

This is the bit I wasn't looking forward to. Zo is entirely right. This is the best way to handle this and keep as low a profile as possible, but they're not going to like it.

"Aurora will be the plant and Ni—"

Before I can finish my sentence, I'm met with the angry cries of, "Like fuck she will," and, "Over my cold dead body," from the other sofa. I go to respond, but before I can get a word in, Aurora is already putting them in their place.

"One night between my legs and you think you have any fucking say over what I will and will not be doing? You can both fuck right off, you misogynistic twats."

They look sheepish as fuck as they realise their mistake. Aurora has had someone deciding for her for far too long, and now that she's free from her husband's clutches, she's unlikely to let a man decide anything for her again. *Rookie fucking error boys.* I can't help but smile at their mistake, bless them. The ignorance of youth.

Because we've all worked together for such a long time, I forget how inexperienced you are at their age. At twenty-three and twenty-four, they're a decade younger than me. Babies in the organisation, really. The next-gen. Although thinking about it, it could also be because they've never been with a woman before...

Idiots.

"As I was saying," I glare at them, hoping they take the hint and shut the fuck up, "Aurora will wait in the room, but she won't be alone. Nico will be in there, too. Since you worked so well together with Carlo, Zo wants you both on this. But this time, you guys have to keep it clean. No torture on site." I nudge Aurora and she gives me a sheepish smile.

"What are we going to do with him?"

"You'll need to get him out of the club without being spotted."

"How are we going to do that?" Nico growls. "I assume he's going to have some sort of protection watching the main areas in the club."

"True, but that's where Benny comes in." Benny's eyes brighten as if he can sense where this is going.

"You need some pyrotechnics to keep people busy and cover your escape," Benedict says, an unsettling smile appearing as he speaks.

"Correct. Aurora and Nico will be in the room closest to the fire escape, and you will light a few distractions that will keep the staff busy and cut off the access to that fire escape. I've emailed you the building plans with notes on the escape routes you need to manage. Study them and come up with a plan by four, you need to know what we're setting on fire and when."

His smile grows, morphing into a malevolent grin. Only mildly disconcerting. We carry on talking out all the other details—escape routes, timings, logistics of getting Marco back here without being tailed.

As we wrap up, Nico becomes uncharacteristically fidgety.

"What's up, Nico?"

He doesn't speak and a look of concern washes over him.

"What's wrong, Nico? You heard me last night, we're good."

Glaring straight at me, his words take me by surprise. "You and Aurora may be fucking good, and Benny and I may be good, but you need to talk to Benny and me if we are all... I don't know what the fuck to call it... we're not dating, it's not just fucking... if we're all together in some way. It doesn't matter if you are not with Benny or me. We still need to talk about it because we will all affect each other in some way."

Huh.

He's not wrong.

I was so busy trying to reassure Aurora, I dismissed out of hand how it might impact others.

Nico continues and makes sure I'm paying attention, "Especially when there are *dynamics* involved. You know it's not just me."

"You're right," I concede and volley my head, "but now is not the time. We need to focus on tonight, and then we'll talk."

He doesn't look happy, but he lets it go for the time being. Benny hops up and pulls out his phone. I assume that he's already studying the building plans. He wanders to the kitchen and pulls open the fridge, burying his head, searching for his first, second, and possibly even third breakfast. He'll set up camp close to the fridge until he's figured out his plan.

Nico leaves him to it and retreats back upstairs, not before kissing the top of his head. That leaves me on the sofa with Aurora.

"So, what am I supposed to do all day?"

I smile because she's looking sheepishly at her hands as she worries the hem of the hoodie she threw on. "Well," I say, running my hand along her sleeve and tugging on one of the ties, "as much as we love seeing you in our clothes," she blushes hard, "we need to go and sort out your wardrobe. Can't get you in and out of the club inconspicuously if you're in sweats."

She hesitates for a minute. "Only on the condition I'm still allowed to steal everyone's clothes. They're comfy," she adds with a coy smile.

"Deal."

I HAD ASSUMED Aurora Bianchi didn't enjoy shopping based on her reaction to being brought on a spree. After dragging her to the mall, I've had to listen to her complain in every damn shop we've been to and she's getting tired. She insisted on leaving the boot off and the crutch at home. I only agreed on the condition that she wore the wig again and took the painkillers Doc Em prescribed. She may be struggling with the amount of effort, but at least she's not in pain.

We've finally found our way into some kind of alternative boutique, and as soon as we entered, her face lit up. I'll be damned if I spoil her fun. In the other stores, all she found were jeans, leggings, and tanks. Here she's all smiles and excitement pulling out all manner of items.

I sneak up behind her while she's staring at a sapphire-blue corset. "Trying to figure out which one of us you'll wear this for?"

Turning slowly, she walks her fingers up my chest before grabbing my chin between her thumb and fore-finger. "Listen here, Sinclair, the sweats I'll wear for you. This, I'll wear for me." She playfully slaps my cheek and then grabs the corset and heads for the changing rooms.

Fuck knows how long she's gone, but I know from the low battery alert on my phone that it must have been longer than I thought. I grab a power bank from my coat pocket to charge it as the idea of my phone dying and my being disconnected from my servers makes me nervous.

The dilation of time makes it seem like she's trying on everything. I don't really need to see every outfit; I'll see it at some point if she buys it. Plus, Aurora doesn't need my approval, she's fucking gorgeous in everything. But there is a part of me that loves that she wants to show me.

Eventually she walks out, and I'm stunned into silence.

She gestures to the shop assistant, who comes straight over. "I'll take everything on the rail on the left and can you show me where your shoe displays are, please?" Taylor, according to her name badge, peers into the dressing room and her eyes widen at the number of clothes. I'm guessing she works on commission.

"Er-sure, follow me."

I trail after them both, still not sure what I'm looking at because never in my life have I ever seen Aurora look like this. Skin-tight black jeans, leather belt with silver studs and the damn blue corset peeking out from under a white collared shirt.

She doesn't simply look *hot*—she's breathtaking. So tantalisingly beautiful I want to lick every inch of her visible skin. I've known for years that she was an attractive woman, but it wasn't until I got to know her that she mesmerised me. In this moment, it's like she's trans-formed herself.

No, that's not right. She hasn't miraculously become someone else because she changed her clothes. She's free to be her again. The smile I can see creeping across her face reminds me of the ball-buster whose team emptied the safe and Renwick's auction house five years ago.

She's magnificent.

I watch as she grabs a selection of shoes, asking for her size. It doesn't take long for Taylor to return, and Aurora tries them all on. The last pair are black leather knee-high boots with laces all the way up the front. They have no heel and look like she could do some serious damage with the thick soles, chunky treads, and steel toed fronts.

"Yes, thank you." Aurora nods, handing back the rest of them.

"Sorry, which ones?"

"I'll wear these boots out with this outfit, and you can add the rest of the shoes to the total."

"All of them?"

"Yes, all of them." Aurora walks over to a rack of leather coats and finds a longish single breasted black leather coat, hooks it off the hanger and tries it on in front of the full-length mirror. "Oh, and this."

I'm laughing out loud now because it's obvious from Taylor's gobsmacked expression that we've broken her.

"Of course, right this way, ma'am."

"Oh, I'm not paying. He's footing the bill."

"Actually, It's on Zo." This little excursion won't put the smallest dent in our bank account, but I'm glad as I pull out the black Amex, that we have the capabilities to look after Aurora, even if it's in this small way. Taylor spends the next twenty minutes bagging everything up. *Thank fuck we brought the truck.*

DON'T GET ME WRONG, I found the shopping entertaining. But after a not insignificant number of hours in a hair salon with Aurora, I'm considering running head-first through the plate-glass windows to relieve the tedium.

We had been heading home when she spotted this place and demanded I stop, jumping out and running in before I could stop her. By the time I parked and caught up with her, she was already in a chair with a stylist—wig tossed on the floor. She had grabbed me by the shirt collar and her exact words were, "If you make me wear this wig one more time, I'll either make you eat it or shove it up your ass, depending on my mood."

The only sensible response given her mood was, "Yes, Ma'am."

So now here I sit, watching hair *process* apparently. It's on a par with watching paint dry. I'm sure it will make sense soon, but right now it looks the same as when she came in, just covered in strips of tinfoil. The look is as effective a disguise as the wig she hates so much.

I've been texting with Enzo about the plan for tonight. We're later than I'd expected to be back, so he's chasing me for an ETA.

CHAPTER THIRTY-ONE

> Fuck knows.

ZO:

> That's unhelpful.

> Take it up with Aurora.

Next thing I know, he adds Aurora to our group chat. *Interesting.*

ZO:

> Aurora, how much longer are you going to be?

HUMMINGBIRD:

> Afternoon, Sleeping Beauty.

ZO:

> ETA?

HUMMINGBIRD:

> When would you like us back by?

ZO:

> Two hours ago

HUMMINGBIRD:

> Time machine broke down, so we'll see you in an hour.

ZO:

> One hour.

Aurora looks up from the chair. "Why do I feel like I'm in trouble, Sin?"

"Because Zo worries and we've been out for longer than you have been since the warehouse."

She winces, and I kick myself for reminding her. "Oh," is all she musters out.

It doesn't take much longer, and I'm transfixed as the stylist blows-out her hair. As her hair dries, it reveals hues of dark green, teal, and blue running through the ends hidden under her ebony black lengths. You can only see them when she moves. She's also had the hair cut shorter at the front to frame her face. It's bold and fierce and in no way helps her blend into the background.

"Zo's still going to make you wear the wig," I admonish and then wipe away my look of mock judgement with a warm smile. "But it's beautiful, Aurora. It suits you." I can't help but step forward and run my hand through it, entranced by watching the colours slip off my fingers. "Hummingbird," I muse.

"Yeah, you kind of inspired me."

Her words tease a smile from me, and the tribute to my nickname for her is unearthing other emotions in me. My feelings for her refuse to be suppressed. She's captivating, and the little thief is doing a phenomenal job of stealing all my resolve. I can't resist her, and I don't think I want to.

Leaning in, I press my mouth to hers. Her lips part and she welcomes me, letting me devour her in long, languid strokes as our tongues duel with each other. It's intoxicating.

A gentle cough sounds behind us, reminding me we're not only in the middle of the salon, but that I need to pay. After flinching at the total for a fraction of a second—fuck me, being a woman is extortionate—we pay and head back to the truck.

After a few minutes, Aurora turns in her seat and dithers over whatever it is she wants to say.

"Spit it out, *colibrì*."

"Is Enzo okay?"

Her question surprises me. "In what way?"

"I don't know. He takes on a lot, and you made a whole thing about letting him sleep today."

"I wouldn't say 'a whole thing', but I see what you mean. Enzo takes on a lot of personal responsibility for, well, everything. He sets a near impossible standard for himself and at the moment the stakes are incredibly high."

Aurora nods along beside me. "It's not just about what's going on with the De Lucas, is it?"

"No, hummingbird, it's not. Finding a lead on your sister's death has thrown him. He won't admit it, but we'd begun to think we'd never find anything. How much do you remember about Gianni?"

"He was head of my sister's protection crew. That's how I've known Zo for so long. He hung with them sometimes when Gianni was watching Isabella. He died not long after my sister, and I didn't see Zo much after that."

I flick a glance her way as I drive, trying to figure out how much an eleven-year-old would have gleaned about how close Isabella and Gianni were.

"Gianni killed himself a few months after her death, Aurora. He blamed himself, but it wasn't his fault. No one could have saved her. He was more than just her bodyguard."

"I-I would have known."

"You were eleven..."

"Fuck, no wonder Zo's so focussed on Isa's death."

"His brother loved her so much and he just couldn't survive losing her. When he died, Enzo was never the same. Then your father asked Zo to keep searching for Isa's killer and it became a crusade for him. To get justice for your family, but also for his. I think your father knew about Gianni and your sister, and that's why he knew Zo would never give up on finding the person who took so much from both of them."

"That's a lot for one man to burden himself with. My father expected too much from him if that's the case."

"You're not wrong, and Zo's been buried under the weight of it for far too long. After so many years, we'd all but resolved we would never get an answer, but Enzo will never let it go and it takes a toll on him."

"Who watches out for him?" she asks.

"We all try to help as much as he allows. It's why I focus as many of my resources as I can on it."

"He's going to break one day under the weight of the expectations he has of himself."

"Unless someone can help lift them," I posit.

She goes quiet and chews on what I've told her.

The minute we found her on the floor of that warehouse, I felt a shift in all of us. Aurora is the missing piece of a puzzle none of us knew needed solving. She brings out a part of each of us that we usually keep hidden. For me, I have an overwhelming desire to support her. Aurora needs someone to nurture her, someone who won't *only* protect her, but encourage her, too. My hummingbird needs to spread her wings and fly, and just like the bird she reminds me of, she needs to do it with all the chaotic energy and vigour that burns through her veins.

Watching her evolve before our eyes is a reward in and of itself but watching her unfurl under my tongue is just as fulfilling.

Unfortunately, that will have to wait until later. We have a turncoat to deal with.

CHAPTER THIRTY-TWO

AURORA

When we walk through the door, three sets of eyes snap to me from the couch and I smirk at the domino effect of jaws hitting the floor.

"Why, thank you, I'll take your faces of shock and awe as a compliment," I say, teasing them a little.

Enzo looks away, Benny smiles broadly, and Nico grumbles while adjusting himself. I can't help but laugh at their individual reactions, so representative of each of them. Enzo the stoic guard dog, Benny the eager puppy, and Nico the feral stray.

I ignore them and take a seat on one of the sofas. I feel different. More like myself that I have in years. For the last few weeks, I've been coming back to a version of who I was before, but I've also been using these men as a security blanket. Hiding in their house, sheltering in the basement. Even wearing their clothes, retreating into the safety of every aspect of them.

But now it's about time I stop hiding. Time for me to remember I'm Rory-fucking-Bianchi.

When Sinclair first told me we were going out today, I was dreading it. But the longer we were out, the more I felt like the old me was returning. At first, every shop reminded me of being Mrs. Aurora De Luca, the wife, the wallflower, the doormat. When we stopped in that last store, it's like I had a flashback to what it was like back when I was my own woman, and I was blown away by the feeling of freedom and empowerment.

With every item I tried on, I felt more and more like me. From the colours breathing life back into me and lighting me up, to the feel of the fabrics. They felt like a second skin and not a noose around my neck.

I left that store feeling like I could breathe again.

I left the hair salon feeling like I could conquer the world. What woman doesn't when she dyes her hair?

Once they've all stopped staring, it doesn't take Benedict long to walk us through where he's going to set the fires, and which escape routes we're going to need to take. Enzo then tells everyone where they'll be. It will fall entirely on Nico and me to snatch Marco. Sinclair will run interference with any protection he brings with him while Enzo will be driving the van. It all seems pretty straightforward, but I'm left with an uneasy feeling in the pit of my stomach.

I may have spent all day making myself look the part, but this will be my first job with a full crew in five years, and it's the most important one. One that brings me a step closer to annihilating my husband. Ugh, calling him that, even in my head, makes me want to vomit.

There's no moniker I could give him that adequately channels the venomous hatred I feel for him and yet, if I were to call him something like *The Devil*, it gives him too much credit or power over me. He's Max De Luca. He's not my husband, he's not my captor, he's not my tormentor, he's nothing but an enemy that needs to be eliminated.

As Enzo finishes up and everyone starts to break away, but I call after him. "Zo, you got a minute?"

He stops in his tracks, turns, and then cocks his head for me to go with him. I follow and realise he's leading me to a room I haven't been in before. As we enter, I realise it must be his office. I've roamed the whole house in the time I've been here, but I assumed this was a pantry since the door is off the kitchen.

It's nothing like Sinclair's command-centre-style office. There's a high-backed leather Chesterfield chair behind a dark wood desk with leather inlay. It's so traditional. There are two tall bookcases behind him, full to the brim and each one neatly arranged by what looks like genre and author. I want to walk over and mis-shelve a few of them. Although taking a second look at the titles, I may also want to borrow a few.

There are no other chairs in here, only a small two-seater sofa off to the side. I perch myself on the arm of it, not knowing how to broach this subject. I return to tracing the scars on my wrist as I search for the words. Thankfully, he doesn't push me.

Eventually, without looking up, I get up the courage

to say, "I need you to show me the file you have on my sister, Zo. I've never seen it and I think I need to understand exactly what happened. My dad told me some of it, but I want to help you track down her killer. To do that, I need to know everything."

I don't look up, but I don't need to. I can hear him take a deep breath as he takes in my request. This can't be easy for him.

"If you're asking me privately, I'm going to assume Sinclair told you about Gianni?" I nod.

"How much did he tell you?"

I finally look up and lock eyes with him. He's stoic as ever, refusing to let his façade crack so I take a deep breath and spare him from having to say it out loud. "That Gianni and Isa were in love, and that when no leads were found in her murder, he took his own life."

He swallows hard but doesn't look away. "Did you know I was the one who found her?"

"No. My father never told me. Any details I have, I got from listening in at his door." The memories of sneaking around my own house, listening at keyholes, running away at the slightest creek of the floorboards come flooding back. The hurt at being forever protected and never trusted is still there, buried deep.

"You were so young; you can't blame him for trying to protect you." He's right, but that doesn't help me now.

"I know, but I need to know what you know. Why the marks we found on the bodies at the morgue are so important. I need to see for myself if her killer is still out there. When no one was found, I just assumed it was some junkie, a robbery gone bad and hoped more than believed her killer was long since dead—overdosed and long forgotten."

He opens his bottom desk drawer and pulls out a far too thin, manilla envelope and slides it across the desk to me. "This is everything that was in Isa's autopsy report."

I stand and cross over to his desk, picking it up, and hugging it to my chest, not ready to open it in front of him. I feel my heart thudding in my chest, the file feeling heavy in my arms, like I'm holding Pandora's box. The contents are a mystery and threaten to unravel me.

I peer into the still open drawer and see another file.

"What's that one?"

"My brother's file. I don't even know why I have it, but all suicides are investigated by the Medical Examiner's office, and it felt wrong not to keep it," he rasps out, the words forced and obviously painful to him.

"I'm so sorry for your loss, Enzo." It's the only thing I can think of to say.

"And I yours, Aurora."

He's a man of so few words, but they're always so meaningful to me. My heart breaks for him, to the extent that I feel a palpable ache in my chest. I nod and turn to leave but pause at the door. I don't face him as I say, "Just because I don't need monitoring anymore doesn't mean you can't still hang out, you know."

No response.

"I only see you when you need coffee these days."

Nothing.

"No one else will let me watch period dramas."

I hear a soft chuckle behind me that I take as an

acceptance of my invitation and leave without another word.

―※――※――※――※――※――※―

WHEN I GET DOWN to my room, I see that not only has Sin brought down the many bags from today's little excursion, but the sofa has been moved away from the wall and behind it there's a dresser and a freestanding wardrobe. He's also put a mirror on top of the dresser.

I approach it carefully and stand in front of it. It's been so long since I've really looked at myself in a mirror that it feels alien to me.

When I take in the reflection before me, I don't see the new clothes and the vibrant hair. I see the bruises on my jaw and cheek that refuse to fully fade. They're more like subtle hints of yellow now, but to me, they are as noticeable as the day they appeared.

I start to unbutton the shirt and expose my collarbone and the dozens of tiny pink slashes decorating my skin. One day, they'll fade and blend with the silver streaks of my previous scars, integrating themselves into this map of my indelible and inescapable history.

I unhook the corset and expose my abdomen. While everything else on my body is fading, the incision from my stab wound is still angry and announces itself jarringly. The corset is the first thing I've worn that has supported the wound site and helps me feel less of an invalid when I move. It's also the first time my breasts have been supported in what feels like an eternity.

When I stand here exposed and look at the catalogue

of injuries so obvious in the reflection, I feel like a victim. It's so different from when I'm naked in front of Nico and Benny, or Sinclair. I didn't feel weak or broken; I didn't feel exposed or vulnerable. I felt like a fucking goddess.

As I start to hook the corset back together, wincing at the pull around my newly forming scar tissue, I channel how they make me feel when they look at me. With every memory of their eyes on me and the fastening of each clasp, I feel like I'm knitting myself back together. I leave the shirt off and go about unpacking everything I've bought.

I come across an unfamiliar bag and when I open it, there's a note on top.

Phoenix, Sin asked me to grab some things for you today. Didn't have the first fucking clue what you'd like, so I got everything.
—Nico.

Beneath the note is a large black box. It's heavy and rattles loudly as I take it out and place it on the dresser. Popping the lid, I can't help but laugh out loud. It's full to the brim with an eclectic assortment of makeup. The thought of Nico traipsing through the drugstore trying to pick out a lipstick for me shouldn't make me smile as hard as it does.

I root through the contents of the box, pulling out what I think I can make work and feel like a weight is lifting from me as I glide the foundation onto my face, masking the bruises. With every sweep of my fingers, the victim in me disappears.

When I'm finished, I'm transfixed by my appearance. It's me. A version of me I haven't seen in so very long. A tear threatens to spill over my lashes, taking my eyeliner with it. Blinking rapidly, I chase it away and a soft smile warms my features as I realise this is the first time in years that I have looked in a mirror and not been ashamed of the woman staring back at me.

I have a lot to thank the guys for. Not just for saving me, but all the little things they've done to remind me who I am. For helping me rediscover the person I buried a long time ago.

Movement catches my eye in the mirror, and I see Enzo entering through the door.

"In need of a caffeine fix?"

He doesn't speak, but he crosses the room and takes a seat on the sofa, tapping the seat next to him. I'm not sure what's going on, but it feels like he's making an effort. I sit beside him, and he flicks on the TV. Before I can suggest anything, he's already selected a period drama we haven't watched before, and I can't stop the broad grin that plasters itself across my face.

I sink into his side, and we enjoy the ramblings of a self-sacrificing Georgian socialite and her embittered sea captain.

"This is our secret, little warrior."

"If you say so, Zo," I say, unable to stifle my giggle. "Just remember, we can all see the watch history on your profile. How do you think I find half of my watchlist?"

"Fuck," he says with mock indignation, but I can see a smile peeking through. One that's meant just for me.

─✳─✳─✳─✳─✳─

BY THE TIME the film finishes, we're not far off needing to regroup, but Zo is up and crossing to my bed. "Have you read this yet?" he asks, picking up the discarded file and returning, holding it out to me.

I blow out a slow breath, steadying my nerves and shake my head.

"I think you need to read it. I'll stay with you if you want."

I stand and slowly reach out and take it from him. "I think I need to do this on my own." If he stays, I know I'll fall apart.

He nods and as he turns to leave, my hand stops him, entwining my fingers in his. He stops and turns. We don't need words. I reach a hand to cup his face and he leans into it, absorbing my touch and visibly relaxing before me and closing his eyes.

I take advantage of my opportunity and reach up on my tiptoes, pulling him down to meet me. As I press my lips to his I lean into the softness of them, and I feel the most overwhelming sense of belonging. I don't paw at him or try to devour him. We don't escalate, we simply sink into the taste of each other. Sweet and delicate, delicious and addictive.

A gentle hum rumbles from his throat as he steals my breath and slides his tongue against the seam of my lips.

I surrender to him and am lost to our tangled breaths and gentle moans. I can feel the moment he hesitates, his doubts overtaking his desire as his lips still and he pulls away leaving me bereft. His brow is drawn, like he's wrestling with himself.

"You are a truly spectacular woman, Aurora." He sweeps a stray tendril back, anchoring it behind my shoulder.

"And you are worthy, Enzo."

He hugs me and kisses my forehead as he lingers. I could swear he's inhaling me, which should be odd, but I'm doing the same thing. My head tucked into his broad chest, brazenly inhaling his scent and letting it engulf me. One day I'll figure out what it is he smells of, but right now it makes me think of floating down a river in a forest. Clean and fresh with dark woodsy undertones. It's uniquely him and I find it soothes every part of my soul. There's no one I feel more at peace with.

He slips out of the room, and I take a deep breath before I open the file in front of me. I don't think it's possible to prepare yourself adequately to see someone you love reduced to cold words and photos of their naked body on a slab. I can't stop the tears that flow, or the aching realisation of the torment Isa was subjected to in her final days.

The anguish flows through me like a torrent of rain, finding the path of least resistance as it demolishes the last of my remaining emotional barriers.

I cry until my eyes run dry and then I return to the mirror. Seeing myself broken, but also seeing myself enlightened. I set to work righting the mess I've made, and brushstroke by brushstroke I don't rebuild myself, I discover myself.

Time to get my game face on.

CHAPTER THIRTY-THREE

NICO

When Aurora appears, she's undergone another transformation, but it's not the obvious one. She found the makeup I left in her room, but that's not why she looks like a new woman. It's the air of confidence she's bolstered by.

She's standing tall, shoulders back, and strides into the room like she owns it and everyone present. I can't speak for the others, but feeling even the slightest bit possessed by this woman makes me hard as a rock.

Given we're about to head out, that's just fucking unhelpful.

We're taking both cars, since we'll be exiting at opposite ends of the building once Benny lights it up. Benny, Sin, and Zo will take the panel van with Benny's supplies while Aurora and I are in a nondescript, dark sedan. We have a few we rotate, stored in various lockups, swapping out the licence plates as needed.

After reminding us of our escape routes, we're good to go and Aurora leads the way. *Fuck me.* Her ass sways as she struts to the passenger door, and it's all I can do to stop myself from spanking it.

Once we're on the road, the silence which starts off comfortably soon grows into something wildly awkward.

"So... we gonna mention the fact that you fucked me so hard I nearly went blind as I came? Or that you spat your lover's cum into my pussy and then had him lick me clean?"

I can't help chuckling at her brutal candour.

"Because I am not complaining—in any way, shape or form—I'd just like to know if we're cool and if we're going to be doing it again?"

"Inquiring minds want to know, huh?"

"Something like that."

"I like this new you. Or rather old you. She's ballsy and bratty."

"And you love to punish a brat."

"Fuck yeah I do."

She's smiling broadly and trying her damndest not to look over at me. "Can you handle two brats, though? Benny *and* me, I reckon we're a handful taken together."

I groan at the image she's conjured in my head. Me taking Benny while Benny takes her. Fucking him into her over and over again. I shake my head, trying to release myself from the hold that fantasy has over me.

"You're a fucking tease, my little cock-warmer."

"Is it teasing when I'd follow through, though?"

"Fair point," I say in a growl that reveals my frustration at not having her riding my dick right now. "But you'll have to wait until later. We'll be pulling up in ten."

"Enough time for you to answer the question then, *sir*." She squeezes my thigh to emphasise her point.

I glance across at her before resuming my focus on the road. I answer her with absolute conviction, "We didn't fuck you, Aurora. We claimed you. There's no way that's not happening again."

"Oh."

"Nothing else to say?"

"What about Sinclair?"

"What about him? He claimed you, too. He has no problem with us wanting you, and we have no problem with him wanting you."

"What about me wanting all of you?"

"Don't think I didn't see what you did there. I have no problem with you wanting *all* of us. Do you have a problem with my relationship with Benny?"

"Of course not. I love what you have together."

"So, there's no issue. We'll figure everything else out as we go."

"Well, okay then," is all she can muster in response, and the silence that settles between us is comfortable again.

As we enter through a shabby side door, we're given the once over by a sorry excuse for a doorman who takes one look at my size and instantly decides it's easier just to let me through than to hold me up.

I inform him I'm escorting a replacement for one of the girls, and he checks a clipboard on the desk in front of him, nodding when he sees a name crossed out. We paid Cherry a boatload of cash to make sure she wouldn't be here tonight. After seeing this place, I hope she takes the money and runs as far away as she can.

From the building plans we'd figured the front-of-house would be a strip club and as I follow Aurora through a threadbare red velvet curtain, we're greeted by a gloomy room full of half-empty seating arranged around a stage that's seen better days. Half of the bulbs are blown in the lighting rigs and the spotlight hardly has enough lumens to highlight the barely-legal stripper doing her best to enthral the lacklustre audience. As fronts for brothels go, this one is piss poor.

Everything about this place feels dirty and the stale smell turns my stomach as we head towards the bar.

I take out my phone and send a text to the group chat.

> Gonna be hard to blend in with the clientele.

BOSS-MAN:

> Shit.

BAMBI:

> Do I need to solo it?

BOSS-MAN:

> No.

SIN:

> No, you won't.

> Fuck no.

BAMBI:

> Thanks for the faith in me.

BOSS-MAN:

> It's not that, and you know it. You'll only have one exit route and that's got the only security.

BAMBI:

> Fine.

> We stick to the plan. Sin goes with you. Zo, we'll meet you out back with our passenger.

BOSS-MAN:

> Agreed

Aurora finishes up with the barman and hands me a bottled beer. She grabs hers and sidles up to me, reading the group chat to catch up. Bottled beer is a wise choice in this place. I don't trust that there's a single clean glass behind that bar.

We're early so we can set up in the room before Marco arrives. I nod towards the door to the left of the bar. It's covered by a grotty grey-black curtain as tattered as the one we entered through.

This place is just fucking delightful.

We move leisurely and I make a show of running my hands over her in a lascivious manner while she plasters the fake smile of an indentured woman on her face. She's able to channel it far too easily, and it makes my already sickened stomach roil.

The stiff curtain scrapes against me—so stained in

fuck-knows-what it barely drapes any longer—and we pass through into a dimly lit hallway. According to the layout Benny showed us, there are six rooms back here and our target is the last one on the left, closest to the fire exit. The fact there's no security strengthens my disdain for the place. Anything could be happening to the girls. There aren't even cameras in the hallway.

Pushing open the door, Aurora retches at the state of the room. I doubt anyone has ever cleaned anything in this room except the bed sheets—and they look dubious.

She looks around, peering suspiciously and refusing to touch a thing.

"Something's not right about this."

"You're not wrong."

"No, I mean it, Nico. This doesn't feel right. Why would Marco, a man of significant influence, be caught dead anywhere near this place?"

"According to our intel, Marco's been seeing Cherry here every week for two years."

"But why? Why not set her up somewhere after all that time? Why come here, of all places?"

I think about it and come up short. Pulling out my phone, I see that we still have ten minutes, so I open the group chat again.

> You sure we can trust our source on this, Zo?

BOSS-MAN:

> Why?

PHOENIX:

> Because the likelihood of a man like
> Marco patronising this establishment
> voluntarily is slim to none. It's a fucking
> dive.

> What she said.

No one replies, no three dots. My unease builds until at last Zo responds.

BOSS-MAN:

> Looks like the intel's good. Marco just
> arrived with two men. Benny and Sin are
> tailing them. They're off comms.

> You're a go.

Aurora nods but still looks unconvinced. We wait. We wait longer than I expect, considering he only has to cross one room, the bar, and a corridor to get here.

My foot taps on the floor and Aurora glares at me, and crooks her head, reminding me I'm supposed to be hiding behind the door. As I move to position, I can hear the sharp clack of pretentious shoes on the creaky floorboards in the hallway. They pause outside the door for a moment, and then I watch as the handle slowly turns. The door creaks painfully, imitating the sound of nails down a chalkboard, sending a shiver down my spine.

As the door opens, an overly cocky Marco saunters through, adjusting his tie in a brash fashion and then reaching into his suit jacket, he arrogantly proclaims, "Which of Enzo's lackeys am I going to have the pleasure of killing tonight?"

My pulse quickens and I feel my stomach drop—he

knew we'd be here, and everything is about to take a turn for the worse.

When his eyes land Aurora, he hesitates and I take that as my opportunity to slam the door shut and barrel into him, disarming him of the gun he was reaching for when he entered.

From under my firm grip, Marco stares at Aurora. Eyebrows raised, incredulous tone revealing his shock at seeing her. "You're supposed to be dead. He said you were dead."

"Well now," interjects Aurora, "one would have thought, if you had any knowledge of your don's daughter being murdered you would have, I don't know, told someone maybe?"

"This is going to be another easy interrogation, isn't it?" I say as I grip Marco's throat. He's choking, but only slightly. I squeeze his rolls of neck fat just hard enough to restrict his windpipe and compress his carotid artery at the same time. I need him lightheaded and pliable, as opposed to agitated or unconscious.

I could carry him out the fire escape, but I don't want to.

His garbled rants fade to an incoherent mumble, so I release him and steer him back towards the door. We need to get him out, but only once Benny and Sinclair take care of his guards. That's when we hear a fire alarm —and that's our cue.

Aurora opens the door, and we can see flames consuming the curtain that leads to the bar, and beyond that is a raging inferno spewing out acrid black smoke into the hallway. While I manhandle Marco, Aurora forces the fire door open, and we burst out into the back alley. The van isn't here. Enzo was supposed to leave the town car for Benny and bring the van to us.

"Shit." I'm searching the street for any sign of the van, but there's nothing. Looking back into the club, there's no one else exiting through the fire escape. That means there was no one else in the five other rooms off that corridor.

We are so fucked. I'm not entirely sure how fucked we are, but we're definitely fucked.

CHAPTER THIRTY-FOUR

AURORA

We tumble out of the fire exit, struggling with the weight of a half-unconscious Marco. He's still slightly loopy from the lack of oxygen, but he's also damn heavy.

Complacent and overconfident capos are usually as overinflated as their egos, yet most have intellects the size of their dicks. I have no idea how some of these men have amassed the power and support they have. My father would never fully explain why men that turned my stomach made up his inner circle, but he would often say, "Just because something is ugly doesn't mean it can't be useful."

He was a clever man, and managed his capos well, but he spent far too much time and energy working a broken system.

Enzo and the van are nowhere to be seen, and I know in the pit of my stomach that something is wrong as I feel the hairs on the back of my neck stand on end. I hear the vehicles before I see them. Tyres screeching as they hoon around the corner and come to a stop in front of us. The doors of three black SUVs with tinted windows, spring open as soon as they stop and eject at least half a dozen men with guns drawn. All trained on us. No matter what Nico has concealed on him, he can't get to it quick enough. We are out-manned and outgunned.

Nico drops our cumbersome guest on the ground and we both raise our hands automatically. Marco rolls around as he tries to right himself. No one moves to help him. These people are not his rescuers. They're here for us.

My pulse races and I struggle to halt the ragged breaths that assault my lungs. I can't be taken—I can't be captive again. I wrestle my traitorous body into submission, refusing to give these assholes the satisfaction, burying my fear.

No one speaks, but the gun closest to us waves its barrel towards the SUV on the far left. *Guess that's our invitation.* Behind me, I can hear our captors manhandle Marco into the back of one of the other vehicles. As we're pushed into the rear passenger doors, I can see that Sin, Benny, and Zo are not here.

I'm desperately hoping they escaped. My teeth are clenched so hard they're beginning to ache under the strain. Saliva pools in my mouth and as I swallow, I realise from the sharp copper taste, that I've bitten my cheek so hard I've drawn blood. *They have to be alive.* Shaking my head, I try to snap myself out of this spiral.

The familiar faces of Salvatore's lackeys register just

before they throw a bag over our heads. It's oppressive and jarring to be suddenly without one of your senses, but it's not foreign and I find it oddly calming. This was one of Max's regular punishments when I was in the basement for any length of time. It's an excellent way to disorient your captive and make them lose their sense of time and reality. After four days chained in darkness, I was usually at my most malleable.

Their scare tactics lighten my mood and make me chuckle—nothing about this situation is funny, but equally there's nothing these men can do to me that would intimidate me—it's like they're following the *Henchmen's Guide to Intimidation*. I receive a swift jab to my ribs from what I assume is the butt of a handgun, but the corset boning does a fantastic job of absorbing a majority of the impact. Nice little bonus there—stylish and practical.

It's ridiculous that they've covered our heads, such a pointless thing to do. Once we get wherever we're going, it's highly likely we're going to be executed, so what's the fucking point in hiding the destination from us? As low-level lackeys go, Salvatore De Luca's are not the smartest.

My best guess is it takes about twenty-five minutes for the cars to come to a stop and we're dragged out of the backseat. Rough hands grab my arms, wrenching me out of the car, before I'm handed off to someone else who makes sure to grip my hips hard enough to bruise when they spin me around and push me forward to walk in front of them. I start a mental tally of exactly how many men I'm going to kill or simply castrate if I get out of this. *Gotta have hope, right?*

I'm pushed from the frosty night air into a warm room, which only serves to highlight the icy claw-like fingers that clutch the back of my neck under the bag—that makes number three. I distract myself by coming up with a list of unique ways to remove someone's balls.

I can hear the scuffles of multiple sets of feet struggle with what I can only guess is an uncooperative Nico. The scratchy, musty-smelling material is wrenched off my head and hands force me down on my knees in front of a familiar desk. My tender ankle objects to the sudden movement and shift in weight.

Well, this is just fucking great. *We are so fucked.*

Forcing Nico to his knees beside me, we are frisked, our phones taken and switched off before the two men assume their sentry behind us and place the barrels of their guns to the back of our skulls. "Don't fucking move."

There's only one positive about this situation. We have not been delivered to Max. The latent fear gripping my chest eases, making it easier for me to plaster on a veneer of cold-heartedness. I'm going to need it.

Taking in my surroundings, I'm reminded how much I detest this house. Every square inch is dripping in reds and golds, deep rich hues, and mahogany furniture. It's like someone googled 'more money than sense' and then bought every piece of furniture in the search results. It's a tasteless blend of Neoclassical, Georgian, and Victorian that's hard to look at without sneering.

It doesn't take long before our host enters behind us. I know from the slink of his gait and the clack of the heels on his overpriced Italian loafers who he is before he even opens his mouth.

"Well, well, well. Imagine my surprise when I was notified my daughter-in-law was alive and well, and in my office." Salvatore De Luca stalks across his office and assumes an overly dramatic position behind his high-backed chair. A menacing yet gleeful expression etched in place by the lines on his face. I've always found his manner oppressive, but now it's outright menacing. I see a ghost of the monster he spawned in his appearance and it catches me off guard, making the confidence I'm forcing myself to project slip, just for a second, but Salvatore doesn't miss it. Shifting on his feet, he takes us in, looking down on us with an air of imperiousness that sits as uncomfortably as it ever has.

"Good evening, Aurora. Welcome home."

I swallow the bile rising in my throat. This never was and never will be my home. Suppressing the urge to shout that at him I force a curt nod, grinding out my response between clenched teeth, "Salvatore."

"Still as graceful as ever. It's no wonder my son is obsessed with you—perhaps if he'd exhibited a fraction of your stoicism, we could have avoided all of this."

I muster every ounce of control it's within my power to wrangle. "I'm afraid I'm at a disadvantage, Salvatore. I've been preoccupied, recovering from my last encounter with your son. You're going to need to elaborate."

His mouth twists up into a smirk as he volleys his head, debating on whether to engage with me. "Alright,

CHAPTER THIRTY-FOUR

I'll indulge you for a little while. What do you want to know?"

"Why now? Why go through the pain of forming an alliance only to attack us? It doesn't make any sense." I ball my fists, having to work hard to keep my tone even, careful not to show the emotion that's trying to drown me.

He laughs, "Why the fuck couldn't you have been a De Luca instead of a Bianchi? Ever the pragmatist."

His comment shocks me and I can't help but retort, "If you admire me so much, why the fuck did you have your son kill me?"

"Well, many reasons, but mostly because you were his consequence," he says, eyes devoid of emotion.

"Elaborate," I demand, clenching my jaw at his callousness, trying not to give him the reaction he so desperately wants from me.

"Well," he says and pulls out his chair, assuming his throne, "you're right, of course you are. The Syndicate was working as intended. There was no real reason to upset the balance. No good one, anyway. We'd finally stopped the infighting, and both families were mostly getting along. It was manageable discontent as opposed to war and it was fucking lucrative." His demeanour shifts and a disquieting look crosses his features. "That is, until my son's unhealthy interest with you became too obvious."

"Unhealthy interest? Is that what we're calling it?" I sneer at him.

"Careful now, Aurora," he warns starkly. "Don't

mistake my candour for fealty of any kind. He is still my heir."

"An heir you have to clean up after. Tell me Salvatore, do you think you will ever trust him enough to hand over the reins?" I force a melodic cadence to my words, hoping my attitude pisses him off.

A flurry of emotions cascade over his features before he schools them. Anger, fear, dread, then nothing.

He levels his glare on me and not a cell in my body is prepared to baulk under the weight of it. "Once your father suspected you were in danger, he wouldn't let it go and any move he was planning would have resulted in the dissolution of The Syndicate. I had no choice but to intervene."

"Intervene?" I arch a brow at him incredulously. "You mean slaughter him?"

"He made plans to eliminate my heir. Any action I took was in defence of our family."

Fuck, of course he did. The realisation that, despite the risk, my dad was fighting for me enfolds me like a warm embrace which fills me with as much solace as it does sorrow.

"And me? Why have Max kill me? Surely, he's more pliable when he has a..." the next part is harder to force out than I would like, "when he has a distraction?"

"You're not wrong. But eliminating you, my dear, was and is a necessity."

"A necessity?" I say, my temper rising, simmering beneath the surface, begging for release.

"Well, if it hadn't been for you, none of this would have happened. My son's obsession with you jeopardised our entire organisation. He evidently can't be trusted to make the necessary sacrifices. He can't be allowed to keep you." His control wavers, his eyes burning with fury, mouth drawn into a thin, venomous sneer.

And now I cannot keep my countenance. Here I was thinking Salvatore had half a grip on reality. The laugh that escapes me starts small and grows to a near hysterical cackle. Nico, who's been still throughout our interaction so far, is staring at me with concern.

"I can tell you right now my patience for you is wearing beyond thin, Miss Bianchi."

I try to collect myself, wiping the tears away from my eyes. Fuck me.

"Sorry," I say cheerfully, still unable to temper my outburst. "I'm fucking sorry, but how are you this delusional?"

Standing, he's around the desk faster than I would expect for a man of his age. He's older than my father was by a fair whack, pushing at least seventy. Pulling a gun out of a shoulder holster under his suit jacket, he presses it to the centre of my forehead.

"It's not wise to mock the man who holds your life in his hands."

"Believe me, I know. It's a lesson I learned quickly from your sadistic progeny."

He removes the safety. "Explain what you mean."

My eyes bore into his as I say the next words. "The only thing that has ever tempered your son's proclivities has been me. You were fucked the minute you ordered him to kill me."

I can see from the slight flinch he knows I'm not wrong, so I continue.

"Tell me. How's he been the last few weeks? Cool? Calm? Collected? Or has he been erratic? Difficult to track down?"

Salvatore pushes the barrel of the gun harder against my forehead, sending me back into the guard behind me. If I have to be on my knees between two massive pricks, I'd rather it were in a more literal sense.

I square up to him, well as much as I can in my current position. "Your son is a fucking psychopath—you know it and I know it. You must have helped him before me, helped cover up his victims. I'd be willing to bet you haven't had to lift a finger to protect him since we got married."

He takes a step back and perches on the top of his desk, hands at either side of him on the desktop, gun still under his right palm.

"Smart girl. When did you figure it out?"

This is the point where Nico pipes up, and when he speaks, I can't meet his eyes. I'm ashamed of myself. How can he bear to look at a woman who allowed herself to be broken?

"Does someone want to tell me what the fuck you two are talking about?" I hate to hear the uncertainty in his voice. Like he's worried that I'm keeping something from him.

Salvatore ignores him and continues to stare me down. "How long, Aurora?"

"I've known exactly what type of monster he was from the day I married him." I shake my head to chase away any emotion from bubbling up at my next words. "But as soon as I saw the photos of my sister's autopsy, I knew." My words ending on a whisper.

I hear the sharp intake of breath to my left from Nico, but I cannot turn my head. If I look away from the cold heartless eyes of Salvatore De Luca, I will shatter into a thousand pieces. The only thing holding me together is the rage I feel. The molten fury that burns through my veins to know that I've been touched, fucked, raped by the man who killed my sister is indescribable.

Nico tries to rise to his feet, but Salvatore lifts his gun, takes aim and shoots without blinking. I cry out and instinctively reach for Nico, only to be held back by the man at my back. My heart is screaming at me to move, to run to his side. But just like with my father, I'm forced to watch as someone I care about is hurt. It's torture— worse than any pain Max could ever inflict.

Nico falls forward on his hands and knees, grunting and grinding his teeth, as if trying to bite back the pain. Blood immediately flows from the entrance and exit wounds above his knee. It looks like a through-and-through, but that doesn't mean he's not in agony.

"Down boy, honestly, I don't understand why we keep you bastards around. You may be useful occasionally, but you're a bitch to train. Stay." Salvatore spits out, nodding to the men behind Nico and they lean over to pull him back up to a kneeling position again.

"He's doing it again." I throw out, hoping to distract him from Nico. I know we're fucked, but the longer we can stay alive, the longer we have to figure a way out of this shit-show. Chances are fucking slim, though. I don't know if Salvatore has all of us or if Enzo, Sin, or Benny are coming.

The only thing I can do is keep Salvatore talking.

"Without me, he's back out there, creating more messes. Do you even know how many there were between my sister and marrying me?" I can't mask the anger any longer, my voice catching as I grind out my words through gritted teeth.

Salvatore is noticeably uncomfortable, flinching at my words, but I keep pushing, revelling in the fact that I can make him squirm.

"Come on, there's no way there weren't others. But there are no bodies from back then, else there would have been connections made to my sister's death. You're telling me there was nothing for a whole fucking decade? What did you do to protect him, Salvatore?" The more playful I force my cadence to be, the more it seems to irk him.

"You think you're so fucking clever, don't you?" He practically spits out the words, sneering at my confidence, disdainful that I have the gall to question him and obviously irritated that I don't show him the fear he expects.

"I am so fucking clever. How many?" I push.

Salvatore makes a show of clenching his jaw, before saying, "Five. But I couldn't prove that they were his, so I just made them disappear. And after the wedding, the problem went away."

"And what did you think was going to happen when he no longer had me as an outlet? He's right back out there. You're losing your touch, De Luca. There are already bodies showing up and he's getting fucking sloppy. Two in four weeks."

"You're lying!"

I raise an eyebrow, daring him to question me and he storms around his desk and sits down, pulling out his phone and making a call. "Get my son here within the hour." He's about to end the call when he says, "And bring Marco to my office." He throws the phone down on the desk and levels his icy blue eyes on mine. They're the same as his son's and it's hard to meet them without being bombarded with images of those same soulless orbs hovering over me, taking everything from me, over and over again.

"What's the plan, Salvatore?"

"Wait and see," is all I get back in response.

Time stretches out and the only noises in the room are the desynchronised breaths of its occupants. What should be imperceptible little huffs become increasingly loud and oppressive to me. Torturous and pulling at my nerve endings. While I have been able to endure complete silence for days, the small noises of the people in this room are slowly building to a rampant crescendo that feels deafening.

Nico's the quietest of them all, despite his injury. The blood from his wounds has seeped into the dark denim, the stain slowly travelling down towards the floor. His jaw is rigid from gritting his teeth so hard. I can see the beads of sweat tumbling from his forehead that he's straining to maintain his composure. There's no way a man like Nico will allow himself to buckle now.

The ornate, gold clock on the mantle behind Salvatore's shoulder tells me it's been a few minutes despite feeling like an eternity when the doors open again, and yet more of Salvatore's men escort Marco into the room. I don't miss the look of disdain he casts over Nico, and the smirk that falls across his features when he realises Nico's bleeding. *Cunt.*

"Tell me, Aurora, as you're so clever. What do you think will be Marco's position in the new organisation when I dissolve The Syndicate and absorb the Bianchis?"

"Do you want me to tell you what he thinks his position will be? Or what it will actually be?" I say with a confidence and flair I don't fully feel.

Salvatore smiles before letting out a genuine laugh. Its authenticity does nothing to dispel the note of menace in it. He nods for me to continue.

I look back at Benny's father and stare him down as I say, "He believes he's going to maintain his position as capo under you, potentially being promoted when the prince ascends his throne." My distaste at his treachery is evident in every word that passes my lips, my tone cold.

"But..." Salvatore prompts. His manner is void of all sentiment. Blank and unfeeling.

I make sure my next words to Marco are felt with the force I intend. Slowly and with relish I say, "You're going to kill him."

At my words there are cries of, "What the fuck?" and, "You can't do this," and, "I did what you asked," while the men beside him hold him back.

"Shut the fuck up," Salvatore barks at him.

"But why?" Is all he gets out before he's forcefully

quieted by a chokehold, that leaves him gasping for breath.

Salvatore chuckles and looks at Nico. "Even you should be able to figure this one out. Tell me, mongrel, why will I kill Marco Romano?"

Nico looks worse for wear. He's applying pressure to the gunshot wounds, clamping his hands around his leg. His voice wavers as he attempts to keep the obvious discomfort from his voice when he answers Salvatore. "Because he's disloyal."

"Bingo."

Marco's body falls to the ground milliseconds after the gunshot rings out. It happens so quickly, I barely register who shot him until I see the guard to his left adjusting the drape of his suit as he returns his piece to his hip holster.

I feel conflicted as I stare at Marco's corpse. He deserved to die, but a part of me mourns for Benedict. Now he's lost his father twice, and it breaks my heart. I look at Nico and see the same turmoil reflected in his eyes.

Salvatore returns to stand in front of me and hooks my chin with his bony finger.

"I'd be a fool to ignore the valuable information you've provided me. It seems I need you alive far more than I need you dead." He looks lost in thought for a moment, and I almost miss it when he whispers. "You have your mother's eyes." Breaking my gaze, he issues instructions. "Lock them up downstairs for the time being." He's already storming out of the office as he hollers back, "And clean up my office before my son arrives."

—※—※—※—※—※—

WE'RE THROWN into a room in the basement, the door locked behind us. I scramble over to Nico and get to work assessing his injuries.

"I'm fine, stop fussing," he grouses, trying to push me away from him.

"Sit your ass down on the floor, back against the wall. Now." I can't hold back the growl that escapes me. I need to know how bad his injury is.

He makes noises that imply I'm overreacting, but I don't give a shit. If we get even the slightest opportunity to get out of here in one piece, then I need him conscious and mobile.

With his good leg extended and the other bent up, being used as an armrest, he stares at me. "Get to work then."

I laugh at him as I check the gunshot wound. "It's a through and through."

"Coulda' told you that."

"Wind your neck in, Nico." I can't help falling into a snarky banter with him. His natural abrasiveness familiar and calming.

"Make me, phoenix." Rolling his head back against the wall, he smiles as playfully as he can given his grey pallor and glistening brow.

I can't help but smile back at him, which feels wrong given the dire situation we're in. He swears profusely as I poke and prod the area around the wound. "Fuck are you doing, woman?"

"Checking the bullet didn't clip anything vital on its way through. You're clotting, but we need to get you out of here and to Doc Em."

"Doubt that's gonna happen, phoenix." His tone is solemn, almost accepting of his fate, and I feel my heart breaking at the thought of losing him. It's a new type of pain, one that lances at my soul. Salvatore will probably kill him, and it looks like me and my smart mouth have bought me a one-way ticket back to my marital bed.

That's not happening. I can't go back. I won't.

Sweat beads along my spine as my heart rate picks up, thundering in my chest. I'd rather die than be at Max's mercy again.

Forcing myself to calm down, I take a deep breath and push all thought of Max from my mind and focus on Nico. My pulse steadies as I take him in. I start removing my belt and he chuckles, pulling me into him. "Odd timing, but I'm not going to say no."

I plant two hands firmly on his chest and push myself away from him. "It's for the tourniquet you, prick."

Leaning forward, he steals a tender kiss and then releases me. "Can't blame a guy for trying."

"I can't." I smile not knowing what else to say. I thread the belt under his thigh, tugging hard to tighten it.

"Argh. Fuck me, you're ruthless, phoenix." His breath is coming in short, strangled gasps and he looks to the ceiling as if to centre his focus.

I'll have to be ruthless if I have to face Max again.

"Why didn't you tell us about your sister?"

"Honestly?" I say with an air of resignation. "A part of me knew as soon as I saw the marks on her body, the sheer volume, the placement. Every pattern was familiar because he did the same to me. But I didn't process it until just now, saying it out loud to Salvatore. Zo only gave me the file this afternoon. It's a lot when you realise you're married to your sister's murderer."

He pulls me to him, dropping his leg and settling me on his lap, drawing me into a koala hug.

"Stop, I'll hurt you."

"Shut the fuck up, Aurora, and sit still."

So, I do. I sink into him and bask in his warmth and comfort. I will hold him for as long as I can.

CHAPTER THIRTY-FIVE

My phone vibrates in my pocket, tearing me out of the moment I'm trying to bask in. This one didn't last long. Her screams rang out across the warehouse like a discordant choir of angels descending into hell. It was magnificent.

I normally hate screamers. They waste their energy and burn themselves out too soon. But her cries were enthralling.

I painted the warehouse floor with arcs of arterial blood, coaxed in plumes out of her slender neck and wrists. Releasing the chain, I smile as her drained shell crumples to the ground, folding in on itself, snapping and breaking like a predated carcass.

I roll her onto the waiting tarpaulin and drag her across to the trunk of my car, hauling her in, and wrapping her as best I can. This is the first one I've brought here. I had hoped she would make a good proxy. That I could relive our last farewell, but no one will ever compare to her.

And she wouldn't stop crying.

My principessa never cried—she was fucking perfect.

CHAPTER THIRTY-FIVE

Crossing over to the controls on the back wall, I set off the hydrants, watching transfixed as crimson streaks spiral and swirl, disappearing into the drains.

So beautiful. Such a shame to erase it all.

Pulling out my phone, I look down at the incoming message alert. He's summoned me.

Time to subjugate myself to the old man.

CHAPTER THIRTY-SIX

ENZO

Fear rampages through my veins. It's frenzied and violent, bordering on uncontrollable. Watching the procession of SUVs pulling away from the rear entrance, I know we're too late.

I hate this feeling of powerlessness. I haven't felt like this since I lost Gianni. Like my family is lost to me. The pain in my chest is palpable, leaving a dull ache that feels like I'm shackled by my failure.

When Sin called, I knew the plan had gone to shit. Marco's men had been prepared for us, and Benedict and Sin lost the element of surprise. Benny was unconscious and Sin needed back-up. I made a choice and went to help them first—now Nico and Aurora are gone.

It's all my fucking fault.

I glance in the rearview mirror to see Sinclair hunched over Benedict who's flat out on his back breathing heavily. He took a helluva beating before I arrived, and we were able to overpower Marco's men. Sin seems to have got away relatively unscathed, but I suspect Benny has a concussion, judging by the bruising on his temple.

I have one man half-battered and two captured. I should never have sent them in tonight. They knew we were coming. Someone betrayed us and my family paid the price for my hubris. That thought settles in my mind and steals my breath.

I will never forgive myself for this. They trusted me, and I failed them.

I'm trying to tail the procession of SUVs discreetly, but it's not easy. I can't lose them. Aurora and Nico are as good as dead if I can't keep up with them or blow my cover.

"Have you got a way to track them?" I bark back at Sin.

"Shit, yes. Give me a minute."

From my glances in the mirror, I can see Sin grab his phone and furiously tap at his screen. It doesn't take long before he leans forward and shoves it in the cradle on the dash. There are two red dots flashing on the map on the screen. Both moving at a consistent pace ahead of me, so I know they're definitely in one of the cars. I just don't know which one.

If I did, I'd probably run the other ones off the road.

"Back off a bit and rely on the tracker. These fuckwits didn't toss Aurora and Nico's phones," Sin mutters as he rubs his face and blows out a breath, obviously relieved that he has a way of tracking them.

I look at the two red dots and it eases my fear, but as I

take my first even breath for a while, it evolves and grows into anger. Anger at myself for letting this happen, fury at the power-hungry traitors who betrayed Mateo in the first place, and incandescent rage at the De Lucas.

They have my people. My family.

If anything happens to either of them, there won't be anywhere on this earth that the De Lucas can hide from me. I will hunt them down and exterminate them.

The sound of my teeth grinding together makes me realise how tightly I'm clenching my jaw while the idea of Aurora being hurt any further by these monsters leaves a bitter taste in my mouth.

I was supposed to protect her from them, and I was fucking derelict in my duty to her.

Sinclair is watching me closely and his scrutiny prickles across my skin. Fuck, I don't need his judgement —I'm judging myself enough right now.

"Speak, Sin," I say, calling him on the way he's tiptoeing around whatever it is he wants to get off his chest.

"We will get them both back," Sinclair says with a confidence that I pray rather than believe is true.

"You don't know that."

"I know you'll do whatever it takes to make sure they survive."

I nod slowly, letting his faith in me quash my anxiety.

"Promise me something?" he asks quietly, his tone as close to begging as Sinclair gets.

"You can ask, but I won't promise."

"Promise me you'll do whatever it takes to make sure you survive, too."

"What the fuck are you talking about?"

"You're the heart of the team, you idiot. Make sure whatever we have to do to get them back includes you walking out with us. No fucking heroics. Do I make myself clear?"

I can't help but laugh at Sin's dramatics. "Fuck off, you prick, I have no plans to sacrifice myself. We're following them, we're getting them back, and then we're all going home. End of story."

Sinclair eyes me dubiously but turns his back and checks on Benny. Benedict rolls his head from side to side and checks his injuries, crying out when he bumps the bruise on his brow.

What the fuck is Sinclair talking about, 'No fucking heroics'? Does he think I'm some fucking martyr—that I believe I'm expendable? I sacrifice a lot for my team, but have I really closed myself off so much that my closest friend thinks I have some kind of death wish?

Shit. Do I? I would sacrifice myself for any one of my team. But Sin has a point. Maybe that shouldn't be my default position. It was my first thought when they were taken—to barter their freedom for mine. How the fuck does he even know that's what I was thinking, anyway?

Fucking asshole, nothing gets by him.

The flashing dots stop moving on the screen and I can't stop the run of expletives that rush out of my mouth.

A feeble voice from the back says, "Tell us how you really feel." Benny rights himself against the side of the van as I pull into a side alley.

"Welcome back, Benny-boy," I snark.

"Fuck off, Zo. That prick smashed me through a fucking wall. I'd like to see you get out of that intact."

"You okay? I need to know if I've gotta bench you."

"They're my... my... they're fucking mine. You're not going in without me, Zo. *You can't fucking stop m—*" Benedict roars, lurching forward to grab at the back of the passenger seat and haul himself up.

Sin seems to realise I'm not just worried about Benny's health when he yanks Benny back to the floor like a disobedient puppy and asks, "What's the issue? Explain."

I point at the map, and Sin joins me in my tirade of swear words.

"Yeah, that's about right," I say before clarifying to Benny, "They've been taken to the De Luca compound."

All Benny says is, "Fuck."

We've been waiting in the alley a few blocks south of our target for a while now. We're all agitated, but there's nothing to do but wait. The three of us can't take on the full De Luca security detail.

"We don't have fucking time for this," Benny screams, punching the side of the van and howling in pain at his own stupidity.

"I swear to fuck, if you blow our cover because you're too busy throwing a tantrum, I will have Nico spank your ass raw when we get him back," I grind out.

Benny immediately shrinks back. That's the first time

I've ever referenced their dynamic to one of them directly, and it feels like I've crossed a line. I shouldn't have called him out like that. It feels like I've shamed him, and my mistake sits like a bitter pill in my mouth. He's quiet, and withdrawn, and decidedly un-Benny-like. I turn in my seat and demand his attention. "Hey, I had no right to say that. What goes on between you and your... partners... is none of my fucking business."

He blanches at my words, and I can't figure out if he's embarrassed or freaked out by my reference to Aurora. Swallowing nervously, he says, "Thank you. You don't need to apologise, though. I just didn't realise you knew so much about mine and Nico's dynamic."

I'm smiling as reassuringly as I can, given our current situation. "*Very* thin walls, Benny. Very thin."

"So fucking thin," Sinclair grumbles.

That gets a weak smile out of Benny, followed by a quiet plea. "Promise me we'll get them back."

"We will do everything we can."

I can't make that promise, as much as every fibre of my being wants to. I can't be the man that makes it and then can't deliver. It will destroy me, just like it did my brother. Benedict nods, but it hurts my soul to see him so lost.

We have a plan. I'm not saying it's a brilliant plan, but it's a plan, and it's the only one we've got. After running it by Sinclair and Benny, it took us thirty minutes to make the necessary calls and pull in every favour we have and now all we can do is wait.

Every minute is torture, not knowing if our waiting is

costing Aurora or Nico minutes they don't have. We can't make a move on that compound without back-up. I just fucking hope it comes soon.

CHAPTER THIRTY-SEVEN

AURORA

I don't know how the fuck I dozed off, but I'm woken up by rough hands circling my biceps and wrenching me from Nico's arms. As I'm pulled from his lap, he collapses to the side, and I see the tourniquet has done a piss-poor job of stemming the flow of blood—there's a pool of deep crimson beneath his knee.

"Leave him, boss just wants her," says one of the assholes behind me.

I'm making life as difficult as possible for them by remaining rigid and unmalleable. Eventually, they tire of my complete lack of cooperation and the stockier of the two hoists me over his shoulder, making sure to swing me into every wall and door frame he can on our way to wherever I've been summoned. I barely feel the bumps, but my ribs ache and I struggle to breath against the shoulder wedged against me.

As we ascend the stairs, I hear a loud voice yelling half in English, half Italian. I don't know what I expected when Salvatore summoned his son, but this was not it and I can't hide the shock from my face.

We stop abruptly and I'm thrown down, landing on with my full weight on my fractured foot which immediately gives way and I collapse to the floor. My pained cry is ignored, and I'm immediately wrenched up and forced to my knees. The pain is fresh and raw but not unmanageable. I clench my jaw, swallowing down the discomfort as I try to reassert an impervious veneer.

I find myself just inside the doorway by a large, ornate fireplace in what Salvatore has always called *the parlour*. I always found it pretentious, but in reality, it did make it easier to distinguish from the four other reception rooms on this floor.

I've spent more time in my father-in-law's house throughout my marriage than I did my father's. Mainly because Max didn't give two shits about hiding his handiwork from Salvatore. In fact, he seemed proud to display my scars for his appreciation. It was in vain though—Salvatore never acknowledged them outwardly.

I associate this house with hopelessness. There was no salvation here, only a momentary reprieve while Max sought his father's approval of my debasement.

And here I am again, still at the mercy of a De Luca. Only this time, I'm not the only one on their knees.

As I take in the scene, I find my husband restrained and being forced to kneel at his father's feet. Salvatore is screaming at him, face red and consumed with rage. I should feel pleased to see him brought to heel, but I know every humiliation Salvatore serves to his son will be meted out on me. From my position behind them, I'm relieved Max can't see me, but I know that won't last.

"What the fuck are you playing at? You're thirty-five years old and I'm still cleaning up your fucking messes. What's so fucking special about the Bianchi whore that the minute she's gone, you're out there slaughtering surrogates?"

"I did what you asked. I killed her and her fucking father. What the fuck does it matter what I do now?" Max spits out, brimming with a venomous anger.

"It matters when you're out of control and leaving bodies at a rate we can't cover up." He grabs Max by the hair and wrenches his head up, yanking him around to make sure Max can see me. "You're such a fucking disappointment. With all the years of practice, when it came down to it, you couldn't even kill her properly."

As our eyes meet, my body freezes in terror. The look in his eyes when he realises he failed—that I'm still alive —is not what I was expecting. He's not angry, he's not disappointed. He's fucking happy. His posture relaxes as relief visibly rolls through him, triggering a shiver that wracks my body from head to toe.

It's then I know if he ever gets his hands on me again, I will be lost to him forever. He doesn't want to destroy me; he wants to keep me.

The fear is overwhelming, and my eyes glisten as I realise the two fates before me. Death at Salvatore's hands, or life at Max's.

I will choose Salvatore. No matter what he does to me, it would be a lifetime quicker than anything Max would do.

He's been watching his son's reaction to me, and he sneers before slapping the odd expression of awe off Max's face. "Her death was the price you were supposed to pay for your incompetence. No whore is worth more than our legacy."

Max starts struggling against the two men holding him down, roaring incoherently like a man possessed.

"Silence," Salvatore bellows as his men grapple Max back to his knees, face pushed into the floor, one with a knee between his shoulder blades.

"If it wasn't for you, none of this would have happened. If you had an ounce of self-control, Mateo would never have made a move against us. You jeopardised our entire fucking operation because you couldn't keep your hands off of one woman. I could have spared her and simply killed Mateo—but look at you. You're pathetic. If you need her to control yourself, I question if you deserve the honour of being a De Luca," Salvatore rants, every word dripping with venom. The disdain for his son's actions is unmistakable.

Salvatore stands up, shaking off his outburst, righting his tie and brushing his lapels like he's trying to wipe off his disappointment at his son. He paces towards a wooden box on the mantelpiece beside me and flips the lid. Max struggles and wrenches his head to the side to watch his father's performance, eyes flaring wide when he sees the gleaming edge of the knife blade while Salvatore turns the dagger over, inspecting it with a cruel smirk.

"Tell me, son, how will it feel knowing that my knife will succeed where yours failed?"

Salvatore chuckles and brings the tip of the blade to my neck, applying enough pressure for it to nick the surface and allow a trickle of blood to run down my collarbone, over the swell of my breast only to be absorbed into the satin binding of the corset. I try to stifle my heavy breathing, limiting the heaving of my chest to avoid the knife going any further. For a moment, I contemplate jerking forward, taking control of my own end, but as I do, I think of the men who risked so much to save me, and all I want is to stay alive long enough to get Nico back to them.

My attention is pulled out of my thoughts by the persistent low growl emanating from Max. I see the moment Max De Luca disappears and the monster I know so well takes control. Salvatore has underestimated his son and will pay the price. He points the knife towards his son in warning and pulls me further in front of him, like a human shield.

Max is free before his guards even realise they're in trouble. Throwing them off him before a blade I'm intimately familiar with, usually concealed within his belt buckle, makes short work of their carotid arteries, leaving Max free to charge forward at his father.

It's like Max was playing a part, waiting for his father to show his hand before striking.

"I'm done prostrating myself at your feet, old man.

Your legacy is meaningless to me. But mine? Mine will be a beautiful carnage. All who oppose me will be destroyed, starting with you."

In that instant, I realise any hope of a quick death at Salvatore's hands is gone, as I feel the blade drop away from my neck.

I'm pushed to the floor, my skull smacking the floorboards hard, as my guards jump to defend Salvatore. My vision blurs and all I can make out is a tangled flurry of limbs rolling in front of me, interspersed with grunts and the occasional flash of blades and splashes of crimson.

As I scramble to avoid the jumble of bodies, I try to stand, struggling against the pain lancing through my ankle.

The thuds and crashes die down and I try to make my eyes focus, but as soon as I hear his voice, I know my fate. A hand grips my hair and I'm forced to meet his gaze. As he drags me up, the terror eclipses any pain I feel.

"I've missed you, *principessa*. No one compares to you. You're my Cinderella. No one wears the glass slipper like you do."

The bile rises in my throat. No matter how much I will my subconscious into action, I don't slip away. I stay here in the moment with him, the bloodshed and carnage devastating. There are five bodies in the centre of the room, all dispatched with alarming efficiency. The sheer volume of blood as they each exsanguinate is unlike anything I've ever witnessed.

Admittedly, it was messy when I killed Carlo, but this is different. I sit and stare as the pool of blood creeps with menace across the floorboards, staining the wood as it travels. The shiny surface breaks in places where the old floorboards have gaps, and I can hear the macabre pattering as the blood drips through the cracks. All I smell is death. So overpowering, I can feel it coating my tongue with a grim metallic aftertaste.

As much as I try, I cannot subdue my reaction when my eyes come to rest on Salvatore's body. I wretch and heave, vomiting at the sight of his tongue, severed and discarded on the floor by his body.

"I hope he burns in hell, tortured for all eternity, screaming out his agony." Max hisses, forcing out a maniacal laugh. "You're not usually so squeamish, princess."

He drags me across the floor, away from the slaughter, taking a seat in one of the high-backed armchairs by the fireplace. Yanking me down, I squeal as I'm forced to kneel at his feet. He covers my mouth with one hand as he uses the other to retrieve his phone to make a call.

"Get to the compound. The old man is dead, and I just got promoted. You report to me now." That's all he says before he hangs up and places another call. "I need at least twelve men inside for a sweep and clean-up. Leave four on the perimeter."

He stares straight ahead, lost in his own thoughts. The smile that spreads across his features is grotesque and ever-widening. I can see every thought that dances through his mind as he processes exactly what he's just done. Not only is he free of any limitations his father placed on him, he is now the most powerful man across both families. His influence is absolute.

I'm held captive by the right hand of the devil, and there will be no escaping him.

This cannot be my fate.

There has to be a way.

I have survived him before. I'll have to do it again.

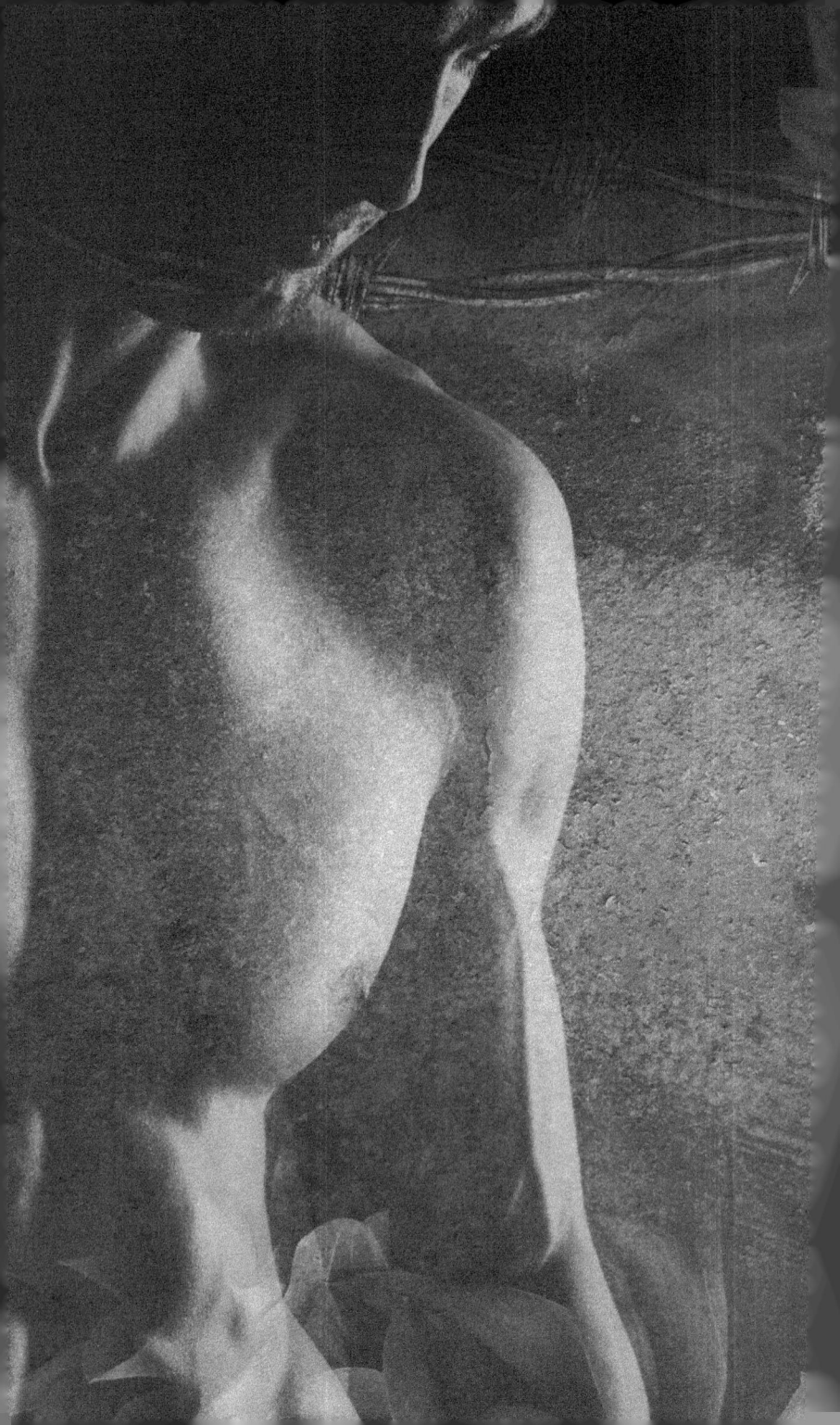

CHAPTER THIRTY-EIGHT

SINCLAIR

It's taken too fucking long for the cavalry to arrive, but fuck me, they arrived. The De Lucas won't see this fucking coming.

Manny and Stefano got here ten minutes ago, and they've brought every loyal Bianchi with them. Turns out that's a shit-ton of people and they're all incensed. The most surprising members of the crowd are not only Marco's son, but his daughter. Luc and Etta are standing beside Stefano, faces stricken with emotion. It's obvious that they're both ashamed and enraged.

I watch as Benedict approaches them with caution. I'm poised, ready to jump in if need be. They didn't approve of how their father treated Benedict, but given their father's position, they couldn't speak out or they would have faced the same fate. They did what they could. I don't think Marco ever knew his daughter had called Nico the night his dad shot him. She risked a lot to save Benedict's life.

They exchange a few words before they lean in and hold each other. I hope that whatever happens, Benny gets some of his family back tonight. Assuming we all survive.

We have more support than I could have hoped for, but an all-out attack on a Syndicate leader is crazy. Putting our surprising numbers aside, another bonus for us is that no one in that compound will be expecting it. It's a civil war between the families. It's unprecedented.

But is it unsurprising? What the fuck did Salvatore expect? They killed Mateo, and they infiltrated our leadership. They have betrayed any trust that was built. The Syndicate is *dead*.

Stefano is heading my way and marching behind him is the last person I expect to see.

"No fucking way you're going in with us," I say as Doc Em comes to a stop in front of me.

"Of course not, you prick. I'm here to triage any casualties and help when you get Aurora and Nico out of there."

I cast her a dubious glance, and she holds up her hands.

"Scouts honour. I'll be in the van with my father's crew backing me up. Besides, this fucking guard dog you sicked on me is making it really hard to have any fun at the moment." She cocks her head sideways at Stefano, who remains expressionless, but I swear I see a glint in his eye flaring to life at her bratty attitude.

"Less talk, more getting in the van, Katerina," Stefano says.

She's already climbing in as she says, "That's Doctor Mancini to you, old man."

"So, she's glad of the protection, then?" I say, unable to hold back the snigger at his expense.

"I'm not above shooting you, Sinclair," Doc Em threatens.

"Understood."

We walk over to Enzo, who's got a satellite view of a map up on his phone, pointing at various points of entry to the people he's designated as team leads. With so many Bianchi capos compromised, Stefano charged Enzo with picking people from the ranks. It wasn't difficult. We have enough information collected on the rank and file to know who's got the best skills. It's far easier now the capo's egos are not part of the equation.

Enzo has given me a team of eight to lead through one of the back entrances to the basement. Our focus is to find our people and destroy any weapons caches. I'll have Luc and Etta on my team. They've never shied away from getting their hands dirty, and their skills with firearms will be an asset. Benedict will be taking a team to take out the front gates. He's working with whatever provisions we have left over from the club earlier, but if I know Benny at all, it will be enough. He's well-known for over-preparing when it comes to pyrotechnics.

Zo is handing out the earpieces Stefano brought, and I raise an eyebrow at him. "Are you finally moving into the twenty-first century?"

"Fuck off, Sin. There are too many bodies on the ground not to upgrade communications."

"It's about time, you fucking luddite."

Enzo calls for everyone's attention and starts the final go command. "Everyone knows where they need to be. Gather up your teams and get in position. When you hear the gate blow, that's your signal. Make sure you're on comms." Enzo pauses and looks around at everyone. They've all stopped and are hanging on his every word, including Stefano and Manny, who are showing him a level of respect that's unprecedented with any of us bastards. It's jarring, and I can see the bob of Zo's throat as the recognition takes him by surprise.

"I want to commend you all for your loyalty. This move against the Bianchis is a threat to everything we have built. The De Lucas have woefully underestimated who they're dealing with, and I thank each one of you for taking a stand tonight."

A flurry of nodding heads return Zo's sentiment in the sea of loyal faces.

"You know what to do. Move out."

My TEAM IS CROUCHED in the alley behind the De Luca compound, waiting for the signal. It doesn't take any more than ten minutes before we all hear a deafening explosion. By the sounds of it, Benedict hit them with a missile, but I know that can't be right because Zo made him get rid of his RPG-7 rocket launcher. Zo's gonna be pissed if he didn't.

I nod at the driver of the van at the end of the alley. They floor it and head straight at the reinforced gates in front of us. We're not lucky enough for them to buckle on the first try, and despite the damage to the front end, our driver gets enough momentum on the second attempt to bust them clear open.

As the van reverses, I hold up my arm and then flick my wrist for the team to follow me. "Team three in," I confirm to Zo.

"Ten-four," he quickly replies.

I see the stairs to the basement and we all move quickly, careful to look out for any stray guards. Gunfire rings out from above and to our left—four of us keep going as the other six in my team take defensive positions and start laying down cover fire. Our attackers are shooting from the second floor. They can't get a good angle on us through the windows, so the rest of the team follows us to the basement door.

A swift kick from Luc and we're in. We're in a vulnerable position at the end of a long, narrow corridor with many doors on either side. Opening the door closest to us, I find a small empty storage room piled high with logs. I signal for two people to take up sentry here to cover the corridor and stairwell.

Leading the rest, we start a systematic sweep and clear the rooms on this level. It's not until we get to the last room that we find anything.

"Oh shit," I say, realising from the clothes that the slumped body on the far wall is Nico. "Etta, Luc, get your asses over here and help me move him."

We roll him over and see that aside from a hole in his

leg, he seems to be injury-free. He's lost a lot of blood, though. I tighten the belt acting as a tourniquet, but it won't hold. I'd bet that's the reason for his current state of unconsciousness.

Looking around, I see nothing better I can replace the strap of leather with, so I lay down my weapon and pull out a knife from my utility vest, keeping it sheathed. Wrapping the ends of the belt around the knife, I then twist till it's tight enough and tuck the handle under the taught leather to hold it. I let out a sigh of relief as it holds fast.

I tap on the in-ear receiver. "Enzo, we need cover across the rear of the property. We found Nico, but I need to get him out to Doc Em now. I have enough to carry him and cover our asses, but I'd like back-up."

"Sending you a team now, get moving. Any sign of Aurora?"

"She's not here, but we've cleared the basement."

"Can you close it off, make sure no one else gets through down there?"

I pause as I have an idea... a terrible idea. "Maybe..."

"What do you mean, *maybe?!*"

"I could torch it. There's a shit-ton of kindling and firewood down here, but until you find Aurora, that's a fucking awful idea."

Zo is quiet on the other end of the comms for longer than makes me comfortable, but eventually he's back. "Get out of there. I sent you back up and I'm sending Benny's team to your current location to wait for my signal before torching the place."

That is a much better plan. Let the pyromaniac play with matches. We're out of here.

With the size of him, it takes four men to carry Nico. This fucker is reducing his bench press from now on. With three in front, and me, Etta and Luc at the rear, we head up the stairs, into the open.

As soon as we reach the top of the stairs, all fucking hell breaks loose. We're caught in a crossfire, and I can't tell which side is friendly, so we have no other option than to run full-pelt across the courtyard to the van waiting in the alley for us.

Losing two of our team in the front within three strides, they drop like stones with headshots taking them out instantly.

"Fuck, Zo, we're sitting ducks out here!" I scream into the receiver.

"I'm on it," is the only response I get. I'm about to scream at him some more before I see him burst out of a window on the second floor and jump down on the first-floor roof. He slides straight down on his front for cover, before taking aim and shooting. He takes a breath and repeats. For every shot, there's a sickening crunch and thud as each enemy shooter falls from the opposite rooftop.

Left only with friendlies in the courtyard, we pick up Nico and haul ass to the waiting van. Throwing open the doors, we find a sheepish-looking Doc Em in the back, and I shake my head while also laughing. "Thank fuck you're here, but you're on your own when Stefano finds out you went rogue."

"Fucking coward," she says and winks at me before

banging on the side of the van. "Close it up and get moving. I need to get him out of here, now."

I slam the doors shut and turn back to the compound. Any relief I feel at knowing Nico is safe is dwarfed by the gut-wrenching anguish I feel knowing Aurora is still in there. I have to get back in there.

"Eyes open, people, and follow me. Our secondary objective is to thin out their defences. If it shoots at us, we shoot back. Be accurate and don't die."

CHAPTER THIRTY-NINE

ENZO

Where the fuck is she?

The basement is clear, and we've taken out most of the exterior hostiles. I was doing a sweep of the first floor when Sin called for backup. I'm back in the main house and flying down the stairs before the last body falls off the roof. This place is a fucking maze.

Calling out over the comms for their location, I catch up with my team in a reception room at the front of the house by the front door. I have four of Manny's men with me, none of which I've worked with before, but I've heard good things.

When we reach the third room... *holy fuck*. It's a massacre.

There's a heap of bodies—skewed limbs branching off of prone torsos—piled like rag dolls on the hearth, a carpet of blood beneath them. Signalling for my team to watch the door, I edge around the glassy crimson pool and grab a poker from the fireplace. I can't get close enough without risking skating through the viscera, so I poke the top body with the iron tool, rolling it over to confirm my suspicions.

Salvatore De Luca's body tumbles to the floor with a dull thud, followed by a thick squelching sound as it disturbs the congealed gore.

I can hear the collective gasp of shock from the men behind me, and I can't help but join them. Shit just got a whole lot worse if the sick-fuck that is Max De Luca is now in charge.

Please, for the love of God, say he doesn't have her.

I turn around a fraction too late to warn my awestruck team of the men coming into the room behind them. Diving behind the pile of corpses, I reach for my weapon, but my angle is wrong, and I can't lay down any cover fire. I can only listen as one by one they drop to the floor, adding to the surrounding carnage.

The voice that rings out makes my blood run cold. "Bring him here."

Hands band around my arms and haul me up and present me to Manny-motherfucking-Ferella.

"*You traitorous cunt,*" I scream, only to be silenced by the butt of his gun.

"You can shut the fuck up right now, you illegitimate bastard. I've tolerated your inferior pedigree polluting our ranks for far too *fucking* long."

He backhands me before spitting in my face. Fighting against the vice-like grips holding me back, I nearly succeed in wrenching myself free before he pulls his gun on me and presses it firmly into the fleshy part of my cheek so hard I can feel a pounding ache in my teeth as the barrel pushes into them.

"Bring him."

I'm dragged behind Manny further into the house. Where the fuck are the other teams? How many are loyal to this prick? Can't be many—if any—Bianchis if he just slaughtered his own men. I've always known Manny was an old-school underboss, but I would never have thought he stood against Mateo.

He drags me into a less gore-strewn sitting room and sits down on the most uncomfortable-looking couch I've ever seen. It looks like it's stuffed with concrete, but the pompous twat makes a show of relaxing, throwing his arms over the back of the sofa and puffing out his chest like some kind of preening peacock.

"You really fucked me, Enzo." I keep my face blank and let him continue his diatribe. "We had a solid plan, cut out all the weak links and make The Syndicate a shining example of how an organisation should run. Then you and your fucking mongrels had to get involved and accelerated the fucking timeline. You've incited a civil war when it could have been an efficient takeover."

He nods to one of the goons behind me, who kicks out my knees and pushes me down, leaving me in a heap at Manny's feet. I grind my teeth, livid to be prostrated before a man with so little honour.

Years he served at Mateo's side, and he sold him out. It makes me nauseous. I can taste the bile rising in my throat and it's all I can do to bite it back down.

"Why show your cards now?"

Manny stands, wrenching my head up off the floor with one hand, only to kick me full across the jaw. I feel the sharp pain as my jaw threatens to dislocate and I have to smother the scream that desperately wants to escape. I won't give this fucker the satisfaction.

"You wiped out every fucking Bianchi ally I had! I've had to assume my new role earlier than planned. You've created fucking chaos and now the fate of this organisation rests is being influenced by a whore and a band of impure bastards?" Manny's words are brimming with a hatred so strong I feel every one of them like a blow to the body.

I spit out the blood that's pooling in my mouth, making sure to cover his pretentious loafers. I can't help but smile as he swears and fusses over the mess. It's the small things in life that make you happy.

My smile is short-lived as I see Max appear at the door, men towing Aurora behind her. She wrestles herself free and half runs, half limps to my side, crouching down to check on me.

"I'm good," I force out through the searing pain in my jaw, hoping I'm muted enough for no one to hear the next part. "Has he hurt you?"

She shakes her head and various hands grab us both and pull us to our feet, restraining us as Max approaches.

"Interesting," he says, tone practically dripping with venom as he addresses Aurora. "It seems my wife has picked up a fondness for strays."

He grabs me by the hair and jerks me down to meet the knife in his other hand.

"I hope you didn't get too attached. Mongrels like this only ever end up getting put down."

Grunting, I try to lean back, away from the blade that he's now pressing at my skin, coaxing out a thin stream of blood that I can feel slip down my throat beneath my collar. I try to shake my head, to tell her to keep quiet, but the blade only slips further around my neck, lengthening the cut.

Aurora gasps and cries out, "What the fuck do you want, Max?"

This grabs his attention, and he pushes me back into the hold of his men.

"What do I want? What do *I* want?" He wanders around the room with a façade of nonchalance, twirling his dagger playfully. He looks as dangerous as he does maniacal.

"You know, honestly, there's not a lot I'm wanting for right now. My wife is back from the dead, I just got one hell of a promotion, and my biggest problem is about to be executed. As days go, this is a pretty fucking good one. It literally couldn't have worked out better if I planned it. All thanks to the monumental fuck-up that is you, my dear Enzo. I might as well have brought you in on this from the start. Fast-tracked every one of my plans, although you have halved my forces by kicking off a fucking civil war."

With my arms held tightly behind my back, I cannot stop the right hook that batters my already fragile jaw.

"You were working with Manny against your father," I spit out.

"Of course I was. Admittedly, we hadn't planned on

ousting Daddy dearest quite so soon, but as soon as Mateo made a move against him and he starting fucking about with my plans for the future, the timeline had to be adjusted. Honestly, I never actually planned on killing the old cunt."

He walks over to Aurora and runs his hand down her face, between her breasts, and grips her hip violently. "But the minute he ordered your death, he sealed his fate. I never should have followed that order. I thought you were a necessary sacrifice in our master plan, but I was wrong. No one compares to you, *principessa*. They are all weak imitations, and I'm never letting you go again."

I see the fear in her eyes, and I lurch forward only to be wrangled to the floor and held down.

"You're a sick and depraved fuck, Max," she growls, but he smiles back at her, eyes glazed appearing almost lost to his frantic glee at having her back. His joy fills me with dread.

I have to find some way to get her out of here. Fuck knows if there's anyone left to help us. I don't know if Sinclair and his team have left with Nico. My team's dead. Benny's is downstairs waiting on my signal to torch the place and I have no fucking clue how many others Manny took out before he got to me.

Fuck.

"You killed Isa," she grinds out before spitting in his face and I hold my breath as she taunts the monster. I feel like my heart has been carved out. The monster I've hunted for years. The man who stole everything from my brother is the same monster who wants to take her from me—from us. He can't have her.

With a depraved laugh that grates down my spine, "Finally figure that out, did you? My-my, that will only make this so much more fun going forward. How does it feel knowing you survived what that weak mongrel-fucking-whore couldn't? She deserved everything she got for fucking that Moretti half-breed." Max grabs Aurora by the throat. "I will punish you for betraying me. For seeking salvation with these worthless fucking half-breeds."

He nods, and on his command, they level a barrage of kicks and punches at me before bringing me back up to my knees. Two men hold me as the others maintain a continuous assault, fists landing hard on my torso, kicks catching me across my back, making my kidneys howl in protest. After a few minutes, the first rib buckles. That's when I let out the first cry, unable to hold back any longer. I lose track of time, trying desperately to maintain focus so that I can find any opportunity to get Aurora to safety.

I only realise the extent of my injuries when Aurora's screams start to drown out sounds of the punches.

"Stop, please, stop!" Her terrified cries wrench me back into my body, and I wish they didn't. There is only agony, and it cuts me to the bone as I know I won't be able to help her. Max will kill me, and she'll be condemned to a living-hell with him.

Blood swells in my mouth. I can't swallow it quickly enough and it overflows from my lip, cascading down my chin and splashing on the floor below. It's absorbed into the rug and obscures the intricate pattern.

As my eyes lose focus, the carpet's motif fading in my vision, I hear gunfire and it snaps my gaze to the door.

I'm shoved to the floor as all the bodies behind me seek cover behind the sofa and high-back chairs. From the corner of my eye, I track Max and he drags Aurora with him behind a desk in the corner.

It's chaos.

It takes every ounce of strength left in me to haul myself across the floor towards the desk. I can't seek cover, but I look up and spot Stefano with a large team of men distracting them and drawing their fire. I realise this is my chance. I nod in Stefano's direction and stand, turning and throwing myself over the desk at Max.

Every muscle in my body feels like it's screaming in protest, but I have no choice but to continue. Landing on him, I reach straight for the gun but turn to Aurora, now thrown free of his grip as he scrambles to defend himself. I scream the only thing I can, hoping she does as I ask.

"Run."

She reaches for the gun, trying to help me, but Max sees and tries to aim at her. My strength is fading fast. I need her safe. I need her gone. It doesn't fucking matter what happens to me. I lurch to the side, forcing her out of our way.

"I said *run!* Fucking run, *mia guerrierotta.*" It's a desperate roar, and I see the moment she understands. Her face pales and her brow furrows, sorrow etched into every anguished crease of her.

She is *my* little warrior, and I will sacrifice myself for her a thousand times over if it means she escapes Max De Luca.

Tears streak her face. She tips her chin in a nod and hauls herself over the desk, running for the door. Stefano's men all start shooting, covering her escape, as she hurtles towards them and bursts out of the room and into their protection.

The sense of relief overwhelms me, and all my strength evaporates. Max finally overpowers me, pistol whipping and rolling me off him then leaving me in a heap on the ground. I try to pick myself up, but my limbs refuse to obey me.

In a last desperate attempt to help her, I scream over the din, "Get her the fuck out of here!"

Through the legs of the desk, I watch Stefano drag her away, struggling in his hold and screaming for me. I hold on firmly to the feeling of comfort, knowing that she is free of Max, as I slip away into the oppressive darkness that engulfs me.

CHAPTER FORTY

AURORA

"Let me go, we have to go back. We can't leave him!" I scream, but no matter my words, Stefano holds me tight as he drags me back out of the house.

As we approach the door, we take fire from four men thundering down the central staircase. Stefano's men are out in the open, caught in the crossfire between Max's men.

We have no choice but to keep going and throw open the front door. As he drags me across the front courtyard as the gunfire continues. Through the open door, I witness our defenders being gunned down as they try to retreat through the front door.

"They're *sitting fucking ducks*, Stefano. We have to help them."

He says nothing, but I feel the moment our luck changes and turn my head to see Benedict running around the side of the building, a team of six heavily-armed people trailing behind him.

"Benny, you have to help. He has Zo. Max has Zo in there." My tone is shrill, and desperation wraps itself around every word.

I see him blanch as my words register a moment before an explosion rings out and the entire house starts to shake and rattle with the force of the blast. I see a soft glow of flames and I sigh in relief as two of Stefano's team manage to escape through the front door before the blaze engulfs the hallway, blocking the exit.

Realising he's just blocked our only way of getting to Zo, I scream, "What the fuck did you do!?" Wrenching myself free of Stefano's iron grasp, I jump forward to beat my clenched fists against Benny's chest.

His face is a mask of devastation—all he can do is repeat the same words over and over again, "I'm sorry, I'm so sorry. He told me to. Zo told me to blow it. I'm so fucking sorry."

"What the fuck do you mean he told you to?"

"He was on comms. He told me to blow it. He said he was clear," Benny explains, his eyes searching for my understanding and finding nothing.

Tears flood my eyes, betraying me and fury consumes me. Fury at Enzo for sacrificing himself for me. We need to go back—we need to see if he survived. I make a run for it, back toward the building. My feet barely make it to the first porch step before arms wrap around my waist and I'm dragged backwards.

"We can't get in that way, Rory. The whole place is

coming down," Benedict shouts over the roar of the flames.

The fire is licking the door frame. There's no way through. While the logical part of my brain knows Benny is right, every part of my soul screams that I can't give up on Enzo. I struggle against them, determined to find another way.

"We can't just leave him..." But they don't let me go and I slump into their grip, levelling them both with my gaze. "I will never forgive you for this."

Stefano and Benny's stricken faces say everything. They're choosing me over Enzo—and I hate them for it.

"Enzo would never forgive us if we didn't save you," Stefano says, holding my gaze and forcing me to face the truth of his words.

I'm pulled to the front gates, away from the rapidly growing inferno, I can see movement behind the windows. I'm filled with a hope that grips my heart and threatens to stop it from beating. The window shatters and a dining room chair bursts through it, crashing to the ground and splintering.

Max and his men climb out, lifting their guns once their feet hit the floor, forcing us to take cover behind what's left of the incinerated front gates. I watch as he turns back to the house and signals to someone.

Moments later, I watch as they toss Enzo's abused body out of the window, putting on a display meant for us all to see. He's not moving. All I can make out are dappled crimson flourishes of blood. Lifting his gun, Max takes aim and unloads what's left of his clip. Shot after shot rings out and I'm blinded by my tears.

The scream that leaves me burns so deep that it incinerates my soul.

The pain. The rage. The hatred. They're indescribable.

Max looks up and smiles. It's a smile I know so well. The unbridled joy he gets when he knows he's broken someone.

When his men open fire at us, I'm dragged away as we retreat. We're too evenly matched for either side to come out of this confrontation well, and the fire will attract too much attention from the emergency services. We have to leave. We have no choice, but I hate it.

With every step we take away from Enzo, my rage builds. Burning wildly within me, blazing an inferno through my core.

I feel like I'm slipping away again, only this time I'm not driven by fear or self-preservation. Fury engulfs me, making me lose myself in a torrent of emotion that will consume me.

When we reach the van, I drag myself into the passenger seat, and I close my eyes. I don't have the first fucking clue who's driving, nor do I fucking care.

I'm lost in a fucking sea of peripheral noise. Completely detached from reality, floating over it, not registering locations and time. I'm vaguely aware of people getting out of the van, continuing back to the safe house. Being led into the living room, and many angry people yelling around me.

I know people try to talk to me, but my throat is too clogged with emotions to allow to choke out my response. When everyone else has worn themselves out, a heavy silence descends, making the air thick and redolent with grief.

I step forward from the grim post I had assumed by the fireplace and look around the room, finally cognisant of my audience.

Sinclair stands behind me to my left, watching over me like a sentinel, guarding my back. In front of me are Nico and Benny. Nico looks haggard, but better than the last time I saw him. He's laid out on the sofa, leg elevated with a rolling IV pole behind him carrying multiple bags, both red and clear.

Doc Em is hunched over the kitchen island, perched on a stool, Stefano behind her, rubbing her shoulders with a tenderness I don't expect. Katerina's face is nothing but shock and sorrow. I've never seen her look so... so unsure, so lost.

There are others here, ones I vaguely recognise as the people that risked everything to come for Nico and me— to avenge my father.

I clear my throat and address them all.

"Salvatore De Luca betrayed The Syndicate. Massimo De Luca murdered my father and butchered my sister. Manny Ferella deceived us all and poisoned our ranks." I pause to cast my gaze across every eye that meets mine. "We have declared war on the De Lucas. We have dissolved any partnership the Bianchis had with them. Salvatore De Luca is dead, and his psychopathic progeny is under the delusion that he is in charge now."

There's a rumble of voices and I hold up a hand to silence them.

"There is only one course of action. They will pay for

what they've done, and we will be the ones to make them. We are motherfucking Bianchis, and we will reign down fucking hellfire if that's what it takes, but not one of those disloyal cunts will be left breathing by the time we are done." I'm met with a sea of nodding faces.

"Stefano, I'm kicking you and everyone who doesn't live here out. You and five of your best will report back here first thing in the morning to organise our ranks and start working on a plan. We are fucking restructuring and if I find even so much as one voice among them that objects to taking orders from the rightful Bianchi heir, I will have them sent to the De Lucas in tiny fucking pieces. Am I fucking understood?"

"Yes, Ms. Bianchi."

I nod and he hurries everyone out until it's just my men, him and Katerina, left. Stefano doesn't say a word. Simply wraps his arms around me in a hug that feels like more than I can handle. I feel everything I'm desperately trying to block right now, so I take a step back and nod, watching as he backs away towards the door.

Doc Em steps forward next. "You call me if Nico's condition changes. He lost a lot of blood, but it was straight through. I've stitched him up, he should be okay until I come back in the morning." She also hugs me, and I wish she wouldn't. I'm so fucking close to crumbling, but if I'm really going to do this, I need everyone to believe the front I'm projecting right now. She goes to say something else, but when she catches the look in my eye, she seems to recognise it for the silent plea it is and turns to leave.

I nod as Stefano adds, "I've left my personal guards

on you tonight. They will remain on the perimeter until we work out more permanent protection for you."

It takes everything I have left in me to remain standing as they leave and the moment the door closes, I collapse in a heap, nothing but a mess of tears and hopelessness. I don't hit the ground as Sin is right there, sweeping me up and taking me to the same sofa as Nico.

Sinclair holds me as I fall apart, and a stream of incoherent words come tumbling out of me. Begging for Zo to be here, sobbing at the injustice, screaming out in rage at the vengeance I will visit on Max. I feel my emotions reflected in every other heart here and I feel comfort wrapped up here in this moment with them. A collective pain that only we understand.

Eventually, I have no more tears left to shed and find myself wrapped in a tangle of limbs. Sinclair holding me, Benny's head in my lap, Nico's head on my shoulder.

"I'm so sorry," I heave out. "If it wasn't for me, he'd still be here."

"This isn't your fault, Aurora," Nico growls out.

"We would save you again in a heartbeat, *colibrì*."

"You shouldn't. The life of some pathetic mafia princess isn't worth more than a man like Enzo. He was one of the most honourable men I ever met. It was an uneven trade." My words are laboured as tears threaten to fill my eyes and I struggle to catch my breath.

"You're not a princess, phoenix. You're our fucking queen," Nico says, turning my face to his and brushing his lips to mine. I can taste my tears on his lips. It's a sweet agony.

"Anyone of us would sacrifice ourselves for you. It's not your place to deny us that honour," Sinclair adds.

We stay wrapped up together until the sun fades and the room darkens. I wake up hours later, nestled in the warmth of the men I don't deserve. The rays of the morning sunrise dance across the room, highlighting that the world has turned, life has gone on, and there's always another day.

But he is gone.

The light is meaningless to me.

I am lost in the darkness.

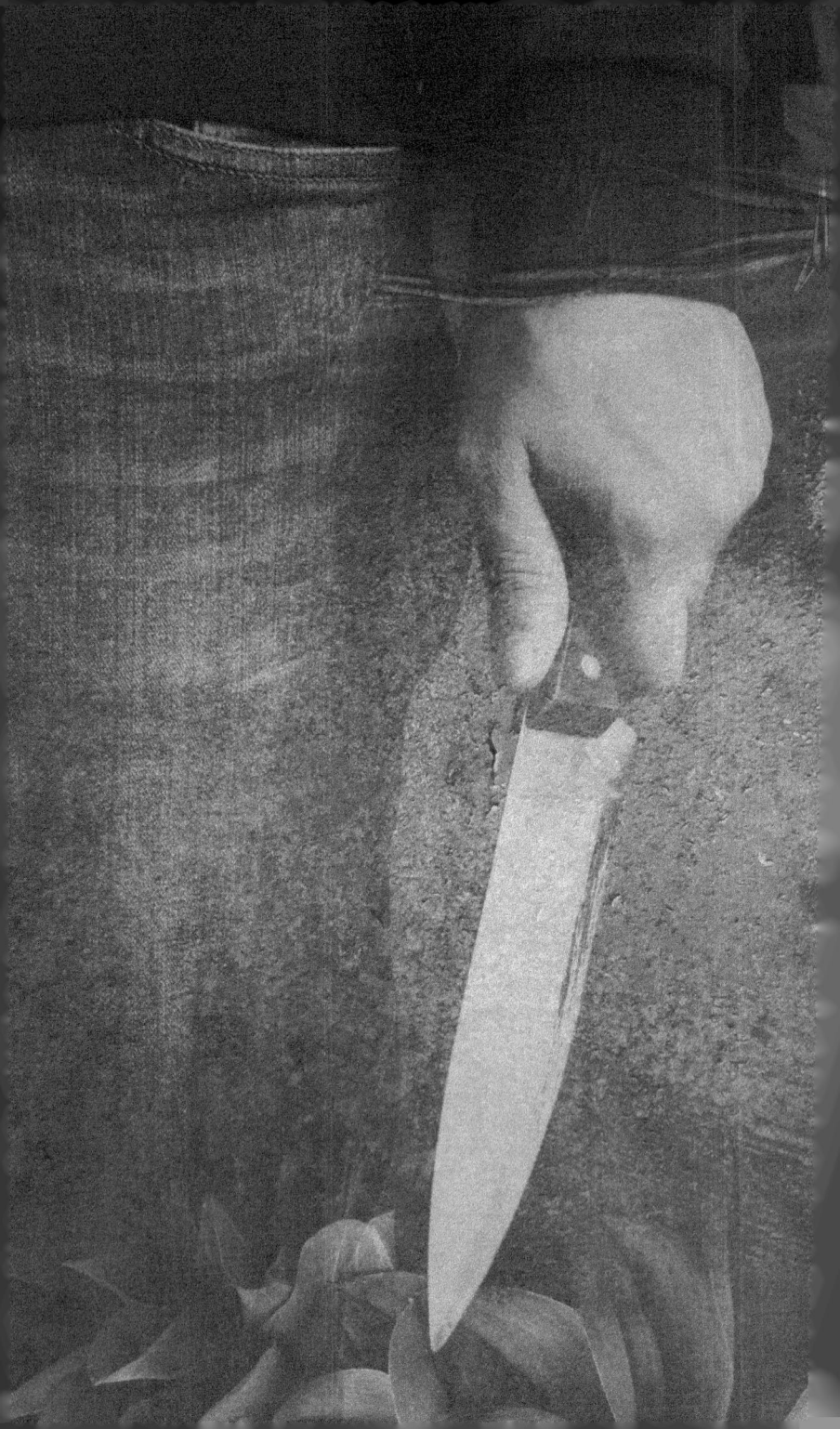

END OF PART TWO

FOUR WEEKS LATER...

I had watched her closely as we came out of the house. The terror etched into her face was so delicious I could practically taste it. However, my pleasure in her pain was fleeting when I realised the cause. She wasn't terrified of me; she was scared for him.

When I called for my men to toss him out, her eyes followed him, not me. When I aimed the gun, I watched as her terror morphed into horror. When I pulled the trigger, her agony was absolute.

The sound of her soul shattering should have been exquisite. But knowing that her pain was driven by the loss of him felt like a hollow victory.

I take solace knowing that her pain is torturing her, at least until I can get my hands on her again. In the meantime, I will simply have to make do with the toy at my disposal.

Opening the basement door, I descend the steps and feel the glaze of serenity wash over me when I see he's exactly where I left him—standing in front of the St. Andrew's Cross, stripped of his clothing and his pride, tethered in barbed wire at his exposed thighs, biceps, and torso. It's secure but loose enough to ensure that every time he sways from exhaustion, he tears into his own flesh.

His body is dripping a tapestry of crimson, masterful enough to rival Jackson Pollock. I approach and run my index finger through the gore, wiping a clear path and exposing the other scars I've left on him. Transfixed by my own artistry I know now why I aimed wide.

He's nearly as perfect as her. In sparing him I've gifted myself with her ideal replacement. He drifts away like she did. He's here to play with, but his mind is gone. An empty vessel I can fill with agony. Every day I have visited a fresh torment on him, ones she always withstood with grace, and he has done the same.

But it's not the same. He doesn't make the right sounds.

My father was right about one thing: I can't be caught playing with toys when I have a legacy to build. A new legacy, not his—mine. Enzo will make the perfect surrogate until I can rid myself of the resistance to De Luca rule and get her back.

Oh, I wonder if he can take the cattle prod?

Only one way to find out.

Need to find out what happens next?
Continue with *Brutal Queen*, the conclusion to the *Broken & Brutal* duet and book 2 in The Bianchi Chronicles

THE BIANCHI CHRONICLES

Novels

Broken & Brutal Duet

1. Broken Princess

2. Brutal Queen

Interconnected Standalones

3. Fierce Protector

4. Wicked Guardian

—✳——✳——✳——✳——✳——✳—

Novellas

0.5. Axe To Grind (Nico & Benedict's First Date)

ABOUT THE AUTHOR

I live in the south of England with my real life book-husband—AKA Mr Bennett—and our two *delightfully* unruly boys. I'm usually found in my writing cave arguing with my characters trying to convince them to follow the outline I spent weeks planning.

For the latest news and to join my mailing list check out my website www.laurabennettauthor.com/links

ACKNOWLEDGEMENTS

There are so many people I need to thank here. I can't start with anyone other than my husband who not only supported my hair-brained notion that I could write a book, but also actively encouraged me at every turn. Listened to all my rants and rambles about misbehaving characters, pacing and plots, and didn't complain when I ignored all his suggestions. There's no one in this world who has my back like he does and I cannot thank him enough. I love you! *More, most, bestiemost.*

There's no way I'm not mentioning Sally here. You're not a #bookbestie, you're quite simply a bestie. I would never have had the confidence to finish this without you in my corner. You make my day on the regular and I love that I found you. But please if you could ask your family if they'd consider moving to within a 20 mile radius of my house that would be great. If not, I'm implementing a mandatory writing retreat in an exotic location each year. I am so grateful for the time you spent hashing out plots with me and reviewing my work. Your insights and suggestions were amazing.

Daisy Jane. You found me on BookTok, you trusted me with your work and you inspired me to be able to do this. I'm so privileged to have met you and cannot thank you enough for your support. I am honoured to have you as a friend. I thank you so much for all your amazing feedback and taking the time to read my work. It meant the world to me.

Sarah Baker. Another one who lives entirely too far away! I love that a comment on a TikTok brought you into my life and that I have the honour of calling you a friend now. You and your crazy-angsty MMC's have tormented me this last year and I've loved every word of your writing. Thank you so much for the time you've taken answering my random texts and reading my work. Your comments brought a smile to my face and joy to my heart.

Vicki Nicolson. Woman, you... you are THE most supportive person I could have ever hoped to meet. Words cannot express how meaningful working with you has been. You not only helped me find my brand, design my book cover, and give me invaluable advice on self publishing but your enthusiasm is infectious and motivating to a level I cannot begin to explain. Thank you. Thank you. Thank you.

Mayhara, working with you has been so fulfilling. Your enthusiasm for my characters and interpretation of them has filled me with joy. Thank you for bringing my babies to life.

Amanda... Thank You! For every animated voice message, DM and piece of feedback. You went above and beyond and brought a smile to my face whether you were shouting at me over one plot point or squealing with glee over another.

Tracy, Taysha & Christine. Thank you so much for

beta reading for me. Your feedback was so helpful and I can't thank you enough for your support.

My ARC readers, your support blew me away. Thank you for taking a chance on a new author and giving me your time and championing my story. The posts, the emails, the DMs... it was truly joyful to hear from you. To every very single one of you who took the time to share your love of Aurora and her men... THANK YOU!

J and T. Thank you for giving mummy so much time to write, for supporting me and for all the hugs. I love you so much and no, you can't read this 'til you're *at least* 16, maybe 21.